More Than An
ECHO

Linda Kay Silva

Bella
BOOKS
2010

Dedication

This one is dedicated to my dad, Ron Silva, who let me turn his house into our house, who encouraged me to build the library of my dreams, and who loves up my princess Lucy and makes her tail nearly wag off her body. He's given me more than a place to park my Harley—he has given me a home filled with love and laughter, frogs and turtles, books and movies, and most of all, a place where I am finally free to be me. I love you.

Acknowledgments

Moving my life and my family back to California was not easy, but so many wonderful things have happened since we've been back. I want to take this time to thank those people who have helped turn California back into our home.

JUGS (Just Us Girls): Lil G, Irish, Easy Breezy, and Peligrosa, otherwise known as Gita, Catherine, Julie and Silvia. Riding with you guys brings me so much joy. Thank you for your friendship and support.

JUGS' men: Rich and Gordon. As guys go, you two totally rock! Thank you for your acceptance, your friendship, and your willingness to hang with five chicks with uber cool rides!

My daughters, Sunnie and Kelley: Without you here with us, it just couldn't be home. I am so proud of both of you. You have grown into fine young women who care about social change. Party on!

Paul and Ellen, Riley and Isaac: As we start a new life, we begin new traditions. Thank you for being part of both. I consider your family an extension of ours.

My cousin Kris: Thank you, thank you, thank you, for being my friend, and for taking care of Uncle Ronnie whenever we go away. You are truly one of the most giving people I know.

My other cousins, Otis, Katie and Tyler: For loving me in spite of myself and for laughing with me through this crazy life of ours!

Aunt Cathy and Uncle Richard: You accepted us when few others did. You'll never know how much that means to me. You are the kind of Christians who make Christ proud.

My editor, Katherine V. Forrest: Thank you for whipping me and Echo into shape. I have learned so much from you and have grown as a writer and woman because of it. Thank you for being my taskmaster.

Finally, my partner in crime, Lori: It takes courage to ride on the back of a Harley and to watch your daughter and partner jump from a plane. Your incredible courage is surpassed only by your capacity for love and your willingness to let me be me: rider, writer, player, traveler, and...sigh...zookeeper. Thank you will never be enough. Will a convertible suffice? LOL.

Thank you for all you do for me and dad. Without you, we'd be living on burnt toast and pop tarts, and wearing dirty clothes. You're the best.

About The Author

Linda Kay and her partner of 13 years have returned to her childhood home in the San Francisco Bay Area to care for her elderly father. There, she has reunited with old friends, met new ones, and fallen in love with her new Harley, Lucky. She belongs to a women's motorcycle club, plays on a tennis team, rescues turtles and tortoises, and travels around the world, having recently returned from Egypt. When she's not Professor Silva teaching Early American and British Literature at a Military University, she is busy working on the third novel of her Across Time Series and her fourth installment of this series. Linda Kay can be found on Facebook and YouTube under Linda Kay Silva, as well as Twitter under iamstorm. She welcomes (and responds to) all email at iamstorm@yahoo.com.

At the age of fourteen I became what I am today.

It nearly drove me insane.

They say your teenage years are the hardest. Imagine being a teenager and coming into a paranormal power no one believes in and you don't even know you possess. Imagine being semi-normal one minute and supernatural the next. Imagine what would happen to your world if suddenly you *knew* what everyone around you was feeling. Every one. Every feeling. All the time.

Just imagine.

It was November of my freshman year in high school, and my best friend, Danica, and I were cutting through Mrs. Jorgensen's creek on our way home. High school had started out great for us. I was in a really nice foster home with two other kids, neither of whom were foster kids. I had been in the home for over a year and finally felt like this one might be the one. Life was good for me. It was even better for Dani.

Danica was a cheerleader and well-liked by everyone. Half -black, half-white, she was considered almost exotic by my new family's white-bread standards. We both attended a private school in Oakland, where most came from upper middle class white families. When I say most, I mean, I didn't. I came from foster care. I could have been born in a mansion or a trailer park, but Danica didn't care. Money and color meant nothing to her because she would never fully be accepted in either community. If the black kids didn't like her, she just flipped them the bird. If the white kids didn't like her, she would just flip them two birds. That was the beauty of Danica. She didn't care who liked her.

Unfortunately for her, on this chilly November afternoon, someone liked her a little bit too much.

That someone had followed us to the creek as we walked and chatted on our way home from school. I'd used the path before without fear or trepidation, so I thought nothing of the pinpricks on the back of my neck as we neared the hole cut open in the cyclone fence.

But as we got closer to the fence, those pinpricks changed into something I had never experienced before. Like a blast of hot air on every nerve in my body, something warned me the person following us wasn't just using the shortcut; whoever it was carried malicious intentions. I don't know *how* I knew, but I knew it as surely as if it had already happened. I knew because I could feel it, as if I were wearing his skin.

Stopping just before the opening, I whirled around to face Todd Abrams, a linebacker on our football team. He was wearing the school uniform of maroon polo shirt and khaki pants. He was also wearing a smile much like the wolf must have worn in *Little Red Riding Hood*. I felt that grin before I saw it, and it made me nauseous.

"Hey," he said, leering at Danica, his eyes traveling up and down her body. He never once looked my way; not once.

I didn't mind. I was used to being invisible; used to people looking over and around me. What I *wasn't* used to was feeling as if I were inside someone else's head. I wasn't used to swimming in an energy field that felt like static electricity a hundred times over. I have to say…it freaked me out big time.

2

Blinking several times, I swallowed back a small pocket of bile. Whatever hot blast I had felt, now radiated from my brain down to my fingertips and toes. It was almost as if I *were* Todd. I knew exactly what he wanted, exactly what his intentions were, exactly what he was feeling. They couldn't have been more real had he whispered them to me. Something weird was going on with me, and if I hadn't been so afraid of Todd's feelings, I would've been scared to death of what was happening *to me*. My heart raced, my palms were sweaty, my breathing became shallow, and I knew... I *knew* we were in trouble.

"Come on, Dani. We're going to be late," I said, never taking my eyes off Todd. My hands were shaking as I reached out to push Danica through the opening before he could get any closer. I could sense his plan through every pore in my body, as if my soul kept jumping from my body to his and back again. It felt creepy and...dirty. When my hand reached out to touch Danica, I suddenly felt *her* emotions as well; it was as if I had leapfrogged from inside Todd to Dani. She was irritated by his interruption. Irritated and pissed off. I felt her emotions as if they were my own, and I had no idea how I was doing it.

It was the first time my powers kicked in and I had no clue what they were or how to stop it.

But I *did* know one thing: we were in danger.

"Beat it, Todd. I already told you I'm not interested." Danica casually tossed this out as she had done so many times before to other guys who didn't quite understand her boundaries.

"Jane," Todd said softly, looking over at me for the first time. His eyes might as well have glowed red. "Why don't you scoot along and let me walk Danica home."

Yes, my real name...the name bestowed upon me at birth, was Jane. Jane Doe. I was born one of many Jane Does that year and actually remained one until my eighteenth birthday when I changed it to something more fitting; something more in line with who I turned out to be. Something which raised its head this very minute.

Fighting back the strange feelings crawling beneath my skin

3

like a bad drug, I tried to shake off the images pinging around my head like a pinball. Was I going crazy? Was there something wrong with me? Could they tell? Danica, bless her heart, was staring at Todd as if *he* were nuts. If she had *wanted* him to walk her home, she would have asked him to. Danica didn't appreciate *anybody* telling her what to do or assuming they knew what *she* wanted.

The emotions rolling over me were definitely from Todd, and were as palpable to me as the very air I breathed. For a second, I thought I was going to faint from the overwhelming sensations whirling through my mind, confusing me, disorienting me. It nearly took my breath away.

When I finally, and with great effort, was able to push the emotions away from me, I managed to say under my breath, "Danica. Please. *Go*." This time, I shoved her with all my might.

Todd took a step toward the hole in the fence and I knew it was now or never. I knew it as if I were standing in his shoes; he wasn't taking no for an answer. He was going to get what he came here for and if Danica wasn't going to give it, he intended on taking it.

Without hesitation, I acted. Swinging my extraordinarily heavy backpack at him, I hit him square on the side of the head, knocking him away from the opening and onto the ground. He landed with a whoosh sound forced from his mouth, and was momentarily stunned. Then, with one final push, I shoved Danica completely through the hole.

"Run!" Turning back to Todd, who was lying on the ground holding his bloody head, I lost my mind. I grabbed my heavy geometry book that had spilled from my pack and continued my assault. Straddling his chest, I brought that book down again and again on his face. I couldn't see where Danica went, but I felt her fear leave as I bashed Todd's head over and over with my five-pound math book. As he struggled beneath my weight, I felt his lust and arousal transform instantly to anger and rage. He wanted to kill me.

I'm sure he would have, too.

So I kept hitting him. And hitting him.

I had to keep him down or he would hurt me. I didn't know how long I was smashing his bloody face, but it was long enough for his blood to end up on my clothes, arms and backpack. I probably would have kept hitting him until I crushed his head into a pancake, but Danica had returned with Mr. Morgan, who had to pull me off Todd.

"Jane!" Danica cried, coming to assist Mr. Morgan.

Something had happened to me; something big and weird and scary and bad. I was like some feral girl completely out of control, lashing out blindly at an enemy only I could see. When Mr. Morgan finally calmed me down, he kept his arms around me, which was wise. I glanced at the unmoving Todd and wondered if I'd killed him. The scariest part was that I didn't think it was such a bad thing if I had.

"Jane?" Danica knelt in front of me and took my hands. They were covered with Todd's blood, but she didn't care. "Are you okay? What...what happened?"

"He...he was going to hurt you, Dani. Don't ask me how I knew, I just did. He...he..." I saw Todd twitch, and started for him again, when I realized that the only emotion I was feeling from him now was pain. "I'm...I'm sorry if I scared you."

Danica glanced over her shoulder at Todd. "Don't be sorry for protecting yourself, Jane. Don't *ever* be sorry."

When the paramedics arrived for Todd, the police came for me. I was nearly incoherent, not because of what I'd done to Todd, but because my brain was frying from all the images and emotions I was getting from Danica, Mr. Morgan, the police, the paramedics and even a few of the bystanders. I was losing my mind feeling all those erratic feelings at once. It was like a dozen different voices in my head at the same time, only I wasn't hearing voices...I was feeling emotions. The strength of those feelings were practically driving me mad.

Apparently, the police thought so as well because the next ambulance that came was for me, and the last thing I remember was being strapped down and given a shot of something I

5

welcomed because it finally calmed the whirlpool of emotions sucking me under.

"Be cool, Jane. Everything's gonna be okay."

As my eyes got heavy, the emotional noises of the crowd began to dissipate, leaving me with the only question going through my mind: What the hell was happening to me?

When I came to after beating Todd's questionable brains in with my math book, I was strapped to a white bed in a white room, under white sheets, with a dark cloud sitting somewhere inside my skull. Whatever drug they had shot in me had given me a horrible headache and a metallic taste in my mouth.

If you've never woken up after being drugged, and found yourself strapped to a bed in a nuthouse, count your blessings. You can't even imagine how incredibly frightening it is to a fourteen-year-old-girl who had just experienced her first psychic moment, her first violent outburst and her first run-in with the cops only to find herself in the looney bin. It was the worst thing in the world; a nightmare of gigantic proportions, and when the fuzz finally drifted from my head, I realized that I was strapped to the bed with these thick leather restraints. My legs were no freer. I was pretty well tied up and trying my hardest not to panic.

One minute, I was walking home with my best friend and talking about homecoming, and the next minute...here I was in this living hell, strapped to a bed in a nuthouse. Alone. Well, alone with only the memory of trying to kill Todd.

Kill Todd?

Oh my God, had I succeeded?

No one wants to be immobile. To wake up and know you cannot move, cannot itch your nose, cannot do a thing for yourself. I did the only thing anyone would have done in my position.

I screamed.

Yep. I started thrashing about like some wild woman; yelling, kicking, fighting against the restraints that weren't going to budge. I don't know how long I flailed around before an enormous black orderly entered the room. With him came this weird calming effect that I felt to the marrow of my bones.

"You gotta calm down, sweetpea," he said, reaching over to touch my arm. I stopped fighting, mostly because I was just so glad that I wasn't alone anymore. I think that was the scariest part.

"Where am I?" I asked, my tongue feeling thick and heavy in my mouth. My heart pounded in my head, but that wasn't the only thing I felt. There was a still strength from the big black man peering down at me with what looked like yellow eyes. It washed over me like a warm blanket, and helped me relax. "Who are you? Where am I? What's going on? Why am I tied up?"

"One question at a time, sweetpea. First off, I'm Big George. We're in the psych ward of Alta Bates Hospital. Do you remember anything that happened before they brought you in here?"

It took a second for me to remember all of it; not because of the actual memory of it, but because of the lingering emotions from my first empathic episode and the drugs still in my system. My throat was killing me and I had that horrible taste in my mouth. "Can I...please...have some water?"

Big George poured some in a plastic cup and bent the straw to my lips. "You ain't gonna spit it at me, are you?"

I frowned. "Uh...no. I think I'd rather just swallow it." As I sipped the water, I calmed down, but I knew the emotions calming me were not mine. I wasn't sure how I could tell the difference between my own emotions and someone else's, but this quiet feeling was *definitely* not mine. I was tied to a bed in the loony bin, for God's sake. What was there to be calm about?

"Thatta girl." Big George put the water at the side of the bed. "How you doin' now?"

"Can you unlock me?"

He shook his head. "Only when a doctor gives the okay. You gotta stay calm, like you are now, and they'll cut you loose quicker. Okay? No more thrashing about."

"How's Todd?"

"Would that be the boy whose head you bashed in?"

Sighing, I nodded. "Is he...is he dead?"

7

"Don't know 'bout that. You want me to go find out?" Big George had an accent I could not place.

"Would you? I'd really appreciate it. I...I didn't mean to..."

"I'm sure you didn't."

"Thank you for the water."

Big George smiled kindly. "You got manners. I'll give you that much. If I go get the doctor, will you promise to stay calm and not do anything stupid?"

"I promise. I don't want any more of whatever it was they shot into me."

"Okay, then. I'll check on that boy and let the doctor know you're awake. Stay calm, sweetpea. I won't let anything happen to you." Big George leaned over and peered hard into my eyes as if he was searching for something. "Be cooperative and you'll be outta those in no time. Trust me. No one wants to see a young gal like you tied down, okay?"

I nodded as two tears rolled down my temples. "Where are my foster parents? Do they know I'm here?"

"The doctors can tell you all that, sweetpea."

"I...I don't know what happened."

"Shh. That's okay. We're gonna get you the help you need." Big George pulled a small packet of tissues out of his pocket and wiped the sides of my face.

"Thank you."

"I'll be back in a jiff. I know it's hard, but just take deep breaths and stay calm. Don't panic. I promise I'll be right back."

"You swear?"

"I give you my word. You do some deep breathing exercises, okay?"

I nodded and watched him leave the room, taking his calm with him and leaving me with a slight panic rising in my throat. There's a sound a door makes when it's locked from the outside and it's far louder than when you lock it yourself. Big. Scary. Click.

Closing my eyes, I inhaled slowly and deeply as Big George had recommended. It really helped. I was finally calming down

8

when Big George returned with the doctor.

"Hi, Jane. I'm Dr. Knowles. How are you doing?" Dr. Knowles was a petite woman around forty-five. She was wearing black pants with a light pink blazer that reminded me of a lollipop. Her salt-and-pepper hair was cut in a short bob. She had these intense hazel eyes that were examining me as she spoke. Big George stood at the foot of the bed and winked at me as the doctor finished her examination.

"Well, I'm in a nuthouse tied to a bed for bashing a guy's head in with my math book. I've had better days."

Dr. Knowles grinned. "I'm sure you have." She took out a penlight and shined it in my eyes. "Headache?"

"Pounding. I'll bet Todd's is far worse than mine. I didn't kill him, did I? Please tell me that I didn't kill him." This last was directed to Big George.

"I got a call in. We'll let you know as soon as they call back."

I licked my parched lips. "Thank you." I could feel Dr. Knowles studying me; assessing my stability. I felt like a lab rat caught in a maze.

"Big George seems to think if we unlock you, you'll be cooperative. What do you think?"

I nodded and licked my lips again. "Believe it or not, doctor, I'm not really a violent person."

She smiled and motioned for Big George to leave. He did. "Then what happened, Jane? It says here," she opened up a file with my name on it. "You were repeatedly striking a young man in the head with your math book. Is that true?"

I nodded.

"Can you tell me why?"

Blinking several times, I exhaled. "He was following us home and I thought... I thought..." What *had* I thought when I hit him with my bag? It wasn't a thought, really; that much I knew. It had been more; so much more, but I had no name for it. I just knew what I knew, and didn't know *how* to explain it without sounding like a nutcase.

"You thought what?"

9

"I thought he was going to hurt us."

"Did he do something or say something that led you to believe this? Was your reaction provoked?"

Before I could answer, Big George reentered with two other orderlies who were just as big as he was.

"Jane?" Dr. Knowles prodded.

"Honestly? I don't know. It was just a feeling I had. It was a really, really bad feeling, and scared me."

Dr. Knowles never took her eyes from mine. "I see. Well, here's what's going to happen. George is going to take your restraints off. You and I will chat for a few more minutes and then he'll take you to your room where we will be observing you for the next forty-eight hours. We'll need to prepare a report for the police should Todd's family press charges. Do you understand what I've said?"

I nodded. "Do my foster parents know where I am?"

"Yes. They will be able to see you at the end of our observation." Dr. Knowles stepped back while the orderlies started unlocking me. My heart was pounding. A flood of emotions that were not mine started pouring over me; boredom, concern, care, even hunger. Yes, someone in this room was hungry, and I knew it... but how?

"Just relax, sweetpea," Big George said from the foot of the bed. "Let the guys get you out and then we'll show you where you are and go over what's going to happen in the next twenty-four hours."

I nodded and laid there trying to block out the confusing mixture of emotions. When they were through unlocking me, the other two orderlies left, shackles in hand, but Big George stayed at the foot of my bed. "There. Better?"

Rubbing my wrists, I sat up and reached for the water, downing it all into one pull on the straw. "Much better. So, you're going to see if I'm nuts."

Dr. Knowles grinned and pulled up the chair. "Something like that. I'm going to ask you some questions just to see what you were thinking and feeling and to try to get a better idea of your general state of mind. Your foster parents are sending us your medical records so we can put all of the pieces of the puzzle together to find out what happened today."

Looking up at Big George, I nodded. "Is my friend, Danica, okay?"

Dr. Knowles glanced over at Big George in question. Big George nodded. "She wanted to go with you in the ambulance, but couldn't."

"She's my best friend."

Dr. Knowles smiled slightly. "Those are always good to have. Are you ready?"

I nodded. About a half an hour later, when the doctor was finished asking me a battery of questions, Big George escorted me to my room. I had never been in a psych ward before, but I had seen plenty on television. Let's just say that Hollywood usually got it right. There were all sorts of hideous noises coming from people I couldn't see, but could definitely feel. It was like being on a soundstage with all of these horrendous sounds coming from every nook and cranny of the ward. I swear to God, human beings aren't supposed to be capable of making such inhuman sounds. It was awful.

"This place is pretty scary your first night here, sweetpea. There are all sorts of screams and noises and sounds that you ain't never heard before. Don't let it get to you. Just breathe through it and try to stay relaxed. That's key here. Stay relaxed. Stay calm. And remember that all of this is temporary." Big George opened a door to a room not unlike the one I'd come from. There was a bed, a bare toilet and a camera high up in the corner of the room. That was it. At least there weren't any shackles.

"Thank you for being so kind to me, Big George."

He stood at the doorway as I sat on the bed. "I get off at eleven, sweetpea, so if you need anything after that, Tony will be on. He ain't as nice as me or as good-looking, but he can help you get something if you can't sleep." Big George winked.

I held my hands up. "No more drugs for this girl. I've had my fill for the rest of my life."

"Good. Now, what did I tell you to do?"

"Relax. Breathe deeply. Stay calm."

"Thatta girl."

"Big George?"

"Yeah, sweetpea?"

"Am I going to jail?"

He stepped back into the room. "I wish I knew, but you can't be worryin' about that right now. Whatever happened to you today needs to be taken care of. Focus on that."

And so I did. When that door closed and locked, I took several deep breaths as I climbed onto the hard bed. Relaxing was difficult. What was happening to me, anyway? What had I done to Todd? Where was Danica? What did my foster parents think? And, more importantly, was I going insane?

These questions banged around in my very tired mind as I closed my eyes. I was still feeling the residual of the drug they had pushed into me. I was exhausted, scared and alone in a psych ward. Still, it didn't take long for sleep to claim me even in the midst of cries that would haunt me for the rest of my life.

My first cold sweat happened the first week I was in the Johnson unit. The Johnson unit is the nickname for the loony bin. I'd been there a couple of days and done little more than eat, sleep and answer question upon question. As kind as Big George was to me, I just didn't have anything left to give. He was always trying to get me to go out into the day room, but one nanosecond in there and I thought I would go insane. Imagine what it would be like to feel *all* of the emotions of a room full of whackos, depressed lunatics, schizos, suicidals, split personalities and generally disturbed people. I could have fallen down the rabbit hole forever.

Instead, I stayed in my room and slept until it was time to talk to a doctor or eat.

The first morning I was there, Big George came in to report that Todd had a concussion, but he would live. Except for his bruised reputation, he had come out of this with just a few stitches here and there. No one was pressing charges because they were all pretty clear that I had lost my mind and might never get it back. My foster parents had already kicked me to the curb. By noon, I was once again a ward of the state.

"And what about Danica? She's my best friend. Has she come or called?"

"She's called a dozen times, sweetpea. If you want to see her, you're gonna have to cooperate with the doctors more. They're just trying to help."

Nodding, I sighed. My head was pounding, as it had been since I arrived. I was exhausted from the night terrors, and I couldn't stop feeling emotions which obviously were not my own. I knew I was sliding into the mental abyss but I was too afraid to share it with anyone. After being shackled to a bed, you'd pull off your own ears to keep from experiencing that again.

"I'm trying, Big George. I don't know what she wants from me."

"The truth. Always the truth."

That *sounded* easy enough, but I didn't know what the truth was. Was I insane and didn't know it? Had something happened in my brain chemistry that made me susceptible to other people's emotions? What was I supposed to say to her? *Hey doc, I know what you're feeling. You're bored, you hate your job, and you wish you had gone to Miami with your sister.* Yeah...that might work if I wanted to be locked away forever.

"I just don't know what truth she wants from me."

Big George cocked his head and leaned against the wall. "You sure you don't want to talk to Big George about it? I don't judge people, sweetpea."

I looked away and nodded. "Thank you for that, but right now, I don't have any truths for you or for the doctors. And believe me, I wish I did."

He left me alone that morning pondering my fate with my door open and my mind closed. I'm pretty sure he meant for me to go through it, not for someone else to slip on in, but that's what happened.

13

"Yo. You the newest nut on the block?"

Opening my eyes, I was staring at a girl about my age with fuchsia hair sticking up like little spikes from her head. Her head reminded me of a flower. "Excuse me?" I quickly sat up; the energy from her was practically knocking me off the bed.

"I'm the Welcome Wagon for all incoming psychos. I'm Celeste. I'm a carver."

"A what?"

"I'm here for carving up my body like a fucking turkey. And you are?"

"Echo."

"Echo? Super cool name. I always wished I had a cool name, but my parents named me after my grandmother, which wouldn't be so bad if she had one remotely nice bone in her body. What a bitch." Celeste took a deep breath before continuing. "What brings you to our humble abode?"

"I beat up a football player with my geometry book."

Celeste's eyebrows rose and she took a step back. "No shit? Cool. I know a few football players I'd like to take a math book to. Why did you do that? You got violent tendencies? Tourette's? Schizo? Manic depression?"

"I thought he was going to hurt us."

"Oh." She stepped back into the room. "Cool. Get to them before they get to you, I say. So, did you kill him?"

"No."

"You going downtown?"

"Downtown?"

"Yeah. You know...jail. They get you for an A and B?"

I shook my head. She had the energy of a half-dozen puppies and it made my head hurt.

"Even better. So, how come you don't come out? Scared of all the cuckoos out there?"

"I keep having these horrible headaches and I just don't feel like visiting, that's all. How come you cut yourself?"

"My version or theirs?"

"Yours."

"My girlfriend wouldn't come out so she dumped me. According to my shrinks, to cover up my broken heart I cut myself. You know, one pain replaces the other, and voilà, here I am. Wanna see?" Before I could say no thank you, she had her wrists and forearms in my face. "It fucking hurt like hell. That's the point."

"You said you had a girlfriend?"

"Yeah, but I'm not gay or anything, so don't think I'm all, you know, hittin' on you or something. I just liked her, that's all." Celeste squinted as she studied me. "You're kind of normal, aren't you?"

Forty-eight hours ago I might have said yes. "I guess that depends on what abnormal looks like to you."

"Bummer. You know what happens to normal kids in psych wards? They go fucking nuts. If you weren't a whack job when you got here, you sure as shit will be when you leave."

"Is there any way out?"

"Out?" Celeste grinned. "Now you're talking. I don't know if there's a way out, but it might be worth looking into. You stay here, and you'll be drooling and twitching in no time. Take my advice and whatever you do, do *not* take any of the meds they give you. Here." Celeste pulled a button off her shirt and handed it to me. "They always look under the tongue but they never check between your cheek and gum. Practice putting the button there in case they decide to start drugging you. Once the drugging starts happening, kiddo, you're fucked. So practice, okay?"

I took the button and nodded. "I will. Thank you."

"If you aren't going to cooperate, then at least pretend to."

As I lay there working the button around my mouth with my tongue, I turned Celeste's words over in my mind. Normal people go crazy in the psych ward? That, I could believe. This place was unlike anything I had ever experienced in any nightmare.

Little did I know my nightmare was just beginning.

"So, I'm back to being a ward of the state again." I was sitting across from Dr. Knowles when she told me what I already knew.

15

"And how do you feel about that?"

I shrugged. "Who could blame them? I beat a kid to a bloody pulp. At this point I am more of a liability than an asset. I'd get rid of me too."

Doctor Knowles' eyebrows rose. "Is that how you see yourself?"

"They cut their losses. End of story."

"How are you sleeping?" Dr. Knowles liked to change subjects quickly. I had a teacher who used to do that because she felt our responses were more sincere.

"Actually, I've been sleeping really well."

Dr. Knowles waited, her sharp blue eyes piercing mine. She knew I was lying, though I didn't know how I knew she knew. "I seem to be having nightmares or something. Of course, I'm living in one so I shouldn't be surprised that I have one at night."

"I've studied your tapes, Jane, and what you're experiencing isn't a nightmare. They're called night terrors."

"What's the difference?"

"Nightmares and night terrors can be differentiated both biologically and psychologically. Nightmares occur largely in REM sleep in the second half of the night. Night terrors usually occur in the first hours of sleep, and the sleeper typically doesn't remember the episode. Night terrors occur during non-REM sleep and don't occur during the dream cycle. They're often accompanied by physical manifestations of the terror."

"Physical manifestation?"

"You're fighting something or someone in every episode."

"Are you sure?"

"It's on the tape, Jane. Every night. Is this news to you?"

"Gee, Doc, I don't know. I've never had twenty-four hour surveillance in my bedroom." It bothered me that I was doing something I couldn't remember. Apparently I was losing my mind in the nighttime as well as the daytime.

"So you have no memory of your episodes?"

I wished she would stop calling them that. "None at all."

"Well, I've prescribed you a sleeping pill. You must be exhausted."

16

The truth was, I felt pretty good and even well rested. I didn't need a sleeping pill, and was thankful Celeste had given me The Magic Button. I was pretty sure I could hide a cereal bowl in my mouth, I had practiced so much.

As if on cue, Dr. Knowles brought up Celeste. "I understand you and Celeste have become friends."

I shrugged. "The only friend I have has come by every day and still I haven't gotten to see her. I would clean every bathroom in here with a toothbrush for only five minutes with Danica. Why can't I see her?"

"It's complicated, Jane, really. You'll get to see her soon, though. I promise. Now, let's talk about your last foster parents."

For the next half-hour, we talked about all my foster parents and how it made me feel to be unwanted. It's funny; I'd never really *felt* unwanted. I felt more uninterested than anything else. Unwanted was for sissies who sat around feeling sorry for themselves because they hadn't been adopted out. I never had time to feel sorry for myself.

Apparently, I was too busy going insane.

My session over, I was heading back to my room when a huge commotion broke out in the dayroom. Normally, I ignore all of the hourly outbursts, but today something drew me closer.

Orderlies were yelling, people were scattering, and someone ran by me with shackles. It was the shackles the drew me closer. I hated those things more than anything else on the planet, but whoever they were intended for actually *feared* them. *That* emotion came through loud and clear and rang in my head like one of those stupid canned horns people use at football games. The feeling was so intense, I didn't even notice when Celeste approached me.

"Come on, J, let's DD outta here." Celeste grabbed my arm.

"Wait."

"For what? The Mute's gone bad, man. She's gonna blow and you don't want to be there when she does."

"The Mute?"

"You need to get out more. Yeah, the Mute. She's gonna

do something stupid. Come on. I'd rather not watch her stab someone with scissors or something."

I pulled my arm away and started back to the dayroom.

"What's the matter with you, J.? Have you fucking lost your mind?"

"Probably." When I got to the dayroom, Big George, Tall Tommy and Small Sal were all cornering the girl known as The Mute. To my horror, she held a pair of scissors to her own neck. She had every intention of pushing them in, too. She wasn't bluffing.

"Get back, Jane!" one of the nurses ordered.

"Stop!" I yelled over them. All three orderlies turned to me. When Big George saw that it was me who was shouting, he muttered something to the other orderlies before approaching me. "Let her through."

The nurses let me go.

"What you doin', sweetpea?"

"She's not bluffing, Big George. Please. If you guys get any closer, she *will* shove those scissors into her neck."

Big George looked hard at me and whispered, "How do you know this, girl?"

"I...I don't know." I lowered my voice. "I just do. You have to believe me, she's not kidding."

Big George peered into my eyes so long, it made me uncomfortable. Finally, he turned back to the dayroom. "Hang on a second, guys. Back off and give her a little breathing room."

One of the younger doctors pushed through the crowd. "What's going on here? I thought I said to sedate her. Can't the three of you handle her? She's just a girl." The doctor was a smallish Asian man who weighed all of one hundred pounds.

Big George cut his eyes over to me. "Jane?"

Making my way over to her, I was nearly knocked down by the fear coming from The Mute. "What's her name?" I whispered to Big George as I walked by.

"Mary. Her name is Mary."

"What in the hell is going on here? I told you how I wanted

18

this handled!" The little doctor was getting irritated that nobody would listen to him.

I ignored the remainder of their conversation and focused on Mary The Mute. Her fear was overpowering; not just because of the shackles, which she hated, but of what she was willing to do to herself.

"I know you're really scared," I said softly as I approached her.

Her eyes were on fire and she looked at me; wild with fear, distress and anxiety. I felt every single emotion she was experiencing, and she was feeling them all loudly in her silence. "I know you're not kidding about using those." I motioned to the scissors. "I had the same thoughts when they had me all trussed up, too. It's the shackles, isn't it?"

Mary swallowed hard and then barely nodded. The scissor tip remained pressed against her throat, but I felt some of her fear ebb.

I stepped closer to her. She blinked several times, but made no move to step away or to use the scissors. "You don't need to be so scared. I don't trust anyone here, either, except Big George. You can trust him. I swear." I watched Mary's eyes move over my shoulder to Big George. "And you can trust me. I'm not a loon or a nutjob. I'm afraid, too."

Mary lowered the scissors a little. It was so very strange. I felt...I felt like I could hear her through her emotions. She couldn't speak...she didn't have to; not to me.

"I'm scared shitless," I said, "because I have no place to go from here. I have no family, no home, nothing. It totally sucks. Do you have a family?"

Mary nodded.

"Lucky you. I know...none of us here are very lucky. I mean, we're here in this horrible place that insists it's helping us with its drugs and restraints. What a joke. I'm sure some of us belong here. Hell, maybe I do, too, but at least *you* have some place to go when this nightmare is over. But you know the beauty of nightmares? Eventually, they end. They all do. This one will, too.

For all of us. And when it does, don't you want to be around?"

Mary hesitated before lowering the scissors. She trusted me... trusted my words. I turned to Big George. "Can you *please* put those shackles away? She doesn't need them. Please don't rush her."

Big George nodded and signaled to the other orderlies to back away. Then, he said something to the doctor, who stepped aside. "Go ahead, Jane."

I sat down at a table near Mary and patted the tabletop. "Come sit, Mary. Leave the scissors there and come sit with me awhile." To my delight, she did. Her fear was much less now that the shackles were out of sight. I felt her exhaustion more than anything else.

"I'm Jane," I said. "I'm here because I beat a kid up with my math book."

She grinned slightly. I guessed her to be closer to my age, maybe a little younger.

"And you're here because..." I closed my eyes and there it was. "Oh. You suddenly stopped talking, huh?"

Her eyes grew wide. She looked as surprised as I felt. Nodding, she blinked back her tears.

"Wow. You just stopped talking and so this was someone's idea of a solution? How shitty is that?" I suddenly felt emotions from someone behind me, so I reached out and gently put my hand on hers. "You go with Big George now, okay? He's a good guy and he'll make sure no one puts those shackles on you any more. Okay?"

She looked over my shoulder and then back at me before nodding.

"Yes, I trust him," I repeated.

She nodded and then ever so slightly smiled. She was pretty when she smiled, her brown eyes shifting from dark to milk chocolate.

"You know what they say...*suicide is a permanent solution to a temporary problem.* Remember that, okay?"

Mary nodded again as she rose.

20

"Good." I rose. "Do you know Celeste?"

She nodded and smiled bigger. "Celeste told me that pretending to cooperate is the best plan for getting out of here fast." I pulled my practice button out and slipped it into her hand. "Don't let them drug you anymore," I whispered. "Practice hiding them with this."

As Mary stood, she nodded and started past me. Just as we were side by side, she whispered so softly I almost missed it. "Thank you." It was the slightest of whispers and meant only for me.

I didn't know why that meant so much to me, but it did, and something changed for me at that moment; I stopped being afraid. Maybe I really *was* going nuts, but even that wasn't so scary anymore.

When I got back to my room, I lay on the bed and wondered if Danica had given up coming to see me. I missed her so much. Away in here, it was as if the world outside wasn't real anymore. You knew it was out there, you knew it went on without you, but every day you were gone you became less and less a part of it, less and less real...almost like you were evaporating.

I was almost asleep when there was a slight knock on my door. It was Big George.

"How is she?" I asked, sitting up.

"Better. Whatever you said to her really helped."

I nodded and looked away. Big George had come to my room seeking answers. I didn't know the specific questions, but I had a pretty good idea of what he was looking for. "That's good. You know, you guys need to ditch those shackles."

He pulled up the chair, his eyes were riveted to mine. "You really believe you're going crazy, don't you?"

I nodded and swallowed hard.

"You're not."

"How do *you* know?"

Big George leaned closer and whispered, "Because I think I know what's happening to you. I think I know what you are."

What I was? Oh, that was just grand.

"What...what do you mean you know *what* I am?" Sitting up, I stared at Big George. He *knew*. I could see it in his eyes.

"Am I nuts?"

Big George smiled a mouthful of long, white teeth. "Not even remotely. What you got is a gift." Big George put his hand out and I put mine in his. He led me out into hall, where we walked a ways until we came to the small quad outside. It was enclosed with a twelve-foot-tall fence.

"You're kidding me, right?"

He slowly shook his head. "If you are what I think you are, it's a gift. You knew what Mary was feeling without her ever saying a word, didn't you?"

I nodded. "What's happening to me?"

"You feel all these emotions from everyone around?"

My jaw dropped. "Yes! That is *exactly* what it feels like. It comes in waves sometimes knocking the wind out of me. Sometimes, I feel it in my head, like I can actually *hear* their feelings in my brain."

Big George patted my leg. "Ain't nothing wrong with you, sweetpea. Trust me. You're so special, God gave you a rare and precious gift." He held his hand up to stop me. "But it's only a gift if you know how to use it, otherwise, it feels like you're losing your mind. I know it feels that way, but I know what I'm talking about."

"I don't know what to trust anymore, Big George. I can barely trust myself. You have no idea."

Big George leaned closer. "Actually...I do."

"Are you—"

"No, but my mother, Melika is."

I blinked several times. "She feels things, too?"

He nodded. "More than most. What you are, sweetpea, is an empath...and probably more. We won't know what all you have until you're checked out."

"An empath?"

"Yeah. You're a feeler. You have the ability to feel the emotions of those around you. I've only met a couple in my life."

"You mean there are...others?"

"Sure. Some are quite powerful. Not all are empaths. Some are telepaths, some clairvoyants. You, little one, are in a select group of individuals known as paranormals or, as my mother likes to call them, supers...for supernaturals. You have a rare and precious gift. The key is learning how to control it."

"Control it? I don't even understand it."

"I know, I know. First thing we have to do is get you out of here."

"Excuse me?"

"What you have, we can't help you with here. Conventional medicine doesn't even recognize what we're talking about. All we'll do is talk at you or drug you up, and neither of those will protect you."

"Protect me? Protect me from what?" I felt a mixture of alarm and relief.

"From all those emotions hammering away at you. You gotta learn about your skill, how to harness your power, how to protect yourself, how to understand who and what you are. You haven't mentioned any of this to Doctor Knowles, have you?"

"Even if I wanted to, which I don't, I wouldn't even know where to begin." I would have cried, but I didn't have time. I was overflowing with questions. "There are so many things I want to know. Oh my God. All this time, I thought I was going crazy."

Big George ran his big hand over his head. "I'd like to answer your questions, but you need answers from someone who has all of them."

"Melika?"

He nodded. "Melika. She's the real deal. I'm just a spotter."

"A spotter?"

"It's my job to help find those like you who don't know what they are yet and get to them before...well...before they do something stupid."

"Like kill themselves?"

He nodded.

"Will she come see me?" I asked.

Big George shook his head. "Can't. She lives in New Orleans. She's the best there is. If you're going to live with this and be sane, you need someone to show you how. You *need* help and Melika can give it to you. She may be the only person who can."

"But how? Can she call me here?"

Big George slowly shook his head. "This ain't something you can learn about in an hour or a day or even a month. We're going to have to get you out of here. I can get you off the floor and out of the hospital, but we're going to need some help getting you from here to New Orleans, especially since you're only fourteen. Is there someone who can help? Do you have any of your own money?"

Yes and yes. There were two people I knew who would help; Danica and Britt Bevelaqua. I hadn't heard from Britt since she ran, but I still had the forty dollars she'd given me. "My best friend, Danica, can help."

"Okay. You give me the number and let me see what I can do. We've got a lot to do and not much time to do it in." Big George reached for my hand and held it tightly as he outlined his plan. When he finished, I sighed.

"But won't they just release me back to the state pretty soon? Can't we just wait until then instead of sneaking out and risking your job?"

He rose and motioned for me to follow. "You beat that boy up because of something you felt, didn't you?"

I nodded as I followed. "I knew as sure as if he'd said it. He was going to really hurt me, so I just kept hitting him so he wouldn't get the chance."

"And what about Mary? You *knew* what was going on with her, huh?"

"She's scared of the shackles and being tied down. She can talk, you know."

"Can, but won't."

"Won't but does. Where are we going?" Big George was taking me down a locked hallway forbidden to the rest of us.

"You'll see."

We took a couple of squeaky turns down hallways filled with moaners, screamers, chatterbugs and singers. I knew where we were now. We were in the J ward where the hopelessly insane awaited removal to some other treatment facility where they would, most likely, live out the remainder of their pitiful lives. When Big George finally stopped, he peered into a small glass window in the door. "Look at this one in here."

I had to stand on tiptoe to see, and I recoiled. A poor, demented young girl was rocking back and forth, mouth hanging open with a foot long string of drool hanging from her chin. She looked no more than fifteen or sixteen. "What's wrong with her?" I turned from the window, feeling chills and goose bumps on my arms. "She's so..."

"Crazy?"

"So young to be crazy."

"She wasn't always nuts. As a matter of fact, she wasn't crazy at all when she got here."

I remembered Celeste's words about this place making people crazy. "Did bringing her here make her mad?"

Big George sadly shook his head. "No, it's not *where* she is that made her insane. It's *what* she is that did that to her. You see...that sad little girl in there is...an empath. She came in here for the same reasons you did, but I couldn't get her out in time. I couldn't get her to Melika in time. And without my mother's help, you'll wind up just like her."

And so it turned out that Big George's mother wasn't just an empath, but a very powerful woman who spent her time teaching people new to the world of psionics how to adjust to and utilize their abilities; telepaths, clairvoyants, empaths and telekinetics came to her from all over the world *if* they were caught in time. The majority of us were not, and usually ended up in a rubber room or worse, like this poor girl.

Fear punched me in the gut. I was trapped in a cage with only one way out.

Life is filled with unlikely heroes and mine is no exception.

After Big George dropped his big bomb about my tenuous future, we got down to planning my escape. He could help me escape at night, but what then? I refused to do anything that would put him at risk. I had really grown to care about the big guy and I wouldn't hear about him risking his job. All he needed to do was get me off the floor and the rest was up to me.

Or so I thought.

When I finally got the chance to talk to Danica, it was by phone and I had very little time for pleasantries. "There's forty bucks in my backpack in the inner pocket. I need you to get me a fake ID. Just use my student body photograph when you go."

"A fake ID? Are you nuts?"

"I will be if you don't get me out of here."

"What about money?"

"Big George is loaning me cash for a ticket, but I need an ID that says I'm eighteen."

"Same name? I mean... Jane Doe already looks like a fake ID, know what I mean?"

I thought about my recently discovered powers and that what I felt from people was a little bit like hearing an echo. "Echo. I want my name to be Echo."

"Sure you haven't already lost your mind?"

"Funny. Echo is perfect. It suits me. Trust me on this. I am so much more of an Echo than I ever was a Jane."

"Fine. Echo it is. And your last name?"

I thought about the only girl who had ever been nice to me in the foster homes I was in. "Branson."

"Echo Branson?"

"Why not? I'm going to be starting a new life."

"Are you ever going to tell me what really happened?"

I had written her several letters attempting to explain to her why I tried to crush Todd's head in. I wanted her to know what I was, but I still didn't have the words for it. It would be quite some time before I did. It's hard to explain something you barely understand yourself.

"But why New Orleans?"

"There's a...school there that specializes in my...issues."

"What issues?"

"I'll tell you as soon as I can explain it better. I'm still adjusting to the idea that I have these issues. You've got to get me out of here."

"Of course I will, she said with the warmth in her voice that made me love her. And there's forty bucks in your backpack."

"Inside the small zipper pocket. Britt gave it to me before she left. She told me to spend it only when I was ready to run. I'm ready to run. Really, really fast."

Our time was up and I hung up knowing that she would do everything she could to make that run possible.

Escape was easier than I thought. Once Big George got me off the floor undetected and wearing regular street clothes, I was able to walk casually out of the hospital as if I were just a visitor.

When I reached the parking lot, I looked around for Danica. I started to panic a little, but then I saw a black Trans Am screech into the parking lot. I felt a familiar presence, but since I had no experience with my "gift," I couldn't really pinpoint it.

"Need a lift?" someone asked from the car. I knew the voice as soon as I heard it.

"Britt?"

"Get in, doofus! You trying to get us busted or what? Come on, girl, we don't have all day!"

The passenger side door opened and Danica stuck her head out and waved me over. "Come on!"

I hopped in next to Danica as Britt peeled away even before I could close the door.

"Parking lot cameras," Britt muttered as an explanation for why she had floored it. "Don't worry. We'll be ditching this ride in a few."

And so we did, snagging a white Explorer left in the middle of a mall parking lot. Hot-wiring cars was something Britt had learned from her time on the street and she was very good at it. We got in and out of that lot in under five minutes.

"Okay ladies, Oakland airport, here we come."

I turned to Danica, but before I could ask my question she answered me.

"Britt wrote her cell number on the bills she gave you in big, red letters. I called her and—"

"Told me you'd finally wised up and decided to run. So, here I am." She cut her eyes over to me. "You look ready to run." Britt flipped her wallet open and pushed my fake ID out with her thumb.

"Echo Branson, eh, Jane?" Britt grinned as she drove. "Cool name. It suits you."

I looked over at Britt. The streets had aged her overnight. She was seventeen going on thirty. Her short blond hair was blonder than I remembered, but her eyes were as blue as ever. She was wearing faded jeans with designer holes in the knees and a gray SFSU sweatshirt. I'd never been happier to see anyone than I was her. "Thank you so much, Britt."

"Hey, we orphan Annies gotta stick together, you know? I'm just glad I could help."

"You got money?" Danica asked.

I nodded. "A paperless ticket. Melika bought it for me."

"Who's that?" Britt asked.

I thought for a minute. "She's the woman who's going to save my life."

Britt smiled. "Then you're all set to go."

And so I was.

Less than twenty-four hours later, I stepped off the plane and into a brand-new life of supernaturals.

For a kid who grew up in California, New Orleans might as well have been another country. Everything about it was unlike anything I had ever experienced; the smells, the sounds, the energy, *everything* was so foreign.

As I made my way through the airport, I found a kid standing at the baggage claim with a sign that read Echo Branson. I nearly walked by, my name not seared into my life yet, but he caught my eye and stopped me in my tracks. I had a headache from the emotions from a plane full of people, so I wasn't thinking clearly. Sleep was my savior and had been the only thing that kept me from hearing the feelings crashing against my brain.

"Echo?" the boy asked.

He was the blackest boy I had ever seen, and I had seen *a lot*. His skin was so dark, it had a purple tinge to it. He was wearing black shorts, black Nike high-tops and a red T-shirt that said something about Alligator Adventures. He looked all of twelve.

"Oh. Yes. I'm sorry. That *is* me."

He grinned with teeth whiter than white. "I know. Come."

We got into a silver Towncar waiting for us at the curb. The air was hot and humid and felt like it clung to me.

"I'm Jacob," the boy said, extending his hand.

I shook it. "Where's Melika?"

"Oh, she hardly ever comes to town."

"Town? Where does she live? Big George said she lives in New Orleans."

Jacob kept grinning. "She does. She lives down in the Bayou."

"The what?"

Jacob groaned. "Ah, man. You don't know what the Bayou is?"

"No. Do you know what the Tenderloin is?"

"Uh...no."

"Then we're even."

Jacob sighed and shook his head. "George shoulda warned you. I mean...the Bayou is...well...it's not like any place on earth. You'll see."

We drove in silence through streets lined with homes that rivaled the Victorians in San Francisco. People of every description were everywhere on the streets and many of the areas reminded me of San Francisco, only older. I mean, this place was *old*. You could smell old heat in the air. It was if I had been transported back in time, and I was mesmerized by the vivid colors of everything from the homes to the clothes people wore. What a charming and wild little place this was. I loved it immediately.

"Pretty cool, eh?"

I nodded, looking out the window. People here were into things like voodoo and palm reading, not to mention food, food, and more food. I'd never seen so many restaurants. There was a restaurant every other building, and each was packed.

"Melika wanted you to see it because she said it would be a long time before you'd see it again. You have a lot of work to do and the city distracts from all that work. In the Bayou, there aren't nearly as many folks around to bother the process."

"The process?"

"That's what we call it."

"We?"

"You'll stay in the Bayou with Melika and the rest of us while she teaches you what you need to know." He shook his head. "Man, Big George musta had to get you outta there fast. Normally people come with a better idea of what we're about."

I nodded and leaned back. His somber tone reminded me this wasn't a vacation. I was here to learn how to live. "How come I don't feel any emotions from you? Ever since…well, for a while now, I've been picking up everything everyone around me is feeling."

"I'm blocking. It's a wall I've constructed to keep you from reading me. Melika will show you how, too."

Sighing, I watched the landscape go by. This was my new life, my new beginning, and I was already realizing that I couldn't have been more out of my element if I'd been on the moon.

"Don't worry if you're feeling overwhelmed. We all felt that way when we first got here."

Watching a new world fly past, I thought about my last couple of days at the hospital. They had been pure torture, and I understood, all too clearly, why that poor drooling girl had cracked. I couldn't get away from the emotional pounding of anyone who came near me. It was as if every one of them was screaming into my brain at the same time. As a result, I stayed in my room, seeing only Big George, and occasionally Celeste, but even then I could only take her in small doses.

So, here I was, coming to empathic boot camp, where I would, hopefully, learn to block out the noises threatening my sanity. This was serious; not a frivolous moment to be squandered. Yes, New Orleans was a most incredible place, but it was so much more than that to me. It was the keeper of a mysterious woman I knew little about, but who offered to teach me how to live with what had driven any number of people like me mad. And as we left New Orleans proper and started to wind our way to the Bayou, I looked forward to meeting this woman who was going to save my life. But as we floated lazily down the river, further and farther from the city, I was beginning to wonder if this was such a good idea.

An hour later, we pulled up to a tiny cinderblock house precariously perched on a sliver of land overlooking the brackish water. It looked like a shed behind one of the more dilapidated houses in the ghetto.

"She lives *here*?"

Jacob shook his head. "Nope. Bones lives here. He's the boatman."

"Boatman? We need to take a boat?"

This seemed to amuse Jacob. "You really don't know much, do you? Where have you been? In a cave?"

"Actually, I've been in a psych ward," I replied, leveling my gaze at him. "Sorry I didn't have time to bone up on my geography."

"Oh. Gee. I'm sorry."

"Ya gone stan' der yakkin' all day, boy?" a tall, bony man asked. He looked like a skeleton with a black plastic bag pulled over his bones. He spoke with an accent I hadn't heard before.

"Hold your horses, Bones. She's one of Melika's newbies. She's new to the whole Bayou thing."

Bones hobbled over to me and bent down to look in my eyes. His were two pieces of coal. "Ain't nuddin' to fear out here less'n you goes inda water. Dun't go inda water."

I swallowed loudly. "What's in the water?"

"Death," Bones said, shaking his head and pulling up a pants

31

leg. He wore a two-foot long scar from his inner knee to the top of his raggedy boot. "Dey kint have old Bones," he said, grinning. He had maybe half his teeth. Maybe.

"Stop scaring her, Bones, you old bag. You know Melika doesn't like it when you scare them."

"Den don't tell her, boy." Bones raised up and sent a warning glare over to Jacob. "You too old to be a tattler, Jacob Marley."

Jacob Marley? Wasn't he a character in the Dickens story?

"I won't tell her, but stop scaring the girl. It's hard enough."

"Fine den. Come on, missy. Get inda boat." He pronounced it boot.

I looked over at "the boat." It looked like a cartoon boat that had been shot at by Elmer Fudd. "You want *me* to get in *that*?"

"It's the only way," Jacob said, heading over to the piece of Swiss cheese Bones called a boat.

"Get on in, missy," Bones said, tossing two oars to Jacob before grabbing a really long pole. "'Gator getter," he said.

Tentatively, I stepped into the rickety raft, my eyes scanning the water for alligators.

"Dey ain't none near here," Bones said, chuckling under his breath. "I sind dem away long time ago. Me and dem…unnerstand what's what."

Glad he did because I sure as hell didn't. "Then what's the stick for?"

"Um…just what he said. In case a 'gator gets curious, then he just pushes them away."

I scooted to the very center of the raft. They had no right calling this thing a boat. It was a raft with punctured sides that looked like a family of termites had it for dinner. "With a goddamned stick? Don't you have a machete or a shotgun or something?"

Bones was chuckling as he pushed away from the shore. "We don't kill sometin' dat lets us live on de land. We're de trespassers here. We leave dem be. It all works out." Bones pushed off from the dock with his big stick. It was then I noticed this crappy boat actually had a motor. I wondered if it even worked.

"You gotta respect de Bayou," Bones said softly. The only other sounds I could hear were insect noises and other wild sounds I knew nothing about. Our wildlife in Oakland were gang members howling at the moon during drive-bys.

I was a long way from home.

"Well, Jacob Marley, educate de girl."

Jacob sighed and nodded. "Bayou comes from the French word meaning small stream and is used when talking about the delta of the Mississippi. It's not a swamp, though folks call it that."

I nodded. Swamp, delta, Bayou, it was all the same to me.

"The water's got creatures in it that'll kill you; 'gators and snakes mostly. Stay outta the water and you'll be safe."

"Um...don't alligators and snakes come to land?"

"Sure, but not to get *you*. They come to land for other reasons, but if you go in the water, you're in *their* home and could end up *their* dinner."

"Respect de Bayou," Bones said to no one in particular. "And stay outta de water."

I looked down at the brackish water and cringed. It looked filthy, like a really muddy mud puddle. At least if an alligator was going to get you, you'd never see it coming.

Looking up at the huge trees stationed near the bank, I saw weird mint-green colored string hanging from nearly every branch like a wedding veil. "What's the green stuff hanging from the trees?"

"Spanish moss. The Cajuns used to use it to stuff their mattresses." Jacob looked at me and sighed. "Don't know what a Cajun is, either, I suppose."

I looked away, suddenly feeling very small...or was it just that the world suddenly got bigger?

"Cajuns were the French speakers who came here from Nova Scotia and preferred the Bayou over the city. Cajun also means a type of cooking. You'll see that a lot here."

"Then what's Creole?" I'd seen plenty of signs in town about authentic Creole cooking.

"Creole means different things to different people. Creoles down here were born in the West Indies or came from French descent. You *do* know that Louisiana is French, right?"

I knew something was French about it, but not exactly. "Yes, I know."

"Creole is a language, a way of cooking and a people. Melika is Creole. Her family is from Haiti." He looked hard at me and shook his head. "It's an island in the Caribbean. There are tons of definitions for both words. Whatever you do, don't confuse a Creole with a Cajun. That really pisses 'em off." Jacob nodded to Bones. "He's Creole. Call him a Cajun and he'll dump you in the water."

Nodding, I ducked my head as we passed under a long strand of Spanish moss. "What are you?"

Bones and Jacob both laughed. "Me? I'm from the Bronx."

"New York?"

Jacob nodded. "Finally, something you *do* know. I've been here since I was eight. Not sure I want to go back to a city. My home is here, and if what I hear is right, I'll probably die here."

I nodded, not understanding what he meant. "And you like it here?" It was beyond me how anyone could like this foreign world with its dinosaurs and deadly snakes.

"Not like. Love. It's my home. It's gonna be yours, too. It may take awhile, but you'll learn to love it, too. You'll see."

What I saw were metal shacks I thought were sheds dotting the banks of the river, and it took me awhile to realize they were actually people's homes. Even in the worst foster home, I lived better than these poor people. "People *live* there?"

"Yes. I told you. This place is unlike anywhere in the world, but don't assume everyone out here is poor. As a matter of fact, don't assume anything until you learn more about this place."

Bones made a sound like he was sucking his teeth. "De boy got dat wrong. Always assume de 'gator is inna water and hungry."

I shuddered and changed the subject. "Can you tell me anything about Melika?"

Jacob shook his head. "She's not like anyone you will ever

34

meet, but that's all I'm gonna say about her. She hates being discussed. And trust me...she'll know."

Nodding once more, I put my hands in my lap just as I heard something kerplunk into the water. I sat up straighter. "What was that?"

"'Gator. Get used to the sound."

"Is it coming toward us? Can you see it? Is it hungry?" Every stupid nature horror movie I'd ever seen flashed through my head.

"Nope. Relax, missy. Bones ain't never lost one a Melika's students, 'specially wid Jacob Marley on board."

I looked over at Jacob. "He's kidding."

I spent the remainder of the time in awe of the human beings living on the Bayou. There were some shacks that made Bones' house look palatial. Each shack had a short wooden dock and a boat even more rickety than the last. As we floated on, the shacks became fewer and fewer until some actually looked like nothing more than lean-tos and I realized there were no more electrical lines.

"How do they get electricity out here?"

"Dey don't."

"No electricity. No plumbing. Nothing like you're used to," Jacob said.

Oh, now I *knew* I was out of my league...maybe even out of my planet.

Unbuttoning my shirt, I fanned myself. The heat, the odd odors, the sounds, all of it made me uncomfortable. "Please tell me you're just messing with me."

"Look around you. You see any telephone poles out here? The Bayou is as primitive and as wild as it gets. You don't come out here for luxury or even rest. Tourists get the nickel ride to see a few 'gators, but the livin' out here is hard." Jacob looked hard into my eyes. "You're here to learn, and you'll learn from the best. Trust me. You'll be really glad you came."

I sat in silence. I could handle alligators, poisonous snakes, mosquitoes and crawdads better than I could the thought of turning into that drooling, rocking nightmare of a girl back at

35

the psych ward. My greatest fear of being burned alive had been replaced by the fear of turning into *that*.

The remainder of the trip was spent in silence, with only the lapping of the water communicating with us. Bones never used the small engine or the oars, preferring the big pole like those guys in Italy. Occasionally, Jacob would row a bit, but not often.

I was missing Danica already. When she asked me when we would see each other again, I honestly didn't know. My friends were my life and I had left both behind under cover of darkness. I didn't just leave them behind...I left the old me as well, and I couldn't think about her going on without me. She swore we would be best friends forever. I had to believe her. She was all I had.

"We're here," Jacob announced after what felt like hours.

Looking up, I saw a tiny woman standing on the end of a dock that looked newer than the other docks we had passed. "That's her?"

Jacob nodded. "She always comes to the boat to greet the newbies. She'll get a feel for you right away."

As we approached the dock and the older woman waiting for us, I was mesmerized by her gorgeous flawless caramel-colored skin. She was wearing a black sundress with big black galoshes. In her right hand was a walking stick that had intricate carvings whose detail I couldn't distinguish from the boat. Though I knew she was Big George's mama, she didn't look a day over forty. Her black hair had no gray in it and hung down to her shoulders in a single, thick braid. Even as the boat pulled alongside the dock, I saw eyes like topaz shining and they were locked intently onto mine. Like Jacob, I felt nothing from her and realized this was the first time in days I hadn't had to deal with others' emotions.

"Afternoon, Madame," Bones said when the boat came to rest at her feet.

Melika smiled knowingly as she reached into the front pocket of her dress. She withdrew a little baggie and handed it to Bones. "Try this on it and make sure you heat it up nice and good, you hear?"

I looked at Jacob and started to ask a question, but he shook his head at me.

"Now, Jacob, just because we have a pretty one doesn't mean you can go and forget your manners." She turned her smile at me and warmth ran from the top of my head to all my extremities. Whether it was from me or her, I couldn't tell. "I'm Melika, dear. You must be Echo."

Jacob scurried off the boat and helped me out.

"Yes, I am. It's a pleasure to meet you."

Melika reached for my hand and held it tightly as she gazed deep into my eyes. I felt like I could stand there forever. "Oh my," she said softly.

"What?"

Releasing my hand, she picked something from my hair and tossed it into the water. "It appears George got to you not a moment too soon." Melika continued looking in my eyes, searching for something. I could barely feel it, but I knew she was there.

"You can barely feel it, my dear, because I am virtually unreadable to any but the strongest of us. Try as you may, you will *never* know what *I* am feeling, just as a telepath will *never* know what I am thinking." Melika took my chin in her hand. She smelled of mint and oranges. "But you *do* have a great gift, to be sure."

"It feels more like a curse every day."

She released my chin and patted me on the shoulder. "Every gift can become a curse and every curse, a gift. It is how we choose to use it that makes the difference."

And so, without taking another step, lessons began that would change the course of the rest of my life.

I met Tiponi Redhawk next. She was sitting on the stairs to the porch of Melika's cute little cottage that looked like something a Keebler elf might have lived in. Unlike so many of the other shacks lining the Bayou that were made out of thin pieces of wood and sheet metal, this cottage was fashioned out of stone. A small wisp of white smoke curled from the chimney, and I wondered if there was a trail of breadcrumbs somewhere. A covered deck wrapped around the front of the house and had a wooden swing hanging at one end and a set of green plastic Adirondack chairs at the other. Quaint.

That was when I noticed Tiponi sitting on the stairs with her arm draped around a bloodhound. I was immediately struck by her exotic and out-of-place looks. Unlike the black folks I'd met or seen so far, Tiponi's perfect complexion was that of a Native American; a golden hue with a slight reddish tint. Her hair was black tar that hung well past her shoulders. Her light hazel eyes looked at me with such intensity, I had to look away. She was at least twenty...maybe older. It was hard to tell. I'd never been good with ages.

"Stop it, Tip," Melika admonished. "Please bring her things to the blue room, Jacob. Tip, please take Zeus for a walk, will you? I don't need you underfoot right now."

Tip rose and seemed to keep rising for several seconds. She was enormous; legs like the trunks of some of the trees we had passed, shoulders that stretched her shirt to the tearing point, and arms that said she did a lot of heavy lifting all made her quite an imposing figure for a woman. "I thought—"

"I know what you thought, Tip, but not now. Can't you see she is a fish out of water? Scoot. Come back when you can be useful."

"Yes, ma'am." Tip and the wrinkly dog strode away, leaving tree branches and leaves bending in their wake.

"Don't pay her any mind for right now. You'll be working closely with her later, but this trip has made you weary. Jacob will take you to your room. Take a little nap before dinner and get your energy back up. My son explained what happened to you in the hospital, but I'll need to hear every single detail of your life from the first moment you felt what that boy was going to do to you. So, rest, my girl. We have a lot of work ahead."

Nodding, I took two steps and then just started bawling. I'm not talking crying and sniffling; I mean an all-out meltdown. I sobbed uncontrollably until Melika put her arms around me and pulled me closer. She was right about me being exhausted. The horror of the hospital, the fear of the escape, the awful goodbye to the only person who loved me, not knowing when I would see her again hit like an elephant kick to my chest. Add to that, feeling all of the emotions of every person on the plane and entering a land as foreign as Ethiopia, and I was ready to collapse.

By the time I got to the blue room, I was more than ready for a nap. I needed to just close the world around me and just sleep.

I did.

"Welcome back," came Jacob's voice from a rocking chair in the corner of the small room.

"What time is it?"

"Two fifteen."

I frowned, trying to remember how the times changed from one time zone to the next.

"Of the next day," Jacob said, smiling. "You've been asleep almost twenty-four hours."

"What?" Sitting up, I looked out the window at the bright sunlight. "It's tomorrow?"

"That's one way of looking at it. Melika has lunch on the table."

Inhaling deeply, I rose and stretched. The smell of something baking hit my nostrils making me instantly hungry. "God," I said, slowly putting my feet on the cold floor. I hadn't slept that well in ages, but twenty hours? Sheesh. "I didn't know I was so tired."

"Everyone does it when they first get here. We call it Bayou Bliss. She just wraps her arms around you and lulls you to sleep. It will help you with your night terrors, for sure."

"My ni—how did you know about those?"

"I was watching."

"All night?"

He shook his head. "We took turns."

"Including Tiponi?" The idea of that huge Indian woman staring at me all night made me nervous.

"Nah. Just me, Mel and Zack."

"Is that how she knew I needed a nap?"

"Melika knows everything about us. That's all I can say right now. Melika will start your lessons after lunch. Be smart and listen carefully to everything she says. When I say she knows everything, I'm not kidding. She can give you your life back. No one else can."

I believed him.

I followed Jacob down the stairs, smelling this incredible aroma with every step. At the bottom, sitting at a small picnic table, were Melika and Tip. There was a huge pot of something that had steam rising off the top. It smelled so good, I couldn't stop salivating.

"I trust you slept well," Melika said, dipping her ladle into the reddish stew. Tip cut a piece of corn bread out of the pan and set it on the table. My stomach made its embarrassing announcement that it was hungry. "Have a seat and eat up. There's plenty."

"I'm sorry I slept so long. It's sort of rude."

"Always listen to your body, my girl. Let that be your first lesson. Your body will always tell you what you need, where you need to go, what to do if only you let it. Primitive man relied more heavily on his body than his mind. He ate when he was hungry, not because someone or some social rules told him it was time for dinner. Sometimes, progress takes us backward."

I sat at the picnic table across from scary Tip, who never took her eyes from me. She was sort of creeping me out with her intensity and I found I could not maintain eye contact with her for longer than a moment.

"I'm Tip," she said, extending her hand to me. "We haven't formally met."

I reached across the table and shook her hand. "Echo."

"Interesting name."

I shrugged, retrieving my hand. "It fits."

Tip motioned with her chin over to Jacob. "As fitting as Jacob Marley?"

I started to ask what she meant, but my stomach continued to make itself known. My plate was loaded down with a yummy red stew and a chunk of corn bread. There was a crab-like thing in the stew that I had never seen before.

"Crawdads," Tip said.

"We eat crawdads the way other people eat chicken. Tip, show her how."

She picked up one of the crawdads, popped her thumb under the head and then pulled it off and sucked it before removing the meat from the shell. "Sucking his brains out is a Cajun thing, but don't do it if you don't feel up to it." Tip went on to explain how there are a lot of Cajun ways and Creole ways and Southern ways and Louisianan ways of doing things. I had never seen so many customs in my life. But no matter whose way was right, they all had one thing in common; an appreciation for fine food that was evident by the way they all dug in.

I jumped into my plateful of food with gusto that almost scared me.

"Always keep your body well-nourished, which is very different from well-fed. Eating well does not mean eat a lot. Treat your body like you would an expensive automobile; give it only the best." Melika sipped her coffee and cut her eyes over to Tip. Something passed between them I could not name.

"And so it begins," Tip said under her breath.

Melika swatted her arm. "Hush, you, unless you want to spend your days with Zeus."

"No, I'm good." Tip held her hands in surrender.

Melika returned her attention to me. "So, my girl, tell me what happened that day with the boy. Don't leave a single detail out no matter how insignificant it may seem."

Tip turned to me. "You'll find that Mel is quite detail-oriented, so the sooner you get used to sharing the details, the better. We have no secrets."

Nodding, I finished my meal and started my story. I wouldn't get three sentences out before Melika would stop with a question or five. Tip wasn't kidding when she said she liked details. She didn't just like them...she demanded them.

When I finally finished telling her every single thing that had transpired since I whacked Todd in the head, it was nearly five o'clock; three hours in the telling.

"Very good. Now, I have a clearer picture of how you came to be. What we *don't* know is how you came to be *what you are.*" Melika motioned to Jacob, who rose and started clearing the table. "Come."

I followed her outside to the porch. We sat in the Adirondacks while Tip took the steps with Zeus.

"What do you mean how I became what I am?"

"Most of us are born one way or the other, Echo. Very few of us come to it in the middle of our lives. It is difficult when that happens because we are incapable of understanding what is happening to us until, more often than not, it's too late."

I looked over at Tip, who was petting Zeus. "Her?"

"Born."

"Jacob?"

"Born."

"You?"

She grinned. "Born. Like I said, very few of us are like you. As you learn and grow here, perhaps we'll discover what it is that brought it out in you."

"Big George said I'm an empath. Is that true?"

"That remains to be seen. At first glance, you appear to be clairempathic; you feel the emotional energies of others. You can read their auras until it becomes a part of you. You can experience their emotions with them. You are overrun by others' emotions."

I nodded. "But...I must have lost it or something because I can't feel anything from any of you. Jacob mentioned something about blocking, but I don't—"

"Blocking means we erect a psychic shield that prevents our energies from leaking to you, and you can't read us because we won't let you. That's what blocking does; it protects us from each other."

"You can actually do that?"

"So can you. At least, you will when I'm done with you."

"So...you're all empaths?"

Tip threw her head back and laughed. It was a sound I would hear repeatedly for the next four years of my life.

My first week with Melika was eye-opening, to say the least. It wasn't just the bizarre food or location in the swamp that was strange, but the lessons I learned from others like me. I had had no idea how close I had come to losing my sanity...of coming to the edge of reason and falling off. Without their help, I would have most assuredly ended up like that frothing girl back in the California psych ward.

I was an empath. Unlike those born with the gift, I had come into mine in a moment of crisis; not uncommon for supers. Because it came upon me so quickly and without notice, it had the potential of quickly consuming me and driving me mad. I owed my sanity as well as my life to Big George...I knew I would end up owing my future to Melika.

"The first lesson is going to be the hardest one, yet the most important," Melika told me the second day there. We'd loaded up a small boat with picnic items as she and I headed out to the Bayou. The Bayou, like I said, was another world unto itself. Out here, there was no hustle or bustle of crowds or people too full of their own self importance. Out here, there was just you and nature. You either learned to become part of the natural world or you'd leave it behind on your way back. For me, there *was* no *back*, there *was* no home. There was only this moment, and I was, at this moment, staring at an enormous alligator basking in the sun on the banks of the Bayou. I couldn't help but hear Linda Ronstadt, though there wasn't anything blue about it, really.

"You tensed up when you saw the 'gator. Do you know why?" Melika adjusted her large straw hat. Today she was wearing another black dress similar to the one she had on when I arrived. The rubber galoshes she had worn seemed to be her shoe of choice. Today, she had a yellow shawl wrapped around her shoulders even though the temperature was already over eighty degrees.

"Because he could eat us."

43

Melika barely glanced at the beast. "Could. The question is does it *want* to?"

I stared at the prehistoric creature as the boat glided silently by. Neither of us were rowing, just floating down the river. I was pleased to see that this boat also had an outboard motor at the rear. Although no one seemed to use them on the Bayou.

"Well...I guess it could, but—"

"Don't guess. Guessing is for naturals. *We're* not naturals, Echo. We're *super*naturals. We can do things they cannot. A natural would make all sorts of assumptions about that 'gator. I don't want you to assume. I want you to read it."

"Read it? You mean—"

"Look at it. Everything has a vibration, an energy, a frequency that others can tune into. Not everyone has the ability to tune into others, and not all empaths can read animals or the natural environment. I want to see if you can."

Nodding, I tried to put my fear of the ugly beast aside long enough to really focus in on it. Sure enough, I was immediately hit with a wave of bored energy from the alligator. He was more interested in napping than he was in eating us. "Oh my God! I did it!"

Melika smiled softly. "Very good. So much of what we're going to be doing for the next couple of weeks is just to determine the strength of your power. You must be patient during this process because we cannot proceed with the education until we know what all you are capable of."

"Wait a second. What do you mean, *all*?"

"Many empaths have additional sight as well as telepathy, clairvoyance—"

"Clair what?"

Melika inhaled deeply. "A telepath can do what you do, only with thoughts. Some telepaths are slightly empathic, some empaths slightly telepathic. Our gifts are as varied as our faces. There are so many varying degrees of our powers. No one knows how or why, and none of us know the true depths of our respective powers until we push the envelope."

"And clairvoyancy?"

"Is the ability to see the past, present and future moments."

"People can really do that?"

Melika tilted her head and when the sunlight caught her face, she looked years younger. "There are all sorts of gifts, Echo. All of you who have come to me have always been dubious about the other gifts even though you possess your own." Melika took her hat off and sighed. "Let me ask you this: do you think the idea of flight was impossible to the people of the Middle Ages? Or that fuel-powered cars seemed like just a silly dream? Do you think men and women of the Wild West ever believed we could walk on the moon?"

I shook my head.

"And what about the idea of reattaching limbs, or transplanting organs? Don't you think there was a time when the majority of people thought these were merely fantastical ideas?"

I nodded.

"And what about computers? Television? Radio? The Internet? Those used to be beyond the scope of man's ability, yet here they are. We can drive, fly, do microscopic surgery and even clone creatures now, but these things were once considered impossibilities."

I nodded, watching another 'gator slip into the water. "But they *weren't* impossible."

"Indeed, because they all happened. Now, we have pills that can keep us from getting pregnant, we can travel at the speed of sound, and even some blindness can be cured. But isn't it funny that with all humankind can accept and do, it still does not believe in the power of the human mind that created all of this." Melika pushed her hat back as I used the pole against a nearby bank. "Humans use less than ten percent of their brain. Apparently, this is a fact. What, then, is the other ninety percent used for? Filler? Clearly, it's used for something, but science hasn't figured it out yet."

My eyes grew wide as I realized where she was going with this. "You're saying—"

"I'm saying that just because society does not believe a thing exists does not mean it doesn't. Before science came along to tell us what to believe and not believe, people believed in the possibilities of witchcraft, of alchemy, of Merlin's power and the mental capabilities of the pagans. But science came along, Christianity grew powerful and soon, what couldn't be explained or proven became an *impossibility*. Those of us with supernatural powers were forced underground by the fear of being hunted and destroyed. People like you and me lived in fear of being found out. *We* are one such impossibility."

I nodded. "I get it."

"Don't you find it interesting how many insane people who are locked up say they hear voices? The belief is that only crazies hear voices. According to modern man and science, these voices must come from within that person. Because it is impossible *for science* to prove that we can do what we do, we've labeled those who actually can hear voices *insane*."

"But it *is* possible. We're proof of that."

"Oh, dear girl, only a small number of us know how very possible it is. It's funny; science tells us animals communicate in any number of ways we can't. But we can only talk? Why, if we're so damn smart, can't we communicate much in the same way dolphins can?"

"Because we can?"

Melika nodded. "Exactly. And we always have been able to. It's possible, once we started using language, we actually devolved away from telepathic communication like the rest of the animal kingdom. But not all of us. Just as there are still some white Bengal tigers left in the world, there are those of us who can do what the rest cannot."

"We're the supernaturals."

Melika nodded. "Yes, we are. We *are* the living, breathing impossibilities of our time." She patted my leg. "Since we are the impossibilities of this age, and if it was ever *proven* that we truly existed, we would all be forced back into hiding. Do you know why?"

I shook my head.

"Because we would be reduced to lab rats. Scientists would *use* us to see how to duplicate or replicate our gifts. We would become a giant human guinea pig."

I was beginning to get it. "Because the government would want to exploit us."

Melika grinned slightly. "Absolutely. Think what it would do for a president to be able to have an aide who could read the minds of everyone in the room."

My stomach lurched at the thought. "We would never be free."

"Never. If governments could tap into what we have, they would do it regardless of what it would mean to our personal freedom. Think about it. We would be poked and prodded like—"

"An alien?"

"Precisely. Our powers are as alien to the world as an extraterrestrial being, so, we must be careful in the real world. Of course, there are those of us who are flashy and out there, but that's because they rely on the public not to actually believe that what they are seeing is actually happening."

"Oh wow. That's scary."

"Indeed. There are those of us who use our powers for personal gain. Unethical use of any of our powers can result in a rather unpleasant visit from some in our community to whom we must all heed."

My eyebrows rose. "We have people we are responsible to?"

Melika cocked her head. "Why to all of us, my dear. Each of us is responsible to the other and to our community as a whole. The protection of our existence is a necessary component of our lives. Those who put others at risk are…dealt with."

"Dealt with? Sounds ominous."

"It can be. We must protect ourselves from society at large as well as from each other. I will show you how to do both." Melika brought her hair forward and began working on a thick braid. "You, my dear, are an incredibly powerful empath, and when we are done with your lessons, it will be up to you to locate

47

those who haven't yet lost their battle with insanity. You will, like my son, become a spotter in order to save those who need help. When you do, you will bring them here, to me, for the same help and guidance you're getting. That is the only *deal* on the table for you. In exchange for the semblance of a normal life, you must agree to help others like you."

"How will I find them?"

"You'll know. Some will be beyond help. Others won't want it. But for those who do, you must reach out to them in the same way Big George did for you."

I nodded and said nothing.

"You will, at times, see those who choose to make money from their gifts. Case in point are two of those men on television who speak to the dead."

"No way. You mean—"

"What I mean, dear girl, is that we are everywhere. Some of us do manage to make a living using our gifts because what we do cannot be scientifically proven, such as speaking to the dead or reading the future. They are, in some ways, safe from the prying eyes of our government, so they are allowed to do what they do."

"Allowed by? You make it sound so mysterious."

"No mystery, Echo, just protectiveness. One day, when you need to know, you will."

Leaning back, I heaved a huge sigh. It was so much to take in.

"Yes, it is, which is why we are just chatting. Before we can even start helping you understand and utilize your powers, you must first understand the nature of the supernatural community to which you now belong."

"Supernatural is such a...weird word."

"I prefer supernatural over paranormal. I try to excise the word normal out of my vocabulary. There is *nothing* normal about us. When we wake up every morning, we must create shields, deal with excessive energies, protect ourselves against psychic vampires, and try not to let our powers ruin our lives."

Psychic vampires?

"A crisis turned your powers on, so to speak. They were always there, laying dormant, waiting for the right chemicals to flip the switch. Your switch was flipped, my dear, and that's why you felt what that boy wanted from you."

I thought about poor Todd's head. "But I think I could have killed him."

"No, you wouldn't have. You would have felt his life ebbing away and come to your senses. You're no killer, Echo."

I bowed my head and tried to keep the tears from coming. Melika reached over and touched my knee. "You're not alone and you're no freak. You have a gift. I'm going to show you just how special that gift is."

"But how did I *get* it?"

"Clairempaths, which is what you are, come by their powers genetically. Somewhere in your family history there are others with similar powers."

"I wouldn't know. I'm an orphan. My birth name is—"

"Jane Doe. Yes, I know. I know a great deal more about you than you realize." She smiled. "I have a few powers of my own."

We stayed on the water talking about life, about other supers she had taught and how each of them managed to find their own way. I told her about Danica and how much I missed her. To my surprise, Melika promised I could talk to her tomorrow, when I went in to town. This perked me up immediately. It was one thing to escape from the psych ward, but I felt so cut-off from the rest of the world out here on the Bayou.

The best part was how calm I had suddenly become. Melika had called it stabilizing. She said it was important for me to clear out the energies from the psych ward and settle down from all the anxiety and fear I had been experiencing. I have to say that sleep really helped. I felt rested for the first time in forever. No night terrors had made their way into my sleep.

When the bugs started eating us, Melika showed me how to start the motor so we could head back up the Bayou more easily. If you've never been in the Louisiana Bayou, the best way I can

49

describe it is a water labyrinth. There are main thoroughfares, side streets, inlets and assorted waterways, none of which were marked with any sort of sign. There was absolutely nothing to let you know where you were and it all looked the same. All of it.

But I quickly realized it only appeared that way. As Melika pointed out various trees and other landmarks, I started to see the Bayou through different eyes. There were too many greens to name, various trees of all sizes, and scenery more stunning than any I had ever seen. I was beginning to understand why some people never left here.

Actually, I was beginning to understand me.

I wasn't a freak after all. I had a chromosome or something natural that gave me supernatural powers I need not be afraid of. I needed training. I needed understanding. I needed to be exactly where I was.

When we finally returned to the cute little cottage, Jacob was waiting on the dock. "What is it, Jacob?"

"Another incoming, ma'am," Jacob said, holding up a cell phone. "TK."

Melika nodded solemnly. "I've been expecting him. Where is he?"

"Atlanta."

She nodded. "Tip packed and ready?"

"Yes, ma'am."

"Thank you, Jacob." Melika took his hand as he helped her from the boat. When she got out, she turned and helped me out. "Tomorrow, we will discuss how to protect yourself, how to reserve your energy, how to make everything work in your life. You need not ever be afraid here. You are safe. I know that you have never had a real family, but I'd like you to consider all of us here one."

I swallowed hard and nodded. "I'd like that. I'd like that a lot."

And with that, for the first time in my life, I had a family.

No wonder I had slept so well.

After I was well-rested and well-fed, it was time to get down to the real lessons. Tip had gone off to Atlanta, leaving me and Jacob to tend to the many chores around the cottage. The weather was mild in the Bayou, but without electricity, Melika had to cook by a fire that was always burning. There was also a brick barbecue on the side that she used as well. Let me tell you, that woman could cook. I think I gained ten pounds the first ten minutes I was there. It was a good thing I had chores or it would have been twenty.

It's weird to think that my Bayou experience was the closest thing to a normal family I had ever had, but that was the truth. Jacob was the most respectful young man I had ever met. Melika, though not motherly in the slightest, was like a parent in that she had expectations for us to fulfill. We had to rest, eat well, do our chores and be respectful of each other and our environment. Once we finished with our morning chores, our first lesson started, and it wasn't at all what I thought it would be.

"The average stay with me is three or four years. I know it seems like a long time, but gaining complete control of your powers is a long and often complicated journey. It is not easy and there are no shortcuts, but it will mean the difference between having a real life and possibly having none at all."

I gulped hard. I couldn't imagine being in the Bayou a year, let alone four. What would happen to my real life? Were those days long gone and I hadn't even grieved its death?

"There are two ways out of your power; suicide and insanity. Many choose the former after long battles with the latter. To successfully master yourselves, you must invest fully in the process. Everyone's process is different just like everyone's powers are different. What I teach Jacob I may not teach you. Do you understand?"

I nodded.

"Good. Now, since Jacob has been here so long, he is in charge of this week's morning lessons. When you finish your work, he will take you out on the water and educate you about this new environment. It is important you understand your surroundings at all times."

"Is that part of the process?"

Melika nodded and ran her hand up and down her walking stick. "Oh yes. You see, a super must always familiarize herself with her environment. It should be the first thing you do wherever you go. Knowing your environment keeps you safer. Always be aware of the hazards and pitfalls of every environment, that way you can be prepared." Melika rose and walked out to the edge of the dock. "Were you prepared when Todd overtook you? Did you see anything in your surroundings you could have used as a weapon? Did you see any way out besides violence?"

I shook my head. "No."

"You felt the threat and acted, correct?"

"Yes."

"Had you been more aware of your environment, you might have had other choices. A life without options is not a life worth living. The more you understand the Bayou, the more you'll know about life. The Bayou *is* life."

At first, I wondered if maybe this was a mistake. I didn't see how knowing about the Bayou was going to help me. I thought maybe this was a big, fat waste of time.

But Melika had been so right about the Bayou being life. That day, Jacob opened my mind and my world. I saw a texture and layers to the world around me I never knew existed. In Oakland, a tree was a tree. Here, every tree served a purpose, every plant important to the whole. If we don't learn the interconnectedness of the universe, how can we ever truly be a part of it? How can you know *yourself* if you haven't combed the depths of your being?

I felt full of life and energy only nature provides. I understood why Melika sent me out on a boat with Jacob, and I started looking forward to it every morning. He was a great teacher and I learned more about biology and life from him in one week than I learned from any teacher in any school.

That afternoon, Melika took me out into the backwoods behind the cottage and there was a firepit with several stumps for sitting. It would become one of my favorite places in the world.

"I come out here because we need to be away from any

potential emotional energies. What we have to do needs to be done undisturbed. You already know shields help empaths keep out extra emotional energy from others so you aren't overwhelmed. The edge of it works as a psychic alarm. The stronger you are, the better and longer the shield holds up. Now, there are many things that will quickly erode a shield: stress, negative emotions from others, and lack of sleep can deteriorate a shield as well, which is why I want you to eat and sleep well. Anytime your physical body is out of balance, you are vulnerable to attack."

"Attack?"

"Yes. An attack can be from the wave of emotions coming in through your shield, or it can be an attack from another psionic being. Rest, time alone and meditation are wise, so before I teach you how to create a shield, I'll need to show you how to meditate effectively. Meditation is a huge key, but it must be done effectively. Many people don't know how to meditate the correct way, and there is definitely a right way for our purpose."

Who would have thought it would take me two months; two long, grueling months just to learn how to meditate. For a while there, I thought I was just slow. Come to find out, energy cannot easily be called upon or contained without the proper mental approach. It just took me awhile to get to that point. It wouldn't be long before I wasn't the only one who couldn't get it, either.

After my first week there, Tip returned to the Bayou from Atlanta with another student. His name was Zack and he had also just come into his powers.

Only his powers were not empathic in nature. Zack was a TK, or a telekinetic. Tip referred to him as a mover; someone who could move objects using the energy from his mind. Zack, a twelve-year-old boy from Savannah, Georgia, was a redheaded boy with freckles and a bad haircut. Tall and lanky, you just knew kids teased him all the time.

Soon I realized it was a mistake to tease someone with out-of-control telekinetic abilities. A TK is a very powerful being, indeed, and I saw how powerful he was the moment he arrived.

When Zack stepped off Bones' boat, he was just like I had

been: disoriented, exhausted and on the edge. I could feel his tender emotions and fear as he got off the boat and looked around. As he started up the steps, he lost his balance, and when Tip reached out to help him, Zack, out of fear, put his arm out straight toward Tip knocking her to the ground without ever touching her. It was the most amazing thing I had seen in my life. From then on, Tip gave him a wide berth, and sometimes when Zack would leave the room, Tip muttered under her breath, "Spoon bender."

I would find out later what that meant.

Shielding was, by far, the hardest lesson I had ever learned. I don't know why I thought it was something I could learn in a day or so, but boy, was I wrong. This was the single most important skill Melika had to teach me. Without it, without being really efficient at erecting it, maintaining it, stabilizing it and lowering it without incident, my chances to live out a semi-normal life were slim-to-none. I wanted a life. No, I wanted a *normal* life insomuch as I had never had one. I'd been in and out of so many foster homes.

Until I came to the Bayou.

Every day was different on the Bayou. The weather changed on an hourly basis, the creatures were unlike anything else I had ever seen, and the river itself seemed to change on a whim. I loved it. I never saw myself as a naturalist, never gave much thought to the world around me. I paid very close attention to *the people* around me. You did that when you lived in the ghetto. It was *ghetto* back then. We didn't pretty up the ugly nature of the ghetto with euphemisms like inner city or 'hood. It was the ghetto.

You can spray gold flecks on a dog turd and it would still be a turd. So, when I lived in turdville, I paid really close attention to gangs of every color, drug dealers of every race, prostitutes of every shape, and pimpmobiles of every make. For your physical safety in the ghetto, you paid attention or you paid a price.

Out in the Bayou, you did the same for the same reasons. I

learned to love the sound of the 'gators as they slid off the muddy banks. They made a distinctive sound in the water that no longer frightened me. There were hawks whose calls were music to my ears, and insects whose nightly serenade sent me to sleep.

And then there were the various characters who came and went. There was the French-speaking woodcutter, a grocery delivery woman with only one eye, and a gardener of sorts who had a boa wrapped around his neck.

And then there was Bishop.

Bishop was Melika's very colorful mother, and it was her powers that had eventually brought the family from the West Indies to a plantation in Georgia. When she was finally able to free herself from the debts of her "boss," Bishop went straight to New Orleans and opened up what was to become one of the most profitable tarot reading businesses in the state of Louisiana. Bigwigs, CEOs, restaurateurs and drag queens came to her for advice, solace and a glimpse into their future. But Bishop wasn't a twenty dollar an hour shill pretending to read cards. Bishop had the sight: the pinnacle of all clairvoyant powers.

The first time I met her was my third week in the Bayou. Melika and I were working on building a shield I could keep up for more than a minute, when Bishop and her boatman pulled up to our dock.

Melika and I walked out to the porch. "Oh Lordy," Melika said under her breath. "She's earlier than usual."

"Is that her?" I whispered. "Your mother?" Jacob had told me about Bishop on one of our morning Bayou trips. She was some big voodoo priestess who scared half the population of New Orleans. They lived and died by her readings, paying a small fortune to see what lay ahead.

What I saw in the boat was a thin woman draped in all black and wearing a hat. She must have stood less than four feet eight. Her boatman helped her out of the boat, but he remained there staring at her.

"Yes, dear girl, that's my mother. She comes to check out the new blood every blue moon. She always knows whenever there's a new one of us in town. It's her way. Now don't let her scare you. That's her way as well."

Zack joined me and Melika on the porch and together the three of us started toward the dock.

Bishop was the most exotic woman I had ever seen. Her skin had a goldenish hue and her complexion was flawless. No wrinkled old hag, Bishop's skin seemed to defy time. As she walked across the pier toward us, I beheld a woman of grace and class. She carried herself like she owned the world. Short in stature, she made up for it in attitude.

"You must be Echo," Bishop said before I could open my mouth. Like everyone else on this side of the Bayou, she was blocking, so I couldn't read her at all. "My, my, Melika, what have we here?" Bishop's low, musical voice mesmerized me but it was her eyes that captured me. Bishop's eyes were yellow. "Do you know what you have here?" she asked Melika without taking her eyes off mine.

"I am well aware, mother."

Bishop released me from her gaze and looked up at Melika. "Nick of time. Good boy, my Georgie. He's a gem, that one. How are her lessons going?"

"She is bright and unafraid." Melika put her arm around my shoulders and pulled me reassuringly closer. "Eager to learn."

"Excellent. Fear is a useless emotion. We need not fear a thing from those who cannot do as we do." Bishop looked over at Zack. "Ah...a mover. Tell me, boy, can you move my hat from my head?"

Zack stared at Melika, who, to my surprise, nodded.

"Take your best shot, boy." Bishop winked.

Blinking a few times, Zack hesitated and Bishop held up her hand.

"Wait," she said, turning back to me. "Can you see it?"

I frowned. As far as I knew, my powers were emotional, not visual. I had never seen— "Not true," Bishop replied, interrupting my thoughts. "You *think* your powers are merely emotive, but you're wrong. My daughter will, of course, show you how to better utilize *all* of your senses, but for the moment, I want you just to look carefully at Zachary."

I nodded and did as she said.

"Now, relax your eyes. Don't focus on the physical being of Zachary, but on his image. If you see him but don't really see him, you'll notice something about him. Like those silly pictures you stare at until you see something else. What is it you see?"

Sure enough, as I relaxed my eyes, I could see a slight haze all around him, as if outlining him. "A haze...like a blur."

"All living things are creatures of energy, Echo, and for those with your gift, it is visible to the naked eye much in the same way night vision goggles zoom in on the heat from our bodies. You have the wonderful skill of being able to read people's auras. This will help you ascertain the integrity of people. It will help you make your way in the world more safely. Now, tell me what color it is."

"Umm...green?"

"Be specific. Is it olive, lime, emerald, kelly, forest—"

"Dark green. Like a forest green, yeah."

Bishop nodded and patted my shoulder. "Good girl. Dark green means mental stress, which is precisely what Zachary is feeling right about now. He is unsure if he can do what I have asked him to do. Isn't that right, Zachary?"

He nodded, but didn't move. Even with his wild red hair, there was something charming and sweet about him. When he looked at me, I immediately felt a kinship with him I'd only felt with Danica. He felt it, too.

"Cool," I murmured, trying my new skill on Bishop.

"He's the only one you can read right now because he has not yet learned how to block. But keep your eyes on him and tell me what happens." To Zack, she said, "My hat, young man."

Zack rubbed his hands together before turning his palms toward Bishop. Zack frowned and I felt him press harder, wanting to please her.

"Color?"

"Orange."

"Meaning?"

"He's trying really hard."

"Good girl. Orange means strong motivation. Keep trying Zack."

I watched him try again.

"Color?"

"Pumpkin."

"Ah, yes. Self-control. Well done. That's good, Zachary."

"But—"

"It's okay, my boy. I asked you to do something I would not let you do."

"*You* stopped me?"

Bishop smiled. "Of course." She stepped closer to him and smiled kindly into his face. "You must remember always that no matter how strong you think you are, there's always someone stronger than yourself. Always. And because you can't identify other supers, you must never assume the people around you are not. Using your particular abilities in public could very well be the last thing you do."

Zack nodded. "Yes, ma'am, but how—"

Bishop held her hand up. "Not now. Later. Be a dear, Zachary, and get me a glass of Melika's lemonade, please."

Zack bolted into the house.

"Mother, stop scaring the boy."

"I'm not scaring him. The boy is a male, Melika. You know how dangerous male movers tend to be when they come into their powers." Bishop turned to me. "What you are going to face is much more difficult than anything you've experienced these last three weeks. Always stay focused. Always be disciplined. Having a power does not give you carte blanche to use it indiscriminately."

I nodded. "You sound so much like Melika."

Bishop chuckled. "Of course I do. Who do you think taught her everything she knows?"

And that was my first meeting with a woman I would come to love as a strict grandmother. I would learn so much about her powers, about mine, about life and my place in it. For a fourteen-year-old girl who had never had a place, this was just about the biggest gift anyone could give me.

And I wasn't going to waste it.

I had been on the Bayou for a little over six months when Melika announced we were finally ready to go into town. I'd only been in that one day when she allowed me to call Danica to let her know I'd arrived safely. Since then, it had been a grueling six months of learning every single day how to read emotions correctly. There was more to it than the learning. Zack, Jacob and I would sit around the firepit with Tip and Melika discussing the moral and ethical issues we faced by being different. There were supers who abused their powers, and when they did, someone from deep within us takes care of them. That was about all Melika was willing to tell us about the ramifications of putting the rest of us at risk. She said when the time was right, she'd tell us.

Of course, we wanted the time to be right now.

"I'm pretty sure it's tough turning down a million dollar Vegas gig," Zack said afterward while twirling a rock on his index finger.

"Don't," Jacob said. "You heard Mel; it's totally uncool to use our power for personal gain."

"That's not what she said, homey. She said it's wrong putting the rest of us at risk. Big difference. Some of us can do shit and get away with it. Like you. Who'd believe that you were talking to the dead?"

I turned to him. "Did you...did you just call Jacob *homey*?" I stepped up to him and was a bit surprised when he didn't back away. Zack never let me invade his personal space.

"He doesn't mind."

"That's not the point."

For a moment, we stood inches apart eyes locked. He couldn't maintain his shield and it dropped just enough for me to realize something I should have known all along: Zack *liked* me.

"Oh. I...uh..."

Turning, Zack walked away, leaving me and Jacob Marley to wonder if he was going to be one of us or one of *them*.

"Don't stress it, Echo," Jacob Marley said. "He's young and foolish. Once he sees his powers are somewhat limited, he oughtta chill."

"Come on, Jacob Marley, it's time for the cit-ayy."

"New Orleans. The Big Easy. The most colorful place in the country. I think you're both ready for the excesses of such a place. It's the perfect testing grounds for all of the lessons you have learned so far."

New Orleans! I had heard so much about it from Tip whenever she deigned to speak to us. She had an odd role at the cottage. She wasn't really a student, wasn't really a teacher, either. She was more like a utility person or substitute teacher/bus driver/school bully. I never got the feeling she liked us; me, in particular. Maybe it was our age difference or maybe she was just a jerk, but she seemed to enjoy teasing if not tormenting me more than anyone else.

I asked Melika one day after a lesson why Tip stayed with us and she told me that Tip was a very powerful telepath who offered to help her take care of the newbies once she learned how to control her very impressive powers. Tip was a projector telepath meaning she could force her way into the minds of others. Not all telepaths could do so and this was when I learned the many variations of our powers.

It was with an open mind that I learned Tip was an exceptional telepath, an avid naturalist, a consummate chess player and a royal pain in my ass. I tried everything to be nice to her, but she treated me like a bothersome little sister, and that pissed me off. I was so glad to be getting away from the way her eyes followed me around the room. No matter what I was doing, if I looked up, I was sure to find her staring at me. If she were a teenager, I'd think she was crushin' on me, but she was too old for shit like that. She was just...invasive.

"Bishop will pick you and Zack up at Bones' place," Tip said, barely looking at me. "This is something the two of you have to do on your own. I'm not always going to be around to help you kids out. You're ready for this. You make sure you construct a strong shield and keep it up for a prolonged period of time with many people around."

"Isn't Jacob Marley coming?" I asked.

"We don't need him," Zack retorted. "Or are you afraid to be alone with me?"

"Hardly," I said. "I just like his company."

"His company or *him*?"

Shaking my head, I pushed Zack away from me a bit. "Don't be an idiot."

"What will we do?" Zack asked.

I had come to love Zack like a little annoying brother. He was respectful toward the process, toward Melika, and toward me. He wasn't at all like the twelve-year-olds I'd grown up with in various foster homes, the kind of boys who pulled wings off butterflies. Zack was kind and gentle, thoughtful before speaking and considerate of everyone's feelings. He was very bright and well aware of his surroundings. He didn't care much for Tip, and steered clear of her ever since their initial meeting.

"Do?" Melika grinned as she handed me a wad of twenties. "What else? Eat! Think of yourselves as two cows and the Big Easy as your pasture. Graze away. In New Orleans the topic of conversation at lunch is where you're going to eat dinner. In between eating, you can shop, shop, and shop some more. Oh, I'm sure you'll find quite a bit to do. You'll love it. I'm sure of it."

And, boy, was she right.

New Orleans was the most amazing place I had ever seen, and now I got the chance to see it up close.

After picking us up near a gorgeous cathedral, Bishop showed us her place. It was just like the tarot reading parlors in Oakland, only with a far more authentic feel. Hers was in the back of a voodoo shop, and when we arrived at her place there was a line waiting for her.

"Now, you know where I am. I shall be here until six and then we'll go grab a bite to eat at the Oyster House. My daughter has a habit of coddling her students, but I don't share that affliction. The Oyster House is well known. Be there at six. Unless there is a dire emergency, I don't want to see your faces until then. I trust Melika gave you ample funds for a good time. Go enjoy yourselves."

We both nodded and had started out of the voodoo shop when Bishop called me back and hooked me under the chin. "Large crowds like the ones you are going to encounter are filled with intense emotional energy. If you ever feel like your defenses are down, find an alley or a quiet place where you can rebuild. If that fails, you must return quickly to me here. Do you understand me?"

"Yes, ma'am." Her dark gaze was mesmerizing.

"You are getting stronger every day, and my daughter believes in you...in your gift. She says you have abilities you haven't even tapped into. Still, you are young and new to handling your powers. Be aware. Always aware."

"Yes, ma'am."

"Now go. Enjoy yourself, and take good care of Zack. It's always the boys who manage to find a way to screw up on their first time out."

I nodded and left.

"What did she say?" Zack asked when I returned to him on the street. There were hundreds...no, thousands of people milling about, most of them carrying beer or red punch in a plastic cup, and it wasn't even noon.

"She told me to make sure I keep my defenses up and to come back if I lose it and can't get it back up."

Zack giggled. "That's funny."

"Don't be a perv. Now, don't lose me, okay? We need to stay together."

"You're not scared, are you?"

Scared wasn't the right word. Apprehensive was more like it. Six months without a lot of people around was a blessing for me. No hassles, no emotions. No problems with foster parents or foster kids. I think I could have lived the rest of my life on the Bayou.

"Not scared. Cautious. Let's do it."

And boy did we. We had so much fun looking in all the voodoo shops and tourist shops. There were so many little shops with cool things in them. There were shops selling everything from alligator heads to hot sauce, and we went into them all. Zack's favorite was the street performers. He couldn't stop staring at the jugglers and magicians.

"Come on," I said, pulling his arm.

Zack stopped and I released him. "I just think it's cool, don't you? It's something I've never been any good at."

It wasn't what he was going to say, but I didn't want to get into it today. Today was going to be just fun. It felt like forever since I'd had any of that.

"Think the juggler would be impressed with this?" Zack called from inside the candy store.

When I looked up from the map I was staring at, I saw him juggling two pieces of candy without either touching his hands. My mouth dropped open and I quickly looked around. "Stop that!" I hissed. Stepping in the store, I scanned the area to see if anyone else had caught it.

That broke his concentration and the candy fell to the floor. "What?"

Grabbing his arm, I pulled him out of the store. "What in the hell are you doing?"

"Nothing! I was just—"

"I *know* what you were you doing. Have you lost your mind? If Melika or Bishop ever found out, they'd kill you."

"Lighten up, Echo. I was just messin' around." He looked at me with wide blue eyes, his freckles heightened in his flushed face.

"Well, don't. She'll send you packing if she so much as suspects—"

"Okay, okay. I'm sorry. It won't happen again."

"Good. Let's get out of here." As we turned to go, three twenty-something men stood in our way blocking the exit.

"Excuse us," I said, feeling my shield waver.

"How'd you do that, dude?" The biggest one asked. He was tall, bald and had a tattoo of something on his neck.

"He didn't do anything." I said, trying to maneuver around them. The short one was wider than he was tall, his arms oak branches hanging at his sides.

"You some sort of freak or something? We saw what you did. How'd you do it?" The shortest one took a step closer. I didn't need to lower my shield to know that this wasn't good.

"He's into magic, you know?" I said, pulling Zack closer to me. "He's not very good yet."

"Bullshit. I know what I saw and that weren't no magic."

I could feel Zack beginning to panic, and that meant I was losing my shield. We were in deep dog shit and I had no idea what to do to get us out of it. If Zack panicked and used his powers, we'd really be screwed.

"I want to see you do it again. I bet Buster here twenty bucks it was real. He says it was a lusion or somethin.'"

I put my hand on Zack's shoulder. If he made a move, we were never going to get out of this unscathed. I had to act before he did. "Leave us alone," I said, squeezing Zack's shoulder. I even called out for Bishop in my head. Somebody had to get us out of here before Zack did something foolish. He was getting that skittish feeling that said he was getting ready to use his powers, and if I didn't get him out of there fast, things were going to go south on us.

"Just show us what you did and you can go."

"Don't," I uttered to Zack, digging my fingers into his shoulder.

"Look, you're really beginning to piss me off," the larger one said. "Just fuckin' do it again."

I felt *her* at the base of my skull and released Zack's shoulder to stand a little straighter. I stopped feeling afraid. We were *not* alone and this wasn't going south.

"So, which is it? The easy way or the hard way?" The short one asked.

"How about the *high* way, fellas."

Without turning around, I knew it was Tip.

64

"Fuck off, Injun Jane. Go find yer own fun."

Tip put one arm around my shoulder and one around Zack's. "That's just it, boys. These two *are* my fun. And I don't share."

I frantically worked on rebuilding my shield, but I couldn't manage. I was feeling their anger, their agitation, their aggression. I couldn't block them out, but what surprised me was that I couldn't block out Tip's ire, either, and she was *pissed*!

"This may be hard to believe, but the two kids and I could drop you like that." Tip snapped her fingers. "And not even get dirty."

The three thugs threw their heads back and laughed. "A freakishly tall injun, a little white girl and a redheaded freak take us on? Are you fuckin' nuts?"

"Yeah. You on drugs or somethin', Chief? Two chicks and Howdy Doody take us?"

To my surprise, Tip chuckled. "Tell you what. I'm gonna give you *boys* a chance to turn around and walk away before we embarrass the hell out of you right here on the street."

My heart was racing as the last remnants of my shield fell away. I had nothing to contribute to our defense and it was taking everything I had to keep up my own. I wondered what the hell Tip was thinking by antagonizing these guys. They were *thugs*!

"You must be mainlinin', Chief, if you fucking think—" The tallest one took one step toward us and then dropped to his knees grabbing his head in pain. He howled in agony. The other two looked at each other before also taking a step toward us. They, too, dropped to their knees. Whatever Tip was doing to them, was causing them a whole lotta mental agony. All three were holding their heads and wailing, their pain rattling the marrow of my bones.

"You boys oughtta lay off those Hurricanes. I hear they can give you a mighty big headache. Come on, kids. Let's get out of here."

The three of us turned and walked away. At the corner, Tip stopped short, released us and turned to look back. "Hang on a sec. Stay here."

I grabbed her arm. When she turned, I saw something in her eyes I'd never seen before. It wasn't fear or trepidation…it was a protectiveness bordering on scary Mama Bearness.

Stepping up to her, I was inches from her face, looking up into brown eyes that truly, deeply cared. "Tip—"

She shook her head and stepped back. "Don't."

"Don't what?"

"Whatever it was you were going to do." She stepped back. "Just don't."

I cocked my head. "You don't know?"

She turned around to check on the three men. "I've been a bit busy."

Zack and I both turned back toward the three guys attempting to get back on their feet.

"Mover?" Tip said to Zack, motioning with her chin to the biggest one.

"The tall guy," I said softly to Zack, feeling his intentions as clearly as if he had been holding a sign that said *I have a gun and I'm going to blow your head off with it.*

"One shot, Zack," Tip whispered. "That's all I'm giving you, and I will totally deny it to Melika if either of you snitch."

Zack looked up at Tip, who nodded.

The big guy reached behind him and before he could move another inch, Zack raised his arm as if he was holding a shot put, and thrust it forward. The guy flew backward about ten feet, crashing against the side of the store. The other two looked at us, then at their friend. They got up and ran, leaving their friend lying on the sidewalk.

"Nice shot," Tip said. "Not one word about this to anyone. Don't talk to each other about it, don't even think about it. It never happened."

Zack and I could barely manage a nod. I was overwhelmed and unprepared for all of this and was beginning to lose my sense of balance. Emotions are one thing; drunken emotions fill you with this weird, hazy feeling. It's ugly and disconcerting, and I was having a real hard time focusing. "Tip…"

"I know. Come on." Taking my arm, she pulled me into a lobby of a hotel room. Tip knelt down and took my hands in hers. It was the most intimate gesture we had shared and the look I'd seen earlier was back. "Can't get your shield back up?" Her voice was softer than I'd ever heard it.

I shook my head, glad to be off the street and inside where there were less people. My knees were weak and I realized for the first time that I'd been scared. "I'm trying, Tip, really I am."

"I know you are. Deep breath, kiddo. Take all the time you need."

I winced. "Tip, how old are you?"

"What?"

"How old are you?"

"Twenty-four, why?"

"So you're not old enough to be my mom?"

She tilted her head. "Don't follow."

"I hate *kiddo*. Could you call me something else?"

A slow smile spread across her face. "I can try." Rising, she slapped Zack on the back of the head. "You and I are going to have a little chat. Echo, you do what you've been taught to do."

"He was just—"

She waved me off. "Don't try to save his ass, kid—what he did back there put you both in danger. Not only that, if Melika found out, she'd send him packing so fast, he'd arrive home yesterday." To Zack, she said, "Showing off is *never* smart. You know better than that. You think you're going to impress Echo with that bullshit, you're wrong." To me she finished. "You get your defenses back up. Zack and I will be waiting for you over at Cafe Du Monde."

It took about ten minutes of quiet to get my defenses back up. Then, I walked over to Cafe Du Monde. After having my fill of the best beignets in the world, I was feeling more like myself again.

"Thank you, Tip," I said, at last.

She nodded as she sipped her coffee, looking away. "No biggie."

"Were you following us?"

She stuffed an entire beignet into her mouth and shook her head. "It's my job."

Zack looked over at Tip and then at me. "She heard you. She heard you call for help."

I looked at Tip, who was still averting her gaze. "You did?"

Shrugging, she sipped more coffee. "You'd stopped blocking, so it was pretty easy to pick up your thoughts. I'm just glad I wasn't far away. But don't worry, Zack swears it'll never happen again, right, Zack?"

Zack nodded contritely.

Laying my hand on hers, I said, "I'm glad you're here, Tip. Thank you for saving us from ourselves."

Tip rose and dropped a twenty on the table. "Next time, you might not be so lucky. Enjoy the rest of your day."

When Tip was gone, Zack slumped down in his chair. "I coulda taken those assholes. I didn't need *her* help."

I thwacked him like Tip had. "Once again, are you *brain dead*? Do you have any idea what you could have done?"

"Yes, but—"

"But nothing. You don't have the *right* to put us at risk with your dumb male ego. Haven't you heard a damn thing Melika taught us about protecting each other? Damn it, Zack, you know better."

"All right, already. Jesus, don't you start lecturing me, too, Echo. Tip totally busted my chops. I said I was sorry."

"You'll really be sorry if Melika sends you packing. Seriously, dude, you can't do that anymore. We have a responsibility to the community."

"A community we've never even met, Echo. We're out here in the middle of nowhere being told there are hundreds of us and yet we never see anyone else. Aren't you curious—"

"No. It's called faith and trust, Zack. I trust Melika, and when it's time to meet more of our community, we will. Until then, we need to be more aware of everything we do."

"I want to meet another mover. I want to see how my powers stack up."

"You will when the time is right. Until then, do us both a favor and behave."

I finally had to just let it go and by six o'clock, we had eaten too much, shopped too much, and had too much fun. We had even had our palms read by a woman who was no psychic, but we were curious about what she would say. My shields held up for the rest of the day, Zack finally stopped pouting, and my feet were killing me from all the walking.

My shields were still holding when I entered the Acme Oyster House, otherwise, I would have known what to expect when I walked in.

As I approached the table where Bishop was sitting, she looked up and gave me a little finger wave. She was talking to a woman whose back was to us. "Right on time!" Bishop said.

When the woman turned around to look at us, I stopped dead in my tracks.

It was Danica.

She had come to New Orleans.

"Danica!"

"Jane!"

I had never been happier to see anyone than I was at that moment. We hugged each other tightly for a really long time. I felt like if I let go, she would vanish, so I held on until she whispered, "I can't...breathe."

Pulling away, I held her face in my hands and just stared into her eyes. "It really is you."

"Goddamn, Jane, what have you been eating? You look fantastic!" Danica stepped back, a grin stretching across her face revealing two perfect rows of teeth. Her eyes were green and slightly almond shaped. At six feet one, she carried her slender frame like a much larger woman and commanded attention everywhere she went. Her mixed race gave her caramel color skin that looked edible and yummy to nearly all who met her. If her interior was as hot as her exterior, Danica would spend her days fighting people off, she was that hot.

I laughed giddily. She laughed. We laughed together, and

nothing ever felt as good as that moment. "Good food, fresh air and great company will do that to a girl."

"Ahem."

We turned around, and I realized I had completely forgotten my manners. "Oh. God. I'm sorry. Zack, this is my best friend in the world, Danica. Danica, my new buddy, Zack. I take it you've already met Bishop."

"Yep, and that big ass Indian chick who picked me up at the airport."

I turned to Bishop. "How—" And stopped when she raised a hand.

"How is hardly ever relevant or important, Echo. What matters is that Melika felt it was time for you to remember there is a whole world outside the Bayou and that you are still a member of that world. It becomes very easy to get lost down here...to become assimilated into our world. The Bayou now feels like home, but it isn't. Your home is back in California, where you will one day return to begin anew. We've brought your lovely friend to New Orleans to remind you of that."

"But...am I..."

Bishop motioned for us to sit. "Sit. Eat. You won't find a better po' boy anywhere in the world. Eat first, and then go to Jackson Square and find yourselves a park bench to sit on and catch up."

My eyes grew wide. "Catch up. You mean...on everything?"

Bishop leaned across the table and took my hand. "There comes a time in our lives when we must decide who to trust and who not to trust. You must always remember how vulnerable we are, as individuals and as a community. We are each responsible for the other and for the safety of both. This is your first test. Only *you* can decide if she's safe, loyal and worthy to possess a secret that could damn us all. Only *you* know the truth about her heart."

Inhaling deeply, I looked over at Danica and nodded. She sat there, wide-eyed, clearly wondering what in the hell we were talking about.

After six months with Melika, I knew the importance of keeping mum about our powers. As long as our gifts were still considered something of myths, we would remain safe. I understood that. However, I also understood that someday I would return to the life I had so quickly left and I would need someone who knew and understood what I was.

But at fifteen, was Danica that person? Were *we* mature enough to handle the truth of who I was and what I was becoming? At this moment, I didn't know, nor did I care. Danica had flown halfway across the country to see me, and that was all that mattered.

We ate our delicious po' boys and waved goodbye to Bishop and Zack before heading off to Jackson Square. We held hands and bounced along like two little sisters, barely stopping to take a breath.

"This place is fucking awesome," Danica said as we walked to the Square. "I've never seen anything like it. You must be having a fucking blast."

"I would be if here is where I lived, but I don't. I live way out in the boondocks. This is the first time I've been here in almost six months."

"This place is so way better than any place I've ever been." Danica laughed as she threw her arms around my neck. "Damn, girl, I have missed you. You look so good, Jane...oops. I guess I should get used to calling you Echo, huh?" Danica sat down and took my hand. "Okay, *Echo*, what the fuckaroonie is going on here? Some humungous, and, might I add, gorgeous Indian chick picks me up at the airport and brings me to this old, superbizarre woman who talks in some kind of code about some kind of secret. What the fuck?"

I threw my head back and laughed. "I have missed you so much!"

"No, you haven't. How could you? This place is so awesome. No wonder you've been too busy to call. I stopped waiting for you to call two weeks after you left. Then, out of the blue, I get a call about coming here, and, of course, I jump for it."

"Your parents?"

"Took some convincing, but they're all about me seeing other black folks and getting a better idea of how others live. They finally agreed to let me come take a look at Tulane and Xavier, but it's really all about the black thang."

I took her hands in mine. She had the longest fingers of anyone I had ever met. "Danica...I'm really sorry—"

She held up both hands. "Hey, I wasn't pissed or anything. I mean, hell, you're here and I was there, and—"

"I have so much to tell you, but first, I just want to listen. Tell me all about school, about your life. Tell me everything I've missed."

I was so happy sitting there, in New Orleans, with my best friend gossiping about people as if I had never left. She told me about Todd having to get stitches, and how everyone teased him for weeks about getting his ass kicked by a girl and how he would never come near her again. She told me who was dating whom and what teachers were bad. And as Danica kept talking, I tried to decide whether or not to tell her the truth. It was such a huge decision for me. I just didn't want to blow it. Melika trusted me, trusted all of us to be selective in whom we told. I used to lay in bed at night wondering about the moment I revealed everything to her. Three months ago, I was sure I would tell her the first chance I got. Now...now I wasn't so sure, especially in light of Zack's outing of himself.

"You gotta be sure, Echo."

I looked around for Tip, but she was nowhere to be seen. Just in my head.

"Stop looking around, goofy girl. I'm not in Jackson Square."

"Where are you?" I thought. The first time you link up with a telepath, it feels a little schizophrenic. You can "hear" the voice in your head and it doesn't feel or sound like your own. It's quite a bizarre feeling, and though this wasn't the first time, I never quite got used to it.

"Not important. Look, if you're going to tell your friend, do it in a setting that will help her understand. She can't understand anything

sitting here in New Orleans. Tell her on the Bayou."

"When? How?"

"Meet Bones at his place tomorrow morning around nine. Take her to Du Monde and then take a cab to Bones' place. You'll know when you're out on the river whether it's the right time. Trust me, kiddo."

"Please stop calling me that."

"Sorry. Habit."

"Well break it. Now go away."

"Not until you tell me you trust me."

Trust her? She scared the crap out of me...out of all of us. And now, here she was, for the second time in a day popping up in my head, giving me unsolicited advice.

"Trust me, kiddo."

Turning all of my attention back to Danica, I listened attentively, asking all the right questions, wanting to be in the moment with her. She had lost weight and colored her hair so it had nice copper streaks in it. She looked really good.

We stayed up half the night cruising Bourbon Street and catching up. It was big fun and I discovered I could relax knowing that somewhere in New Orleans, Tip was lurking, listening, reading, keeping tabs on Melika's students. I discovered that I could feel whenever she had popped in and out of my mind. I decided then and there to learn more about the strengths of telepaths, because from what I'd seen on this trip, Tip was, by far, the most powerful of all of us.

We were allowed to stay at Bishop's fine Victorian home for the night, which was such a blast. We baked cookies and just sat and talked. Danica wanted to hear all about the loony bin and the people who were now my family. We didn't get to sleep until four in the morning, and were back up at the crack of dawn when we set out for Bones' place. We were never allowed to take anyone to Melika's, so I told Bones we just wanted to go out to the Bayou.

"Ummm...Echo, are you serious about getting in that thing?" Danica stepped away from the boat as if it might bite her.

I chuckled. "It's okay, Dani, really. I thought exactly what you're thinking, but I know from experience that it floats. It'll take us where we want to go."

"Which is where? Where *are* we?"

"The Bayou, baby. I'm going to show you where I've really been for the last six months, and...well...to explain what's been going on with me."

Danica nodded. "Hey, I'm up for an adventure."

I grinned. "Oh, Danica, you have no idea what you're in for."

Turning to me, she grinned. "Oh yeah? Try me." There was no one braver than Danica Johnson.

Ten minutes later, I did.

"You've been living all the fucking way out here?" She asked, looking around. "You have got to be shitting me. No TV?"

"Nope. That's why I wanted you to come out here. You think I've been partying away in New Orleans when the truth is, I've been living in a cottage all the way out here. Not quite the party environment you pictured, is it?"

"No. Fucking. Way." Danica looked around the Bayou all big-eyed. "Here? Out *here*?"

I nodded, noting how six months made Danica look six years older. She was beautiful. "Farther out, actually, but it's all the same after you get to a certain point."

"Holy shit. People can't live out here, can they?"

"Can and do. That's why I haven't called. This is the first time I've been to the city since I called you shortly after I got here."

"What in the hell have you been doing all this time? You can't..." And then she heard that familiar sound. "What in the hell was that?"

"Just a 'gator."

"A what? Don't fuck with me, Jane!" Danica scooted toward the center of the boat, her eyes darting about. "Are you telling me there are *alligators* in the water?"

I nodded. "But don't worry. They're not after us."

Danica's eyes were wide. "How do you know? Maybe they're ready for breakfast." Danica was looking all around the boat trying to make herself smaller.

This was the moment of truth. Since Danica trusted me enough to come out into this foreign land in this rickety boat, I needed to trust her enough with *my* truth. I needed to trust *her*. "I know because...because I'm not like everybody else, Dani. That's why I'm here. I didn't come here by accident. I was brought here to learn how to handle my...special abilities."

"Abilities?" She stopped looking for alligators and stared intently into my eyes. "What in the hell are you talking about?"

I went for it. "Let me get this out first, okay? It's not easy to understand, and I know you'll have a bunch of questions, but—"

"Just say it."

"I'm an empath. There." The word hung in the air like a helium balloon waiting to be popped.

"Is that what it sounds like?"

I nodded. "I have the ability to feel people's emotions. I read them like someone might read minds. That's what happened with Todd. I read his emotions. I read his intent. I knew what he wanted. It was the first time I had ever felt my—"

"Wait." Danica held her hands up again, her face working to understand. "You *feel* people's emotions? Do you feel them feel them or just see them?"

"Both. All. If there's an emotion near me, I pick up on it like some weird magnet drawing it to me. Then I feel it."

"Wow. Like a superpower. How cool is that?"

I shrugged. "Not so cool, sometimes. That's why I'm here; to learn how to use it, hide it, defend against all incoming emotions from people around me."

Danica looked around. "Are we on *Candid Camera* or something?"

"Dani this is serious. I have these—"

"Superpowers. I got that. You're sitting here telling me you can feel other people's emotions...that you knew what Todd wanted so you bashed his head in. Sorry if it doesn't sound a little like a Lifetime movie."

"I've rehearsed this over and over, and still, when it came out of my mouth just now, it sounds so—"

"Twilight Zonish?"

I nodded and looked away. "It's true nonetheless. It's what I do and what I am."

She blinked several times before nodding slowly. "Okay. Okay. So you knew what Todd wanted, you beat his head in, and now you're here."

"Yes. Melika teaches us out here so we can focus on learning what we need to without going insane."

"Us. So you go to school with that Zack kid to learn how to be a superhero? What's the big Indian? Super Amazon Woman?"

I didn't want to say. It was outside our code of conduct to reveal someone else's power. "She's not an empath, if that's what you're asking."

"I don't really know what I'm asking, Jane. You bring me out into the middle of a fucking swamp and..." She stopped in mid-sentence and started looking frantically around. "Who the hell? What the fuck was that?"

I realized at once what was happening. *"Stop that!"* I ordered. *"You're scaring her!"*

"She'll never believe your words, kiddo, and unless you want Zack to kick her ass, there may be only one way to get her to believe."

I thought for a moment. *"Can I tell her?"*

"You're probably going to have to. If she's that important to you, out me. I trust your judgment."

I don't know what amazed me more: that she was going to let me out her or that she actually trusted me. *"Thank you. And stop calling me kiddo."* Reaching out, I held Danica's hand. "That voice in your head is Tip, the big Indian."

Danica's mouth dropped open. "No way." She glanced quickly around. "That is so fucking creepy."

I told Tip to stop. She responded by telling me to call if I needed more help.

"She should be gone now."

Dani cocked her head and listened for a moment and then nodded. "Fucking A, Jane, what the fuck?"

"You ready to hear this, now?"

76

She nodded. "That was so fucking weird."

"It gets weirder, believe me. Me, Zack and another kid named Jacob are all here to learn how to handle our powers. No, they're not superpowers like in a comic book." I quoted Melika. "These are real powers genetically woven into who we are. My power allows me to pick up the emotions of others. It would have driven me insane because I didn't know how to block all of the emotions coming at me. The first time it happened was with Todd. The crisis I felt coming triggered the recessive nature of it."

Danica simply shook her head. "And this is no joke."

"I know this is a lot to take in, but I wanted you to know why I am here and why I hadn't been able to call you. I wanted to, but what could I say? *Hi, I know you're my best friend and all, and you saved me from going crazy, but I'm not the girl you think I am?*"

"So...you really *can* feel people's emotions?"

I nodded. "And apparently a few animals as well, which is why I knew that alligator had no interest in us."

"Holy shit, Jane...er...Echo. This is weird, but pretty fucking cool at the same time."

"I'm here trying to get my life together...to be normal."

"Oh, this is rich. You have some sort of superpowers and now you want to be normal? Are you insane?"

We both looked at each other and laughed.

"This is serious, Dani."

"Oh, right. I'm sitting on a holey boat with the Boatman from hell, and my best friend has just told me she knows what alligators are thinking, and I'm supposed to be serious? Come on, Jane! Give me a break."

"I just need you to know how serious this is, because telling other people would put our lives at stake. I trusted you with my life once, and now I'm trusting you with my future."

She looked over at me, her eyes locking onto mine. I would not lower my shield to read her. Rule number one in Melika's universe: don't invade the private emotions of the ones you love.

"If you can do what you say you can, then do it now. You'll know how much you can trust me."

I looked at her a long time before asking, "Are you sure?"

"Have I ever lied to you?"

"No."

"Ever let you down?"

"Never."

"Then do it."

So I did. I read her and knew that she would never tell, never betray me, never let me down.

She never did.

Not once.

We spent a wonderful couple of days together, and after Danica left the Bayou, it was back to work. I spent the next six months learning more blocking and shielding techniques. Melika wanted me to be able to block naturals as well as other supers.

After Tip's intrusion into my mind, I decided blocking was a necessary evil. I didn't like her rooting around in my brain. I was incredibly uncomfortable with the whole notion of telepathy. It was one thing to feel what people were feeling, but to hear their thoughts and then be able to project myself into their minds? That was on a whole other level.

So, I asked Melika about it on our daily walk through the swamp. The morning rays streamed in through the trees and moss. "Tip must be a more powerful telepath than I realized, huh?"

"Oh yes. She's quite strong, perhaps one of the strongest telepaths I have ever met. I must apologize for what happened in town. I never intended for you to find out she was watching over you. I apologize for that. I just can't risk the young ones doing what Zachary did. I've seen it happen too often. I'm sorry."

"It was a good thing, I guess. I mean, I'm glad she was skulking around..." I stopped talking. I didn't wish to give away anything.

"Don't worry, my girl, I am well aware of Zack's little indiscretion in the shop and have already spoken to him about it."

"Oh." I heard Jacob's voice in the back of my head about Melika knowing everything.

"It happens to the boys...especially TKs."

"Tip calls them movers."

"Tip is a snob. She doesn't believe anyone's powers are as strong as hers. She might be right. Anyway, she was charged, as she always is, with watching over you both and she did her job. If you want to be angry with anyone, be angry with me."

"I wasn't angry. I was taken by surprise. Her voice in my head felt very..."

"Disquieting? Invasive? It takes some getting used to, I know."

"It might not have been so weird if it was someone else. Tip is so intense. Sometimes she looks at me and I feel like a bug under a microscope."

"Tip never does anything without reason. Every move she makes is thought out or planned. If you find her staring at you, she is working something out in her own mind. Don't let it get to you."

"*She* gets to me. Like under my skin gets to me."

"It comes with her telepathic abilities. That's one of the pieces you'll learn while you're here—other sorts of psionic powers."

I nodded.

Melika stopped and looked hard into my eyes. "You are no longer responsible just for yourself, Echo. We are a family, a community of beings who need each other; who need to be understood. Who need to protect each other. Someday, you might be called upon to help someone much in the same way you've been helped. You can't do that if you know nothing."

"Useful? Melika, I can barely erect a shield."

"Now, yes, but believe me, there will come a time when you can do that and so much more. We must always look beyond the moment, beyond our own distorted sense of self. Someday, you will need to give back."

And so, my next set of lessons began. I came to understand how Zack could do what he did. Well, no one really knew the exact way it was done, but I got the general idea. He was able to manipulate energy to the point of making it react like a solid. Both Melika and Tip had tried giving me the scientific explanation, but I'd never gotten higher than a C in science.

Melika really had to work closely with him to keep his powers in check. Because he could use energy to move things about, he thought nothing about pulling something to him that was just out of reach. She had to reteach him how to think about his way in the world. It was fascinating, really, because TKs were more of an anomaly than telepaths or empaths, and therefore, more at risk. We were all at risk, but Melika felt the younger male TKs more so because they had a tendency to act out in public just as Zack had done. A TK in the presence of the wrong people could be a disaster.

Melika had warned us that our government had several departments looking into the possibility of paranormal activity. They wanted one of us in a big way, and it was rumored they were "interviewing" everyone from tarot readers to magicians trying to get a bead on one of us, preferably a mover or a reader, like Tip. They hadn't seen any use for a necromancer, and couldn't prove their powers truly existed.

I did not quite understand necromancy, and wasn't at all sure I ever really wanted to. Most of the time, Jacob Marley seemed like he was in a daze, but then maybe he was listening to somebody's dead grandpa. I could never tell.

"You must remember, my dear, that much of what we all do is a matter of manipulating energy. It's all about energy. Understand that and you have half the puzzle. The other half is understanding that no two supers are alike. Each of us comes to the table with a different set of abilities and limitations. There are quite a few wiccans with the same ability to do so."

"But if people found out…if they saw us doing what Zack did…" I shook my head. "I never considered that we could be in danger."

"Only in recent history have witches decided to hide in plain sight. Now, they write books, hold open meetings, and even advertise in the Yellow Pages. They can do so because the Christian segment of our country has led people to believe they no longer exist, that they are powerless. Isn't it ironic that the very people who burned them at the stake have made it possible for them to live in the open?" Melika chuckled, a rare event.

"No longer...then you mean..."

Melika nodded. "They went underground. Now, hundreds of years later, they have been able to resurface because of the very faith that forced them underground in the first place. Irony at its finest."

I whistled and shook my head. "Hiding in plain sight. It's brilliant."

"It's what we all do. The Bishops of this world are able to do what they do because no one believes the truth—well, no one except those who pay for her readings."

"How come she doesn't get in trouble for it?"

Melika chuckled. "Bishop isn't out there making money. She is on the lookout for others. As you can imagine, New Orleans is a gathering place for many supernatural types. She uses her vantage point to find those who need to be found."

"You think that someday people will believe?"

"Oh yes, but believing is not the same as understanding. It is incumbent upon you to understand because there is a component to your powers we have yet to discuss."

Melika's countenance was heavy. I swallowed hard. "There is?"

"Yes, my dear. You have the unique ability to read the truth about people, and once I show you how, you will be able to know the moment you meet another one of us. You will be able to look at someone and know whether they are telling the truth. You are a truth seeker, Echo, as surely as if you were born to it. In your life, you will find a career that will allow that part of you full play, and you will be prepared." Melika stopped and took my hand. "Echo, it is incredibly important to be able to do what you can do. I don't want to frighten you with this, but you are far more than empathic. Your powers are like layers of an onion and we've only removed a couple layers."

81

"I can do more than read emotions and seek the truth?"

Melika nodded. "Oh yes. Much, much more. You, my girl, are the most powerful empath I have ever met."

I had been in the Bayou a year when it happened. I had successfully learned how to shield and block, which delighted everyone. I had learned how to read some animals in the surrounding vicinity, and I read up and studied everything Melika handed me about telepaths and telekinetics. There were other paranormal powers, of course, but my immediate concern was to learn about the powers of those I was learning with. Finally, Tip and Mel could relax; I had found my comfort zone where my powers were concerned, and it felt great.

"I couldn't be more proud of you, my girl, but now, we must step up a little."

"Step up? Melika, we've been going 24-7 for a year." I smiled as I said this. I wasn't just learning about my powers. Every day for three hours, the three of us were tutored in every subject from algebra to Latin. We were drilled, tested and put through the educational wringer. Our tutor was an old Cajun professor who had taught at Xavier forever. Every day, Bones delivered Professor Mathias to our dock, and every day he rigorously demanded excellence from us.

I might have preferred his lessons over some of those Melika threw at us. One day, she decided it was time to see if I had really bought into the process, if I was really ready to expand my knowledge.

"What would you do if that alligator over there decided to make a run at us?"

I glanced at the ten-foot beast, remembering Jacob Marley's instructions in the event one ever came at me. "Climb that tree?"

"Perhaps. But you have a power, and you're not here just to understand your powers, but to make the most of them." Melika waded into the water, her dress floating all around her.

"What are you doing?" Fear gripped my throat as I watched her get closer to the alligator.

"Hand me that bag."

I handed her a bag that felt like it had a bowling ball in it. When she reached into it, she pulled out a whole chicken. "Let's get his attention."

To say I was scared to death would have been an understatement. There was my mentor, waist deep in the water, about fifty feet from an alligator, waving a chicken at him.

"Mel—"

"Like martial arts, there are two main styles that can be used to defend one's self. There are hard and soft shields. You erect a hard one when you need a more solid barrier."

I gasped when the alligator slid off the bank and into the water. I stepped back, knowing that if it went under the water, it would eat more than the chicken.

"Hard shielding is done by extending the energy of the psychic forces into a sort of barrier around you. In an ideal situation, the barrier width would be equal strength at all points around your body, thereby protecting you from harm." Melika put the chicken back in the bag and backed away from the alligator now gliding across the water. I gasped even louder when the alligator came to such an abrupt halt it looked as if someone had yanked his tail.

"She doesn't know what hit her nose, but she doesn't want to hit it again because it's not really solid. It's an energy that acts like a solid. Animals have an aversion to unfamiliar energies, which is why so many act so strange just before a natural disaster. They sense the change in the earth's energy and it throws them off a little bit."

I watched in amazement as the alligator retreated back to her bank, without either the chicken or a piece of Melika. "That was...incredible."

Melika waded back to the bank and I helped her out from the water. Water dripping from her clothes, she addressed me intently. "That was necessary. Oftentimes, when we are faced with a threat, we don't have time to do anything more than erect hard shields. The more powerful you are, the farther out you can cast a hard shield. It might take you years to cast your energy as far as I did, but you will learn how to create one that does more than protect you emotionally and mentally."

It was at that moment I realized I did not understand a damn thing about my abilities or the energy necessary to perform them. Energy, like that used when you turn on the light, will always remain a mystery to me. I don't know how it works. I just know that touching a switch makes a light come on.

"This is what we will be working on for the next few months. It will take more energy, both mentally and physically, and you'll be exhausted at the end of every day. It's vital to get plenty of rest at night."

I nodded.

"Now it is time for your first lesson in personal defense." She pointed in the distance, and I saw Tip leaning against a tree. Now, I'm not one to stereotype, but that woman could walk in complete silence through the swamp and never be heard. I had no idea how long she'd been standing there or how she got there.

"Why is Tip here?"

"We need a third person: the attacker, as it were. That will come later. She is going to teach you what you need to do to create and maintain a hard shield. She also has incredible skills in energy maintenance. I found she often succeeds with students where I fail."

I couldn't imagine Melika failing at anything.

My next big task was to learn how to create and maintain a hard shield. Every day, we went out to different areas around the house and worked until I was a sweaty, exhausted mess. This was really hard work requiring a level of concentration that made my first year look like a party. I would create a shield through various distractions, like Tip tossing pebbles at the back of my head, and then I would have to shift my energy focus to strengthen the shield and make it hard.

Hard was just a term that meant it was more capable of deflecting physical properties and not just emotional energies. For the first two weeks, I couldn't stop a feather. But around week three, I was finally able to stop a pebble. Constructing

84

and maintaining that energy wrecked me for two whole days. I could not believe how it had sucked the life out of me. Although supernaturals manipulate energy, there wasn't an infinite amount of it within us, so erecting barriers against physical threats meant we had to push *our own* energy away from us. It felt like someone had drained me of my life force.

By the end of week four, I thought I was getting better at it, but I was wrong. I only had a fifty-fifty chance of erecting a wall strong enough to stop a very small pebble. This went on for two months until I became physically exhausted and eventually sick.

Really, really sick.

For the first two days, I stayed in bed. Poor Zack worried nonstop about me and wouldn't even go into town. We had become very close in our year together, and though I was pretty sure he wanted something more than just friendship, he'd always kept a respectful distance. I was now sixteen and Zack was fourteen and going through those awful growth spurts boys go through. His hands and feet looked like they belonged to someone else and his voice and hormones were all over the charts. Some days he wanted to kiss me, other days, he wanted to punch me, like a brother. It was both cute and annoying.

I had been in bed about four days when Zack came by for his hourly check-up. He had to be dragged out to his own lessons, so intent he was on watching over me. "How are you feeling today?"

"Getting better and better. How were your lessons?"

He shrugged. "Not bad. I have to work with Tip and she just bugs the crap out of me. She thinks she is so hot. I hate the way she talks down to us like we're stupid or something."

"Don't be so hard on her, Zack. She just wants the best from us."

"She wants something, all right."

I struggled to sit up a bit. "What does *that* mean?"

He scuffed his foot on the ground. "Never mind. Someday, *we'll* be that strong."

I sighed. "Someday. I just can't seem to get this hard shield thing down. I suck."

"No, you don't. Sometimes, you just don't have the right intent."

"Intent?"

Zack sat on the edge of the bed. "Yeah. Melika calls it focus, but it was Jacob who taught me about intent."

"What's the difference?"

For the next three days, after his own lessons, Zack came in and taught me about intent. The way he was able to manipulate the energy often required use of his telekinesis. I needed to know within myself what it was I wanted the energy to *do*. Finally, after a great deal of hard work, I was beginning to get it.

"Energy is energy, Echo, but you'll never get there if you don't accept who you are. *Who* you are, Echo, not *what* you are. God gives each of us a toolbox. Some of those toolboxes are full and some of them are empty. Ours are overflowing, and the first thing we have to do is figure out what tools are in our toolbox and then pick the ones that are going to be the best defense and the more perfect offense."

After a week in bed, I finally got up. It had taken me that long to fight the fatigue, I slept more than didn't, and ate only when Tip or Zack brought me food. I could have sworn I heard them bickering over who was going to bring it up the stairs, but I couldn't be sure.

"I think you have the power it takes to do this, Echo," Zack said, laying his hand on mine. "You just have to believe."

"Show me."

And he did.

I learned about defense shields and combat shields and how to layer them on top of each other. Shields of this sort were made and maintained by concentration and energy. Some shields required less energy and more concentration and vice versa. Zack knew a great deal more than I about something he called the human energy field or HEF.

We all have a human energy field. It varies, of course, in size, shape and color. Everything alive has energy and this energy travels in waves and bounces off objects and other living things.

This energy is absorbed by the object it hits, while others bounce off. As an empath, I have the capability of absorbing that energy, reading it and even feeling it. Since energy naturally travels outward, it is possible to gather that energy and, with proper concentration, force it outward. It was this shield Zack spent days showing me how to construct. I wish I could say I was a quick learner, but the truth is, I was a sorry student. Luckily for me, he was a very patient tutor and never got angry or frustrated. He really believed in me and this made me believe in myself, which was a good thing because I soon discovered that he was a really good teacher and maybe I wasn't as slow as I thought.

Slowly, but surely, I started getting the hang of it until one day, I successfully stopped a rock. I know...big deal, right?

Wrong.

It was a super big deal and I found out just how big when, around eleven o'clock at night, I heard Tip come upstairs.

Tip never came upstairs unless she was bringing me food, and it freaked me out just thinking about her creeping around. Melika had gone to help the birth of one of Queenie's babies, and wasn't supposed to return until morning. That meant she left the big Indian in charge.

Then why was she coming upstairs now?

My palms got sweaty and my heart was racing as I felt her presence in the doorway. She was just standing there blocking all light. Then, she moved into the room and I panicked. I didn't know whether I should sit up and ask her what the hell she was doing, or just lay there and pretend to be asleep. By the time I decided which to do, Tip was leaning over me.

"No!" I cried, pushing my combat shield out as far as I could. The strength of that shield surprised both of us as it knocked her backward and against the doorframe.

"Get away!" I ordered, reaching over and turning the light on. "What in the hell are you doing in here?"

Tip righted herself and brushed off the seat of her pants. "Jesus, Echo, it took you long enough."

"What are you talking about?"

"Take it easy, kiddo," she said, holding her hands up in surrender. "I wasn't going to do anything."

I looked into her eyes, and this time, I lowered my shields just long enough to see she wasn't lying.

"She's telling the truth," Zack announced from the doorway. "It was time to see if you were able to put any of your lessons to good use."

"And you passed," Tip said over her shoulder, starting down the stairs.

"Tip?"

She turned back to me and waited.

I nodded to Zack he could go, but he hesitated a second and then, almost angrily, went downstairs.

"I'm sorry," I said to Tip standing in the doorway. "I didn't mean to yell at you."

She shrugged and jammed her hands in her pockets. She must have felt me reading her, because her shields were back up and in place. "Yeah you did, but that was the point. You gotta do what you gotta do, Echo, and you have to protect yourself. Mel has big plans for you." She took half a step in and then stopped. "You did great, kid...uh...Echo. Really. I'm proud of you."

She stood there a moment, hands in her pockets, air thick with a tension I couldn't define.

When she left, Zack came back up the stairs.

"Zack, does she hate me or what?"

Zack looked at me and shook his head. "You're so busy struggling with your lessons, you don't see it. I'm thinking it's the *or what*."

Three years had come and gone in the Bayou and I was such a different person than the frightened little girl who first floated into Melika's place. Some of the changes were subtle, while others were quite distinctive. Physically, I was taller, now nearly five feet eight. I had sprouted three inches in as many years. I had really filled out from all of the manual labor required of us: chopping wood, repairing the dock, schlepping garbage here and there. All of it kept me slim and tight, and I liked that feeling. My hair was well beyond my shoulders, and all the outdoor sun had changed it from mousy brown to a golden honey.

I had also taken and passed my GED, which was a requirement of all of us. It was embarrassingly easy, but Melika and Tip had still been proud of me. I wanted Danica there with me, but the number one rule was no naturals on the Bayou. It was one thing not to have Danica, but an entirely different thing to have to say goodbye to Jacob, who had learned all he could from Melika and Tip and had to go back into the real world.

He had done his best to keep a stiff upper lip during our tearful goodbye, but he failed miserably...so did I. I would miss our morning boat rides, our philosophical conversations about life and death...our fun times together. Jacob would grow to be a good man. He had a big heart and a warm personality. If only he could battle the demons of the dead who haunted him daily, he might actually learn to enjoy life. He would probably be one of the few of us who would bury his gift deep inside him so he could have as normal a life as possible. I could not even imagine what life would be like as a necromancer. The dead, in my opinion, ought to be left alone, in peace, to do whatever the dead do. Jacob agreed.

When we returned from taking Jacob to the bus stop, I was surprised that Tip was gone as well. She remained gone for quite a few days, longer than she'd ever been gone in the years I'd been on the river. This was when Zack explained that Tip was a hunter. Her job was to see if rumors about other supers were true and to bring them the help they needed. Sometimes, the help was not wanted, other times, it was too late. According to Zack, Tip was one of the best hunters in the country.

This surprised me. Hell, *Tip* surprised me. It seemed the older I got, the longer her eyes lingered over me. I had thought that Mel saw that smoldering look in her eyes and sent her away to cool her off. I had no idea that she was *a hunter*. I wondered if she was hunting me sometimes, the way her eyes followed my every movement, and while I didn't hate it, I wasn't sure what it meant.

Anyway, by the end of my third year, I had begun preparing for my own insertion back into reality. It was scary thinking about leaving the only real home I had ever known, my only real family. Melika had been the one adult in my life who had made me feel wanted. I may have had to work my ass off, but at least I knew where I belonged.

So, when it came time for me to think about college, it surprised no one that she invited Danica to town for a conversation about where *we* wanted to go. Prior to this visit, Danica and I talked about going to a women's college on the East Coast. We both loved the idea of ivory towers and all that tradition. So, when we met up with Bishop in New Orleans for a powwow about college, Danica and I had no clue just what they had in mind.

"Danica," Bishop began, leaning forward so that her glasses hanging around her neck stroked the table. "You have proven yourself to be a very loyal and true friend to our Echo. It is not every day that a normal of such integrity and strength of character comes into our lives, but you, my dear, are one such person. That sort of loyalty and friendship should not go unrewarded." Bishop took both of her hands. When she did, I felt a cold chill go up my spine. "And you have come to trust us as well, have you not?"

Danica nodded. "Absolutely."

"Then, please know I share this piece of life with you because of all the two of you have gone through. Since you have proven complete and total trust, I am giving you a gift few others on this planet ever could: the gift of time."

The chills turned into something more ominous. Something was coming and Danica wasn't ready.

"Time?"

"I want you and Echo to consider Cal or Mills College back in Oakland."

"Oakland? But we wanted to go away for college."

"And you still can, if you want. But...my dear..." Bishop ripped the Band-Aid off as fast as she could, "...your mother will be diagnosed with cancer while you're in college."

My breath caught as I stared first at Bishop and then at Danica. Time stood still in that moment.

Bishop continued. "It is a vision I've had more than once since you've been coming to New Orleans. I know it comes as a shock, but I wanted you to know so that you can remain closer to home and be with her during her last years."

The gift of time. Wow.

Danica blinked back her tears and then looked at me. I could barely manage a nod. I could barely move. "So...my mother is going to die from cancer while I'm in college?"

"I do not know precisely when she will pass, my dear, but I do know that if she passes while you're in college, it will turn your life around in ways you cannot even imagine; and none of them for the better. Believe me, Danica. You are meant to do wonderful things; great things."

I reached for Danica's hand and laid mine on top of it.

"But...what about Echo? She can't afford a school like Mills."

Bishop simply smiled. It was so like Danica to worry about whether or not I would be able to go. "Don't worry about Echo. Her SAT scores, while not as good as yours, will help get her in, as will my contacts there."

"You have contacts at Mills?"

"Oh yes. I did a reading for the president a long time ago and, well, it kept the school from having to go co-ed. She owes me a few chits."

Danica looked at me, her eyes filled with tears.

If Bishop was giving her the gift of more time with her mother, who was I to take that away? "Then Mills it is."

And that was it.

It was at this moment I realized just how far-reaching the supernatural world extended, because when Melika and Bishop asked people to do something, they were never turned down. Whatever it was they did to get Danica and me into Mills was a godsend because life happened just like Bishop had said; Danica's mother was diagnosed with brain cancer in our sophomore year, and it was only months before she succumbed to it. Because of

Bishop's generosity and trust of Danica, Danica was able to spend quality time with her mother before she passed; a priceless and wonderful gift.

It was just the first of many gifts coming from the Bayou.

When the time came for me to graduate from the Bayou and Melika, I couldn't believe that four years had gone by so quickly. I had learned so much and grown up in ways I never imagined. Suddenly, I was eighteen and had finally gained control of my powers and learned all Melika could teach me. Of course, that knowledge didn't make it any easier to leave the Bayou and my new family.

Truth was I was petrified of leaving. I had fallen in love with the darkness and wetness and heat of the river. I loved everything about it, including the fresh, clean scent to the odors of alligators floating on the water. Once I had gotten used to the harsh realities of no electricity or plumbing, it didn't even faze me. What happens in a place like the Bayou when there's no television or computers are conversation and a great deal of reading. Zack and I must have read over a thousand novels, and I firmly believe it was all that reading that prepared me for college. By the time I got to Mills, I had read over half the books on most of the required reading lists.

Four years in one place was also a record for me, and I couldn't picture myself going back to Oakland. I hadn't been back in the years since I'd left. Other than Danica, there wasn't anything there for me. I really didn't want to leave Louisiana. I guess in a way I felt like I still wasn't ready. I had sunk my roots deep into the rich soil of the Louisiana Bayou and it didn't seem fair that I had to pull them out. I just couldn't imagine what life would be like not being there; not waking up to the sounds of the birds and the gentle lapping of the water as it sloshed against the bank. I had had a taste of how rich life can be. Maybe the best lesson I'd learned was not to settle for anything less than greatness.

"Now you know what a well-lived life looks like," Tip said to me the day before I was getting ready to go back to Oakland.

"Once you know that, you are obligated to live one."

I'm pretty sure that was the moment the walls around my heart began to crack where she was concerned. After four years of feeling her eyes one me like hands caressing every inch of my body, it finally dawned on me why she had always called me kiddo: to remind herself that I was underage. It was the moat around the fortress protecting her heart.

"I never knew you were so poetic."

She grinned. "There's a lot you don't know about me. I may not be as bad as you like to think, but my role here was never to be anyone's friend. I do what Mel tells me to. I go where she tells me to go, and I teach what she tells me to teach. But there's a helluva lot more to me than all of that."

"I *do* know that, Tip, but—"

"I don't think you do. Up until your eighteenth birthday, you were just a little girl who thought I was this big, scary Indian who crept around spying on you."

"Weren't you?"

Tip chuckled. "Yeah, but that's only a fraction of who I am and what I do here. Who I am when you're here is the woman who makes sure you stay safe, who helps you with your telepathic abilities, and who is going to miss you more than you could possibly know when you go back." She reached out and tucked a strand of hair behind my ear.

"Thank you for not calling it home. I'm not going *home*."

She nodded, but said nothing, her eyes raking over my face. I wished I could feel her emotions.

"Home is here. I feel so much like a stupid high school kid who's getting ready to go off to college and is scared to death. Does that sound dumb?"

"Not at all. You're leaving the first real home you've ever known, but college...that's where you belong. That's the one thing I never understood about you. You've got it all going on and you don't even know it. The world will lay prostrate at your feet some day, Echo Branson. It's time for you to spread your wings and fly. Trust me. You're ready for this."

I think this was the first real conversation we had ever had. "Thanks. That means a lot."

Tip rose, picked up a rock, and threw it in the river. "See those ripples? That's how you're going to affect the world... waves that ripple farther than the eye can see. I've looked into Mills. It's perfect for you."

I looked at her back as she tossed another rock. I had never looked at Tip as anything other than a big, scary and sometimes mean Indian, but at this moment I saw her for the first time as a softhearted, somewhat romantic woman who possessed feelings she probably shouldn't have had.

And that thought scared the crap out of me.

Turning around, she wore an odd smile on her face and I wondered if she had managed to read my thoughts. "Echo, this place has been brighter since you arrived, and it's been a helluva lot of fun having you here. I'm...really going to miss you."

I rose and picked up a rock and tossed it in. "I'm going to miss you, too."

She laughed. "No, you won't. You'll get into Mills and begin a new life, leaving the Bayou and all of its memories behind. Everyone does."

"Haven't you heard? I'm not like everyone."

Her smile softened as she turned to me. "Don't I know it." Leaning over, she bent down and, ever so softly, kissed my cheek, her lips lingering there long enough for me to turn my face into them.

Our lips barely touched as we stood together, fingers intertwined. I parted my lips and let my tongue slide into hers, over hers, around hers, our breaths commingling in rhythm. She stepped into the kiss, or maybe I did, it was hard to tell. All I knew was my body was on fire, starting at my lips. And traveling like St. Elmo's Fire down my limbs.

When she pulled away, she caressed my cheek with the back of her fingers and whispered, "Remember who you are." And with that, she disappeared, taking something with her I would never get back.

I left Melika and the Bayou in one of the most heartwrenching goodbyes of my life. Saying goodbye to Zack was much harder than I anticipated as well. There wasn't anything I wouldn't have done for him. He'd always had one eye out for me whenever we went to town and he had always been there to bounce ideas off. He would make some lucky girl a great boyfriend because, to say the least, he knew how to listen. There had always been a little tension between us, but through it all, I knew I was not his type.

I was pretty sure I was gay; a fact I hadn't had any time to explore due to the other skeleton in my closet. There was only one pair of eyes I wanted to undress me and they weren't Zack's. We cried and promised to write.

Zack ended up in a doctoral program at Cornell majoring in philosophy. I wasn't surprised; after all, we had spent many hours philosophizing on the river.

Tip's goodbye was the strangest of all. She refused to come to the airport, insisting she had too much to do. Instead, she joined me out by the firepit.

"I just wanted to tell you I'm really going to miss you."

I didn't know what to say.

Opening her palm, she showed me a necklace with a silver feather pendant. "I didn't know what you'd like, but this is an eagle feather from my tribe. It symbolizes courage. I know it's hard to leave the Bayou, so I hope it brings you the courage needed to start your new life."

I started to reach for it, then thought otherwise. "Would you do the honors?" I asked, turning around.

She did not touch me as she clasped the necklace around my neck, but once the necklace hung there, I felt her arms slide around me as she gently pulled me back against her. "I know you may not understand this, but I've only been so hard on you because I care. I care a lot. More than I should. More than I knew what to do with."

Turning in her arms, I reached up and wrapped mine around her neck. Her body was warm against mine. "You've never fooled me, Tiponi Redhawk. You think I didn't feel your eyes on me day after day? You may be unsurpassed as a telepath, but I'm no slouch in the empath department." Standing on my tiptoes, I kissed her, softly at first, as her hands pressed me closer, as if she wanted to meld with me.

My hands slid from her hair to beneath her shirt, her skin was softer than anything I had ever experienced. Her hands were all over my back, pressing me harder against her, almost desperate to keep me in her arms—where I would have gladly remained had Melika not mentally thrown water on us both, telling me to get to the dock, we were leaving.

"Stay true to yourself. Trust no one but whom your instincts tell you to," Tip whispered, stroking my cheek with the back of her fingers.

Releasing her, I stepped back, my heart feeling the slight cracks of being almost broken. "Will you promise me one thing?"

"Maybe."

"Promise me you'll find a new nickname for me. I am no longer a child and you need not straight-arm me any longer."

Smiling her lopsided grin, she shook her head. "That's where you're wrong, Echo Branson. If I didn't keep you at bay, Melika would have had to toss me out long ago. No, it's safest for us both if *I* remember who you are. Mel would…well…let's just say she laid down the law long ago where you are concerned."

"But—"

"No buts. Go. Take care. Know I think the world of you and will miss you more than you can imagine."

I left, but wasn't happy about it.

It was my goodbyes to Melika and Bishop that felt like someone had reached into my chest and pulled my heart out through a sieve. Oh my God, if a person could actually feel their heart breaking, that's what it felt like.

Melika and I took a long walk my last day on the Bayou. We shared our deepest thoughts about my time here and we talked about everything for hours. I wrote her last words to me on a Post-it and kept it on my bathroom mirror for my daily affirmation:

"Echo, my dear girl, you are a very powerful young woman, and not just because of your innate powers. You are powerful because of who you are in here. I want you to remember this one very important phrase from Confucius. *To know that what we know is what we know and what we do not know we do not know... that is true wisdom.*"

That line resonated through my spirit and was my motto all the way through college. I took more with me to Oakland than just the lessons I had learned in Louisiana; I brought with me the entire Bayou.

Returning to the concrete jungle of Oakland was much harder than I thought it would be. I was more than an alligator out of the water; I was rootless. After digging my roots in for the last four years into the soft earth, it was incredibly hard to find any at all in the cement. Still, Mills wasn't a jungle, and there were plenty of trees and bushes within its safe confines.

I was surprised at how easy it was to fit in and to finally be able to relax and be myself. Foster care had scarred me for life and even four years in the Bayou hadn't lightened those scars. So the first six months I kept waiting for the other shoe to drop; for someone to take me out of my classes or send me away. That fear drove me to work morning, noon and night, much to Danica's chagrin. She was on the party circuit and loved every second of it. I don't know how she ever had time to get any of her work done, but she managed to get fairly decent grades.

I desperately missed the Bayou and everyone in it that first year away. Oakland was just so bland compared to New Orleans. I missed the smells, the heat, the wonderful calm that fell over the Bayou at dusk. I missed the color and spice of the food, the way the sunlight streamed through the trees, and even the way the 'gators kerplunked into the water. Life there was to be savored. In Oakland life was fast food; devoured without any decorum; seldom tasted and never appreciated. I had left a place that was alive and vibrant and returned to a place that felt dark and dreary.

Nothing shook the homesickness that descended upon me that first year. I wanted to go home.

At month three, home came to me.

I was coming from an English class when I heard her. It was the first time I was actually glad Tip could reach me. Melika had often told me that if Tip wanted to reach me, she could and that no matter how strong I got, she could get through any block or shield. For once, I was glad.

"Hey, darlin'. Feeling homesick?"

I stopped walking and sat down, my heart suddenly racing. *"More than you know. My god, I miss you."* I had tried to call her cell on more than one occasion, but her voicemail always picked up and I never left a message.

"Oh, I think I know. Melika wouldn't let me contact you sooner. She said it would only make the homesickness worse. You hungry?"

I looked around, but couldn't see her. *"I could eat. Please tell me you are nearby."*

"I'm in the cafeteria, darlin'. I'll buy you a burger, maybe even fries if you are nice."

I practically ran to the cafeteria. When I saw her big frame leaning against a stone pillar, I threw my arms around her hugging her tightly. I never wanted to let go. "God, it's good to see you." She smelled of lilac and mint, the familiar shampoo I'd loved.

Tip laughed as she pulled away. "Well, that's a first. I was a little nervous I'd get here and be sent away before I could even unpack."

"Unpack?" My heart beat harder. "You're staying awhile?"

Her eyes danced. "Would you like that?"

I kissed her deeply, uncaring about prying eyes. "I'd *love* that."

Taking her hand, I led us to the nearest table. "Mel sent you?"

She nodded. "There's a possible PK running around setting things on fire and Mel wants me to reel her in before she hurts someone."

"A PK, really?" A PK was a pyrokinetic, a fire starter. They were the rarest of all of us. Most PKs died before puberty as a result of burning themselves up in a little kid tantrum or fit of rage. Pyros who don't understand how to control their flames were usually consumed by them. I knew why Melika wanted to get her hands on this girl; she wanted to save her before she burned herself up.

"She has wanted confirmation on this kid ever since she heard. She wanted to send you, but she wants you to get settled in first. I need to teach you how to spot first and then—"

"I *know* how to spot."

She brought my hand to her full lips and kissed the back of it. "Spotting is one thing; hunting is an entirely different ball game." She stepped back and studied me a moment. "You *are* getting settled in, aren't you?"

I took her hand and led her away from the cafeteria and the gawking eyes of other women. "You don't want to eat here. There's a great rib place down the road. Where's your car?"

Tip led me to her rental car, a convertible Sebring. She kept her hand on my lower back the entire time—a feeling of warmth expanding down my limbs.

"A convertible? Nice touch."

"It's Cal-ee-for-nia, darlin'! Hop in and take me to your rib joint." She opened the door for me, but I didn't get in. Instead, I turned around and wrapped my arms around her neck.

"Where's this PK?"

She put her arms around my waist, and the cold from her black leather jacket felt good against the inside of my arms. "Santa Cruz. I'll buzz down there in the morning to check her out."

"How long are you staying?" Reaching out, I ran my fingers along her eyebrow and tucked a strand of hair behind her ear. It was as if we had always been comfortable with each other. I could have stayed in her arms forever. It was so good to have the Bayou standing before me—my Bayou.

Tip looked down at me, her big brown eyes twinkling. "You missed me."

Laying my head on her chest, I said, "So? You okay with that?"

Tip kissed the top of my head and got into the driver's seat.

"More than okay. Being homesick is a natural response, darlin'. There's no place on earth like the Bayou, and we haven't forgotten you. It takes awhile to assimilate back into our old lives. It's been four years, Echo. You just have to give it time."

"Time? How much time? I feel like a prisoner in my own life. Everywhere I turn, I see things I don't understand. I have to work daily on keeping my shield up because there are so many negative emotions around. Take that left."

"Don't look backward. That's the kiss of death. You need to remember the lessons you learned and apply them in this place. Everything can be applied. You just have to remember the lessons."

"Take that right. You sound like Melika."

"I should. She and I have been doing this gig a long time, and she's usually one hundred percent correct one hundred percent of the time."

"That's it over there." I pointed to a small corner cafe. Tip pulled in and then smiled at me. "Look, I know this is hard. Maybe it would help to know..." She reached out and took my hands. In that singular moment, when her hands touched mine, she took my breath away.

Tip loved me.

"Big," Tip said softly.

"Oh," I said as she tightened her grip. "I...uh..."

Then she smiled a smile I had never seen before. It was warm and soft and changed the shape of her face. That smile made her eyes sparkle and it was the first time I noticed the yellow flecks in them. "I have fought it for a long time; not just because you were underage, but because...because I just figured it was a passing thing; that once you were gone, I'd be able to get my feelings under control. I fought it hard, and sometimes I acted like a jerk, just hoping it would go away. I had to work double time to keep you from reading me, from seeing how much I care."

I swallowed hard. "Does Melika know?" Then I held my hands up. "Of course she does." It all made sense to me now. "That's why she kept sending you away."

Tip nodded and sighed. "Nothing I've done in the last three months has been able to change how I feel. Even with new blood to work with, you're always there. Always." Tip shook her head. "Melika thought it would dissipate in time also, and when it didn't, she said I could come here and let you know how I feel. She said you were a big girl now capable of making your own decisions." Her eyes watered. "I'm here hoping you decide in my favor."

Leaning in, I kissed her softy. "As if there was another choice for me, Tip."

Touching my face gently, she memorized it. "We miss you."

I nodded. "I miss her so much."

"I know. She misses you, too; more than she would ever admit. You were one of her very favorites. Are. You *still* are. The place has been really quiet without you."

"I thought—"

"That I hated you? I had to do *something* to make you keep your distance. You were fourteen when you came to us for God's sake. Have you any idea how many nights I wrestled with my feelings for you? I'm not always such a jerk, but I had to keep you at bay."

"Then why were you so mean to Zack?"

She bowed her head. "Because he got to see a side of you I never did. He got to spend time with you and laugh, play, just be with you. He *got* you in ways I never could, and I wanted to strangle him." She shook her head as if doing so would help her find the words. "You took my breath away, but he got to be close to you. I didn't want to feel this way, but every time I was gone, I couldn't wait to get back to you...to see you again. I knew I was in serious trouble."

"Because of my age?"

She looked at me with eyes I'd never seen before. Like chocolate melting. "Because you would have to leave me someday." She blinked several times. "So, I bided my time waiting for you to go back to California so I could return to my evil ways." Tip shook her head. "You may have gone away, but you never left me."

101

"So you came today to tell me?"

She shook her head again. "I've been here a month. Mel always sends me for a first month checkup to make sure everything goes smoothly. I was here when she got the PK call, but when I saw you...I knew it wasn't over for me. I couldn't leave here without letting you know how I felt...how I have *always* felt about you."

I swallowed hard.

"It's okay, really. I don't expect you to suddenly fall madly in love with me or gush on about your feelings. I know how I've been. I did what I needed to do to keep you at arm's length. I just wanted you to know how I felt. It was time, that's all."

"Tip, to be honest, I don't know how I feel. For so long, you were a big, scary telepath lurking around the shadows like some ghost. There was one time when you stopped being so scary and that was when I looked at your ass and thought you had a great one."

"Oh great...you see me as a piece of meat." She chuckled, her eyes dancing as she laughed.

We both laughed and finally broke my shield. I *did* feel something for Tip, but I didn't know what it was. I just knew it was fresh and warm and wonderful, like a loaf of bread right out of the oven.

I was already nineteen and had never really been in love. I didn't really know what that kind of love felt like except from afar, when others felt it. "Maybe we could just spend some time getting to know each other as people rather than as supers. You know take some time...see where this leads us?"

She took my hands in hers and kissed the backs of them. "I'd like that. I'd like that a lot."

Looking into her eyes I suddenly felt all of the emotions she had so carefully hidden from me rush like the tide over the sand. She really did love me.

"It doesn't have to be scary, Echo. Let's just do as you say and let the chips fall where they may."

It was at that moment I realized I could love her back.

Tip and I didn't wind up in bed together that first night or even the second. She stayed for ten days and we spent the first three getting to know one another. We stayed out that first night in her hotel room laughing about all the things that happened in the Bayou. We hung out in Jack London Square eating, walking, laughing and reliving the good old days. Once in awhile, I'd slip my arm through hers, but other than that, she made no move that might be construed as overtly sexual or even intimate.

As an empath, I had one of two choices during a romantic interlude: I could keep my shields up and not experience any emotional exchange or I could lower them completely and feel every single emotional truth. I used to be afraid of Tip's truth. Maybe I was even afraid of my own. It was one thing to be in the closet as an empath, but I wasn't about to be placed in another one because of who I chose to love. No way.

At least sex with another super who could block would mean I could have a semi-normal sex life, and that option was quickly becoming a reality the longer we spent time getting to know each other. I was having the time of my life...and I was beginning to feel very deeply for this woman who had been my savior, my hero and the bane of my existence all rolled into one.

Funny thing was I wasn't the least bit fazed by the fact that I was falling in love with a woman. It was perfectly natural to me.

We were taking a walk around the lake one day when Tip took my hands in hers. "I think now is the time to be brave. Now is the time to let go of any fear and really live life on the edge. And you know why? Because you are amazing. You are bright, confident, funny and caring. You're the complete package, Echo with so much to offer.. Maybe now is the time for you to finally let someone in."

"That someone being you?" I said, smiling.

"I just want you to be happy. If that happiness includes me... well... then I'm a really lucky woman."

A really lucky woman? Did I even *know* this woman? So much about how she had been toward me since she arrived had surprised the hell out of me. She was no longer the distant, brooding Indian I had never understood or much liked. This woman was displaying a gentleness and an insightfulness that shocked me.

"The day I followed you and Zack into town, I was in love with you. I couldn't stand the thought of you being vulnerable out there. I had to follow you. I begged Mel to let me come."

"I thought it was standard operating procedure."

"It was, but she wanted to send Jacob. I talked her out of it."

"Because you were worried?"

She nodded. "Hell yes. I know how hard that first city trip is for newbies. I had to promise her to stay far away. Melika threatened me within an inch of my life. She would have strung me up if I so much as made a move. I may be powerful, but Mel..." She shook her head... "You have no idea."

"Is *she* why you don't have a woman? I mean, does she forbid it?"

"Hell no. I don't have a girlfriend because I love living in the Bayou. I love helping Melika with the newbies. It's what I do best. I can't imagine giving it up...even for love."

I leaned into her. "Love, eh?"

"Don't worry. I'm not asking for a commitment or rose petals or anything lasting. I just want you to know how important you are to me. I didn't...I don't want you going out into the world not knowing how much you are loved. And I do love you."

She said it. She actually said it. If the emotion reached me, I didn't feel it. I was too busy blocking, bobbing and weaving to feel anything.

But I *wanted* to feel it.

We walked a little more in silence and I realized that this woman...this woman who had traveled all this way to reveal feelings she had kept under lock and key for over five years was probably the one person who understood me the most. That revelation surprised the hell out of me. I thought Danica was the only one who really got me; but I was wrong. She was my best friend, of course, but she wasn't a super. She couldn't relate to much of what I had experienced.

But Tip could.

And did.

And this changed everything.

What we forget when we leave a place is that life still charges ahead there, and Danica's was no exception. When she came to visit twice a year on the Bayou, it was just the two of us on my turf on my terms. Even though I mentally understood her life still went on, I never felt it in my heart until I saw her life in Oakland and Berkeley. Everyone knew her. Everyone liked her, and her social calendar was always full. Always. I wasn't used to being fourth or fifth on the totem pole, but what did I expect? Of course her life went on while I was in the Bayou. Of course she was well-liked and popular; she was a great person. Still...to know this in the vacuum of the Bayou and to see it happening were two different things. A lot had happened in my absence. A whole lot.

First off, Danica had shown an incredible aptitude in computer programming in her junior year in high school, and I was surprised to learn that she was allowed to take advanced courses in computer science at Cal. This, of course, opened social doors for her and gave her ins to social circles well out of reach of most high school students.

Like Bishop had said, she was destined for great things. It was strange to see how she and her life had changed so drastically. She was no longer living on the island of misfit toys.

Computer geeks are a breed apart from the rest of us. They speak a different language, they see the world through a different pair of glasses. Their world is a four foot-by-four foot space with a flat monitor in front of their faces. It couldn't have been more different from my nature-driven world. While I craved fresh air, deep conversation and sunlight, Danica loved the solitude and isolation of a computer cubicle. We couldn't have been in such diametrically opposed corners had we tried. Her world consisted of ones and zeros. Mine consisted of trying to fit back into a life

I had left behind. And I was still feeling left behind.

That was why seeing Tip had been so important to me. As much as I loved Danica, she had her own gig going. She had no time for anyone. She and some nerds were developing a computer game that was supposed to be revolutionary, and so she ate, slept and drank at the computer lab. Danica wasn't interested in the guys, no matter how smart, unless they had computer skills better than hers...and that was a tough row to hoe.

In the end, I was feeling left out, so having someone there who put me first was just what I needed. Maybe it just felt good to be held, to be comforted and to be understood. Maybe somewhere deep down inside, I returned her affections more than I let myself admit; and before I could stop myself, I let everything between us get out of hand and just like that, I was no longer a virgin and no longer alone.

Making love with Tip was unlike anything I'd ever experienced. She was soft and gentle, always making sure I was comfortable. I have never felt safer in my life than lying in her arms, and I laid there every chance I got. She would kiss me like every kiss was the last. She had a mouth that could do miracles, and she ran her lips over my entire body over and over. I didn't know what I loved more: her hands on my body or her mouth. We spent a great deal of time in bed, just exploring each other. Had I known how good love-filled sex could be, I'd have jumped all over her long ago. We spent in bed every moment I wasn't in class or working. I devoured her like a starving person. She opened up a whole new world of sensations for me. I used to be afraid of what love would be like for me as an empath, but when Tip taught me how to read her just as she was climaxing, I was flooded with such intense emotions that I could experience an orgasm without ever being touched. It was amazing. I was like a newborn addict, counting the minutes to my next fix. Our lovemaking was surreal, romantic and filled with a passion I never knew existed.

For the moment.

I think I was just too naive or just plain stupid to see where this was going. It was nobody's fault, really. Tip and I were simply geographically incompatible, so I'm not sure what I was expecting; for her to stay in Oakland? Hadn't she made it crystal clear the Bayou was her home? She would have been a fish out of water flopping around with its mouth opening and closing. Even with empathic powers, I had failed to actually *hear* her when she told me not even love could move her from her beloved Louisiana.

"My powers know no distance, you know. We don't even need a phone. How cool is that?"

How cool is that? In the throes of new love, it was very cool, but I was a fool. In my need to reconnect with the Bayou, to be loved, I had made a huge mistake of hooking up with someone far more dangerous than any swamp alligator. Yes, Tip cared for me, and maybe she did really love me, but I wasn't ready for the kind of relationship she was proposing. I didn't want long distance. I didn't want a phone relationship.

It was the iceberg approaching the Titanic.

Tip stayed for three wonderful weeks; you know those first crazy days where you can't get enough? The hot and sexy kind where you exist on nothing but the pure adrenaline of sex.

At the end of three weeks Melika called her home. She didn't want to go, but when Melika calls you go. It was time for Tip to go, and when she left, she took a piece of my heart with her.

I finally began to acclimate to my new life and began enjoying myself. What had happened between me and Tip had settled me down and given me the confidence to go on and give my new life a real shot. Before she came to me, I had just gone through the motions; but after she left, I turned one hundred percent of my attention to making Oakland and Mills College my home again.

After being a nomadic foster child and then a 24-7, 365-days-a-year student of the Bayou, I realized I had no idea who *I* was. Being an empath was about power and skill, not character and soul. I had been lost because I didn't know anything about *me*. Once I started to learn who I was, my life at Mills caught fire. My grades improved, my social life opened up, and I was finally happy.

And this threatened Tip. She had been used to me relying on

her. Once I started being more independent, she started crowding me. Our mental connection was becoming more intrusive than supportive and I started resenting it. I started resenting her and her listening in on my life, and she resented me for being so happy without her I bolstered my shields and blocks to keep her from reading me and spying on my life, and she did what she always did: she went on a mission.

It saddened me that this was how it ended up, but we hadn't really given ourselves any other choice. She was there and I was here. Tip was pretty angry when I broke it off because she never saw it coming. She assumed I was completely open for her to read, but I had learned a lot more from Melika than she realized. I needed to learn to love myself before getting that deeply involved with anybody, least of all a telepath. I hoped she would understand.

She didn't.

It took her almost four years to get over it, and almost two years before she would speak to me again. We managed to get beyond the hurt and pain, but it was pretty obvious to us both that she was really in love with me. So, we went our own ways; I dove into my studies and she dove into hers, which was what took her to places like Australia; she loved learning about other people's powers. Tip became a student of the supernatural and I became a student of the truth. We existed under a tenuous truce and every now and then, she would pop in to checkup on me and my life. We settled into an uneasy friendship that was probably less fulfilling to her than it was to me. I loved her, after all, but not with the depth and intensity that she loved me. It was best we had broken up.

I just wasn't sure I completely believed that.

At the age of twenty-eight, I was standing in the office of a man who had recently fired me asking myself the same question I'd asked after I bashed Todd's head in. Was I crazy? What in the hell I was thinking? It's not like me to give someone a second chance to bury yet another dagger between my shoulder blades.

It wasn't like me at all. So what was I doing here? Curiosity maybe? Wasn't the road to Hell paved with the dead bodies of cats, or was I mixing my metaphors? I grinned to myself at the image. Okay...so I was a little curious as to why my old boss had summoned me.

A week ago, my boss, Wes Bentley, who is as snooty as his name suggests, fired me from my lowly peon position as a stringer for the Police Beat section of the *San Francisco Chronicle*. I know...how hard can it be to report on the numerous criminal activities in a place like the City by the Bay? Well, I wasn't fired for incompetence. I was fired for suggesting a well-known CEO who was being interviewed by our top investigative reporter was lying. Lying through his ten thousand dollar DaVinci veneers.

Okay...so maybe I should have waited before blurting it out right in front of this prominent citizen, but I just couldn't help it. A foster parent once told me my biggest problem was I lacked stoplights between my brains and my mouth. She was right about me not having stoplights, but wrong about it being my *biggest* problem. My greatest problem was also my biggest gift, and it was this double-edged sword I wielded daily. Unfortunately for me, on the day I called out *liar, liar, pants on fire*, it was a sword I stabbed myself with.

I knew Mr. Bentley didn't want to fire me that dark day, but his star reporter, Carter Ellsworth, had demanded my head on a rusty platter. Apparently, my pronouncement about his source's lies had humiliated Carter in front of the scheming, embezzling CEO; and being shown up was one thing that Carter Ellsworth could not abide.

I had just returned from the police station and was walking by my favorite fountain out in front of our building. I have a thing for running water because it often blocks out extraneous emotions. That's why I wandered over there in the first place. I couldn't have cared less who he was interviewing or what he was doing because my focus was on the fountain. I hadn't realized Carter was conducting his interview on the other side of it. As I started by them, I was slammed with a huge wave of deceit, dishonesty and dissembling. Normally, I have mental shields up to protect myself from inadvertent reading. Dealing with everyone else's emotions is an exhausting endeavor.

On that day, I felt them like a baseball bat to the back of my legs. The darkness of the CEO's emotions hit me with such force I could not stop myself from blurting out, "What a crock of shit," as I strolled by. Jumped right out of my potty mouth and landed on a pink slip with my name on it. It didn't matter I was right, because as an empath, I was in the closet. Out as a lesbian, in as an empath.

Anyway, Carter got what he wanted, and I was let go.

So, why was I here?

When Wes walked in, I did a quick read and decided against raising my shields. Raising and lowering psychic energy forces is a little like the regular Joe putting his hands over his ears to keep from hearing someone. The only thing missing was the "Lalalalala," and believe me, there were days when I wanted to add that as well.

"Thank you so much for coming in, Branson. I wasn't sure... well...never mind. It was good of you to come." Wes Bentley stood in front of me and extended his well-manicured hand. Wes always wore a tanning booth glow; a little too much George Hamilton meets Bob Barker. I shook his hand and took note of his new Christian Dior suit and thousand dollar hand-painted tie. Wes was one of the best dressed men in the city and commanded attention wherever he went. At this moment, however, all pretense of command had been replaced by something I had never seen or felt from him in the seven months I'd been at the paper; contriteness. Yes, the man who cut me loose with the weak explanation, "If Carter wants you gone, you're gone," was standing there with his hat in his hand.

Now wasn't *this* an interesting turn of events?

Carter Ellsworth wielded that sort of power because he had won a Pulitzer for a series of reports he did during the Iraq War and that pretty much gave him *carte blanche* to destroy the nobodies of the world like me. Pulitzer winners are a rare breed, and the majority of them, from what I gather, prefer to keep their fame and fortune on the East Coast, preferably New York. For whatever reason, Carter preferred foggy San Francisco.

"I'm here mostly out of curiosity, Wes."

Wes moved around to the other side of his desk. "Well, I do appreciate your time, so let me get down to brass tacks. Have you found another job yet?"

Oh, how I wanted to lie; to say, yeah, the *New Yorker* picked me up and offered me my own column and I'm moving there tomorrow. But the sad truth was, I couldn't even get an interview with any of the smaller papers in the area and was working part-time at Luigi's Bakery, the bakery directly below my tiny apartment.

"I'm still looking for something in my field, yes." I read a sense of relief from him. He wanted something from me. This was getting more interesting every second.

"I see." Wes folded his leather-tanned hands on the desk and leaned forward. "I'm going to be straight up with you, Branson. Tomorrow, you're going to be reading Carter's retraction of the story about Glasco's embezzlement." He eyed me carefully as if trying to read *me*.

Wes could look all he wanted, he would never *know* how I was feeling. Looking into his light blue eyes, I understood he was trolling; feeling me out before laying the rest of his cards out on the table. There really was no need to since I saw what was coming next. A retraction for the editor-in-chief of a big newspaper is a little bit like having your pants pulled down in public without any underwear to hide the family jewels. What it means is you didn't fully do your job. Whenever a story suffers a retraction, *everybody* looks bad, and worse...amateurish. Well, the only amateur who had been fired over this story was me. Apparently, the truth had come out somewhere and now both Carter and Wes were eating crow.

I wondered what crow tasted like and if you served it with white wine.

"So, you found out he *was* lying." It wasn't a question, and

I made sure it sounded like a statement of fact. I knew it was a fact, but Wes had cut me off so quickly there had been no time to prove it; someone else had obviously done the job for me. My guess is it was one of the fact-checkers who so often bump heads with investigative reporters. One of the best fact-checkers on the staff was Jennifer Ridge. I would have bet my last dollar Jennifer was the one who found out the truth about the lying CEO.

"Near as I can tell, the man has no idea what the truth looks like." Wes shook his head sadly. He hated retractions.

"Jennifer?"

Wes nodded. "It took her longer than Carter wanted, so he pressured her to sign off on his story. You know how Carter can be."

I nodded. Jennifer was so good at her job our editors actually invented editorial marks to include her. If an editor was unsure of the fact, she would write AJ in the margin which stood for Ask Jennifer.

"Well, now that we've covered that, let's get down to business. I don't know what you've heard about me, Branson, but I am a man who owns his own mistakes. It's not easy, mind you, but you don't get to be in a position of power without taking responsibility for both the good decisions and the bad. Under the circumstances, I was wrong to fire you. I assumed Carter's story had checked out and you had not only been unprofessional, but had made him look bad. Wrong on both counts. I would like to right those wrongs."

"What did you have in mind?"

"I would like to offer you your job back."

The beauties of my gift are the subtleties of emotions peeking around the obvious ones so I get a clearer picture of what's going on with the person. Wes was offering me my job back, hoping I would accept it without playing hardball.

Unfortunately for him, hardball is my specialty. What little I remember of my childhood, I did not grow up in a warm and loving environment. I did not grow up in a soft cushy life. I grew up moving from one home to another in the ghettos of Oakland,

California. You don't last there as a white kid if you can't hit a fastball, and I was one hell of a hardball player. I knew I had been unjustly fired, but the problem with my power is it's impossible to explain without uncovering exactly what I am. Few people in my life know what I am. I wasn't about to unveil that part of me to anyone other than my closest friends. So no, I wasn't going to make this easy on him. "I appreciate your offer, Wes, but the police beat isn't really for me. I came here with the idea of being a journalist. I have the drive, the talent and the instincts for it. I think I would rather wait until a real offer comes along." I rose and extended my hand. "But thank you. I do appreciate knowing I was right about Glasco."

Wes quickly rose and scooted around the enormous desk. "Well then, consider yourself offered a real position here. I like your style, Branson. You don't miss a beat, you're quite astute, and you don't mince your words. You're right about those instincts, too. All of those are essential ingredients in being a top-notch reporter working for me."

The swing and a miss sound you heard was *my* bat whiffing at the curveball Wes just threw past me. I was so stunned I barely knew what to say. "Reporter?"

Wes nodded. "Liz Pensky is going to the *Post*, so I need a new IR. The job is yours if you want a shot at it."

Now *that* was a job offer...and one I wasn't expecting. I could tell by the look in his eyes he enjoyed the surprise. I blinked several times and thought carefully about my response. I could be a good investigative reporter; a *really* good one. I wanted to use my expensive Mills College education for something other than running around collecting short pieces for the Police Beat. This was my chance.

"What about Carter? Won't he have something to say about this?"

Wes got all puffed up. "I run this paper and I make the decisions around here. I gave him what he wanted when I thought he was right. He wasn't. I checked on his *source* and the guy was looking for a better business advantage. He was willing to use *my* paper to get it, the little prick. Ellsworth should have dug deeper."

"Can we recover from it?"

"Oh hell yes. The little worm isn't going to put us in any trouble. Glasco has waved a slander suit in my face, but all they really want now is positive PR, which I willingly give them. Don't worry. I've handled worse threats. So, do you want the job or not?"

"I accept." I reached out and shook his hand. "When do I start?"

"How does tomorrow morning sound?"

"I'll be here."

"Excellent. Then stop by HR before I saddle you with a pro. You'll be working with someone until you get the hang of it."

Nodding, I opened the door to his office. "I appreciate the opportunity, Wes. I swear you won't regret it."

Wes stepped so close to me I could smell the coffee he had had for breakfast. "How did you *know*?"

"That Glasco was lying?"

"Yes. Carter said you sounded so cocksure of yourself. How could you have been so sure?"

Grinning, I stood on tiptoe and whispered, "Like you said, I have great instincts. Would you believe me if I told you I read his emotions?"

Wes pulled away and eyed me once again. "Read? Like telepathically?"

I nodded. "Yep. I looked at him and knew he was lying. It's a gift I have."

Wes tossed his head back and laughed, as I knew he would. "You know, Branson, I like your style. You can read my mind any day."

I already had.

When I finished up with Mrs. Malone at Luigi's Bakery, I grabbed the day olds and took a hard left to the stairway leading up to my apartment.

Luigi's Bakery had been in the same place for sixty years. His father, Luigi Sr., opened it shortly after landing in San Francisco, when Luigi was about eight. I managed to get the apartment when Luigi's mother passed away and he inherited her house on Nob Hill. He rented it to me for a song because he didn't need the money and because I do errands for him. I also covered whenever he needed a break to go to the bank or the store. Anyone who thinks running a bakery sounds easy is a fool. It's hard work and a labor of love that is quite physically demanding. Since I moved in several years ago, shortly after my graduation from Mills, Luigi and I have looked after each other.

Opening my front door, I was greeted, as I always am, by my Siamese cat, Tripod.

"Hey cutie," I said, kneeling down to scritch his ears.

I rose and checked my messages. There was one from Danica, still my best friend, and two from telemarketers. As I erased the messages, Tripod rubbed up against my legs as best he could. Tripod, as his name suggests, only has three legs. He lost his back leg to a rare form of cancer. The vet recommended I put him down, but for reasons I couldn't explain to her, I was going to give him a chance. I had found him on the bakery doorsteps, cold, wet and dehydrated one foggy morning. Luigi said I could keep him if I had him checked out by a vet. So, I bundled him up and took him to Dr. Elaine for a full battery of tests. When he lived through the amputation, she told me that everything in her was against trying to save him.

She had mad skills as a surgeon. I have mad skills as an empath. Two years later, Tripod is cancer free and manages quite nicely with three legs. As a result of keeping him alive, he has been the best pet in the world even if he is addicted to catnip.

Picking up my phone, I called Danica's office. Her secretary put me right through as she always does.

"Hey there unemployed chick. How's the job hunting going? Any bites?"

"I bagged one; a really good one, too."

"Excellent! Do tell."

So I did. Danica was truly delighted. After five years together at Mills, we both had decided to stay in the Bay Area and make our fortunes. So far, Danica was the only one of us who understood how to actually do that.

After graduating with a Master's degree in computer science, Danica opened her own software firm and it took off like the proverbial rocket. She had created a program which instantly alerted a company whenever someone was trying to break through a firewall or other security system. Unlike other programs, hers alerted via audio as well as video before slamming a wall around all files. The program was aptly named The Echo after me. She didn't name it after me because I was her best friend; but because when I had finally learned how to shield myself from the onslaught of emotions from people near me, she thought it was pretty cool. The Echo was patented, Danica had made a bundle, and now she was the sole owner and CEO of Savvy Software, an up-and-coming company beginning to be noticed by the likes of Apple, Microsoft and *Wired* magazine.

"I can't believe old man Bentley admitted he made a mistake," Danica said, crunching something in my ear.

"Carrot?"

"Bingo."

"Diet?" Danica had tried every diet on record, not because she needed to, but because her geek squad of computer programmers were working on a dietary software program even the biggest diet imbecile could use.

"Not this time. So, when do you go to work, Clark?"

I grinned. Danica had been calling me Clark Kent ever since I was the editor of the newspaper at Mills College. She had always called my gift my *superpowers* and was somewhat enamored with them.

"Tomorrow morning. They'll probably apprentice me with a seasoned veteran for a while until I learn the ropes. I am totally excited."

"It's what you've always wanted, Clark, though it's beyond me what you get out of digging around in people's dirty laundry.

116

Quite frankly, I've never really understood the pull."

"You just don't have any appreciation for the press."

Danica made a few derisive noises. "If I want the truth, the *real* truth, I sure as hell won't get it from the news. Anyway, congratulations on your ladder climbing. It's about time your superpowers gave you a leg up on the competition."

"The last time I used my ability I got fired."

"You got fired because Carter Ellsworth is a dick. Uh-oh, my red lights are blinking, so I better scoot along. A boss's work is never done. The boys are all excited about our first role-playing game and they keep bombarding me with questions. You know how they are. I want them to focus on the diet program, and all they can talk about is some dumb role-playing game."

The boys were a trio of Berkeley graduates who had been rejected by a number of top firms because they wanted to be hired as a package deal, unheard-of in the oversaturated computer nerd market of Silicon Valley. After being rejected by just about every major software company, they arrived on Danica's doorstep. She took one look at their resumes and hired all three on the spot. In a way, they were to Danica the way Tripod was to me; grateful to have been given the opportunity to work together, they rewarded Savvy Software with some of the best programs on the market.

Now, the three of them shared an enormous office where they spent far more than the requisite forty hours developing programs that would put Savvy Software on a bigger technological map. Their office, nicknamed the Bat Cave, was a technological and electronic marvel. Danica gave them whatever they needed to get the job done which they did often and well.

"Let's have dinner after your big day so you can tell me what it's like to finally be on the A team."

I didn't know much about being on the A team, but I knew it was a long way from the D list.

Entering the Bat Cave was a little like entering the bedroom of triplets. There were electronic and digital toys everywhere, and three of everything; three remote-control cars, three robots,

117

three Game Boys, three PlayStations, three Xboxes, three laptops, three computers, three plasma screen TVs, and, yes, there were even three virtual-reality stations complete with goggles and headphones. If it was electronic and had bright lights, they owned it. Like three little boys, they would take extended breaks in order to race their cars or play their video games. That was one of the reasons why their work week was well over seventy hours; the emphasis wasn't ever on the work. Ever. The boys got their best ideas when they were either playing on the foosball table or beating each other up in some arcane video game.

They were well worth the hefty salaries Danica paid them. That was why they were my first stop. There wasn't anything they couldn't do with a computer.

"Hey, guys, Princess is here!" Roger said when I opened the door. They had no secretary, no reception area, nothing. They preferred to deal solely with their incredibly lenient boss, and unless otherwise bothered, they seldom left the Bat Cave.

"Hi Roger," I said, shaking his clammy hand. Roger was the coolest of the geeks. He wore his hair in a brown ponytail and subsisted mainly on corn nuts and Diet Coke. There was a warmth about Roger that drew women to him, but he was uncomfortable around most females. I was an exception because I was not just Danica's best friend, I was the Princess to her Queen. "What's shakin'?"

Before he could answer, Franklin set the controls to his Xbox down in order to come greet me. "Princess! We're working on a program that helps kids read better. What brings you to the Bat Cave?" Franklin pushed his black-rimmed glasses back up the bridge of his long nose. He had been wearing the same style of glasses since he was seven years old. I could only surmise how many times he had been beaten up as a kid. I imagined it was a lot.

"Here on business, Franklin, and I could use your help."

"Fun business or adult business?" This came from Carl, who was still playing on the computer. His mop of red curly hair always looked like an oversized wig. When he rose, he unfolded like a cartoon paper doll. Carl ate all day long and never put an ounce on his six-foot-four inch frame.

"I'm afraid this is going to be dull adult business, guys."

The three of them looked at each other. The word *adult* was like a swear word to them. "What do you need?"

Sighing, I told them about my plight. "I need a story. I need something big; something that—" All three jumped behind their computers, fingers flying at breakneck speed over their respective keyboards. "We're all over it. You want something spectacular." Carl explained that information was like a snowball; once they started it rolling, it not only picked up speed, but grew proportionately to what was out there.

"Give us a few, Princess, go bother the boss," Carl said, pushing his glasses back up.

Turning to leave, I was almost out the door when Franklin called me back.

"There's a lot that goes down in this city, hon. You want something dangerous? Something provocative, or both?"

"Sex sells, sistah," Roger said, winking.

I turned slowly. "I want something that will prove to Wes Bentley he didn't make a mistake in hiring me back."

All three of them grinned. "Gotcha," Roger said, returning his attention to his computer. "Then sex it is."

I grinned back. "Knock yourselves out, guys. I'll be back in a half an hour."

As I left the Bat Cave, I made my way to Heidi's desk. "Hey Heidi."

"Oh, Echo. She's in a meeting right now."

"Let her know I am borrowing the boys for a little research project."

Heidi shook her head, a slight smile playing at the corners of her newly collagened lips. She reminded me of every high school cheerleader I had ever met; all legs and teeth and perfect hair. She had been a great secretary to Danica, who was not an easy boss by any means. "You mean they're actually *working*?" Heidi laughed. "She pays them a king's ransom and all they do is sit around in there all day and play."

"Well, just tell her that they're screwing around for me."

She nodded and checked her schedule. "Are you two still on for dinner?"

I nodded.

Heidi's phone beeped. "That was fast. The boys beckon."

In the short time I was gone, the boys had compiled over a hundred printed pages.

Carl was thumbing through them and talking without looking up. "These are some of the issues happening right now. Some are seriously scary, others are like cold cases. Is that sorta what you were after?" He handed me a printout of strange stories around the globe.

I looked down at the paper and saw all sorts of headlines, and blogs and other articles about interesting cases and issues. "That was so fast."

Carl shook his head as he pulled more paper from the printer. "Don't forget who we are, Princess. *We* are the reason the Boss created the The Echo in the first place...well...guys *like* us. We can get through anything."

"What about The Echo? Can you breach that?"

Franklin nodded. "Breach it, yes. Get *away* with breaching it, nope. The Boss designed a program that leaves hackers' fingerprints, so to speak. Unless we tossed our machines, we'd be busted for sure. That's the beauty of her program. You may get your info, but it'll cost you your machine if we don't catch you and your freedom if we do."

I saw a couple of topics of interest, but nothing that reached out and grabbed me. "Good work, guys. I'm sure I can dig my teeth into some of these."

"Be careful, Princess," Carl admonished. "No snake likes to be poked in the eye."

I nodded. "Gotcha." Straightening my papers, I started for the door. "This is great. I owe you guys."

Carl jumped up to get the door. Carl had a little crush on me that Danica thought was cute. "The Boss has been telling us ever since you got hired at the paper that you're going to be a star reporter someday. Anything we can do to help that along... we're here."

"Want us to keep digging? See if any bodies come up?"

"I think you better get some real work done. Aren't you developing a game or something?"

"Games, plural. Roger is working on a more accurate voice-to-text program that's better than anything on the market. Franklin is working on an accounting program, and I am this close to finishing my latest RPG. That means role-playing game."

"But aren't there plenty of voice-to-text programs out there already?"

"Sure, but the Boss wants one that is voice activated for handicapped folks and has an accuracy rate of close to ninety-eight percent."

Franklin nodded. "Yeah, she wants to give the program away to handicapped peeps, the elderly, quadraplegics, people with MS, you name it. It's easy to set up and easier to use and will make it much easier for them to e-mail and write. I just finished designing an app for it for the iPhone and iPod. Pretty cool, huh?"

"She never said anything."

"Because it's not done. When it's finished, she'll be crowing about it to anyone who will listen."

"Well...you guys get back to work. Thanks, again, for all the work. You really do rock."

As I took my bundle of articles out to Ladybug, my 1965 Bug. I realized I had yet to deliver Luigi's day olds. There they were, still sitting in the back of my car glaring at me with their little donut hole eyes. I felt slightly ashamed. Getting into Ladybug, I headed for the Mission District where I knew the little extra staleness wouldn't bother anyone. I had been fortunate enough to get a job...it was incumbent on me to spread that wealth any way I could, starting with the day olds in my backseat.

I read an article that said many of the homeless beggars on

the streets of San Francisco earned an average of thirty thousand a year. I remember scoffing at that figure until a professor of mine pointed out that many of the panhandlers were out on the streets fourteen to seventeen hours a day, seven days a week, three hundred sixty-five days a year. She estimated that a panhandler needed to pull in a little over four dollars an hour to meet that mark; a goal which was quite attainable especially during feel-good holidays like Valentine's Day, Thanksgiving, Mother's Day, and Christmas. Of course, money is a moot point if you spend it on alcohol or an addiction of another sort, as many homeless do. I know because one homeless guy was a friend of mine. His name was Bob.

Bob and I had been in the same foster home in the seventh grade; he was a year older than me, but had missed a lot of school because of his foster care hopping. Like me, Bob had been in and out of foster home after foster home. Unlike me, he struggled in school and those struggles led to some behavioral issues that made him hard to deal with.

I helped him as much as I could, but poor Bob could barely sit still. Our foster parents didn't believe in medicating children, so they refused any sort of help for his hyperactivity. So he continued acting out in class, getting multiple detentions and usually failing every single class. Bob wasn't stupid. He just needed help that wasn't going to come.

Eventually, our foster parents sent Bob back. He was just too much for them to handle. I didn't see him again until I moved into the city. The first time I took Luigi's day olds to the Mission District, I ran into Bob. Quite literally. I was fighting with this enormous bag of pumpkin bagels that hadn't gone over very well when I nearly knocked him over with the bag. He immediately recognized me, but I have to admit, it took me a couple of moments to see through the long hair and ratty beard. He was too thin and had aged terribly. Bob had opted to live on the streets rather than endure another failure in a foster home. In a way, I couldn't blame him. A kid can only take so many rejections and beatings.

Bob became one of the many nameless faces we all walk by every day, hoping that they don't speak to us or ask us for money. It was almost too hard to believe that someone I had grown up with would rather be homeless and alone than be forced to live in a family that didn't want him.

At that time, I didn't have much money on me, but the ten dollars I offered him wasn't accepted. Bobby didn't want my money, but he *did* want my bag of bagels. I've been delivering Luigi's day-old bagels to him ever since.

"Hey, Jane, you're late." Bob waved at me as I handed him the plastic bag.

"Haven't you heard? Beggars can't be choosers."

Bob tossed his head back and guffawed. "You slay me, Jane." Bob peered in the bag as he always did. "Damn. Raisins. You like raisins, Jane?"

I shook my head. "I don't."

"In the day olds, raisins are like little stones." Bob closed the bag and smiled at me. "But don't worry, this beggar likes gift horses. Thank you. You have no idea how much the guys 'preciate these. It's something we look forward to."

Bob was a little like the Pied Piper of the panhandlers. His constituents loved him. The business owners liked him. He may have been a drunk, but he wasn't a nutcase and he didn't steal. He was just a good guy who had gotten lost in the shuffle as a kid and never found his way out.

"How are you doing today, Bob?"

Bob looked down the street both ways before pulling me into the nearest alley. He had never done this before, so it took me by surprise.

"A friend of mine's missing," he said so softly I almost didn't hear him.

"Missing? What do you mean, *missing*?"

"His name is Rusty and he plays chess at the park every day. Every single day. But he hasn't shown up in the last two days and we're worried. All of us."

Leveling my gaze at Bob, I lowered my shield to read more of him. He was neither drunk nor crazy; just really scared. I didn't need to lower my shield to see that. It was etched all over his face.

"Nobody has seen him?"

Bob shook his head. "Not a soul. The last person to see him was Oreo, and that was at the liquor store two days ago. As long as I've known him, Jane, he has never missed a day of chess."

"You don't think he's just sleeping off a drunk?"

Bob shook his head. "Rusty drinks before he sleeps, but never during the day. He takes his chess seriously and alcohol clouds his thinking."

"What do you think has happened to him?"

"I don't know what to think. I just know he's missing and I don't know where else to turn. Can you check with the hospitals in the area? Maybe he got rolled."

"I can do that. I'll check with the SFPD as well." I handed my card to Bob and patted his back. "Be sure to call me if he shows up. I've got this new job and I'm really busy running around trying to impress people."

"Oh yeah? What's the gig?"

"I'm training to be an investigative reporter. It's going to take a lot of time to get where I want to be in my career, but this is my first real break."

Bob's face lit up. "Oh wow. Good for you, Jane. You deserve it. Nobody I've ever met works harder than you." When we were kids, he used to laugh and say that I would always be his plain Jane. "Then I really appreciate you taking the time to look. I know you're real busy."

"If I find anything out, I'll come down here. I'll get on it this evening and see what I can see."

"I really 'preciate it. Nobody's saying anything, but we're all getting a little jumpy down here. I don't know. I've been sleeping with one eye open because something don't feel right. Everyone feels it, too."

Touching his shoulder, I said, "You stay safe, okay? I'll see what I can find out. Do you have a last name for him? Maybe a description?"

"We don't really do last names, but he has long red hair, freckles and wears his 'Nam dog tags."

"Clothing?"

He shrugged. "The usual. Army jacket. Boots. Torn jeans. That's all I know."

I jotted this information down. "Got it. If you remember anything else, call me."

We said our goodbyes and when I returned to Ladybug, I had to shake off Bob's jumpy nature; Rusty's disappearance had really spooked a guy who didn't spook easily.

With a couple of hours to kill before my dinner with Danica, I decided to return to the office to make the calls to the hospitals in the area. When I arrived at our floor, I received a very unpleasant surprise. I had just walked in on the end of one of Carter's stories starring none other than me.

"Can you even believe that? She thinks she can just waltz out there and be an investigative reporter! Shit, old man Bentley's paired me up with Inspector Clouseau! Or is it Inspector Clue*less*?"

The three lackeys listening to his story laughed as if they were watching the Comedy Channel. Then, one of them saw me and his eyes grew so wide that the others, including Carter, turned to see what he was staring at.

"Go on, Carter," I said, folding my arms. "Go ahead and finish your character assassination."

The three now very uncomfortable audience members bowed their heads and slunk away with their tails between their legs. Served them right.

"Oh come on, Branson. Have a sense of humor. You have to admit—"

"You. Are. An. Asshole." I said, stepping up to him. The room became still and thick with tension. "Is this how big people with tiny minds spend their time?"

Carter pulled himself up to his full height, hoping to intimidate me into silence. No such luck. I hadn't been this pissed off in a long time. "I believe you would do well to note the manner in which you speak to me, Branson. After all, I am a man of—"

"Little integrity? No class? Big mouth? Stop me when I hit a wrong answer."

Carter looked over my shoulder at the people who were watching our show. I was pretty sure that he wasn't used to anyone taking him on face-to-face. What he needed to know was that I wasn't just anyone.

"You have to admit, Branson, you're only here because Old Man Bentley likes you."

Glaring at him, I did something I never do. "I'm willing to put *my* money where *your* mouth is. I'll bet you my car that I can come up with a bigger story than you."

"You're kidding, right?"

I inhaled deeply and took the plunge. "I'm so confident, I'll put up my 'sixty-five bug."

"Against my Lexus? That's not even close."

"It's collector's car. It's a classic. It's a—"

"Volkswagen!"

Shrugging, I pushed past him. "Coward."

"Fine. You can put up your *classic* bug for my *expensive* Lexus, but you'll have to do better than that. You want to go up against me, you're gonna have to play hardball."

I looked at him. I'd played hardball on the hard streets in Oakland. This white man wasn't in the same league as any of the guys I'd played ball with. "Bring it."

His upper lip curled into a snarl he wasn't feigning. "Fine. Here's the deal. You come up with a better story to follow or I get your red car *and* your pink slip."

Now *that* was unexpected. "You want my...resignation?"

Folding his arms across his chest triumphantly, he nodded. "Absolutely. You are nothing more than a thorn in my side who doesn't know shit about journalism. If you can't produce the goods, I want you out of here. Go make someone else's life miserable."

Well, I'd pretty much asked for that hadn't I? What could I do? Back out and apologize? Pretend like I never said it? No, I

126

knew I had the chops for this job. All I had to do was prove it. Pushing my hand out at him I nodded. "You're on."

"I can't believe you painted yourself into such a damn tight corner." Danica pushed her salad around on her plate until she found the croutons she was looking for. "What in the hell were you thinking?"

"I wasn't. I was just so ticked off he was making fun of me in front of everyone, I just popped off without thinking."

"And now you've got to put up or shut up. I cannot believe you bet Ladybug. You love that car." Crunching on the crouton, she made a face. Danica had more food issues than there was food.

"I'd love to keep my job even more." Shaking my head, I sighed. "He is just such an ass."

Returning her gaze to me, her light green eyes were intense. She could go from comic to philosopher in a heartbeat. A chameleon didn't stand a chance against her. "Be that as it may, you've really done yourself in this time. Were the boys able to get you any usable information?"

"I've gone through about half of it. There's a helluva lot of creepy shit going on out there. I'm sure I'll find something."

"No kidding. Any story or cold case strike your fancy?"

"Well, I did call the police department and spoke with a Sergeant Finn about possible cases to look into when I called about Rusty."

Danica ran her hand through her close-cropped blond hair that drew both men and women alike to her. "Rusty? Who in the hell is Rusty?"

"He's one of Bob's homeless buddies. Bob is worried because Rusty is missing. I told Bob I would check out the hospitals and see if the cops knew anything."

"And do they?"

I shook my head. "No on both counts. Without a last name, no one was very cooperative. No one remembered a long-haired, redheaded guy with dog tags from Vietnam."

"Kinda hard to locate a missing person who has probably been missing for over ten years, don't you think?" She glanced over at a man who had been staring our way since we sat down. "Needle in the haystack, Clark, even for the boys."

"I know, but I couldn't say no to Bob. He had a real hinky feeling going on about him that I haven't been able to shake. He is really scared."

When she looked back at me, her gaze melted from the cold stare at the probing eyes into one light and airy. "Hinky? One day as an investigative reporter and already you've got a whole new lingo? You've known me for how many years, and I can't even get one *girl fren'* out of you?" Danica laughed before finishing the rest of the croutons in her salad. "So, maybe this is your story."

I looked at her. "A missing homeless guy is so not a story."

Shrugging, she shooed the waiter away who was delivering a drink to the table. "Mayoral reelections are coming up, Clark, and what to do with the city's homeless is one of the items on the docket."

"The mayor is Carter's baby. I need to stay far away from that story."

"So...how are you going to keep your car and your job?"

Shrugging, I bit into my sandwich. "I need a real story; something to shut Carter's mouth up for good. Something that will impress Wes Bentley."

"Impress your audience first, Clark, the rest will follow. Or have you forgotten everything Prof. Rosenberg taught you in journalism one oh one?"

She had a point, as she always did.

"Well, the boys are at your disposal if you need anything. If there's any story in or out of cyberspace, they *can* and *will* find it for you. Just consider them your own personal research team. You know how they love working for you."

"Thanks."

We ate our dinner and chatted more about our lives. We'd sworn off talking about Tip, so we discussed her sex life instead. Danica was a power dater. She only dated powerful men and even

128

then, the rule was they couldn't stay the night. Ever. We weren't sure whether or not she had commitment issues, but no one man had ever managed to be enough for Danica Johnson. If a man lasted to the fourth date, he had overstayed his welcome. I, on the other hand, had a handful of failed relationships to my credit. I had yet to find a woman I trusted enough with my secret, which made a real relationship almost impossible to pull off. Even with my guards and shields up, I knew when a woman just wasn't my emotional match. There's no getting around that fact when you're an empath. It was a little like having X-ray vision; sometimes you saw things you just didn't want to see even when you weren't looking.

So, there we were, discussing the lack of love in our lives, when someone sent over an expensive bottle of champagne.

"I already waved you off once," Danica said, annoyed.

"This one is not for you, miss," he said, turning to me. "It is for you."

"What? Who?" Men seldom gave me a second glance when Danica was in the room. I was a pale five foot eight brunette whose most outstanding feature was big brown eyes with yellow flakes in them. Of course, most men aren't into eyes, yellow flakes or not.

I knew it was from a man because women never send champagne. Too pretentious.

"That gentleman at the bar sent it."

Before I could say anything, Danica wheeled around. "Oh, Clark, he's a cute one. Toss him over to me."

"He's the asshole," I muttered under my breath as I handed the champagne bottle back to the waiter. "Tell him I'm not interested."

Danica turned back to me. "*That's* Carter?"

I nodded as I shooed the waiter away. "Send it back, please."

I'm sure this waiter had not seen anyone turn down a hundred dollar bottle of champagne. "Send. It. Back."

To my surprise, Danica plucked the bottle out of the waiter's hand and poured herself some. "Never let a bottle of good Dom go to waste. Why not accept it and enjoy? Look at this as your last meal." Danica turned her flute to Carter and tipped it toward him. "Besides, maybe it's a peace offering."

"Like an Indian with a tomahawk was a peace offering to the settlers?"

"Oh goodie! Here he comes." She lowered her voice. "He's hunky. I love cleft-chinned men. It's so virile, so—"

"He is a jerk."

"Nobody's perfect."

I groaned. "Please don't do this to me. Not now. Not tonight when I have already suffered humiliation at the hands of that jackass."

"Do what? You better not be reading me."

"I don't have to read you to know when you're up to no good. I can tell by that look in your—"

"Good evening, ladies." Carter said ladies, but he was staring into Danica's face. "Branson."

"Are you following me?"

Carter turned to me, his eyes sparkling with every flicker of the candle in the middle of our table. "Isn't that a tad self-absorbed? Believe it or not, Branson, I'm not the least bit interested in either you or your puny little life." Then, he turned to Danica and grinned like the wolf from *Little Red Riding Hood*. "Unless of course you would like me to be."

Now I just felt plain foolish.

"Introduce me to your lovely dinner companion, Branson."

Lovely? What man ever uses the word lovely? "Carter Ellsworth, the Grand Pooh-Bah of Assholes, this is my best friend, Danica Johnson. There. You've met. Now go away."

He was unmoved and unmoving. "It's a pleasure." Carter extended his hand, but Danica merely looked at it in that way many black women have that says *you're kidding me, right?* Danica and some of her friends had tried to teach me *the look*, but I had never been able to master the moment. I *had* managed to pick up the five-minute French braid, but other than that I was an utter failure as a black woman.

Retracting his hand, Carter was undaunted. "Don't believe everything Branson says about me. She's biased."

Danica sipped her champagne and gave me *the signal*. The signal was something we invented our first year at Mills when she wanted to be read. We had started it as something fun to do at a party. Guys hit on her a lot. A lot. Lots of guys. All the time. Even weird guys who were out of their league. She has these exotic green eyes and this beautiful caramel-colored complexion that draws men like moths to the proverbial flame. Although I'm pretty sure moths have a better chance against the flame than most men have against Danica. She was brutal where men were concerned. Anyway, to prevent any unnecessary lingerers from hanging on too long, she would signal me with the twitch of her left eyebrow. Then I would read her and either swoop in for the save or find my own way home. With Danica, it was six of one, a half dozen of the other.

She wanted me to read her now because she was obviously feeling one way while acting another. A quick shield lower and I could see she didn't care for Carter at all. She was just enjoying toying with him and sizing him up. You don't embarrass the friend of a black woman and expect to walk away unscathed. Black women have this unique ability to knock people off their pedestals like no other. Carter was now dangling from his.

"Mr. Ellsworth." Danica started in her polished ghetto girl voice. "Echo's best friend is half black. She belongs to every environmental group on the West Coast, and she volunteers at the shelter. She doesn't have a biased bone in her body; tad or otherwise, but since I decided for myself that you are worthy of her disdain, it was a decision I made all by herself."

Carter looked at me. "Are all of your friends this fiery?"

"You have fiery and loyal confused," Danica retorted. "For a man who makes a living using and abusing words, I'd say you just abused that one. Thank you for the Dom and for allowing me to meet the jerk-off who talks shit about someone as good as Echo behind her back. Now, be off with you. You're blocking my light." She made a shooing motion with her hands.

131

Carter was unfazed. "Talking shit implies I wasn't telling the truth about her, and I was. It was a funny story. Branson simply didn't think so."

"Know what I think?" Danica leaned forward. "I think you are a bully with an undeserved superiority complex. And if I were a man half your size, I would kick your balls so hard they would fly out the top of your head. Now move along before you piss off the ghetto side of this girl."

Carter laughed. He actually laughed! "That might be interesting to see. You met me and came to this conclusion in what? Thirty seconds?"

"It takes less than two seconds to call a dog a dog." Danica finished her champagne and handed Carter the flute. "And I'll tell you this much, Mr. Ellsworth: Echo is going to kick your sorry ass all over the place. You might want to wear protection."

"Oh, really? Would *you* like to make a friendly wager on that?"

"Friendly wagers are for friends, Mr. Ellsworth, and *we* are most definitely not that."

"Then how about an unfriendly one?"

Danica cut her eyes over to me. I knew enough to keep my mouth shut. Ghetto girl needed no help from me. "What do you have in mind?"

Carter grinned. "You really think she's going to find a better story than anything I write? Get real. Or are you living in the same alternate universe as she is?"

"I am and I do."

"Then make your wager."

Danica's aura fairly glowed. "When she smokes you, and she will, I want my company on the front page of the business section on a Sunday."

"The company you work for?"

"Come out of your cave once in a while, paperboy. The company I *own*. I've been trying to get on that cover section of yours forever."

"What's the company?"

132

"Savvy Software."

Carter looked surprised. "You *own* Savvy Software?"

She didn't even twitch. "Is it because I'm black or because I'm a woman that surprises you so much?" Danica snapped her fingers. "Oh, I know...it's because I'm a black woman."

"I'm not surprised...I just—"

"That's what *I* want when I win, paperboy. Now, what's your wager? What do you want if a miracle occurs?"

He chuckled. "A miracle, huh? You have that much faith in the nubile Branson?"

A slight grin formed on her lips. "Absolutely."

"Enough to risk going on a six-hour date including dinner, dancing and delicious dessert with me?"

"Six hours? That's not a date. That's a marriage."

Shrugging, Carter grinned. "You want the cover, I want six hours to change your mind about me. It's your call."

Danica held her hand out and shook his. "It's a deal."

Carter took her hand and stepped closer. Like most men who looked into her eyes, Carter was riveted. If it wasn't so pathetic it might have been enjoyable. Little did he know he was looking into the eyes of a woman who could and would eat him for lunch.

Danica held her hand up and backed him off her. "Don't underestimate my best friend, paperboy. The last guy who did that..." Danica shrugged as she looked away and pulled her hand from his.

"I will look forward to our date, then."

Danica gave him a look she usually saved for the ghettos of Oakland. "You'll be looking a long time. Thanks again for the bubbly. Now, if you don't mind."

As Carter turned away, she called him back. "Yo, paperboy!"

"Yes?"

"And the word is *neophyte*, not nubile. If you're going to toss out sixty-four-cent words, at least know what the hell they mean."

Once Carter was gone, Danica leaned back and poured herself more champagne in my glass. "I want that front page, Clark."

"I know you do."

"Can you do it?"

I swallowed hard, thinking of the pages and pages of computer printouts back at my place. "In a week? I don't know. I think so."

"Excellent. I want you to kick his ass all over the court leaving body parts behind."

I grinned and tinked her flute with my water glass. "I'm pretty sure you just did."

After dinner, I pored over every printout the boys had given to me. I was astounded by the depth of the information they had managed to come by in such a short amount of time. I had it all. Now, it was up to me to put it all together and see if I could find a story that would captivate the minds of every San Franciscan.

With paper strewn everywhere, I rose and stretched. Maybe I was going at this the wrong way. Maybe what I needed was an inside angle; someone who could give me a hint or point me in the right direction.

Picking up the phone, I called Sergeant Finn.

"Hello there, Ms. Branson. What can I do for you?"

"Echo. Please call me Echo."

"Okay, Echo, before you get started with the million and one questions you reporters are so fond of, I don't want to be rude, but it's my dinnertime."

"Oh. I'm sorry." I looked at the clock. It was almost eleven thirty. Cops' hours must suck if they have to eat dinner at midnight. "Would you mind if I met you for dinner? I promise I won't bother you after that...it's just...I need a break. I bet Carter Ellsworth I could get a better story than he can. I sort of bet my car and my job on it."

The line was quiet for a moment.

"Carter Ellsworth, eh? Do you have any idea how much we *hate* that guy's guts?"

I grinned. "Who doesn't?"

She chuckled. "Look, I'll be eating at the Del Mar Cafe in about fifteen minutes. I can't promise I have any scoop for you, but I'd hate to see you go down without a fight. That guy's a grade A jerk."

"Thank you so much. I'll be there in ten minutes."

"Excellent. See you there."

Snatching the rest of the catnip out of the paws of my stoner cat, I grabbed my keys and headed downstairs.

Did I mention that Sergeant Marist Finn is really cute?

Eleven minutes later, I walked into the Del Mar and waved to Sergeant Finn who was sitting alone in a booth. She rose as I neared the table, a huge grin on her face as if we were old friends. I had seen her on several of my Police Beat runs and always thought she was remarkably cute in a studly sort of way. She was a rectangle of a woman with broad shoulders, a flat stomach and long legs. Her tight-fitting dark blue uniform shirt looked painted on, and her wavy brown hair begged to be stroked. She was smoking hot. I glanced down in search of a ring, but she wore none.

"Sergeant Finn."

"If I call you Echo, would you call me Finn? I hate Sergeant from civilians almost as much as I hate my first name. Marist is my mom's name, my grandmother's name, my great-grandmother's name, and—"

"Your daughter's?" I sat down when she motioned at the booth.

"Oh hell no. I made a promise to myself in high school that I would be the last in a long line of Marists. There are so many great names to choose from, like yours."

I fished around a little bit more. "And what does your wife think about this?" Okay, so I read her before I sat down. Not that I needed to. Every fiber of her being screamed lesbian. All she was missing was a truck, a dog and a big watch.

"My—" she stopped and smiled softly. "I don't have one of those. Would you like something to eat? I know it's late and all..." Her smile was disarming and warmed up the room.

"How's the pie here?"

"I like that in a woman. Nowadays when you go out to dinner

with someone, they order a crouton with a glass of water. They have excellent pie here. I recommend apple."

I ordered apple pie à la mode before looking over at Finn. She was still grinning. "What?"

"I'm not used to a woman eating like a normal person. Bless you."

I smiled back at her. Normal was such a relative term in my life. "Maybe you didn't catch my name; there's nothing *normal* about me. I'm a very healthy eater."

She ordered a bacon cheeseburger with a side salad and Coke. She was incredibly handsome in her uniform. Those Kevlar vests ride high when a cop sits down, giving her that puffed up look. Her skin was a dark olive color and she had sandy brown hair waving to her shoulders. I was glad she didn't wear a buzz cut like a lot of other cops. Her eyes were a deep chocolate brown that took in the whole room. I had no doubt Sergeant Finn knew exactly who was in the cafe and how long they had been there.

Two deep dimples adorned her cheeks whenever she smiled, which was a lot for someone in such a depressing profession. It took a special person to be a walking target these days, and I had the feeling she was very special.

When she finished ordering, she turned those soft eyes on me. "Normally, I'm the one assessing a room, but you're good. I like that."

I poured sugar in my coffee. "You're not listening. I'm *not* normal."

She laughed at this. "Something tells me you're probably not kidding." Leaning forward, she lowered her voice. "I'm going to be honest with you here, Echo. There's no love lost between Carter Ellsworth and me. He's gotten into my way or in the department's way more times than I can count. If there is any way I can help you, I will."

There was so much I liked about her, not just her willingness to help, but the warmth of her words. She was one of the most authentic people I'd ever met.

"I really appreciate your time."

She nodded a hello to someone behind me who had just walked in. "If anything comes up, you'll be the first to know. I would really love to help you get the drop on that wiener."

I laughed out loud. Danica used to call dumb boys *wieners*. "Thanks."

"No, I mean it. You know, cops aren't very fond of the reporters. We never get a fair shake from you folks no matter how much of our blood is spilled on the streets. We can never do it right enough, never get there fast enough, never be fair enough. Guys like Ellsworth get off on rubbing our noses in some story he cracked before we did; as if he could do so without an inside in the department." Finn shook her head sadly. "I hate that guy."

"Well, just as long as you don't put me in the same category. My career hasn't gotten off the ground yet, but when it does, I'll be sure to give you that fair shake."

Her eyes scanned the room once more, as if she was looking for someone, but I knew she was just being a cop. "I would just like to see the department get some praise every now and then, but with guys like that dirtbag Ellsworth, we're just fodder for the papers."

I smiled. Her use of the word fodder made my stomach tingle. She was one of the good guys. Integrity and loyalty were as vital to her as eating and drinking. She was the kind of person you could trust; the kind you called when you needed your car jumped or a shoulder to lean on. I needed more Marist Finns in my life. "Maybe I can help paint a different picture."

She grinned and those dimples jumped out at me. "Excellent. I'll comb through the files and see if I can find anything you can use. Here's my cell number. I don't have to tell you it's frowned upon for us to be talking to reporters. You guys aren't our favorite people, so discretion is in order."

I reached for the card. "I understand. Here's mine," I said, writing my personal cell number on the back before sliding it discreetly across the table. "Because you know..." I lowered my voice. "It's frowned upon for us to be seen eating doughnuts with hot women in blue."

Finn threw her head back and laughed. "So, tell me about Echo. Besides being a reporter, what do you do for fun?"

"Fun? What's that?"

We finished the rest of dinner on more personal notes. She was twenty-nine and had been a cop for almost eight years. She was the oldest of eight kids in a typically Irish Catholic family. She loved her job, lived alone off Market Street and confessed to being somewhat of a movie buff. She was close to her parents, loved the city and wasn't addicted to anything.

So why was she still single?

There was a good give-and-take to our conversation, a nice ebb and flow. So many women just blathered on about themselves, but she asked questions and listened attentively. It was really quite enjoyable. When her pager went off, we both sighed.

"Well, I'm up." Locking eyes with me, she smiled softly. "I've had a really good time."

"I'm glad. So have I." I rose. "Have you heard anything about a missing homeless guy?"

"You're kidding me, right?"

"I wish I was. I know it sounds nuts, but—"

"Nuts is an understatement. Do you have any idea how many homeless people there are in the city?"

"I know. It's just...a good friend of mine said a friend of his from the streets is missing. I told him I would see what I could find out."

"You have... homeless friends?" She cocked her head. "There's more to you than meets the eye, Echo Branson."

I flashed her my best grin. "I told you, I am not normal. I have all sorts of friends... including women in uniform."

She looked me up and down, settling on my eyes. "I can see that. Well, Echo Branson, I'm glad you include one SFPD sergeant among them."

"I believe I do, Officer Finn. I believe I do."

"Goddamn it," I growled, leaning against the car.

"Bad morning?"

Whirling around, I almost punched Bob. "You're far from home. Are you lost, little boy?"

Bob forced a grin and shook his head. "Someone else has gone missing, Jane. Gone without a trace. Donnie's wife said he went to get something for them to eat and never returned. She's sick with worry, Jane. She said this is not like him at all. I have to agree. Donnie is crazy about her. He would never want her to worry."

"And no one else has seen him?"

Bob shook his head slowly, and then I heard his stomach rumble.

"Come on. Let's see if Luigi's got a little something to quiet that belly of yours."

Luigi was in the back as he always was until about nine. His brother, Franko, waited on customers and handled the counter in the morning. He was a good baker, but not in the same league as Luigi.

I ordered a coffee and bagel with cream cheese, and Bob ordered a coffee with a bear claw. I tried to get him to order more, but he wouldn't.

"What's really going on down there?"

"If you want to know what's going on in the city of San Francisco, ask a homeless guy. But Jane, none of us have seen a Goddamn thing. We see everything that happens in this city whether it wants to be seen or not. So...to *not* see two of our own go missing...well...it rattles our cages."

"I'm not sure I can help. I've already checked the hospitals. I've even talked to SFPD, but—"

"Try the morgue."

I blinked several times before replying. "I'll check it out, but Bob, without real first and last names, I'm just spitting in the wind. You have to get me more than just first names."

Reaching his dirty fingers into his jacket pocket, Bob carefully extracted a folded bar napkin. "I did a lot of asking around and found out Rusty's last name was...is Van Pelt." He handed the napkin to me with only a slight tremble.

"And Donnie's last name is Jack? His last name is Jack?"

Bob shrugged. "We all called him Donnie, but I suppose his name could be Jack Donnie. I just don't know."

Taking the napkin, I put it in my notebook. I have always carried a notebook around ever since I was a kid. I could draw in it, write poems or even make games. When you're in a foster home, it's always good to look like you're really busy or really smart. "I'll look into it today. In the meantime, why don't you spend the next few nights at the shelter? You look awful."

He grinned and nodded his thanks to Frank who waved back. "I'm a little tired is all. We spent most of the night looking for Donnie." Bob shook his head.

I dropped Bob back in the Mission District and checked my phone messages. Finn left one saying that she had enjoyed dinner and hoped we could do it again sometime. I have to say, I am a sucker for manners and gentility, so I made a mental note to ask her out to dinner. I am always suspicious when someone appears too good to be true, and when that happens, I lower my shields. Hey, all bets are off when it comes to protecting my heart.

Turning Ladybug around, I headed to Danica's office, sure the boys had found something for me by now.

"So, did you do it?" Carl asked when I arrived at the Bat Cave.

I looked over at Franklin, who was playing some sort of army computer game. He turned and winked at me. "You can tell us. Did you ask her out?"

"What on earth are you—" Then I stopped and stared at all three of them. They were three little boys with a secret.

I watched Franklin's computer generated soldier toss what looked like a grenade into a building. When it blew up, the smoke-filled abandoned building blew up and a bunch of soldiers ran out into the smoke, where his one soldier picked them off one-by-one.

"I did not."

Franklin extended his hand to the other two. "Pay up."

140

"Okay, guys, what the hell is going on here?" I moved my gaze to each one in turn, and each time, they looked away.

Carl walked over and reached for my purse, which I snatched away. "What are you doing?"

"Well…we…um…traced you."

"You. Did. What?"

Roger cleared his throat. "Traced you. It's a bug we've been working on that is a GPS with audio. We needed to try it out, but we only got half of the conversation."

"Enough to hear the proverbial sparks flying," Franklin chuckled like a little boy who heard the word boob for the first time.

I punched his arm. "There were no sparks, but there's gonna be in a second. You *eavesdropped* on my conversation?"

"Not really. Like we said, the audio was a bit unstable." Carl plucked a small device from my purse strap. "If we'd known you were going on a date—"

"It wasn't a date."

"Then we would have told you."

Roger nodded. "When's the last time you were even on a date?"

"It wasn't a date!"

Franklin nodded. "Sure sounded like a date."

"Well it wasn't." I wasn't angry with the boys; they were too cute to get mad at. I was, however, impressed with whatever technology they had used to trace me. "Look, I came by to see if you guys came up with anything for me. I'm getting desperate."

Carl grinned. "You're never desperate. We think we might have something for you. Come over here."

I walked over to his computer. He was playing a game with a beautiful landscape on the monitor. I had never known any of the boys to play a game that wasn't full of fire and destruction, blood and guts. Typical boys.

"Wow, that's beautiful."

"The object of this game is that we are looking for a key that will get us to the next level. We have to search the whole area first. Tell me, Princess, if you were playing this game where would you start looking?"

There were a hundred different places I could look. Up in a tree, in the tree trunk, in the river, by the roots of the huge oak tree or in the bushes. I was still thinking of where I would look when Carl moved the cursor on the screen to a rock. The cursor turned into a hand and grabbed the rock. Underneath was a golden key.

"Sometimes, it pays to look in the obvious places before rooting around and really getting lost. Advanced gamers know that game creators are always trying to fool us. If you get stumped looking for a story, we suggest doing what we do."

"Focus on the obvious?"

"Bingo."

I smiled. "I'll keep that in mind. Thanks."

Carl paused his game and looked up at me. "You're not getting it, are you?"

"'Cause she's not recovered from her date."

They all snickered.

"It wasn't a…oh shit, never mind. What am I not getting?"

Carl motioned to my notepad. "The story you're looking for is right in front of your face."

I looked down at my notepad. "The missing homeless?"

They all nodded, but it was Roger who spoke. "We started doing a little digging on that front. Missing homeless might not seem like a hot story, but the lack of care about them is a perfect venue for you to show off your wares."

Carl joined in. "Think about it. People still have soft spots for the homeless. The fact that one goes missing? No story because no one cares. Make them care, Princess. Make them care because *you* do."

I looked at all three of them, their cumulative IQ probably hovering near five hundred, and I realized that anyone who wouldn't listen to three geniuses must be obtuse.

"But there are a lot of San Franciscans who *want* them to go away. It's a dead-in-the-water story."

142

"The homeless is a story affecting every city in the country. Do San Franciscans want them gone? Sure. Can you paint a different picture to make them care? Sure you can. That's the beauty of a piece like that. You do what no other reporter can."

Franklin held out a memo. "A friend of mine kyped this from the mayor's office."

Reading it, I lowered it and looked at the boys. "This might do it."

"Everyone will read a not-in-my-backyard story. If the mayor opens up a soup kitchen or flophouse anywhere in the city, the people are going to be rabid. So far, that memo is hush-hush. Only his inner circle knows so far."

"Don't ask how we got it. We don't want to have to kill you."

Hugging each one in turn, I left with a glimmer of hope.

After I got home, I made a timeline of Rusty's and Donnie's disappearances on a map of San Francisco and taped it to the wall. Then, I made a few phone calls. The morgue was a big zero, which was a good thing, I suppose. They hadn't had any homeless people in over a month, and no one of Rusty's description had been in. The hospitals were also a big blank, and the lady on the phone practically laughed at me when I told her who I was looking for.

The homeless shelters were no better. They couldn't tell me anything.

I was poring over my paperwork for a third time when the phone rang. Officer Finn. "Why, hello there, my new friend, Officer Finn. To what do I owe this pleasure?"

"Hi there wanna-be-reporter. I spoke to the chief about your missing homeless guy. Apparently, he's not the first to have been reported missing, but we have nothing to go on."

"Yeah, I got that much."

"See? What do you need me for?"

Loaded question. I let it slide.

"Two or three days ago, some drunk guy stumbled in with the same story you told. I guess his buddy was missing, but we blew it off because of how drunk he was. Nobody thought much about it until I brought it up. One missing homeless guy is nothing to write home about, but two or more could mean we have a serial killer on our hands. Wouldn't be the first time killers used the homeless for target practice."

I shook my head in frustration. "How come everyone is so cavalier about this? These are people we are talking about."

"Look, I understand your frustration, but this is San Francisco, and the majority of the population thinks the fewer homeless the better. We're not bleeding heart liberals, Echo. We just want cleaner streets."

"It's three now. I saw my friend Bob this morning. The missing guy's name is either Donnie Jack or Jack Donnie."

"You sure?"

"Bob's a pretty reliable source. He doesn't exaggerate or engage in melodrama. He has nothing to gain by being dishonest."

"You'd stake your as-of-yet unknown reputation on this Bob?"

I nodded. "Yes I would. He's no liar."

"Let me see what I can do. I can't promise anything, mind you, but I'll do my best to see if we can't get some kind of investigation opened here. We could have a serial killer of some psycho running around. Hard to say yet."

"I appreciate that, Finn, really, and not because it's a possible story for me. Bob is really scared of whatever is going on out there. I don't know how much you know about the homeless culture in this city, but it takes a lot to frighten them."

"It sure does. I make no promises. I just wanted you to know that I gave it my best shot." Her voice had softened a bit, as if earlier, someone else had been in the room. "If I can do more, Lois Lane, I'll call you."

Yep. She had me at Lois.

I had been running on fumes since Wes gave me the job. I searched the Internet, the local newspapers, anything that might give me the lead to a story. When I felt my energy waning, I did what most women do when they need a shot in the arm: I called the only mother I knew.

"Hi, Mel. It's me."

"Echo! How are you, dear girl? You've been creeping into my thoughts a lot this past week. Are you all right?"

"I'm good. It's just...well...I have the chance to get this investigator's job and I'm having a hard time finding a story that will grab the readers and my boss."

"Ah. Well then, that explains the confusion I'm getting from you. You cannot see anything clearly through a haze of confusion, my dear. The first thing you need to do is clear yourself of the fog surrounding you. Your spirit cannot see clearly those things you're feeling from others. You know as well as I do that it is not the presence of facts that quells confusion, but the willingness to see all of the possibilities. Take a deep breath and close your eyes. Tell me what all you think you know."

So I did. When I finished, I felt a huge weight lift off my shoulders. "I think I'm operating out of fear and not logic or reason."

"And where does that usually lead us?" Melika asked when I finished my tale.

"Lost."

"Exactly. What do *you* believe might make a great story?"

"That's just it. I don't know."

"Yes, you do. Don't let your mind convince you of something your spirit knows to be a fact. If you believe something is amiss... then consider yourself correct."

"But I don't even know which way to turn. This is my big chance, Mel, and I'm afraid I've really put myself on the short stick with this stupid bet."

"No, you haven't. My dear, you spent four years with me constantly wanting me to clear the way for you and give you answers you already had." Mel chuckled. "Some things never change, child."

I watched as Tripod rolled around on his back in yet another

145

catnip stupor. "They need to change, though, don't they?"

"Growing up is never easy...even for us."

"Is that what this is? A growing pain?"

"I am quite sure it feels that way. You need to meditate on *what* you know. Open your mind and see what comes to you."

"Meditate."

"Yes. Your skills allow you to pick up energies you may not have been searching for. Remember my dear, keep your mind open to all possibilities. If you do that, the answers will come like fish to a light."

I grinned. Melika was the wisest person I'd ever met; not just as an empath of incredible abilities, but as a person. I had learned more from her in four years than I had the rest of my life put together.

"I'll do that, Mel. Thanks."

"It's what I'm here for. Have you spoken to that son of mine lately?"

"Last week. Big George said he's doing a lot of overtime because of the nurses' strike."

"Next time you see him, tell him to come home soon. His grandmother thinks she's not going to be around much longer and wants to spend some time with him."

I felt something seize my heart. "Is there something wrong with Bishop?"

"Wrong? Oh no, there's nothing to be concerned about yet. She's just been playing with a necromancer who has her convinced that she'd like it better on the other side. She's doing something she's unwilling to talk to me about, and that is always worrisome."

I sighed with relief. Bishop was the most colorful woman I had ever met. Born in Haiti, she was brought to New Orleans by a wealthy landowner when she predicted he would suffer a great fall if he attempted to sail to the United States within the next month. He did anyway, nearly dying in the process. His ship sunk off the Haitian coast, but his servants managed to drag him to shore with not one but two broken legs. He spent the next three months searching for "that little dark girl with the big yellow eyes," in the hopes of bringing her to the United States with him. When he finally found her, he offered to bring her entire family to the new plantation he was having built, but no one except Bishop wanted to go. After considerable dickering and haggling, Bishop boarded a ship bound for America.

"Why are necros so incredibly bizarre?"

Melika chuckled softly into the phone. "I reckon being able to talk to those who have passed would tend to make one a tad batty, don't you? I keep telling her to stay away from that one, but you know how Bishop can be; nobody can tell her a damn thing."

"I'll be sure to tell Big George the next time I see him. You don't think she—"

"Hon, I never know what to think where that old woman is concerned. This could just be another ploy to see her grandson. Who knows?"

"I appreciate your wisdom, as usual, Mel. Thank you."

"Perhaps, in the future, you won't shoot your mouth off and put yourself in such a bind." Her words may have been harsh, but her voice was warm.

"I know. I got cocky. I guess I just wanted to show this turd up."

"That's never been our way, child. Whenever we step onto a path that is not true to our calling, our way becomes hazy, as yours is now. You need to remedy that, and you know how. Once you do, your way will become clear. Now...who's the young woman?"

"Young woman?"

Melika's soft laughter floated through the airwaves. "Oh child, we empaths spend so much time guarding against other people's emotions we forget to both feel and examine our own. There's a woman you've got a soft spot for. The sooner you admit it to yourself, the better."

"There's no woman." I knew better than to lie to her, but it wouldn't be any fun for her if I gave in so quickly. It was a silly game we had been playing for years.

She chuckled again. "Oh...I think there is. But never mind. You've got plenty on your plate. It's no wonder I was thinking of you so much. You remember what I told you. You'll find your answers once you have clarity. Seek clarity always."

"Please tell Bishop she has to stay on this side until I have a chance to say goodbye to her."

She laughed.

I hung up feeling better than I had in days. Closing my eyes, I started one of the many meditation techniques Melika had shown me over my four-year stay in the Bayou. Breathing deeply now, I felt my entire body relax completely. No facts, no data, no printouts, no forms, nothing in my mind but calm waters. I saw it now; confirmation of what had been plainly sitting in front of my face and was, indeed, the only story I wanted to write about. The story nobody cared about.

Scanning the map of the city, I wondered if maybe there weren't more missing when there came three hard pounds at my door.

I answered the door to a whirlwind who blew right by me. "Be straight with me, Clark. I'm going to have to go out with that dick head, aren't I? I would rather eat a turd."

Closing the door, I marveled at Danica's gorgeous silk Dior pantsuit. Her shoes were Jimmy Cho and the light lavender color matched perfectly. Long ago Danica had tried to groom me, but soon determined I wasn't built for designer anything. I would always be a fashion don't. I was a woman in comfortable shoes.

"Hold onto that turd thought. I'm not out of this game yet."

She turned on me, eyes ablaze. "Don't toy with me. Ellsworth called to let me know he had a great story on the table. That jerk-off was practically orgasmic."

I could imagine. "Hold on..."

"Which is the only orgasm he'll ever have around me! I swear to God, Clark—"

"Down girl. We're not done yet."

"No? Do you have *any story?* Anything at all?"

"I think I do." I told her about my discussion with the boys.

"Looks like my boys have been busy helping you. I think they fear my wrath if I have to go out with that pinhead. If anyone can make people care, it's you."

"They have. Of course, for them, it takes one-tenth the time to gather information that would take me days."

She bent over and scratched Tripod. "Okay, human interest is a good way to go, I'll give you that, but what if there is no story? What if they just migrated to a warmer climate?"

Shrugging, I sighed. "Then I guess I walk to work and you go out with Carter."

"On no no no. That will never do. You come by tomorrow and put my boys to work with what you have. They're bound to come up with something."

Nodding, I stuck my hand out for an M&M. "My gut tells me there's a good story here, Dani."

She handed me two yellow candies. "Then go with it, Clark. It's been a really long time since your gut was wrong. Besides, even if there isn't a scoop here, a story about the homeless would still be worth it, right?"

I nodded, both of us knowing the only story worth writing was the one that saved my job.

"I've got your pink slip all filled out for you," Carter said from his computer when I walked in. That meant he had the germ of a good story happening.

"Game's not over yet."

"Come on, Branson, don't be pathetic. You don't have squat. I, on the other hand, have bigger fish to fry. I'm going after Mayor Lee. Word has it he's hired illegal aliens to work for him."

"Oohh, *that's* your hard-hitting story. I think I hear the *Enquirer* calling. Or is that the *Globe*?"

"That's not all of the story, Branson. When I finish with him, he'll be lucky go get a job as a greeter at Wal-Mart."

"You really think it's wise to go after a beloved mayor?"

He practically snarled at me. "That right there is why you don't have the chops for this job. Nobody is beyond reproach and everybody loves to see the top dogs fall. I'm going to take Mayor Lee down."

"Not with a lame story on illegal aliens you aren't."

His eyes seemed to turn red. "It will when I prove he's sleeping with one."

I swallowed a lump in my throat. "That's not investigative work, Carter. That's mudslinging."

His lip curled like Billy Idol's. "Then I suggest you put on a raincoat, because my story is going to bury you in that mud. Now, scoot along and let the real reporters work."

I turned to walk away and he called after me.

"You would be better off spending this time preparing your ultra thin résumé. I hear they're hiring at Burger King."

Turning on my heel, I started for the conference room where I flipped open my cell, and called Danica and told her about Carter's story. Danica loved Mayor Lee. He had done so much for the small business owners in the city as well as put up a good fight for gay marriage. He was a love him or hate him kind of politician, leaving few straddling the fence over his policy-making.

"He wants to bury our mayor? What an ass! You do know what you have to do, right?"

I shook my head.

"Are you shaking your head?"

"Yes. Sorry."

"You need to discredit his story before it gets out of the gate. He is going for the sensational angle. He is going for what appears to be a juicy story, when it is, in fact, nothing but a burnt hot dog. You need to pull that rug out before he gets started."

Nodding, I started taking notes.

"Mayor Lee is a good man and has done so much for San Franciscans. He deserves better than to have to defend harmful allegations. You need to cut that jerk off at the pass, Clark."

"I suppose I can do that."

"Know what you need?"

"Don't say it."

"You need Tip."

"I said don't say it."

"Clark, she's the best telepath you know. If she could get in there and read Lee's mind, see if there's even a hint of truth to it, at least you'll know whether to pack your bags or fight. Maybe if you can get close enough, you'll know for yourself."

She added, "If I have to go out with that pecker head, you are going to owe me until the day you die."

"I know."

"Then go on out there see whether Lee is innocent and get your proof if he's not. I'll see if there's anything the boys can get you."

I picked up the phone all right. I called Rupert James, a local necromancer who owned one of the nicest yachts in the Berkeley Marina. Rupert and I met my junior year in college, when there had been a haunting of a local boy. Melika had sent us to put a lid on the situation and see if the boy was also a necromancer. Turned out, the boy was not. He was being haunted by a kid he had killed in a gang fight in Oakland. That's what a necromancer does...they talk to the dead.

And I thought *I* was cursed.

I had enjoyed working with Rupert and he said I could call him anytime for a nice sail out on the bay. I needed a nice sail, right about now, but unfortunately, I got his voice mail saying he was in Catalina and would be returning tomorrow. I left a message telling him I was in bind and to call me as soon as he got back.

Rupert had some of the best connections in the city. Well, around the city. You see, dead men *do* tell tales, and if I couldn't find the truth out about Mayor Lee from the living, maybe the dead could tell me a thing or two.

In a recent story, one of the Hispanic workers at the mayor's home had died of a heart attack. It was that worker I wanted Rupert to talk to; see if there was anything to Carter's charges.

I started off toward my own car and unlocked Ladybug, trying to push Tip from my mind. She was the last thing I needed right now. I spend a great deal of energy trying to convince myself Tip had never been anything more than a good-looking complication in my life. Like most telepaths, she felt superior to the rest of us. She always had. It pissed me off back then, and it pissed me off now. Calling her to come help me would just open doors I didn't need open.

Me need Tip?

Never.

Luigi from the bakery nabbed me as I made my way up the stairs with two bags of day olds in either hand. Flour dusted his thick moustache and floated off it when he explained how he ended up with two bags of day old pumpkin spice bagels.

When I got to the Mission, Bob was nowhere to be seen. My senses were firing off impulses telling me all was not well in the Haight.

Ditching my day olds into the hands of a perplexed drunk, I headed deeper into the Tenderloin. Everyone I stopped to ask about Bob was either too drunk, too strung out or too oblivious to even know who Bob was. I had been on the streets for over an hour before someone finally remembered seeing him.

"Bob? Saw him two days ago. Or was it three? No, two." He shook his head. "Coulda been four. Anyway, he was talking to some guy in a van."

"A van? What color van?"

"You a cop or somethin'?"

"I'm the bagel lady."

His eyes lit up and his face softened. "Oh! Bob talks about you all the time. You're...uh..."

"Echo. Echo Branson." I handed him my business card.

"No, that's not it." Suspicion returned to his eyes.

"He calls me Jane. My...um...street name is Echo."

"Yeah! That's it. Man, Bob thinks you fuckin' hung the moon. Goes on and on about what a good friend you are."

I smiled politely, but my senses were tingling. Something was wrong. "Do you remember the color of the van?"

"It was dark." He stuffed my card in his back pocket.

"Okay...do you happen to remember where you were?"
He scratched his nine o'clock shadowed chin. "Wait. Yeah. I remember...he was wearing them really cool hiking boots some do-gooder gave him. Columbus or something. Bob really loved them boots. Always yammering about them and the friend who gave them to him." He squinted at me. "It was you who gave them boots to him, wadn't it?"

I sighed. I *was* that do-gooder and he did love those boots. "It was. Your name is?"

"Leroy. Leroy Brown. You probably heard of me. I'm the baddest guy in the whole damn town."

I wrote his *nom de plume* down, lowered my shield, and knew, of course, that he was lying. It's not uncommon for street folk to make up names, or, as was more common, have them foisted upon them by someone else. I imagined that at some point in time Leroy here probably *was* a bad ass.

"Thank you, Leroy. Look, if you see anything, call me any time, day or night."

Leroy nodded and started away. Then he stopped and turned around. "You really want to know anything that goes on down here, you oughtta ask Shirley. She knows everybody and everything that goes on down here."

"Where can I find her?"

"This time a day, she's napping in the park. Can't miss her. She got a white dog, a black cat and a green bird. Be careful a them animals. If that dog growls at you, she won't talk to you. You gotta pass muster with them animals before she'll give you the time of day. So, if the dog barks, just keep goin'."

I found Shirley and her menagerie sleeping on a park bench. The white dog, which looked like a dalmatian with one black spot right between his eyes, was curled up under the bench. The black cat was asleep on what appeared to be a pile of rags. Perched on the back of the bench was the green bird, a parrot of some sort. The parrot had a yellow head and eyes that were studying me. I can read many animals, but not birds.

153

The dog rose and ambled toward me. His nose was pink and his eyes were blue, and there wasn't an ounce of fat on his sleek frame. I put my hand out for him to sniff, which he did.

"Cotton doesn't usually warm up to strangers that quickly." Shirley looked a hundred and five years old; like one of those apple dolls with a thousand folds and wrinkles. She had a green kerchief in her hair, which was completely white and heavy like straw. Like most homeless along the Tenderloin, she was wearing different outfits. She had on a green dress, a purple skirt, red stockings, blue leggings, several white socks, a multi-colored macramé vest and a pair of brown shoes. When she sat up, the cat rose and stretched before walking over to me and checking me out.

I realized Shirley had one blue eye and one green eye, and I nearly fell over. One of two things was happening here; either she was one of my kind, or she possessed some other psychic ability because my shield was *always* up. Just to make sure, I put a wall around my mental energies as well. Tip had taught me how to do so after long, tedious and grueling hours of frustration, yelling, and even throwing things. My powers did not extend to telepathy, but Tip and Melika insisted I learn how to protect myself from them. I was not a quick study, but I did eventually learn how to perform even the most rudimentary mental telepathic block.

Shirley grinned. "My. I don't see that move very often. Of course, it's not often I'm coherent enough to notice. Whoever sent you...did they tell you I'm a loon? A nutjob? I fade in and out of sanity like the San Francisco fog. Mostly in. In. Sanity." She chuckled. "You're getting me on an upswing, but that could change at a moment's notice. I'm not kidding you, either. So, out with it."

I told her, and when I finished, I handed her my card, which she tucked into her layers of socks.

"I'll check around and see what I can find out. The missing guys are Rusty, Don Jack and Bob?"

I nodded. "And a fourth guy, but no one seems to know his name."

"I'll see what I can…see."

"Good. Thanks for your help." I started for my car when she called out to me.

"There's evil afoot out here. Don't know what it is, but it's there and it's very powerful, Echo Branson. If it's not after you now, it soon will be."

A cold breeze blew across my arms as I ducked into my car. What was I getting myself into?

Finn called and left a message. I returned it.

She told me without preamble, "I filled out an incident report on those guys, so at least we're working on it."

"Thank you. It mea—"

"Look, I have to run, but if you find a few evenings that work for you, can we make a date?"

"You do know that people don't go out on dates anymore, right?"

"What can I say? I'm old-fashioned. Talk to you soon."

"Be careful out there."

No sooner had I hung up than my phone rang again. "What the fuck have you done?" It was Carter.

"I've done a lot. I showered, I've eaten, I've played with my cat. Can you be a tad more specific?"

"You know what the hell I am talking about. Wes won't run my mayor piece. He didn't say why, but I'm pretty damn sure you had something to do with it."

"So?" I hadn't, but I wasn't about to tell him that.

"God. Damn. You. Branson! Who the hell do you think you are? You've got nothing! This is professional suicide! You can't make something out of nothing, and stopping me from going to print is an amateurish move at best."

"Apparently, whatever trash you wrote, Wes doesn't want or he'd take it to press. That's not my fault."

"Being incompetent is one thing, but making an enemy of me is a foolish, foolish mistake."

"Carter, I was your enemy before Wes held your story."

"You're going to regret this, Branson. When this all comes out in the wash, you won't be able to get a job as a paperboy."

I hung up on him. The truth was, he was probably right. If I didn't come up with a real story, Carter had enough clout to make me invisible.

By the time I got home, I was mentally drained. Too much noise in my head exhausted me. I needed to meditate, to get centered, to quiet my spirit.

At the front door, there was a huge Tupperware container filled with lasagna. I smiled. Luigi was the best.

My belly full, my mind finally beginning to quiet, I quickly fell into a meditative state where all those bad energies slowly dissipated. I was there for a long, long time, regenerating my spiritual energy and just cleansing my soul.

When I was coming out of it, I could hear Franklin's voice saying something about seeing the obvious. Had I missed the obvious? Had I looked through it instead of *at* it?

Opening my eyes, I rose and stretched. Tripod sat in the window ignoring me.

I pulled my pen out and started writing down words that were coming to me. Addict was at the top of the list. So far, the commonalities of the disappearances were they were homeless guys who were drunks, but interestingly not drug users. All were from the general vicinity. All disappeared at night. If they had been killed, if someone was just out to roll a drunk, they'd have been left where they were murdered. Who would move a dead homeless body around, and why? If they'd been killed, someone would have found their bodies.

Did that mean they were still alive?

And if so, for what purpose?

Kneeling down, I gently stroked Tripod as I stared at the stump of his missing leg. What wasn't I seeing here? It was like the lyrics of a song you know but can't quite come up with the title; barely out of reach, I shook my head and hoped whatever I was missing would come to me sooner than later.

I had a feeling Bob's life depended on it.

156

Chuck's Rib Joint was just the kind of place you'd expect a cop to hang out: Gritty, old, paper napkins and plastic cups. Budweiser calendars from days long past papered two walls. The perfect man cave.

Holding my file to my chest, I immediately spotted the enormous Samoan taking up an entire corner booth. He was pretty hard to miss. In front of him was a plate of ribs reminiscent of the ribs that tipped over the Flintstones' car.

Detective Jardine looked up from his plate. He had barbecue sauce on his chin. "You Finn's girl?"

"Excuse me?"

He held up the rib he was eating. "I'd shake your hand, but... please, sit down. Want to order something?"

I shook my head. "No thank you. I'm good." I sat across from him.

"Vegetarian?" He said it as if he asked if I had leprosy.

"Carnivore."

He liked this. I could tell. Detective Jardine wasn't nearly as ugly as Finn had alluded. He was darker than I thought he would be, with black, wavy hair and chocolate brown eyes. He had an enormous face, like a cartoon face on silly putty that had been stretched. It was his smile that was disarming, and when he grinned at me, his whole big face grinned. "Finn didn't tell me you'd be so cute. She trying to keep you all to herself?"

Why do men think that cute is a compliment? Cute applies to babies, puppies and smart three-year-olds. "Hardly. I appreciate you taking the time to see me. Finn told me you're not crazy about reporters."

"Hate Ellsworth the most." Jardine set his picked clean bone on his plate and wiped his hands on numerous napkins. "Finn said you needed some help. If anyone but her asked me to sit here with a reporter, I would have slapped the shit outta her. So, what can I do for you?"

I told him about the missing homeless. He listened, nodding occasionally. When I finished, I shrugged. "If they were killed, wouldn't their bodies have surfaced? I mean, who's going to try to hide a homeless corpse?"

Jardine sighed and toyed with another rib. "I dunno, but I'm sure you got an idea or five."

"I just need to know if there's anything to this. I need some help; something, anything that I can use to find my friend, Bob." I pushed the file over to him. "These are just my ideas so far."

Jardine rubbed his chin. "I'll look through your stuff here and see if I can't pin the tail on the donkey." He took the file and smiled at me. "I understand you're under the gun and your job is on the line. I'll look through it all and see what I can see." He pulled a twenty out and tossed it on the table. I didn't think it was nearly enough and when he saw my eyes, he grinned. "They won't charge me here, so I leave her a nice tip."

I smiled. I liked him more and more.

When I got home, I was exhausted. My hopes of keeping my dream job now lay in the hands of Detective Jardine. He believed me. That much I knew. But cops wanted hard evidence, and unless my skimpy information led him to that evidence, I was going to be shit out of luck.

As I trudged up the stairs, Luigi followed. "Some crazy old woman with a bunch of animals came by looking for you."

"What did she say?" I dusted some flour off his shoulder.

"Just that she hadda summa news."

"Did she say where she was going?"

"Backa to the gutter, I suppose."

I slapped his arm and flour dust went everywhere. "You're terrible." I checked my messages and found one from Danica, one from Finn and yet another one from Carter.

"Smug bastard," I muttered, pressing delete. Finn told me that Jardine really enjoyed his meeting with me and that he was going to get right on it. I wondered if right on it meant tomorrow or in a week. I didn't have a week. Hell, I barely had tomorrow.

Danica's message was music to my ears. She complained of working too hard and wanted to get out for a drink. I changed, hopped in Ladybug and drove over to her office.

I picked her up and announced I had a few errands to run beforehand. She didn't mind. Danica was always up for anything. Everyone needs a friend like Dani.

Half an hour later, we were in the Tenderloin.

"This is one of your errands? Jesus, Clark, you trying to get us killed?"

"You can stay in the car if you're afraid."

Danica reached into her purse and pulled out a small revolver. "I'm never afraid as long as I have my leetle fren'."

Danica's father had given her a gun shortly after I bashed Todd's head in. She didn't carry it until our sophomore year in college when there was a rape near campus. Mills College is one of the safer colleges on the West Coast, but it sits in a questionable neighborhood in Oakland. I wasn't surprised that she still carried it.

"So, what are we doing here this beautiful evening?"

"Looking for a woman named Shirley and her three pets." We got out and started down the street. The Tenderloin reminded me a lot of the Bayou; creepy, dark alleyways and unfamiliar creatures, some of which were deadly. It was easy to get lost, there were freaky sounds you never wanted to hear again, and you had to watch where you walked.

When we got to Geary, we heard Shirley before we saw her. Apparently, she was in one of her "in" moments of in-sanity because she was ranting at nothing.

"There she is."

Danica stopped. "*That's* your source?"

"Hush. She's...she's one of us."

Danica stared over at Shirley, disbelieving. "Oh God, is that..."

"*That's* what you and Britt saved me from becoming, yes."

As we approached Shirley, I could hear her ranting something about Catholic priests and George W. with a little Rush Limbaugh thrown in for good measure. "No gun," I said between gritted teeth.

"Can I mace her?"

I didn't bother to respond. When Cotton spotted me, he sat up and wagged his tail. When Shirley saw the dog's reaction to me, she stopped ranting and cocked her head at me. She was no longer blocking and I lowered my shields to feel every psychotic emotion she was experiencing. She did not quite remember who I was and was perplexed as to her animal's response to me.

"Shirley, it's me, Echo. Remember?"

She squinted at me with her head still cocked to one side and then she turned to Cotton. "I don't, but my dog does. Seems to like you, too, which is odd. He don't like many people. You from the government?" She lowered her voice. "CIA maybe?"

"Why CIA?" Danica blurted. I sent her another *shut up* glare.

"The CIA has been looking for me for a long time. If you're from the government, you can just move along because I'm not going with anyone ever again unless I'm in a goddamned pine box, you hear me? Well? Are you or aren't you?"

"No, Shirley, we're not."

Shirley looked over at Danica. "You afraid?"

Danica threw her shoulders back. "Of you? No."

Shirley tossed her hair back and laughed like a lunatic. "Don't imagine you'd say that if you weren't packin' heat."

Danica looked over at me and I shook my head.

"Shirley, do you remember talking to me the other day about missing homeless guys?"

She scratched her head. "I don't think I know you."

"Come on, Clark, we're wasting our time here. She's got nothing." Danica turned back to the car, but I stayed.

"Check your sock, Shirley. I gave you a card and you put it in your sock. That sock," I said, pointing.

"Really?" Shirley reached into her pocket and came up empty. "Who sent you? The Secret Service? Oh yes, they're always looking under the wrong rocks. Do you know how many times I tried to warn them about nine-eleven? Then, when it happened, *then* they were finally interested, but it was too late." She chuckled. "They been looking for me ever since."

Danica was suddenly back at my side. "You didn't say she was clairvoyant," she whispered.

"Hush," I said.

"We're all in danger, you know? They're not just after me. They *know* we exist. They just can't get their hands on any of us. But they keep tryin'. Once they get a seeker, we're all fucked. Fucked I say!"

"Come on, Clark. Let's get out of here. Whatever it is you wanted you're not going to find it here."

Sighing sadly, I had to agree. The lucid woman I met had been replaced by this ranting woman before us. "Damn."

Danica tugged my arm and Cotton responded by baring his teeth and letting out a low, threatening growl.

Shirley quieted Cotton. "He's taken a fancy to you, Echo." When she said my name, everything about her seemed to change. "Oh. Wait. We *did* speak, didn't we?"

I nodded. "About the missing guys from the street."

Closing her eyes, she breathed in slowly. "Yes. Yes, we did. As you can see, I'm not quite sane at the moment. I apologize." Her eyes transformed back to their earlier crazed stage. "Come tomorrow...I must have something to say to you...didn't I...don't you live in a bakery?"

I nodded, feeling her revert back to her insane self.

"I have something...did you know the CIA uses bakers all the time? It's the hours they keep...people don't get suspicious. You're suspicious, aren't you? Good. You *should* be. It's safer that way. Go on. Come back in the daylight when it's safer."

"Come on, Clark."

Danica was right. "Okay, Shirley. I'll come back later."

As we walked away, Danica let out a low whistle. "Wowee, Clark, you sure know how to pick 'em. All that crazy talk about the CIA."

"It's serious stuff, Danica. If they knew...I mean, what if they got their hands on me? What if they threatened to kill everyone I loved if I didn't point out the other supers I knew? What do you think I would do?"

Danica looked hard into my eyes. "You? You'd take your chances and throw me to the dogs."

"Danica!"

"Am I wrong? I'm not saying you don't love me, because I know you do. I also know that you are part of something larger than your own life, or mine for that matter. You'd have to protect those who protected you."

"*You* protected me!"

"Once, Clark. Look, it's no big deal. It wouldn't happen that way, would it? I mean, they wouldn't threaten the people you love, would they?"

I said nothing.

"Oh shit."

"I know you saw a loon back there, but *something* scares her. I feel it and it's very real."

"Oh puhlease, are you actually saying you think the fucking CIA is after her?"

"I don't know. I just know that her fear is real; that doesn't mean that the threat is."

"Fine. Where are we off to now? The soup kitchen? Goodwill?"

"Close enough. No, we're going to where Bob used to hang out and see if anyone knows anything."

"You think anyone will talk to you?"

I shrugged. "Good thing they don't have to."

No one had seen Bob or heard from him. Two more homeless had gone missing from the Tenderloin. It dawned on me that maybe these disappearances weren't exclusive to the city. Maybe there were others missing from Oakland or Berkeley.

I needed to turn something in, so I decided I would run with this story first and hope that it didn't lead to a dead end. I spent all night typing up the story and coming from an angle that might pique Wes's curiosity. In the end, I realized I was turning in a story that had next to no real meat and when I woke up the next morning, it was time to face the music. I was going to lose my car, my job and a lot of points with my best friend. I wasn't looking forward to this day. Maybe if I just stayed in bed all day, no one would notice.

Two seconds later, someone noticed. I let the machine get it. "Branson? Looks like your time is up. Bring that pink slip and the little red car by the office before noon, will you? And no hard feelings. Someone somewhere will hire you."

I groaned. Then I just lay there feeling sorry for myself for a couple of minutes before finally forcing myself out of bed.

After showering and prettying myself up, I finally made it out of the house by fifteen after ten. Most homeless don't start moving around until well after nine, and I was determined to get to Shirley before she went back around the bend. She was my last hope.

She was in the same place she was when I saw her in the park.

Fortunately, she was on an upswing today.

"Echo? Is that you?" Shirley shielded her eyes from the sun. Cotton came over, tail wagging, eyes happy to see me. "Come take a load off. You wanted my help." Snapping her fingers, Shirley jumped to her feet, scaring all three animals. "Now I remember. Someone came to me to about Smiley."

"Smiley?"

"Yeah. I vaguely recall someone telling me they hadn't seen him in a few days. You probably have seen him. He's the old black guy who holds out one of those plastic Halloween pumpkins for money."

I shook my head. "I don't think I know him."

"A real sweetheart, that one. Wouldn't hurt a fly. Autism or something."

"And he's missing?"

"Smiley's people live in Oakland, off MacArthur somewhere. They're street folks and he visits them at least every other week, sometimes more. If he's not with them, and I don't believe he is, bring me something of his back. Maybe I can pick something up.

163

Don't hold your breath, though. Like my sanity, my powers come and go, but I'm willing to give it a try."

"Is Smiley his real name?"

She shrugged. "Only his people would know."

"I appreciate your help on this, Shirl."

"It's been a long time since I've met anyone like me. I know we have very different powers, Echo, but it's nice to meet one as sweet as you."

"When's the last time?"

She sighed and looked away. "I met a man once, a nasty sort of guy, a telepath, if I recall correctly. He came at me wanting something...I don't remember what it was. Anyway, he was the last one of us I've officially met until you." She fed the bird a chip. "Don't go to Oakland at night alone. It's far more dangerous there than it is here."

I nodded. Oakland, California had a reputation from the Angela Davis Black Panther days that it never managed to outgrow. People see it as one big ghetto, one huge gang fest, but it's more than that; so much more.

I left Shirley and her animals and climbed into Ladybug. There was one message from Danica telling me the boys were staying late and wanted me to bring a pizza. I thought pizza was the very least I could do.

My second message was from Finn, who wanted to meet me for coffee.

Less than half an hour later, we were sitting in a small corner table at Starbucks. She looked so good in her uniform.

"I just wanted you to know I called in a few markers and I think you might have something of a story, and we, a case." Her eyes locked onto mine and I needed no empathic skills to feel her interest. "They aren't in any morgue, hospital or shelter. That's the good news. The bad news is, without public outcry, the chief won't put anyone on it."

"So far, I have a possible six guys missing. That's not enough?"

"Is it six now?" Finn leaned forward.

I nodded. "There's some guy named Smiley whose people are in Oakland. I'll check—"

"Please don't tell me you're going to cruise around Oakland at night looking for this guy?"

"I grew up there, Finn. It's only dangerous in certain areas, and I have no intention of going there. I'll be fine."

"Let me go with you."

I had to laugh. "Everything about you screams *I'm a cop!*"

Flipping open her leather holder, she pulled out a can of mace. Sliding it across the table, she said, "Take it."

So I did. "You worry too much. Is that the cop in you?"

"Not this time." She smiled softly. "It's the...friend in me. A white woman going into the belly of one of the meanest places in the Bay Area is reason to worry, don't you think? Hell, Echo, if I could outfit you with Kevlar and an automatic, I would."

"I appreciate your concern, Finn, really I do, but I'll be fine. When you grow up in Oakland, you just don't look at it the way others do. Honestly it's not that bad."

"When are you going?"

"Tonight. When my story is done."

Rising, she started for the check, but I swiped it first. "My turn. I hear you have to pay your confidantes."

She shook her head. "This one you don't. It's always free of charge." Finn took me by the shoulders and leaned into my face. Her breath was warm and her lips inches from my face. "Be careful out there, Echo. This world is a better place with you in it."

Standing on tiptoe, I kissed her cheek before whispering, "I'll call you, Officer Finn. Don't wait up."

She looked deep into my eyes in a way that might have mesmerized me had I been anyone else. Without thinking, I wrapped one hand around her neck and pulled her to me, kissing her softly. She returned the kiss, leaving her arms at her side.

"How about if I just wait?"

After we both set out on our separate ways, I headed to the office to finish writing up my "story." I wasn't the least bit sure this would get off of Wes's desk, but it was all I had and was better than what I thought Carter was working on.

My cell buzzed. Danica.

"I think the boys found something to help."

I perked up and pulled over. "On my missing guys?"

"I wish. No. On Mayor Lee and the immigrant story."

Now she had my attention. "I put Roger on it and he dug and dug and finally came up with information buried so deep, not even Carter's connections would be able to find it." She inhaled. "He's not sleeping with the illegal woman who is his maid, although I can see where it might look like that from a distance. She's not really even the maid, but his masseuse."

"His masseuse lives with him?"

"Long story. Back in college, he was in a Mexican bar and things got out of hand for some reason, I guess no one knows why. Anyway, I guess Lee was getting his ass kicked when Maria busted a bottle on the assailant's head, keeping Lee from getting seriously hurt. He told her if he could ever pay her back, he would."

"Oh my God. Why doesn't Lee tell that story?"

"Because she was a hooker at the time. The bar was in a whorehouse."

I put my hand to my mouth. How could Carter be so off-base? "But Carter must have something on Lee or he wouldn't risk telling another unsubstantiated story."

"There are a few photos of them together floating around on the Internet. He's on his belly on the massage table. The photos have, no doubt, been doctored. The boys were able to see that right off. They'll show you. You show Bentley. Game over."

"Is she an illegal, though?"

"Yes, she is. The boys did find that she started her paperwork already."

"How…never mind. I don't want to know."

"So it appears that Carter is so blinded by both his dislike of you as well as his quest to pummel you into the ground that he hasn't dug deep enough for the truth. Of course, he doesn't have my guys on his team. All they did was look into Lee's past and saw that he went on spring break as a college student to Mexico. They pulled up a few Mexican newspapers and found a little story about the incident. They went from there. The main thing they found out was Carter's got nothing for proof except doctored photos."

I was scribbling as fast as I could. "This is perfect. Perfect!"

"It's sitting in your e-mail box as we speak. But what are you going to do with it?"

"Warn Wes. I figure if I let him know that Carter's story is bogus or that he should at least dig deeper, maybe he'll print mine instead. At the very least, this should stall Carter's story long enough for me to make some headway on mine. Thank you so much."

"I did this one for me, Clark. No way am I going out with that dildo. Speaking of which, my date just arrived, so I gotta split. What are you up to?"

If I told her I was going to Oakland, she'd have left her date standing at the door, so I hedged a little. "Me? Oh, just doing a little digging on my own. Thank the boys for me, will you?"

When I hung up, I felt some of the stress I'd been feeling lift from my shoulders. As I started to open my e-mail from my iPhone, I realized the fine line I was walking on this one.

Wes-

My sources tell me to hold Carter's story until further proof. He has bogus sources. I don't. See attached doctored photos. Second retraction imminent if it goes to press tonight. Explain more later. Trust me.

The ball had landed deeply in Wes's side of the court. He hated retractions. He'd cut me enough time I needed to get my story together.

Reentering the freeway, I headed for the bridge and the town I once called home.

When you have the ability to defend yourself, you tend to be less afraid. This was the attitude I took with me to Oakland. Bordering Berkeley, one of this country's most bizarre and

167

colorful cities, Oakland has a flavor all its own, and there was a lot to like. There was also a lot to be cautious about. But a city like Oakland didn't get its reputation without incident.

MacArthur Boulevard is over ten miles long and runs from one end of the city to the other. I knew the areas where most of the homeless hung out and aimed my little car in that direction.

Leaving Ladybug in a Pizza Hut parking lot, I grabbed my purse, then I put my Mickey Mouse jacket on so that my purse wasn't visible or accessible. I made sure to put Finn's mace in my jacket pocket. I didn't think I would need it. I had pretty much perfected my combat shield, but had only a fifty-fifty chance of pulling it up under extreme stress. I had managed to do that one night and two more times after that, but I wasn't sure I could do it outside the Bayou and hoped I wouldn't have to.

I didn't have to walk long before I found my first homeless woman. It was just smarter and safer to approach a woman, even though so many of them tended to be mentally ill or drunk. A woman on the streets was seldom mentally or physically healthy.

"I'm looking for Smiley's people," I said to a woman who looked a little like Granny on the *Beverly Hillbillies*. She was rail thin, had her hair pulled back in a gray bun and wore glasses too small for her face. On tiptoe, she was probably four foot eleven inches at best.

She looked me up and down. "You a cop?"

"No. Smiley has disappeared and there are people in San Francisco who are concerned. I'm looking for his people to see if maybe he came here."

She raised an eyebrow at me and I read exactly what she wanted; money. I pulled out a ten. "Point me in the right direction. If I end up there, I'll come back with one just like it."

"They don't like folks snooping around their business, so you best tell them what it is you want and fast." Her eyes never left the money. "They hang out in an alley off of High Street. Ask for Dante."

I left her and drove down to High Street. I knew of a decent

168

place to park Ladybug that kept me from having to walk too far in the belly of the beast.

"Excuse me," I said, asking the first nondrunk I came to. There were times when I thanked my lucky stars I was an empath. "Can you tell me where Dante hangs out?"

"Why?"

"I borrowed some money from him before he hit the skids and I'd like to pay him back."

"How much money?"

"None of your business." Okay, so maybe I shouldn't have bluffed with the money. I had mace. I also had combat shields. When I felt his energy change, I leaned in a little and said, "Don't make me kick your ass in front of your friends." I took a step toward him and he backed off. Ordinarily, that would be foolish for a normal woman to do, but I am neither foolish nor normal. I knew he did not have the ability to hurt me.

"Down the street. Talkin'."

"Thank you." I started down the street, stepping over trash and debris along the way. When, at last, I came to a crowd, there was a tall, rather slim black man standing at the center of it. He appeared to be telling some kind of story.

"There I was...at the very edge of a dark..." This sounded familiar.

"...I stood erect, brave, unafraid of what was to come, when suddenly there he was: Phlegyas, the boat man of the river Styx. He was nothing but a skeleton racing toward me at breakneck speed. He was on fire with excitement that he was coming to collect a new soul for torment, and he howled with a rage that pierced my soul when he realized that I was not yet dead."

I imagined he would have gone on, but a cop car whooped its siren, sending creatures of the night in all directions. When the car slid silently back onto MacArthur, Dante was gathering up his things.

"Excuse me, Dante?"

"Yes?" He turned and his face fell when he saw some little white girl.

169

"That was wonderful," I said. "Canto eight?" His energy changed immediately. I had recognized Dante's *Inferno* from my work with Professor Mathias.

"A fellow thespian, I take it?"

I grinned as I sent out a wave of friendliness to him. He was neither drunk nor was he on any medication. Medication greatly affects one's HEF and aura color. He was very clear. "I went to Mills," I said, as if that would explain it all.

"Ah yes. Professor LaBoskey is quite the Allegherian."

I was immediately impressed. Allegheri was Dante's last name. Few knew that. "Yes, she sure was. Do you know her?" I knelt down to help him pack up his things, most of which were books.

"My oldest daughter took courses from her." He finished packing and straightened up. He was tall, slightly over six feet with short salt-and-pepper hair. "You know my name, young lady, but I'm afraid I don't know yours." His voice had a theatrical lilt to it like James Earl Jones's.

"Echo. Echo Branson."

"Well, Miss Branson, what brings you to our gritty little corner of the world?"

"Smiley. I was wondering if you've heard from him lately."

Dante shook his head. "Haven't seen him since last week. He usually comes to visit every Sunday." His comportment transformed from actor to guardian. "He in some kind of trouble?"

"According to his friends, he's missing."

"Missing? What does *that* mean?"

I explained. "Homeless people have been missing from the Tenderloin the last few days and I was wondering—"

He held up his hand for me to stop. "How many?"

"Smiley makes six by my count."

He nodded, but said nothing.

"I was wondering if maybe you had something of his. I...I know this sounds weird, but—"

"But you're going to give it to a psychic?"

170

"Something like that."

Dante reached into his pocket and pulled out a small key. "I think it's to a bike lock, but I'm not sure. Smiley gave it to me to hold in case he lost his other one. I trust you'll bring it back."

I nodded, taking the key.

"Good. Come with me."

"Where are we going?"

"Someone else needs to hear this."

When we reached *someone else*, he was a six-foot-six black man wearing green fatigues and a green beret hat. "Yo, Dante, my man!" The guy shook Dante's hand in one of those street handshakes I can never do and pulled him into an embrace. "Whatcha got here?"

Dante straightened up and turned to me. "Echo, this is Sarge. Sarge, Echo. Echo here says my nephew has been missing and that he's not the only one."

The grin fell from Sarge's large face. "No shit? How many?"

"Six. Maybe. It's hard to tell. One is a friend of mine. Bob. He told me about the missing men one day and the next, he was one of them." I noticed the exchange of looks between the two men. "What? What is it?"

"We're missing some, too," Sarge said softly. "Five in the last week. That happened in them jungles a lot. One minute, you're sittin' next to your buddy, the next, he's gone and you find his head a hundred yards away."

I pulled out my pad and pen. "Can you tell me anything at all about your missing people? Maybe if I had—"

"You a reporter?"

I nodded. "I'm not here in the capacity of a reporter. I'm here because a friend of mine is one of the missing and I owe it to him to see if I can find him. He's a good guy."

Sarge scratched his head. "Well, there's Rayban, Boston, Lemming..."

"Lemming? When did he go missing?" Dante asked.

"Week ago. Someone found his dog walking by the lake."

"Aww, man. Who would do something to old Lemming?"

"Can you describe him for me?"

They did, and gave me the names Montana and Danny Boy.

"Danny Boy isn't really homeless. He's choosin' to be on the street. It's trendy and hip these days among the younger, dumber set."

I'd heard that before, so I made a mental note to do a story on it. Kids who have it all just throw it away so they can be different. It would be a great piece. "What does he look like?"

"White kid, brown hair, goatee, skin and bones, about yea tall. Wears one of those long black trench coat thingies."

"How old?"

"Just a kid. He doesn't even shave yet. Fifteen, maybe sixteen."

"Anything else?"

"Smokes clove cigarettes. Yuck. Anyway, that's about all. The others I only heard about."

"So what in the Sam Hill is going on?" Dante asked.

"I haven't a clue," I said, putting my pad away. "I was hoping for some leads."

"Wish we could help, but the truth is, people come and go so quickly out here."

"But we'll spread the word that somethin' is definitely goin' on. Smiley's liked by a lotta folks."

"Yeah, but none of us will change our ways. Crap happens. You're just lucky if it doesn't happen to you."

I understood that mentality from all my years in foster care. If you weren't the one getting beaten, you were just glad it wasn't you and stepped out of the line of fire. "Okay, fellas, here's my card. If you see anything, hear anything, or just want to talk, please call me. Day or night, it doesn't matter."

Sarge nodded slowly. "Day or night."

"You wouldn't happen to know any of their real names, would you?"

"I'm pretty sure Danny Boy's real name is Danny."

"No last name?"

He shook his head. "No way."

"Think maybe you can find out? Anything. Where he went to high school. Was he a local kid? Any nugget that might help us get the ball rolling would be great."

"We'll give it our best," Dante said. "Sarge'll walk you back to your car. He's like a free pass around here. No one will mess with you as long as he's near."

Fifteen minutes later, I was on my way back to the city, feeling even more disheartened than ever. I called Finn to let her know I had made it back in one piece. "And...you might be surprised to hear there are homeless people missing here as well. Do you have any connections with OPD? Something is going on, Finn. I just know it." I wanted to add a more personal note, but thought that might be pushing it. Discretion was her word, not mine.

I called the Bat Cave, expecting the answering machine, but Carl answered. "Yo, Princess. How goes it?"

I told him what I knew about the guys missing in Oakland. "I need real names. I need something to be able to take to the police department. Without real names, no one will listen to me."

"This sounds like a job for your boys. His name?"

"It's Danny Boy."

"And you think he's a rich kid who's playing homeless?"

"That's the word, yeah."

"You know, even without a last name, we'll be able to come up with a couple hundred Danny's in that area. Kid might have a blog or a Facebook account."

"That's a start."

"Always here if you need us."

"Thanks." I hung up. I had one story that needed a rewrite and one that could be even bigger than the last. I could only hope I had what it took to bring it all together.

My inbox had a reply from Wes that simply said, *Prove it* about the doctored photo. I had the boys send me the real picture and the explanation as to how the photo had been fixed to make it look like something sordid. This time, I didn't send the picture via e-mail. This time, I left it under his door.

When I finished the final rewrite of my story, I had less than ten minutes left until the end of my first real deadline. It was almost midnight and I was exhausted. My borrowed desk was a mess of notepads, and my mouth tasted like a troop of soldiers had walked through it with muddy boots. It had been a long day and it was time to put my first story to bed. In spite of my tired bones, I felt wonderful...until Carter popped in.

"Branson! I'm surprised to see you here. Did you manage to come up with a story?"

"A better one than yours."

He smiled and shook his head. "May the better man win," he said, extending his hand.

I looked at it, lowered my shields, and realized he was being sincere. Shaking his hand, I was taken aback by this turn of events. "Thank you."

"I thought you'd bow out by now, but I hear you actually have a story. Good for you."

"But?"

He released my hand. "No buts. It's no fun winning a race against a lame opponent, and though I am quite sure I have the better story, you stayed in it until the very end. Bravo."

I wasn't sure if he was being condescending or not but didn't want to lower my shields to find out. Some things are better left unknown. "Thanks...I think."

"Well, Wes will choose the story he wants to run tomorrow, so why don't you go on home and get some rest."

He was being too nice, but I wasn't going to look a gift reporter in the mouth even if it was him. "Carter, can I ask your opinion on something?"

"Mine? Sure." Pulling up a chair, he turned it around and sat astride it.

"If you were on a story about a suspected serial killer and you had a list of the possible victims, how would you best utilize the list?"

Carter toyed with the cleft in his chin. "What all is on the list?"

"Just their first names."

"Hmmm. Not much to go on. I guess I'd start looking for similarities in the victims. Serials like patterns and have very predictable habits. Are they all the same sex?"

I nodded.

"Okay. I'd line up their physical characteristics first. Look for commonalities. Then I'd use a city map and pinpoint where they lived, where they were found et cetera. You have to act like a forensic profiler and get as much detailed information on each individual as you can. Then you step back and examine the whole picture."

"But without last names?"

"Names are only part of the picture, Branson. If you look at the bigger picture, sometimes it's clear enough to lead you to the smaller details. Go with what you have until you can dig up some more. That's Journalism one-oh-one."

I thanked him and then started for the door.

"You working on a serial killer story, Branson?"

I shook my head. "I don't think so."

"Well, be careful." He held the door open for me. "If you scoop my next story, I'm going to have to kill you."

I nodded. "Fair enough. Are you still on the story about Mayor Lee and illegals?"

"Maybe."

I groaned. "That's tabloid crap, Carter. Can't you do better than that?"

"It's an election year, Branson. People want to know if our city's leader is on the up-and-up before reelecting him."

I shook my head. "Dirt is dirt."

"And your story is clean?"

I nodded. "It is."

"Well, good luck with that. Someday you'll realize that clean is lean, and if it bleeds it leads. Again--"

"I know...Journalism one-oh-one." Pushing out the door, I realized something. Suddenly, I was really missing Tip's help.

I woke up the next morning and flew out of bed to get my paper. I couldn't wait to see if my first byline had hit the stands or if I would be hitting the unemployment line again. Ripping the rubber band off the paper, I was stunned to see that my story had made the the front page. The front page!

Grabbing the phone, I called Wes Bentley.

"It's a little early, Echo," his secretary informed me. "Oh, wait. I see he has a message for you. It says: *proof received. Well done. Not why your piece made it, however. It was a better story.*"

"Thanks," I said, hanging up and doing my happy dance. I even gave Tripod some catnip so he could dance with me. Then I called Danica and left a message thanking her and the boys for a job well done and to pick up the paper and read my story about the missing homeless guys.

After showering and doing more happy dancing, I grabbed some day olds from Luigi drove Ladybug to the office parking lot and waited next to Carter's parking space. I didn't have to wait long. He came roaring up and slammed on the brakes of the beautiful silver Lexus.

I also got out and joined him behind the car.

He looked at me. He hadn't shaved and his eyes were red. "Old Man Bentley must be losing it to pass up a story like that. I wonder if you must have dirt on Wes."

"It couldn't just be that I have a better story, huh? That supposed exposé on a story that doesn't exist? Truth is, Carter, I may have just saved your job."

He laughed derisively. "Don't get too full of yourself, Branson."

I shrugged. "It's true. Dig a little deeper, Carter. You'll see. What appeared to be a sexual relationship was not. You'd have had another retraction on your hands for sure."

He studied me a moment as he reached in his back pocket. "Moot point. Wes quashed it for your...umm...story. You won. I honor my bets." Handing me the pink slip and the keys to the Lexus, he shook his head. "I can't figure you out, Branson."

Taking the keys and the pink slip, I shrugged. "I'm not a story,

176

Carter. I am just a woman trying to get her footing in a job I've always wanted. You seem compelled to try to get in my way or at least prevent that. It would please me to no end if we could bury the hatchet and move forward as colleagues."

"Colleagues? Branson, you're barely a stringer who's on a hot streak. We all get lucky from time to time. Do not presume that your winning has anything to do with real investigative skill. The homeless as a lead story? Puhlease."

"Maybe so, but I've kicked your ass twice. You now have the choice of being on my side or against me. I see no reason why there has to be so much tension. I think I have a lot to learn from you. It's your call."

Rubbing his face, he started for the office. "That's one call I am too tired to make at this moment. Enjoy your victory, Branson. Let's hope it's not a Pyrrhic one."

When he entered the building, I opened the Lexus door and jumped in. Guilt-Be-Gone. I may have *earned* this, but I had no intention of keeping it. I promised myself a long time ago, if there was ever a time I could repay Big George for saving my life, I would. That time was now. He was the one who saved me; who gave me a chance at a new life. You don't give crumbs to someone who does that while you eat the lion's share. He deserved the best money had to offer, and right now, I was sitting in it: gray leather interior, dark wood on the dash, this car was something you could live in.

Before I started across the bay, I had one very important stop to make: a lady who might be the key to finding Bob.

"Good morning!" Shirley said with perfect sanity when she saw me. "I take it your journey through the hinterlands of Oakland was a safe one?" She patted the space on the bench next to her. "So, how did it go?"

I smiled and tossed her cat some lox I'd brought from the bakery. "It went well, I think." I pulled out Smiley's key and dropped it into her palm. "This was all they had."

She stared at it as it lay in her palm. "Ah, good. Metal is a good conductor for me. Not for everyone, mind you. We're all a little bit different, but metal works nicely." Shirley reached out and gently took the key from her palm. "You've done very well." She smiled at me with her one blue eye and one green eye.

What she was about to perform was called psychometry, the fancy word for scrying and generally referred to as the ability to get information about a person who belongs to the object in question. The term was coined in 1842 when an American physiologist determined that students given an empty bottle of medicine had the same reaction as if they had taken the medication. He believed all things gave off an emanation that carried with it a sort of record of the activities of that object. A scryer can often play back those emanations in their mind in order to get a better idea of what the object was involved in. It was an interesting process because there's no preparation or any sort of induced trance. Psychometric impressions can come in the form of emotions, sounds, scents, tastes or images. The visions are usually very rapid in nature and are often in no logical sequence. I knew that metal worked best because Professor Mathias had taught us that we exist in an electromagnetic world, so metal maintains a better hold on the emanations than other substances.

Looking over at Shirley, I watched her "seeing" whatever history the key held. Apparently, there was a great deal because she didn't blink as she stared at it. She was definitely picking something up. The energy around her was palpable, her animals moved away.

When at last she turned to me, she inhaled slowly and handed the key back to me. "There is definitely trouble afoot where Smiley is concerned, but I'm afraid I can't uncover any of it right now."

"Damn. I was hoping—"

"Don't throw in the towel yet, my dear. I may not to be able to tell you *what* happened to Smiley, but I *can* tell you what he was doing just before he disappeared." Shirley wiped her hand off. "He gave the key to some older man with a historical name."

"Dante."

"Yes, that's it. The key is to a bike lock."

I nodded. She was good. "A bike lock."

Shirley nodded. "It's a red bike and is locked next to a blue fire hydrant in front of a building with a green awning. I tried to get a better read on where the bike is, but that's the best I could do for the moment. Sometimes, images come later, but for now, that's all I can see."

I remembered Carter's words about commonalities. "Was he a drinker?"

"Of course." Shirley put her hand on my leg. "Who isn't out here? If his bike is near a liquor store, he'll always know where it is and if he doesn't, he'll eventually stumble upon it. That's where I'd look first."

I rose. "You know, if I was half the reporter Carter is, I would have figured that out on my own. Thank you."

Reaching out, she touched my wrist. "Wait. There's one more thing." Closing her eyes, she said, "I couldn't tell what he was doing at first, but I think...yes...I'm pretty sure he...it was such an odd image, and please remember that I am unsure of the order of things, but I believe he was kneeling down next to the bike. I don't know if he was working on it or what but he stayed down there quite a while, and did so more than once. There is something...yes...there is something *on* the bike that is important to him."

My heart picked up a beat. "He's looking at something?"

"More like reading it. I wish I saw more, but his drunkenness blurs everything."

I nodded. "Red bike, green trash can, blue awning. Hell, that could be anywhere in this city."

"Could be, but isn't. Homeless people have a certain territory we feel comfortable in. Unless you have family like Smiley, you'll rarely see us on a bus or on BART. Smiley must take BART under the water to Oakland, right? You can rest assured that his bike is one of two places: near his watering hole or near a BART station; possibly both. I wish I could have given you more, but that's the best this foggy mind can do."

"You did really well. Thanks."

"I want to help, Echo. I don't know what's going on, but it's not good. You know, it's hard enough being a homeless, jobless, loveless person, but being friendless...well that would push those of us with a tenuous grasp on reality right over the edge."

"Hang on a sec, will you?" Running to my car, I grabbed the day olds and a small paper bag I had filled up at home. "These bagels are for you and your friends." I handed her the bag. "But the catnip is something I snatched from my cat. There's catnip and two cans of cat food in there...as a way of appreciating all you've done."

I turned to leave, but she called out. "It was a wonderful story, Echo."

I stopped and looked at her as she pulled the paper out from inside her coat.

I called to see if Finn was in. I knew it was too early for her shift, but some cops practically live at the station. I wasn't able to reach Finn, but they did patch me over to Jardine.

"Echo Branson, famous journalist. Great article, girl. You should be proud."

"Thank you." I smiled as I leaned back in the luxury seat of the Lexus.

"I've put a few calls in and after your article this morning, everyone has been told to make contact with the homeless on their beat and see if they can't rustle up some real names."

I heaved a sigh of relief. "Thank you."

"You come file a report, I'll make sure someone besides me reads it."

"You are the bomb."

I went to the police station. Once the report was finished, I jumped in the Lexus I was quickly falling in love with and drove back across the Bay. Since it was after rush hour, the bridge flowed a little bit easier and I reached the hospital in no time at all. Time is a blur when you're sitting in the comfort of a Lexus. I almost had second thoughts. Almost. This was the first time I had been back since that night I escaped. Well...actually...Echo

Branson escaped. Jane Doe was forever left behind, never to be heard from again.

Big George and I had seen each other off and on in the years since I had left, but never here. He came to the Bayou at least twice a year to visit Melika and his grandmother. When I was at Mills, we had dinner together once a month and I would see him at special events on campus. Hospital orderlies don't make a lot of money, so I would always give him tickets to any of Mills' plays, dance performances and athletic events. Big George loved it, and Mills loved him. I explained his presence in my life by calling him my uncle, and Mills being what it is, didn't bat an eye that my "uncle" was a huge black man.

Big George even came to my graduation, bringing with him the best graduation present ever; Melika, Bishop and Zack, who had left the Bayou only months before. It was more fun than I could have ever imagined, as we showed them our own inner city Bayou.

I couldn't believe how incredibly excited I was. You know how it is when you've bought someone you love the perfect gift? When you know how happy it's going to make them? Big George drove a Plymouth Duster that looked like it was out-of-date two years before it came off the assembly line, a broken brown wreck, dog poo brown with areas of rust and an interior that looked like wild tigers had a fight in there. It needed to be put down.

But Big George wasn't working for money. He was a spotter. Melika's three other sons worked comparable jobs and were also spotters in different parts of the country. One is a very powerful TK, but I never met him. In my four years on the river, he had never come home. I think there were some mother issues. I'd never met her daughter, Jasmine, because she was over in Europe painting. Little was said about Jasmine; only that she was a fine artist with extraordinary powers. I had lain in bed many nights wondering what Melika's daughter was like. If she was anything like Big George, she had a heart of gold.

I took the stairs up and went straight to the front desk.

I waited less than a minute before Big George came out. As

usual, he was all smiles. "Echo! How are you doing, sweetpea?" He came over and gave me one of his famous bear hugs that made my ribs crack.

"I'm employed. I've lost five pounds and I think I've met a woman I might like."

Big George threw his head back and laughed. "Sweetpea, she must not be all that if she came in third behind weight loss."

Grinning, I took his big hand. "Come downstairs for a minute. There's something I want to show you."

"What you got up your sleeve, girl?"

When the elevator door opened, we walked out to the parking lot. "Wait till you see this." I pointed my keys at the silver Lexus and it made that fun whooping sound.

"Holy mother of Mary, sweetpea. You done bought yourself a beautiful car!" Big George walked up to the car, his face lit up and he touched it like a man touching a naked woman. "It's beautiful." Stepping up to the window, he peered in. "Ah man..."

Tears came to my eyes. He was so excited about the car my heart felt like it would burst. "You've got to sit in her, Big George. Those seats are like butter."

"What are they paying you at the paper? Oh, and congratulations on your story. Is this how you paid yourself for a job well done?" Big George slid into the driver's seat while I eased myself into the passenger side. He was in awe.

"Oh, it's repayment, to be sure. So, what do you think? You like it?"

"Like it? Girl, this is something else." Big George looked all over the inside, shaking his head. "This car could be somebody's mistress, she's so damn gorgeous."

I handed him the keys. "She's not *somebody's* mistress, Big George. She's *yours*."

He took the keys and laughed. "Yeah, right. Her and Halle Berry."

Reaching out, I touched his thick forearm. "I'm not kidding. I won this car in a bet and I'm giving it to you...for all you've done for me."

Big George opened his mouth and blinked, but that was all.

"I want you to have it. You saved my life. I waited all these years to find the perfect gift that could possibly convey to you how deeply I care and how much it means to me that you reached out when I needed it most. Not one day goes by that I don't think about that Rachel girl and how close I came to ending up like her. You gave me my life. My *life*, Big George. This car is the very least I could do to repay you for that gift."

"But sweetpea—"

"I already have a car that I love and is me. And since it was the first thing I bought with my own money, I love it too much to part with it. But you...for as long as I've known you, you have always needed a car. Now you have one befitting the kind of man you are."

Tears came to his eyes. "I don't know what to say."

"Say you'll drive me to BART so I can get back to work."

And that's exactly what he did putting the car through its paces, murmuring all the way there as if he were enjoying an expensive meal. When we got to the station, he turned to me with such warmth and tenderness in his eyes. "My mama...my mama told me the first time she laid eyes on you that you were special. Not just because you're a super, but because of what's in here." He pointed to my heart. "You're one special sweetpea, girl. No matter what happens in our lives, Big George will always have your back."

I kissed his cheek and got out, watching with joy as he drove away. It may have taken nearly fifteen years for me to pay him back, but I was pretty sure he thought it was well worth the wait.

I know *I* did.

I made it home, got Ladybug, and was back in traffic when my cell phone rang. Wes Bentley.

"Branson! I can't tell you how many calls I've received about this homeless piece. I just wanted to let you know it was a great job."

"It sure looks good on the front page, Wes. Thanks for putting me there."

"I expected to go with Carter, but when that fell through, I felt your piece had heartstring merit."

"Thank you, sir."

"Carter even thought it is a good start, which is high praise coming from him. So where do you plan on going with it?"

"Homeless people are still missing in the city and now I've discovered they're also missing in Oakland. They're vanishing without a trace. I think there is someone hunting them and I'm going to prove it."

"Hunting them?" His voice rose. "Now that sounds like a story that can go somewhere. I like it.

"You gotta be able to juggle more than one ball. A good reporter has a bunch of stories in the air at once. Missing homeless is soft and fuzzy, but it's a dead end unless you have some sort of follow up. If you follow up with the idea there's a killer on the street, you'll have more front page exposure in your future."

"As much as I hope it's not true, I am leaning in that direction."

"Excellent. Just remember who your audience is. This isn't a community who particularly loves their streets littered with human debris."

Human debris?

"The missing people *are* a community, and as hard as it may be for *regular folks* to believe, they are their own social unit who deserve the same respect and legal help as any other. They know what's going on out there. They have friends. They pull together. Just because it isn't *your* community or one that *our* pristine community doesn't care about doesn't mean we can't *make* them care."

The line was silent on the other end.

Wes cleared his throat. "You say this is happening in Oakland as well? Prove it then. Get a jump on what's behind this before the Trib does. This is your story to tell, Branson. Be the first to tell it." If anything motivated Wes Bentley it was scooping the *Oakland Tribune.*

"I've done my legwork. We're talking about at least a dozen, maybe more on both sides of the bridge. No one has seen or heard a thing, yet there is no blood, no sign of a struggle and no bodies. These people are there one night and gone the next morning. If you were just robbing the homeless, or hell, even killing them for sport, you wouldn't waste time with body disposal."

"Go on."

"That may mean they've taken them somewhere. It may mean they are still alive. I don't know yet, but I will find out."

"All right. While this story of yours unfolds, I want you to write a series of articles putting a face to the homeless. You want our readers to *care* Miss Branson? Then *make* them care. Give them something or someone to care about. You say they are a community? Then I want a story about this community on my desk before the morning. Oh...and no mention of Oakland. Stick with *our* homeless. Do interviews, get some photos of them that will grab people's hearts. Think of this as a three-or four-part series before your story breaks. You need to grab their interest, put a face on the issue, warm the cockles of their goddamn hearts, and by that time you had better have something that blows the story wide open."

The news industry has no soft side, no tenderness. You're only as good as your last good story. No one cares about what you did do or are going to do. It's all about the here and now. Unless you won one of the few prizes reserved for journalists, you're jumping from one story to the next. This is an unforgiving profession where precision is vital, where research must be impeccable, and the truth is everything.

"Fine. I can do that. You going to keep sitting on Carter's story as well?"

"I've given him time to rethink it, yes."

"Trust me, Wes. The story is not solid. Let it go."

"Ms. Branson, you are just a rookie. And while I appreciate you catching the error in the Glasco story, that does not give you *carte blanc* to dip into every story he is working on. Carter seems to think there is probably a lot of dirt under the rug, and I have to agree."

"Carter needs to go back to school. San Franciscans love the mayor. He has done so much for this city. He deserves more than being muck-raked. He—"

"Is a politician, not a saint. "You focus on your story and let me worry about Carter Ellsworth."

"But Mayor Lee is—"

"Don't be so naive. Just because the people *like* him doesn't mean he is a good politician. I don't care if Mayor Lee is well-liked. It's our *job* to churn up the crystal-clear water to see what really lies beneath it. You have to get your hands dirty in the process."

"Getting your hands dirty is very different than smearing someone's good name for the sake of journalistic revenue, especially if your information is not correct or factual. Whatever Carter thinks is happening, isn't."

"Perhaps you were absent that day in Journalism one-oh-one when they told you that the bottom line is about selling papers. Selling papers is about making money. Money is what we give you for a good story. If a story on your good Mayor Lee sells papers, then that is the story we'll run with. Put your philosophic side in your briefcase and try to remember the bottom line: money. I'll quash that story for two more days. In the meantime, get some human interest on my desk."

My profession could be really ugly. My only hope was to counter some of that ugliness with a more caring angle…or the truth, whichever came first.

Grabbing my notes and calling in for a photographer, I headed out to find just that.

"Why don't you just use stock photos of homeless people? I've got bigger fish to shoot." Jeff Simmons was one of the best photographers at the paper. He and I had taken a journalism course together at Cal.

"I don't want stocks, Jeff. I need one really powerful image that will make San Franciscans care…*really* care, but first, I need your drawing expertise."

"Drawing? What the hell for?"

"I need something that's in someone's head. Just go with me

186

on this."

We walked to the park and I had him wait a little behind me to make sure Shirley wasn't having one of her moments. She wasn't.

I looked over at Jeff, who was walking toward Cotton. "I'm a dog person, ma'am," Jeff explained, holding one hand out for Cotton to sniff. "They love me." It appeared he was right because Cotton sniffed his hand before wagging his long tail. "Cool dog. I've never seen one so white." Jeff wandered over and extended his hand to Shirley. "String Bean," he said, taking her hand.

Shirley laughed. "I'm Shirley. That's Cotton, Midnight and Emerald. You came here to take pictures right?"

He nodded. "And to draw."

"Draw?" She cut her eyes over to me.

I nodded. "What I need for you to describe is the image you got of the bike and the surrounding areas. He'll draw a picture so I have something better to go on."

Shirley nodded. "You just sit here next to old Shirley, String Bean, and listen carefully."

He did, and as Shirley described what she saw, String Bean began sketching, lightly at first, and then filling with more details as Shirley continued on with her scry vision. When they were done, we had a very detailed picture of a red bike next to a green awning and a blue fire hydrant. On the bike, there was something stuck to the bottom of the frame. In the windows of the store were bottles of alcohol for sale. His bike was locked in one of those old-style gray bike parking areas where you could secure your bike.

"So, what's this drawing all about?" Jeff asked me. With Shirley's permission he was taking pictures of Shirley and the animals.

"It's just a place I'm trying to find."

String Bean nodded, placing the camera to his thin face. He looked like a cartoon cutout of a person, he was that thin. "Who do you think sees everything that goes on in this city? Who has eyes everywhere?"

I watched in fascination as the animals appeared to be posing for him. "Photographers?"

"Ding! Ding! Ding! Give the girl a gold star! I'll scan this baby with one simple caption: Fifty bucks to the first shooter who can tell me where it is within the next twelve hours."

"Are you serious?"

"Trust me on this, Echo. If anyone knows where this is, we'll know before the twelve hours are up. There are a few things in that drawing my guys will find in a nano."

"Such as?"

"The blue hydrant. Not many of those in the city. Don't know what they stand for, but that one is so obviously not the right color. There was one other thing." He pointed to a pole near the bike. There was no sign I could see. "I'm betting this is either a BART stop or a MUNI. Either way, I'll have this place to you in no time."

I felt a sense of hope I hadn't felt since I started my story. "If that's true, I so owe you."

Jeff nodded and sighed. "Wait until you see these shots, Echo. They'll get somebody's attention."

And he was right.

I was meeting Finn for dinner shortly after I finished the first installment of my series "Invisible No More." I liked the article and thought the story a good one. It would make people who had a heart care; all others were already too far off the grid to bring back.

"Hey there," Finn said, rising when I approached the booth. And I thought chivalry was dead. "Great story."

I grinned. Damn she looked good. I had never seen her in street clothes and she was even hotter than when wearing her tight little uniform. She had on a black turtleneck, light blue jeans and Doc Marten boots. A hint of a spicy cologne barely caressed my nostrils.

"Thank you. Thanks to you and Jardine, I was able to crank out one hell of a first story."

She grinned and there were those two dimples. "Glad to hear it." She perused the menu and then we ordered. "It's nice to have the night off, but even nicer to have someone to share it with." Leaning forward, she smiled softly. "So, let's not talk about our jobs. What is it you do when you're not being Lois Lane?"

I smiled at the reference. First I was Clark Kent and now Lois Lane. Interesting.

We spent the entire dinner talking about our hobbies, our passions, our dreams.

She loved being a cop and couldn't imagine doing anything else. When not on the beat, she played in a softball league, took two-step lessons and made mosaics and stained glass. I was enthralled just listening to her. She was animated, eloquent and very, very funny.

When she asked about my childhood, I got a little jumpy, as I usually do. How much do you tell someone about a past like mine? My foster child days were sad and pathetic, so I never spoke about those times. I couldn't very well tell her that I'd spent time in a mental hospital. *That* was a conversation stopper to be sure. And of course, what could I say about my time on the Bayou?

I had absolutely no memory from before I was five years old, so there was no need to go there, either.

Fortunately for me, Finn wasn't interested so much in my past as she was in my present, and for that I was grateful. She loved that I lived alone with a three-legged stoner cat. She owned a boxer named Lucy, and even carried pictures of her in her wallet.

After dinner, we strolled down to Fisherman's Wharf to walk off our expensive dinner and to just keep talking. We talked a lot, but could also share those comfortable moments of silence as well. I could see how easy it was to fall in love with her, but I was curious about something first.

"If I may be so bold. How is it you are so smokin' hot and still single?"

Turning to me, she lightly stroked my cheek. I melted then

and there. "You're very sweet, but I'm not a great partner. I'm a cop twenty-four-seven. It's not a vocation or a hobby, or a job. It's a lifestyle. It's who *and* what I am. A lot of women fall for the uniform expecting me to shuck it off at the end of a day and act like a regular Joe. That doesn't happen. I see things out here I wish I never had to revisit. But I do. There are times I can talk about my job, but I usually prefer not to. Most women feel closed off from me after a while." She shrugged. "Long story short, the badge gets in the way of everything except the sex."

I stepped closer to her, our breaths mingling together in the late San Francisco fog. "Sounds to me like you haven't been with the right women."

Lacing her fingers together behind my neck, she pulled me to her. "Oh is that right? What does the right woman look like?"

"Someone who is as invested in her own job as you are. Someone not expecting you to entertain her. Someone who," I stood on tiptoe to kiss her soft lips. "Loves you for all of the different people you are. Unconditionally."

She leaned down and kissed me deeply, pulling me to her, almost too tightly. "Oh, Lois, how I wish that woman existed. I'd snap her up in a heartbeat. But trust me. They all start out that way—believing they can handle the highs and lows and ups and downs, but once the honeymoon wears off…" She shrugged. "It's been the same time in and time out. I decided it was best to save everyone the trouble. And just stay single."

I nodded and pulled out of her grasp. "Good to know."

She stuffed her hands in her pockets. "Doesn't mean it has to stay this way."

I smiled and kissed her again. "That's more like it."

We pressed together, kissing, running our hands in each other's hair, touching each other's faces, until she finally came up for air.

"Okay, I know we weren't going to talk about our jobs, but—"

Finn laughed. "Can't stand it any more, can you?" She glanced at her watch. "I was wondering how long you'd hold out. You did better than I imagined. Okay, Lois, go ahead."

I threaded my arm through hers as we walked. "I still have my list of missing homeless people from both Oakland and the Tenderloin, but I don't know what to do with it to make it work for me. I know I should be looking for similarities..."

She laughed. "And who told you that? Jardine?"

"No. Carter."

"Ellsworth? You two on good terms now?"

"Something like that. Call it an uneasy truce."

"Well...I hate to say that cretin is right, but he is. Tell me more about your list."

"It's just street names and in each case, what little I know about each of them."

Finn nodded. "Can I see it?"

She looked at it carefully. "Pretty good. Have you found any connections other than they're all homeless men, they drink and some, not all, are vets?"

I shook my head. "No one has found their bodies. There's been no blood found."

Walking over to a bench, we sat down and she held the list up for us both to see. "Let's see what the two of us can do with this list."

I sat next to her and studied it, my chin on her shoulder, scooting closer to her and she threaded her fingers through mine. I really liked having Marist Finn in my corner. I wondered how much longer it would be before I found her in my bed.

I waited until after ten in the morning before calling Danica.

"Hey, Clark. How's Metropolis's greatest reporter?"

"Good. Any plans for tonight?"

"Why? Are we supersleuthing again? You know how I love sneaking around in the dark and spying on people."

"The sad thing is I know you really dig sneaking around in the dark, but what about sneaking around in the dark Tenderloin?"

"Oh, heart be still. Not another lovely junket into the sleazy underbelly of the city. Damn, are you getting any of this down? I say some pretty quotable lines, you know?"

"Aren't you in a mood? What happened?"

"We sold the boys' newest computer game to Epic Studios for a buttload of money and a movie option. Can you say cha-ching."

"They option computer games for movies now?"

"Oh, Clark, you are a technological throwback. You really need to get out more. Of course they option games. Haven't you ever heard of Lara Croft?"

"Lara who?"

"Never mind. Geez, you are out of the pop culture loop. Do you ever go to the movies?"

"Yes, but not to watch movies twelve-year-old boys watch."

"Then you're missing out, Clark. Those twelve-to twenty-five-year-old boys make Momma money. I'll not have you denigrating my customer base."

"Fine. Congratulations on another success...Momma."

She chuckled. "They're already talking about a spin-off from the original game and everything. We are going to make a bundle. But you want to know the best part? They're willing to package our educational CD with it."

"Excellent."

"Yeah, it's a good start for a great product and a new market. Carl has got a great series for new readers that he's working on. Blows *Hooked on Phonic*s to pieces. It's exciting. Anyway, back to you. Do you need some muscle for the trip into the dark expanse of—"

"Please...no more quotable lines. Yes, I need backup. We need to find out more about these missing guys. Find the tie that binds. There's something I am missing."

"Sounds like this could take all night. I'll wear my high-tops and bring plenty of mace. Should I bring energy food in case we need it?"

I laughed. It was always about food with her. "Sure. Bring sweets too. Only *you* could make a picnic out of a job. Meet me at my place around ten."

"You'll know it's me. I'll be wearing all black and smelling of Coco Chanel."

"Nerd." I hung up, smiling. As I was feeding Tripod, the phone rang.

"Hey Echo, it's Darryl Jardine. You got a minute?"

"For you, I have ten."

"Thanks. Look, I was just thinking about what you said about nobody listening to you and I wondered if you've tried going to the mayor about this."

"The mayor."

"Well, he's looking at reelection and like it or not he has a homeless population that needs tending to. Who knows? You might just give him a cause to hang his hat on."

"Have you ever met him?"

"Of course. He is a regular guy and he truly cares about this city of ours. The brass really likes him. The guy is full of integrity, he backs up the cops, and he gets high marks on his stance on crime."

I hadn't thought about the mayor, except to cover his ass where Carter was concerned, but maybe he would find my information interesting enough to get the police department off *its* ass.

Packing up my gear and my notes, I threw a can of tuna at the cat, who acted like I hadn't fed him in a month. I was almost in Ladybug when I saw a white dog running toward me. I knelt down and patted Cotton.

"Lost another one last night. I thought you'd want to know," Shirley said, hobbling toward me.

"Who?"

"Name was Stinky Pete. Real sweetheart. Other than his stench, he is a wonderful young man. Well-liked."

"What happened?"

She shrugged. "No witnesses. Stinky does the same routine night after night. When he didn't show up to drink and play cards with his buddies, they went looking for him. Nothing." Shirley shook her head. "Vanished like a ghost. Poof."

"Anyone know his real name?"

193

"You got me, sweetie. About all I can tell you is that he's an old, smelly, white guy with a beard down to here. Wears this smelly peacoat, hence his name. I came as soon as I could."

"Thank you." I pulled out my list and added Stinky Pete to it. "Can I drop you off somewhere?"

"I would rather you find who's doing this. People are getting nervous, starting to carry knives and pipes and stuff. The Tenderloin isn't a safe place, at the best of times. Don't turn your back on anyone, not even me. Where there's fear, there's danger, and the community is very afraid."

I shared her cautions with Danica that evening.

"I got all the protection we're going to need right here," Danica said, pointing to the gun she had placed in the small of her back. True to her word, she had arrived at my house wearing a Donna Karan black turtleneck, a black leather jacket from Polo, Hilfiger black jeans and her black high-tops with silver studs from Nordstrom. The only thing missing was a black ski mask, and I had no doubt she could produce one if necessary.

She looked at my attire and asked, "Are you wearing *that*?"

I looked at my clothes. I was wearing blue jeans, tennis shoes and a denim blazer. "What's wrong with what I'm wearing?"

"We're going to a pretty gross place in the middle of the night and you're dressed like Mary Poppins. Come on, Clark. Get in character!"

Once I was dressed in the appropriate black attire we opted for the Tenderloin first, and after nearly an hour we had managed to find only one person who had anything of value.

"Look, Clark, nobody down here can help you if you don't have people's real names. Without real names, we got nothing. Have you tried the police department?"

I looked at her as if she were stupid. "Duh, I'm practically dating one of them."

"I didn't ask you about your boring and pathetic love life. I was wondering if you had anyone *look* at the mug shots."

"The mug..." I threw my arms around her and hugged her tightly. "Oh my God, you really are a genius!"

"It just makes sense that most of your homeless people have been arrested for either drunk and disorderly or under the influence of something. All you need is someone who can recognize their faces and then we can put real names to them."

Ten minutes later we found Shirley giving a Tarot reading near the park. She was more than happy to go down to the station and claim she had been mugged by another homeless person, and she wanted to look at the books. It was a brilliant idea, really, and I was a little bummed out I hadn't thought of it.

I watched as Shirley flipped through page after page of mug shots, nodding and pointing whenever she saw a picture that registered to her powers. About an hour into it, we had eight names. Eight real names. Shirley surprised me by being far more lucid and far more powerful with her visions than I initially gauged.

We dropped Shirley off at the park. She turned to me and put her hand on my arm. "I can tell you this much, sweetie. They're all still alive. For how much longer, I don't know. Not one of them is dead. Not one. You need to find them, Echo. You need to find them and quickly. Time is of the essence."

Danica and I drove away in silence, both of us nursing our own thoughts and fears.

It was Danica who broke the silence first. "If they're still alive then where the hell are they? Who has them? And why? Why would anyone want over a dozen homeless guys?"

I started toward the office with the same questions beating at my brain. "I haven't a clue, but at least now that we have the names of some of the missing..."

"My guys are all over it." Danica pulled out the list and started text messaging on what looked like a compact computer. "They'll be all over it by the morning. They eat research for you with a spoon the size of a shovel. I think it breaks the monotony of being so creative all the time." She texted all nine names before asking me, "So what do we know?"

"Well, color or ethnicity isn't an issue. Four whites, three blacks, a Hispanic, and a possible Asian pretty much rules that out."

"How about ages?"

"Danny Boy is in his late teens, and Stinky Pete is in his late fifties, so age doesn't seem to be a consistent factor."

"Okay, what about military service?"

"Two Vietnam vets, one Gulf War vet, other than that, nothing else. Their jail time wasn't enough to merit a look. Most of them were let go after less than twenty-four hours."

"All are men. I find that interesting. That probably rules out sexual assault as a motive."

"True." I sighed. We still couldn't find a connection. "It seems the more we know the less we know."

"Hang in there, Clark. We'll get some answers."

My next stop was the office, where Danica and I pored over microfilm and had three computers going at once. None of their names produced anything online. That didn't mean they weren't out there in cyberspace, it just meant that I wasn't going to find information on them that easily. Since we knew we could leave cyberspace to the boys, we concentrated on microfilm.

Three hours and two pairs of blurry eyes later, we were still empty-handed. About the only thing I got was a headache. By the time I got home, I was exhausted and felt like I wasn't any closer to finding Bob than when I woke up this morning.

Time was of the essence, and it was running out.

I woke up four hours later to the ringing of my phone. I had to reach over my drugged cat to get to it. I looked at the clock. It was 6:37.

"It's String Bean. I was checking my e-mail this morning and we got a hit on the drawing with the bike."

I was a wide awake now and sitting up in bed.

"A buddy of mine is pretty sure it's a liquor store on Hyde called Fast Freddy's. He recognized the damn fire hydrant."

I was out of the bed. "Way to go!"

"I told you photographers are the best eyes in the city. I also got some really great shots of your street people for the story. I'll leave copies on your desk this morning."

"Thank you so much. Be sure to thank your buddies."

"The photos I took of Cotton and Midnight are awesome. I see a separate story built around those photos. Echo, if you want people to care, those two animals would make even the hardest heart melt. People can watch the *Texas Chainsaw Massacre* without batting an eye, but watch a pet bunny stuffed into a pot of boiling water, and they go apeshit."

I nodded, thinking about his *Basic Instincts* reference. "True."

"Well, think about it."

"I don't have to think about it, Jeff. It's a great idea."

"Well, let me know if there's anything else I can do."

I got dressed, checked to make sure Tripod hadn't overdosed on catnip and then headed for Fast Freddy's. When I pulled around the corner and saw the green awning, I actually gasped. There it was. And there, chained to a post just like Shirley had said, was Smiley's bike. I pulled Ladybug into the red zone next to the bike. As I searched the bike, my heart beat an extra beat when I realized what it was Shirley thought she saw. She thought he had been working on the bike, but that wasn't what Smiley had been doing. Taped to the underside of the crossbar was a sheet of paper the size of a stick of gum. Only the ends were taped to the bike, and the rest of it had writing scribbled all over it. Thank God it hadn't rained.

Carefully peeling the paper off of the bike, I rose and leaned against Ladybug's bumper. I don't know what I was expecting... a note that read *Here's who's taking our people?* This wasn't even close. What I got was some sort of bizarre encryption. On the paper was a weird list of numbers: 3, 9, 7, 30, 24, 93, 34, 62, 26, 86, 26, 22{B}.

"What in the hell?" In the car, I sat and stared at the numbers. It would have taken divine intervention to figure out what these numbers stood for. Taking my lump of coal with me, I headed to the office.

When String Bean said his photos were good, he wasn't kidding. They were incredible; made even more so by the use of black-and-white film. Jeff had the touch of a master. One photo had Cotton and Midnight touching noses as if they were communicating with each other. Another had Midnight sitting in between Cotton's paws and both were looking in opposite directions. I must have been engrossed in my conversation with Shirley because I don't remember him taking these photos.

When I finished looking at all of the pictures, I picked three that were outstanding and started my story on them. With photos like these, the story wrote itself. This would be a great water cooler story. The perfect dovetail into my homeless people series.

There are those people who care deeply for other people, and then there are those people who care even more deeply for pets. In a country that spends over four billion per year on their animal companions, this story would make them sit up and take notice.

After sending Jeff an e-mail telling him how brilliant his photos were, I called Danica and left a message that I was going to Oakland and not to worry. Then I left one for the boys: I had a little puzzle for them I would be e-mailing over. In the meantime, I would finish my story, and then see if Finn would put a call into OPD for me. My to-do list never seemed to dwindle.

My story finished writing itself, and I e-mailed it to Wes Bentley. He and I had exchanged e-mails regarding my story as well as the backseat piece on Mayor Lee Carter was trying to write. Apparently, he refused to believe the photos had been doctored. He wanted more proof. I just shook my head and wished Wes luck with that piece. Then I picked up the phone and called Finn with the intention of leaving another message. I was surprised when she picked up.

"Good morning to you," she said. "Isn't caller ID a great thing? I wasn't going to answer."

"Good morning. I'm so glad I made the cut. How are you?"

"I'm wearing a big goose egg over my left eye, but other than that I'm good. And you?"

"What happened? Are you okay?"

"I'm fine. Someone clocked me with a rock. Hurt like hell.

The goose egg is the reason I'm awake. It's throbbing like a son-of-a-bitch. It's telling me I need to take some Advil or something. And as much as I would love to think this is a personal call... something tells me otherwise. What's up?" There was a slight tinge of resentment in her voice.

"A rock?" I said, softly. "Did you need stitches? Are you sure you don't need some TLC? I can come over and administer CPR or something."

She chuckled. "CPR sounds great. I could use a little TLC."

"Seriously, though, are you okay? What happened?"

"I was breaking up a bar fight and someone chucked a rock toward us. My face got in the way. Twelve stitches. No biggie. What's up?"

"I've got names for nine of the homeless guys. I was hoping—"

"That I could shake some trees and see what falls out? I can give it a try, Echo. Let's face it. We have no proof any crime was committed. And even though I believe you, and I believe in your story and your instincts, I'm just a bottom feeder. If you really want action, you need to go to the top."

"And by that you mean—"

"Mayor Lee would be able to put some heat on the chief. We have a saying in law enforcement—shit runs downhill. If you can get the mayor's interest, he might lean on the chief. The chief would turn around and lean on the captains until finally, someone would be assigned. Off the record, of course."

"The police department won't look good if I do it that way."

"What else is new? We all know the score, Echo. We are short-staffed, overworked, underpaid and have more rules to follow than a dozen jobs added together. It's an uphill battle for supplies, for money, for backing of any sort. You do what you need to do to get action. The department may initially take a hit when it becomes clear that we didn't do anything to investigate, but don't worry. We cover well."

"Then you wouldn't be mad? I hate the thought this might come between us."

"Something can come between us if we only let it. Hell no.

199

I'm on your side. I wish there was more I could do for you. All I ask is that you have a real dinner with me once this is all over. A real date. I'd like to get to know you better. I'm your biggest fan, Echo. You can trust me."

Once I hung up, I realized for the first time since Tip, I actually trusted another woman, and it felt really, really good.

When I handed Shirley the photographs, I included my story with them. Her hand went to her mouth and her eyes welled with tears as she slowly and deliberately looked at each picture.

"Oh my...my babies have never looked so good. These are simply..." She shook her head and wiped her tears. "Please convey my appreciation to String Bean. He did a wonderful job. These are simply wonderful."

"I thought so as well. I wanted you to see the story first, along with the photos. I'm putting faces to the homeless that haven't quite been captured like this."

Shirley stared at them for a very long time before looking up. "What a wonderful gift. Thank you so much."

"I'm the one who should be thanking you. I really appreciate all the help with my story. As a matter of fact, I was wondering—"

Shirley looked up from the photos. "You've got something?" she held her hand out. I had no doubt she had probably been *watching* me from afar, using her sight to see if I was anywhere close. I hadn't had many encounters with clairvoyers, so I wasn't quite sure how they operated. Most people would be freaked out knowing someone could close their eyes and get a vision of where they were and what they were doing, but I'm a supernatural. It takes a lot to freak me out.

Reaching into my pocket, I pulled out Smiley's note. "I found this on Smiley's bike, but you probably already knew that, huh?"

Shirley waited, palm open. "Can't blame an old woman for caring. You've been so kind to me and my critters. Yes I knew, and yes, I knew you would bring it to me." She kept her hand out and I put the slip of paper with the numbers carefully in her palm.

"So this is what I saw Smiley doing with the bike?"

I nodded. "Apparently."

She closed her eyes and sat very still for a long time. When she opened them, she shook her head. "All I can tell you is that he saw something...something that frightened him so much he felt the need to write it down...but he is...different, *n'est-ce pas?*

"Oh yes. A savant of some sort. No one knows precisely what kind."

"But these are just numbers."

Shirley handed the paper back to me. "Maybe they are, maybe they aren't. This Smiley was a special man...special abilities. He saw the world so much differently than the rest of us and his communication style was not at all like yours and mine." Shirley sighed. "One of his people might know how he communicates. Now, can a batty old woman give you a piece of unsolicited advice?"

"Absolutely."

"Don't let this job be ivy in your life."

"Ivy?"

"Ivy looks pretty enough, but left unchecked it will kill all of the surrounding plants in an area until it is the only thing alive. From where I sit, and granted it's no palace on high, I see a beautiful young girl working and working and working. Hamster on a treadmill. Ivy." She reached for my hand and held it. "A yard is much prettier when it has a variety of plants. Your yard is... well... rife with ivy. That may seem fine now, but it can be a very lonely place after a while. Don't become so involved in your stories that you forget to live your own."

Smiling, I nodded. "Good advice. I just wish I knew how to take it."

"Give yourself some time. Balance, Echo. Keep your life in balance."

It was odd the way I could hear Melika's voice, and a small part of me wondered if Melika hadn't contacted her. "You sound like my mentor."

I thought about our conversation as I drove to Oakland. I *did* feel driven. I just never felt good enough. It was the typical stigma of a foster care kid. I wanted to be better than good enough...I

201

wanted to be the best. I wanted to prove to Wes and Carter, and yeah, myself, that I had the chops to do this job really well.

When I finally found Dante, he was reading another one of his namesake's books. Looking up, he frowned. "Is this good news or bad news?"

I shrugged, sitting down next to him. "I can tell you this much: I don't believe he is dead."

"Why not?"

"No bodies. No evidence of violence. Nothing to suggest they were hurt. What's important is finding out what the hell this means." I handed him a copy of the paper with the numbers. "I found this taped to his bike. I was hoping you might know what it means."

Dante looked at the piece of paper and rubbed his face. "He wrote these down? That's odd. Smiley never writes."

"Then maybe they're really important."

Dante looked at them again and squinted before looking back up. "No maybe about it. Smiley never writes. Wasn't even sure the kid knew how."

I bowed my head. I had been so sure the piece of paper was written by Smiley.

"You know, Echo, a bunch of us were talking the other day and the one thing we kept coming back to was the fact that these kidnappings seemed so organized."

I cocked my head at him. "Gangs?"

He shook his head. "To swipe a grown man off the street without anyone saying or hearing anything would take an organized group with the proper vehicle for a quick in and out. Gangs are sloppy. Gangs don't drag dead bodies with 'em. There is an organization that requires leadership and equipment."

"Like a van?" Leroy had mentioned a van.

He nodded. "It's probably a large cargo or something with double doors because they've got to be able to get a struggling man into it quickly."

I nodded again. "You're saying there's more than one guy, right?"

"Way more than one. We were thinking along the lines of three or four. To do a snatch and grab without being seen or heard would require at least three grown men: a driver and two, maybe three others." Dante looked down at the numbers. "This is a fairly covert operation, my friend. They know who they're looking for and what they want. My guess is this is not a snatch and grab. They have targeted certain guys."

"Wait. If that's true, then they're doing their homework." I paced across the alley. "And that would mean—" Stopping I looked up at Dante. "Oh my God."

Sighing, he ran his hand over his bald head. "Someone is giving them up. Someone is leading them to the guys they've been scouting. That's what we've come up with."

"So, you don't think these are random kidnappings at all?"

He looked at me a long time before answering. "Echo, *we* are everywhere. We're smoke on the water. For someone to take as many of us from two cities as you say, this is a very organized endeavor that has inside intel. Someone is giving them that intel, and when we find out who it is..." He made a throat-slitting motion. "Ain't gonna be pretty."

"Very good. I'll keep working my side. Do those numbers mean anything at all to you?"

He shook his head and then proceeded to write them down on the inside cover of *Paradise Lost.* "No, but let me ruminate on them for a spell. I don't know if anyone told you much about my nephew, but he's never been right in the head. Some people call him an idiot. I prefer to call him a savant."

"So you said. Autism?"

He chuckled. "Something like that. We never got the whole diagnosis. Anyway, if he wrote it down it meant something to him. I mean..." He shook his head. "He must have been trying real hard to get something out in his own way."

"Well, if you can think of anything, let me know. Please don't—" I made the same throat-slitting motion he had, "before I have a chance to talk to whoever it is."

"I can't promise that, Echo. Vets down here tend to act first and talk later. If someone has been giving us up, there's gonna be blood. It's become a search-and-destroy mission."

That, in a nutshell, was the way of the street. As I left the old man alone on the stoop, my mind was racing. Who would want to kidnap homeless people, and why? What did they have to offer? Was it their anonymity? The fact that no one really cared?

Getting into Ladybug, I dialed Finn's number and invited her to a quick dinner.

By the time our meal came, we had discussed the various paths to our careers, what we did in high school, and some of our favorite favorites. I found her to be a wonderful dinner companion and an excellent conversationalist. The more I was around her the more I liked her. She was a great listener, asked good questions (as befitting a cop), and was well-read; something that had always been important to me. She told me some of the most hilarious police stories I had ever heard, and we laughed right on through to dessert.

While I was laughing, Finn leaned forward and laid her hand on top of mine. "Can't say I've ever seen you laugh so hard. It's nice." She studied me a moment before squeezing my hand under hers. "As much as I would like to believe you asked me to dinner for a date, I can see the many question marks in your gorgeous eyes. What business do you need to attend to?"

Ivy, ivy, everywhere. Damn that Shirley. Damn my eyes. "Maybe I just wanted to spend some time with you."

Her smile was perfect. "And maybe that's only part of the truth. You know, for a truth seeker, you sure sidestep it a lot."

I stared at her. "Truth seeker? Where did you get that?"

She studied me a minute. "It's written all over your face. It's in your eyes. You live for the truth. It's the bread and butter of your diet." She shrugged. "It's one of the things I like most about you: your integrity."

I felt a catch in my breath, but I let that conversation go. I could not deal with the fact that I was so far inside the paranormal closet I might never get out. "I've decided to go to the mayor's press conference tomorrow. After tomorrow, the police department will see me as Typhoid Mary. I don't imagine that will go down well with your buddies in blue to know that you're consorting with the enemy."

She blew out a breath and ran her hand through her hair. "Maybe not, but I can handle them." Taking my hand in both of hers, she squeezed harder. "I think you're worth it."

Staring into her eyes, I smiled softly. "Thank you, but that's just it. I don't want you to have to *handle* them. I don't want them seeing me as a thorn in your side. That's not a great way to start."

She thought about it a long time. "You might be right." She scooted closer. "Do what you need to do, Echo, just let me help. Even if I can only help from the sidelines, let me help."

I nodded. Then I told her what I had so far and about the van. "It needs to be big enough to be able to throw a guy in and go. How do we narrow down the possibilities?"

"You would need a list of all van owners in the city and, of course, since people are missing from Oakland as well—you need to know all of the van owners in a hundred-mile radius."

"Damn. Impossible, huh?"

"Yep."

"I'm at my wit's end here. It feels like I have a dozen different puzzle pieces I'm trying to fit into one puzzle. It's goddamned frustrating."

"Welcome to investigative work. You just keep your eyes on the prize and keep turning all the evidence around in your head like a Rubik's Cube. One day something will click and you'll have the whole side complete just like that." She snapped her fingers.

"And in the meantime?"

"You take what you have to the top. You believe in your evidence enough to stand by it no matter what."

"And you promise you won't hate me?"

She brought my hand to her lips and let them linger there. "That could never happen."

"Promise?"

Taking my chin in her hand, she kissed me softly. "I promise."

I rolled back into Oakland still feeling Finn on my lips.

I had a feeling it was Dante who kept bringing me back to Oakland. It wasn't that I was reading him as much as the situation seemed to be beckoning me to him. When I found Dante again, he was standing in an alleyway with about twelve onlookers enraptured by his performance. I have to say he was truly captivating with his James Earl Jones voice and his Samuel L. Jackson presence. The man could have played Othello without competition.

He was very good, and though I did not know my Dante well, I did know a grand performance when I saw one.

"Turn your back and keep your eyes shut tight;
for should the Gorgon come and you look at her,
never again would you return to light.

"This was my guide's command. And he turned to me about himself
and would not trust my hands alone, but, with his placed on mine, held
my eyes shut."

I stole a look at members of the audience and couldn't help but smile. Dante held them in the palm of his hand with his theatrical flair. When he spoke, he moved with the words. He stood there now, with both of his hands over his eyes.

...suddenly, there broke on the dirty swell of the dark Marsh a squall
of terrible sound that sent a tremor through both shores of Hell."

As he spoke, his voice pitched and rose like a professional thespian. I was enthralled.

When at last it was time for an intermission, he accepted a small bottle of water from an older woman. "Virgil was afraid, wasn't he?" she asked. Virgil was Dante's guide through Hell in this particular epic tale.

"Indeed he was, but Virgil tried to hide it."

She shook her head. "But Dante wasn't fooled, was he?"

Dante smiled softly at her. "What do you think, Jenny?"

She thought for a moment, like a student in class might, before finally shaking her head. "I think Dante's not so sure Virgil knows the way."

Dante patted her on the back. "And you would be right. Bravo!"

I rose and walked over to him. I sure could use a Virgil now. "This is quite a performance you put on. Do you do these every night?"

"Every single night. Consistency is key to the folks out here, so I'm here first and then I go down the street a bit and do a shorter version down there. Gives them something to do."

"And always Dante's *Inferno*?"

"Oh heavens, no. It's seasonal, really. I do Dante in the summer months from June to September. From September to October I do the *Legend of Sleepy Hollow*. In November and December, of course, I do the *Night Before Christmas* and other tales. And January through April I do *Paradise Lost*."

"Wow."

"The *Inferno* is everyone's favorite. It's been Smiley's favorite since before he could walk. That kid knows the story like the back of his hand. I've never seen a kid love a story so much. He can recite it verse for verse. It's pretty amazing for a kid who seldom talks."

I grinned. "You still call him a kid."

"He always will be to me. It was Smiley who got me to start performing in the first place. He wanted other people to feel what he felt whenever I told a story. At the beginning, only a few folks gathered around. Most thought I was crazy. Can't say I blame them. When one of us starts orating on a corner somewhere, we usually sound quite insane."

Something in my stomach turned. "He...*feels* the story?"

"Well...I don't know that he really does, but that was the way he put it to me."

I blinked several times and let the thought linger a bit.

I stayed for the next piece, but it was getting cold and I hadn't brought a jacket. Whatever was nagging the edges of my mind wouldn't come up, so I waved goodbye to Dante and headed home.

Nothing on my phone from the boys. Nothing from Danica.

207

Nothing at all. By the time I got home, I had a headache the size of Texas. Whatever was poking at me was in a part of my brain I couldn't locate. It reminded me of a song playing over and over in your head but you can't name it. So, I did what every other red-blooded American did when that happened...I took a shower, brushed my teeth, filed my nails, fed the cat, cleaned out my refrigerator, and did everything I could to keep my mind off whatever it was playing hide-and-seek with me. When it didn't come, I cleaned the house and surfed the Internet until I could barely keep my eyes open.

They had been closed for half a second when the phone rang. Checking the caller ID as well as the time, I grinned. Finn.

"Normal women don't call after midnight," I said, yawning.

"Who said *I* was normal? You've been given erroneous information if you think that. Sorry I woke you, but I needed to know you were okay."

"I am fine and I wasn't asleep. Really." Now I was sitting up. There was something in her voice I hadn't heard before and couldn't place it.

"I worried about you all night. I only worry about people I truly care about. I...uh...just wanted to say it seems like you're ready to start a new chapter in your life and I would really like to be part of it."

"I'd like that as well, Finn. I know I am preoccupied with my story and my career, but maybe once this gets off the ground, so can we."

"Once the story is over. Echo, I think you're an incredible woman, and I hope you feel the same way about me."

"Officer Finn, I think you rock. Don't you know? Can't you tell? If I wasn't so interested in finding Bob, I'd be making up other reasons to call you. I'm sorry if I haven't been sending out the right vibes. I would love to spend time getting to know you."

She chuckled goodheartedly. "That's good to hear. I was hoping this wasn't a one-way thing."

"It isn't. I enjoy spending time with you, too." I heard her radio in the background.

"Damn, I gotta roll. Oh, and Echo? If you ever want to feel safe at night...sleep with a cop." With that, she hung up, leaving me smiling and feeling a little tingly.

Rolling over, I sighed contentedly, my eyelids getting heavy again. I don't know how Finn could do that job. It must have been hell day in and out dealing with nothing but tragedy. I was just about asleep when suddenly I sat up straight and turned on the light so fast Tripod ran under the bed. "That's it!" Jumping out of bed, I ran to my bookshelves and rifled through all of my old college textbooks, spilling them to the floor. "Where is it?"

When I finally found the one I needed, I pulled it out and held it to my chest. "This *has* to be it."

I was holding Dante's *Inferno;* my key to the clue kingdom.

I was sure of it.

Turning on my desk lamp, I grabbed the slip of paper with numbers on it and studied it for a moment. "I *knew* there was something there." The moment Finn said the word chapter, all the doors started to unlock for me.

"Okay, Echo, calm. Calm down." My heart was pounding so I took a deep breath, pulled a pen and pad out, and then opened my copy of the *Inferno*.

It had all my earlier chicken-scratch notes from when I had taken a Milton course from Dr. LaBoskey. I remembered how difficult I'd found the class in college. I may not have gotten it, but Smiley the Savant did.

Rainman was a savant who was exceptional with numbers. He couldn't hold a conversation or drive a car or even make his own meals, but he could count cards in Vegas, memorize lists and compute almost faster than a calculator or computer.

Smiley knew the *Inferno* like the back of his hand. He had used it to send some kind of message to his people. Dante's *Inferno* was a story about his trip to hell and the different people who occupied the layers of each region. According to Dante's version of hell, people ended up in the appropriate situation depending on what kind of sinner they were.

I started reading from the first of Smiley's number 3:9. Canto

III. It was called the *Opportunists*, people whose souls are neither good nor evil, but self-centered. It had the most famous line in the work, and most of us had heard it at one time or another: *Abandon all hope, ye who enter here.* That was the sign above the gates to Hell.

Why had Smiley written this down on a piece of paper? Quickly, I flipped to the next set of numbers. Seven was Canto VII, which dealt with the Hoarders and Wasters, The Wrathful and Sullen. The Hoarders and Wasters lacked all moderation and thought nothing was as important as money. Turning to line 30, I read the next ten lines out loud:

Why do you hoard? Why do you waste? So back around that ring they puff and blow, each faction to its course, until they reach opposite sides, and screaming as they go, the madmen turn and start their weights again to crash against the maniacs. And I, watching, felt my heart contract of pain.

Sighing, I leaned against the back of the sofa and scratched Tripod's ahead. At the moment, he wasn't stoned, so he liked me a little bit. "What was Smiley trying to say?" I was beginning to think I was way off base; that I had reached too far in an effort to find an answer.

I jammed a three-by-five card into both cantos and moved on to 24, Canto XXIV, which was about thieves. That was pretty self-explanatory, so I pressed on. There was one line from Smiley's notes: line 93: *In that swarm, naked and without hope, people ran terrified, not even dreaming of a hole to hide in or of heliotrope.*

Heliotrope? I flipped to the notes in the back of my translation and saw that a heliotrope was some sort of stone. A bloodstone believed to be capable of making the wearer of it invisible.

Okay...

With the exception of people running terrified, the idea that Smiley had used the *Inferno* as a way of communicating what he saw was a quantum leap, but I couldn't let go. Not yet. Canto XXXIV, Smiley's 34 dealt with Satan and others. The one line, line 62 read: *That soul that suffers most, explained my guide, is Judas Iscariot, he who kicks his legs on the fiery chin and has his head inside."*

My glimmer of hope was quickly fading. "What are you trying to say? What did you see?" Flipping back to the notes in the book, I read that Judas's punishment was patterned after the Simoniacs. The who? I made a note and continued.

I looked at the last sets of numbers 26, 86; they were a reference to Circe. I knew that one well. Circe was a woman Ulysses stayed with for a year when he was trying to get home. The final set of numbers, 22 {B} made a reference to a bridge: *by the bridge and among a shapeless crew.* Now, *that* caught my attention. San Francisco is known for the Golden Gate Bridge. Was Smiley making a reference to that? And if that was true, then was the reference to Judas about the person who was giving over our guys to those possibly driving a van? If all of this was true, then where was Smiley? Why was he able to even *give* any clues?

My headache had returned. I either had a whole lot or a whole lotta nothing.

Feeling defeated, I decided maybe the boys could find something, so I e-mailed my notes to them with a note. *Guys- I hope you're up to this task. The numbers I sent might be sections of Smiley's favorite novel, Dante's Inferno. I've been banging my head against the wall for an hour, and I can't come up with anything. Maybe you can. Princess.*

If anyone could decode Dante's lines, those three would. I decided after my press conference with the mayor I would see what my fellow thespian could come up with. Maybe he could sort this out. Maybe I was so far off track I could never get back on it. At least I had one thing going for me; I still had a press conference to attend.

"Come to watch a pro in action?" Carter said when he saw me at the Center.

"Something like that."

"Why don't you sit with me? I will lend you some much needed credibility."

I was not in the least insulted. In the journalism field, there

211

is a definite pecking order. If Carter could get me in the door, I would've sat on his shoulders if it meant getting the mayor's attention.

When we took our seats, I looked around and finger-waved to a few people I knew. There were camera crews, light guys and print media there. I didn't stand a chance in this crowd. Sure, I was with a damned Pulitzer winner, but there were also daytime Emmy winners as well as other power journalists who had been around the block long before I was born.

Carter had gotten a seat right in the center. The podium stood in the middle of the stage with three chairs on either side of it. When the crowd quieted down you could see everyone jockeying for space. The truth was, I was really excited to be there.

When the mayor's press secretary came out, I got butterflies in my stomach. He was just a mayor, but there was an energy swirling around the room that swept me up in it like Dorothy's tornado.

"Just wait," Carter whispered. "His mother will be coming out in a second. Everyone thinks it's bizarre the way she goes everywhere he goes, but I'm sure it's a cultural thing."

"Of course it's a cultural thing, and not necessarily a bad one."

"Oh, it's bad," he replied, straightening his bright red silk tie. "The old bag goes everywhere with him. It's weird. Look. There she is."

I watched an elderly Chinese woman walk out and sit on the chair closest to the podium. Her keen, clear eyes slowly inspected the crowd, like a mother bear surveying the territory before her cubs can play there. Her eyes made a slow, methodical pass over every face. When her eyes locked onto mine, I knew *exactly* why she was her son's greatest adviser, and why she creeped people out.

"Weird, huh?" Carter whispered. "Almost like she's looking at *you*, Branson."

I said nothing, but kept my eyes on Mrs. Lee. Only when her son came out did her intense gaze shift from mine.

"Thank you for coming," he said, loosening his maroon tie. Mayor Lee possessed the carriage of a higher ranking official than just mayor. He stood erect as he looked out over the standing room only crowd, confident, poised, yet not arrogant or challenging. His hair was like shiny black tar on his head, and caressed his expressive eyebrows. He looked like a man who had come to claim his second tour of mayoral duty. "Thank you all for coming. I know some of you are here to help me win reelection while others of you would love nothing more than to help me out the door. Well, I would like both sides to know that I am not bowing down to any kind of external pressure from you, my opponent, or the ugly rumor mills. I am proud of the work I've done and will continue as long as the people of this great city allow. We only just started making some of the necessary changes that will keep this city in step with the changing times. I intend to see those programs to fruition. To that end, I'm willing to answer whatever questions you may have. But let's be civil, shall we? Try to keep the mudslinging to a minimum." He smiled, but the truth behind that smile spoke volumes.

"Sounds like he knows you're gunning for him," I whispered to Carter.

"Yeah, well, watch and learn."

I did. All the big names asked questions about gay marriage, domestic partnerships, the possibility of Microsoft returning to the Bay Area, jobs, the security of BART in light of recent terrorist activities and ways to clean up the downtown business district. One by one, Mayor Lee patiently answered every question. I found it incredibly interesting that he had yet to call on Carter, whose hand kept shooting in the air as if he had a spasm.

When the mayor finished with a question about parking, I figured it was time for me to throw my hat in the ring, so up went by hand.

"What in the hell are you doing?" Carter demanded under his breath. "Put your fool hand down."

"Not a chance. Why do you think I came here? To watch you?" I didn't hear his caustic response because I was too focused on Mrs. Lee. She motioned to her son, who bent down to listen to her. When he stood back at the podium, he was staring right at me and pointing. Carter stood up.

"Mr. Mayor..."

"I'm sorry, Mr. Ellsworth. I was not motioning to you. I would like to hear from your colleague in the beautiful red suit."

The look on Carter's face was worth my weight in gold. His head slowly turned toward me, eyes blazing, nostrils flaring.

I turned from him and smiled at the mayor as I stood up. "Mr. Mayor, Echo Branson from the *Chronicle*. Are you aware someone has been abducting our homeless people right off the street and after repeated requests for an investigation into these disappearances, your police department has refused to get involved?" My heart was banging so loudly in my ears I could barely hear myself. My mouth had that dry, *I'm too nervous to speak feel*, and my palms were all clammy.

He frowned for a moment. "Miss Branson, you wrote the article with that photo of the homeless animals, didn't you?"

I nodded and felt a blush rise from my shoulders to the top of my head. "Yes, sir."

"Wonderful story. Fabulous photographs."

"Thank you, sir. I'll let the photographer know you thought so."

He leaned forward on the podium. "So let me get this straight. You are saying that even after the article and requests for help, our police department still has done nothing about these missing people?"

I nodded. "I've done everything I can as a journalist and concerned citizen to get someone to help me figure out what is going on. I'm here because I'm hoping you can help. They may be homeless, sir, but they are our citizens, nonetheless. They deserve the same actions you'd give to someone living on Nob Hill."

The crowd tittered slightly at this, but his gaze silenced them. He took notes and then turned to his mother. I couldn't tell if there was an exchange or not, but when he turned around she smiled politely at me. "Miss Branson, I assure you I will be in contact with the chief of police before the day is through. If what you say is happening, you have my word I will do whatever I can to get to the bottom of it, and I appreciate you bringing it to my attention."

Nodding, I sat down. "Thank you, Mr. Mayor."

The press conference went on and I could feel the heat emanating off Carter, who was no longer raising his hand. He was livid and could barely contain himself. The mayor never looked our way again.

When it was all over, Carter grabbed my elbow and pushed me through the crowd. We were practically out the door when what looked like a bodyguard or security stopped us.

"Excuse me, Miss Branson? Mayor Lee would like to see you right now if you have the time."

"Me? Absolutely." Turning to Carter, who was so stunned he'd turned mute, I shrugged before detaching myself from him. Following the bodyguard, I was surprised when he took me into a small conference room.

"He'll be right in. Can I get you a coffee or tea, or something?"

"Thank you. I'm good."

The mayor and his mother came in shortly after I sat down. Out of deference to Mrs. Lee, I started to rise, but she waved me back down. "Sit. Sit."

I sat.

"I wanted to hear more about what's happening with the homeless population. I would have done this at the conference, but...well...you saw how it was. There are those journalists who would like to put me into a meat grinder."

I nodded. "I'm not one of them. I have a friend who is one of the missing men from the Tenderloin and I am really worried something terrible has happened to him."

Mayor Lee started for the door. "I need some water. Can I get you anything?"

"I'm fine, thanks," I said, wondering why he didn't call for an aide.

When he left, Mrs. Lee turned her chair to me. For the longest time, she didn't say anything. She just kept staring hard into my face with her probing brown eyes. I didn't have to lower my shield to know what was going on.

Mrs. Lee was one of us.

"You know, don't you?" she said softly, eyes never leaving mine. Her face was that of an apple head doll.

I gazed back into eyes which reminded me of Melika's. "Actually, I do. It's one of my gifts."

She squinted her already tiny eyes and nodded. Dressed in a blue business suit, she did not appear anywhere near her reported age of eighty. "You're quite strong. I sensed your presence right away even with all the others in the room."

I didn't reply, but I *did* understand now why she went everywhere with him and why Carter, a Pulitzer Prize winning journalist hadn't been called on; she knew which side of the political fence he sat on and purposely avoided him. What a wonderful ally Kai Lee had in his mother.

"I haven't met an empath of your kind in many years, but you were not trained in the Orient."

I shook my head. "No, I wasn't, but I was taught very well by a woman in the Bayou."

She continued to look in my eyes. "Yes. Yes you were. Good to respect your mentor. I felt you right off. But you are not here to compare powers, as much as I would like to. There are not many of us in this part of the country." She closed her eyes a second and then slowly opened them. "The missing men. They mean something more to you than just your friend."

"Bob is a friend of mine, yes. The others, though not friends, deserve no less attention. Because they are homeless, I can't get anyone at the police station to listen to me. Nobody cares."

"My son is very good at getting people to listen to him." She leaned forward. "And he cares, but there are those who would prevent him from making this city a better place. I would like to help you. Can you help us in return?"

"Me help? How can I help?"

216

She glared in the direction of the auditorium. "That man. Carter Ellsworth. Mr. High and Mighty. He does not like my son or his politics. Whatever lies he is after, whatever dirt he is busy digging up, we would like stopped."

I looked at her and wondered how strong a super *she* was. "Don't you know?"

She waved the question away. "Of course I know. Knowing and stopping his self-serving ways are two different things. That man...people listen to him. People think he is wise, but he is not. He is a little man given a big stage with a large microphone. I do not want that man's voice preventing my son's reelection."

Oh God.

"I am not asking you to silence this voice on your own. It will take more than one muzzle to silence that yipping dog."

I nodded. "He's not necessarily evil, Mrs. Lee, but he is incredibly myopic."

"He is the kind of man who will put his needs before those of the people...of *my* people. I am not asking you to do anything immoral or against your own code of ethics, which I suspect is quite high. I am asking that you simply keep an eye on him and inform me if he is going somewhere dark and ugly." She leaned closer. "This city needs my son, Miss Branson. It needs him more than it needs a self-absorbed journalist. Surely you understand that."

"I do, and you have my word I will do whatever I can to make sure that Carter Ellsworth isn't given that stage." I paused. "I've actually been involved in that very endeavor, ma'am."

"Good. We can help each other then."

The mayor came back with a tray of water and sodas. "I hope my mother hasn't strong-armed you into anything. Sometimes, she can get carried away." He exchanged a smile with his mother.

I doubted that. I could sense a very calculating, precise woman who did nothing without thinking about every angle and every consequence. She knew even before he called me back into this meeting how it would end up. She sat there during that press conference and picked out the reporter she felt could do the most damage and then she made sure her son steered clear of him. Then, she studied us like bugs under a microscope, and she knew. In the time it took the press conference to end, Mrs. Lee knew all she needed to know—about me, about Carter, about anyone who possessed a threat to her son's reelection.

"My mother has impeccable taste in people, and her judgment is seldom wrong. That is why we called you back. Tell me more about these abductions."

It was easy to see why this man was so well-liked. He had a smooth, polished tone like that of a trained stage actor, no hint of Ivy League snobbery. His voice was more like warm honey. He also had very gentle eyes and hair that was graying on one side of his head. He had just turned forty, but what really captivated me was the warmth of his spirit. This man genuinely cared about his job and the people. Even if they hadn't asked, I would have protected him from the likes of the Carter Ellsworths.

About a third of the way through my story, the mayor stopped me.

"You say they're missing from Oakland as well?"

I nodded and was surprised when he pulled out of his cell phone and started dialing. "Excuse me a moment, Miss Branson." He waited a moment then pressed the speaker button before setting the phone down between us. "It's to Deacon Smith's private line."

Deacon Smith was the mayor of Oakland. He and Mayor Lee had put their heads together in recent years to pull off some of the most amazing fundraisers on the West Coast.

"Did you call for another golf whuppin'?" came a deep, baritone voice.

"Name the time, you lucky dog. I'm afraid this is a business call. I have a reporter here who has some disturbing news I think you'll want to hear."

"I'm all ears."

Mayor Lee nodded for me to begin. So I did; uninterrupted. I wondered if maybe the line had gone dead.

"What do you think, Kai?" Deacon asked when I finished.

Mayor Lee sighed loudly. "My sources say she's reliable. She's not out to gain anything here, Deacon, other than to find her friend and maybe even save some lives. If we have a sicko out there and do nothing...well...you know how bad that looks."

Deacon chuckled. "Your sources, eh? You mean your mama?"

"Did you read the story about the homeless in the *Chronicle*?"

"Those her pieces?"

I answered. "Yes, sir, they are."

"Great photo of that dog and cat. Touching really. Excellent story."

"Thank you. Look, I know my colleagues and I can be hard to trust, but this stopped being about the story a long time ago. I've come to know these people well enough to care whether they're healthy and safe or not. All I'm asking is for you to put an investigator on it. That's all."

"That's it? You reporters never have one simple request."

"Mayor Smith, I grew up in Oakland. Graduated from Mills College. Believe it or not, I care. I'm just looking for your respective police departments to care as well."

"I'll take your lead on this, Kai. What do you think?"

"I think Miss Branson has the ability to enlist the population of both our cities with just a few strokes of her pen. For my part, I plan on speaking with the chief this afternoon. If someone is snatching our vulnerable homeless and we're seen as do-nothing politicians it won't bode well for either of our careers, Deacon. I say we go with her on this one. Help her out."

"Gotcha. I'll contact my boys, get the ball rolling on this end. Have your men call OPD and let's set up a task force between the two cities. People love the idea of task forces."

My eyebrows shot up. "Task force? Really?"

"Miss Branson, other than preying on children and the elderly, victimizing the homeless is the lowest of lows. Kai and I can't afford to sit around passively uninvolved. You'll get your task force Miss Branson."

"And you will get the golden ink from my pen Mayor Smith."

He laughed a laugh that sounded like it was coming from the bottom of a barrel. "It looks like we've got our bases covered. Anything else, Kai?"

"We still have that sewage dumping issue, but we can discuss that later. Maybe after I kick your butt on the links. Thanks, Deacon."

"Any time. Nice meeting you, Miss Branson." Then he clicked off.

"Deacon Smith is a very good man," Mrs. Lee said softly. "He is probably on the phone to the Oakland Police Department as we speak."

I rose. "I don't know how to thank you."

Mayor Lee looked over at his mother. "Oh, I think you do." He rose and shook my hand. "This time of year good press is hard to come by, but do know I am not just doing this because it makes me look good. I'm doing this because my mother believes you're a woman of integrity and you truly care about those missing people. They are my people as well, and if someone is... hunting them, we need to put a stop to it. As a public servant, I have discovered that few people are truly altruistic. You are one of them."

"I try, Mayor. Thank you so much for your time."

"Thank you for caring."

Handing him my card, I turned and bowed to Mrs. Lee.

When I finally got in my car, I had three missed calls with no message left from any of them; one call from Danica, and one from Finn. I called Finn first as I headed back to work. She wasn't there, so I left a brief message saying I didn't think the police department took a hit today; that I had effectively gotten what I needed without casting aspersions. Yes, I used the word aspersions. I grinned. She would like it, too.

Before I could even pull out of the parking lot, my phone rang. It was Carl.

"Yo, Princess! Where you been? We've been trying to call you all morning."

Ahh...my third missed message. "Sorry, guys. They make us

220

turn our cell phones off for press conferences. Please tell me you whiz kids have something for me."

"Well, we've come up with something for you, Princess, but we don't know if any of it's any good."

I snapped on my Bluetooth and switched over to it. "I'm listening."

"We've spent all morning working on this. Puff and Blow in the Hoarders' section has a direct correlation to the Judas Iscariot line."

I uncapped my pen and rolled down my window. "What do you mean?"

"Judas Iscariot was a traitor, right? Well, we searched all over the place to see if there was anything else to the name. We tried anagrams, Biblical references, the whole nine yards. We worked so hard on that one, our computers were smoking. Then, Roger input Judas. Just Judas. Do you know what Judas means on the street, Princess?"

"What?"

"Heroin. H. Horse. Shit. Nixon. Chick. China White. If this guy was writing in some kind of code, we think he saw something...something to do with heroin or drugs, maybe."

"How do you make that connection to the puff and blow section?"

"We think the kid could be talking about himself in the line, *and I watching felt my heart contract with pain.* As you know, the *Inferno* is Dante's idea of what walking through hell would be like. We think this kid likens his situation to hell, only *he* is the one describing everything to us using lines from the novel. As a savant, he doesn't have words himself, so he's using the text to say what he means."

It made complete sense for Smiley to communicate that way. "Keep going."

"Next, we looked up heliotrope. It's also known as a bloodstone and is used by warriors to become invisible in battle. The other attribute about a heliotrope is that it turns blood red when immersed in water. We think he means not one but both of the references."

"Good, good. Keep going."

"Do you remember Circe changed Ulysses' men to swine before keeping him prisoner for a year? Could be a clue. Could be nothing, but he does have a couple lines in here that deal with one thing turning into another, such as the swine and the heliotrope. He seems focused on something that isn't what it appears to be. I wish I had more for you, but we're still working on it. Roger thinks your little clue maker is brilliant and that we're just too dim to get it."

"He's not brilliant in the conventional way. He's a savant. Brilliant minds are often found behind the prison bars of autism."

"We'll go back to the drawing board and see if we can't figure out what he's trying to say, but I wanted you to know we're making headway."

"I appreciate this, Carl. Really."

"Don't count us out of the race yet, Princess. I'll call back when we get something."

I hung up and called Wes to tell him about my meeting with the mayor. Of course, he had already been informed about the first part of the press conference. Carter had called up ranting and raving about how unprofessional I was and what a rookie I looked like and how I had embarrassed the paper. That man had no boundaries.

"Of course he was steamed, Wes. I stole his thunder. Look, we're working on two completely different stories. I'm not going to apologize for the mayor preferring to hear my question over Carter's. You think he doesn't know Carter is out to get him?"

"Is he?"

"Come on, Wes. He's digging for dirt in a landfill. It's disgusting and I can't believe you're condoning it."

He laughed. "You either have the biggest balls on the planet or—"

"Or I'm right. Look, I happen to have the attention of the mayors on both sides of the bridge. I have their ear. They are creating a task force to look into what's going on with the homeless on both sides of the bridge. I'm not going to apologize for that."

"No one is asking you to, but that press conference was Carter's."

"With all due respect, Wes, Mayor Lee knows he's out for blood. He wouldn't have called on Carter if he was the only reporter in the room."

"I understand that, but how could the mayor have known? Carter usually flies pretty low under the radar."

"Not this time. Believe me, the tip-off did not come from me, but Kai Lee is well aware that Carter is gunning for him. It's absurd Carter is even crying foul."

"You have the go-ahead on your story, Branson. Let me worry about Carter. If you nail this story, Miss Branson, if you keep scooping the Trib, your life around here is going to get a helluva lot better. Keep me posted."

No sooner had I hung up than the phone rang again.

"Is this the magician?" It was Finn.

"Excuse me?"

"You must be some kind of magician to get people to jump through the hoops they're jumping through. Hats off to you. What in the hell did you say to Mayor Lee?"

"The truth. I decided to go right at him with it. The guy is a winner, Finn."

"Well, guess who is in charge of the task force?"

"You?"

She laughed. "I'm a beat cop. Try Jardine."

"You're kidding? That's excellent."

"I think he has a crush on you."

"Well, I can only handle one cop at a time."

She paused. "You think so? I hear cops can be a handful."

"I'm counting on it. So, tell me about the task force."

"We've got a coupla guys on it and OPD matched it. They're meeting this afternoon to see what's what. They'll be contacting you for sure. I know I'm always busting Jardine's chops, but the guy is a helluva detective. If anyone can get you where you need to go, it's him."

I nodded. I didn't doubt that. "Thank you for your support.

It means a lot to me."

"Well, you're beginning to mean a lot to me. I told you...if there was anything I could do, I will."

"Yeah, I remember some line about if I wanted to feel safe at night to sleep with a cop."

She laughed loudly. "I did say that, didn't I?"

"Was that an invitation?"

"Do you want it to be?"

I grinned. "I have work to do, so I better scoot."

"Be safe out there, Echo Branson."

I started to say goodbye, when I slipped in, "And Officer Finn? I do so want to feel safe at night," before hanging up with a smile on my face.

I flew across the bridge faster than I should have after I received a 911 call from Big George. He'd done an intake with a live one. All he would say about her was that she wouldn't talk and was afraid of him and everyone else. He was afraid she might hurt herself if we couldn't get her out of there.

"I came as soon as I could," I said when Big George met me at reception in his usual green scrubs.

"Thanks for coming, sweetpea. This one is a head shaker. Can't talk." Big George ran his hand over his bald head to wipe the perspiration away.

"Can't or won't?"

"Wish I knew. Hasn't said a single word since she got here. Kinda like that little gal you helped when you were here."

I was not yet a spotter like Big George, nor was I a hunter like Tip, but I *was* a very strong empath. I could possibly reach her where others couldn't. I was a communicator who hadn't yet earned my spotter's stripes. I wanted to. I wanted to help as many of us as I could. Maybe it was my Mills education or just the fact that I loved being a sane and healthy super, but I wanted to play the biggest role I could among my people. "I'll give it my best, Big George."

"I know you will."

"What was she brought in for?"

"She just stopped talking. Apparently, it was a slow progression from an outgoing, cute little girl, to this stoic, emotionless ten-year-old who says nothin' to nobody."

"She's only ten? What's she done so far?"

"She just sits there and watches the crazies. Doesn't interact, doesn't act out. Just watches." He strode along, rubber-soled shoes squeaking against the shiny white floor. I hurried to keep up with his long strides.

The elevator dinged and we got off. A cold chill swept over me, and for a nanoscecond, I thought about getting back in the elevator.

"It's okay, sweetpea. You ain't never comin' back here."

I worked to shrug off the anxiety and panic creeping through my veins. I'd never been as afraid as when I was in here, facing an uncertain future and small white cups of medication. "I'm sorry."

"Don't be. Take a deep breath. You'll be fine."

I did as he suggested, and threw my shoulders back. "What makes you think she's one of us?"

"It's in her eyes. It's the way she looks at me; like she knows I know, but doesn't know how to confirm it for me. There's no trust there like there was with you. This one will be quick to go on the offensive if threatened, so I've stepped lightly."

I nodded. "Good idea." A sharp screech from my left stopped me in my tracks. God, how I hated being here. It felt like yesterday a fourteen-year-old me walked these haunted hallways empty and alone. "Have they started drugging her?"

"Not yet."

"How bright is she?"

"From what I can tell...very...but that's just an old man's educated guess. Her aunt and uncle brought her in, dropped her off, and haven't been back. Haven't called, haven't done a goddamn thing."

I looked at my watch. I had a meeting with the task force at two. The sooner I could get out of this place, the better. Every time I came back to the hospital, I got the same cold chills, the same feelings of fear and despair in the pit of my stomach, and when the odors from the ward hit me, I was a frightened teenager all over again. "Give me the rundown." I tried shaking off the feelings and focusing on the job at hand.

"No violent tendencies, no history of seizures or depression."

"Meds?"

"Ritalin at eight. She stopped taking them just before she quit speaking."

"Depression?"

"Not that we can tell, no. She appears interested in the world around her; she's just stopped living in it. Aunt says she never interacts with other kids. She just...watches."

"Sounds familiar, eh, big guy?"

"I don't think she belongs here one way or the other. We gotta get her out."

"I'll see what I can do."

He put his arm around me and hugged me. "By the way...I love that car. The only problem is I keep gettin' eyeballed by the cops whenever I'm in the bad part of town. Racial profiling and all."

"I'm really glad you like it. It's a beautiful car and one you deserve."

"Here we are. I've kept her in her room in case you just want to read her through the window."

I shook my head. "You say she's not violent?"

"Not yet." He sighed. "But you know how that can change at a moment's notice. You want in there don't you?"

I stood in front of the door and peered in. "Please."

"I figured as much. I'll be right outside. Anything you need?"

"Her name?"

"Cindy."

Nodding, I opened the door, feeling every ounce of teenage anxiety coming back at me. If it had been scary for a fourteen-year-old, it must be frightening as hell to a ten-year-old.

When I walked in, Cindy was sitting in a chair, her legs dangling. She was wearing red Nike high-tops, jeans and a red WNBA T-shirt. She looked much younger than ten. Maybe it was her long blond hair and big blue eyes, but she seemed swallowed up by the chair.

"Hi," I said softly, kneeling down in front of her. I was careful to lower my shields very slowly. You never know when a newbie will pick up everything you're thinking or feeling, so I reinforced my blocks, lowered my shields, and yep, sure enough, little Cindy was one of us. She was trying to block, but was too young and inexperienced to actually succeed. She wasn't afraid, which surprised me. More...annoyed.

Interesting.

"My name is Echo and I am here to help you. Big George is a really good friend of mine and he asked me to come talk to you. Would you mind that?"

She shook her head, then she turned those big blue eyes toward me and they said more than any words ever could have. I had been very afraid when I was here and I was four years older, but she was not afraid at all. There was also no curiosity, as if she knew exactly who I was and why I was there. Her eyes were clear, focused and undeniably super. It unnerved me.

"I understand you don't like to talk to people."

She didn't take her eyes off mine as she shook her head.

"That's fair. There aren't many people worth talking to, huh?"

She surprised me with a wry grin, then shook her head.

"But you *can* talk, can't you?"

Barely a nod, then she looked away.

"Mind if I have a seat?"

She shook her head. I was picking up a lot of mixed emotions from her. She was nervous, but tentative, and was far calmer than I expected her to be. Truth to tell, she was incredibly composed for a ten-year-old.

"I was in here what I was fourteen."

She cocked her head and looked at me, one eyebrow raised

in question. She believed me and was curious to know more. A good sign.

"Yep, I thought I was going nuts. Loony. Whacko. You see, I can feel people's emotions. I can feel yours right now, and I know you're not afraid."

She slowly shook her head. No, she was not scared.

"This ability of mine was driving me insane because I didn't know what was happening to me. I belong to a special group of people with a special gifts. Some of us hear other people's thoughts, some of us can move objects without touching them. We all feel like we're going crazy until someone like Big George spots us and offers to help us out. He spotted you and called me to come help you. Do you want my help?"

Her blue eyes seemed to change color as she slowly nodded. She didn't want my help with her powers. She wanted help getting out of here.

"Fair enough. You know you can trust me, don't you?"

She blinked a couple of times, nodded again. I read her aura clearly and it indicated trust and acceptance, but something else. *She* was reading *me*, only not in the conventional sense. She was looking for hostility or aggression.

"Good. Because you can. I'm here to help. Now I need to ask you some questions. If you don't feel like answering you can just nod or shake your head, okay?"

Nod.

"Are you hearing voices?"

Shake.

"Can you move objects without touching them?"

Shake.

"Does it feel like you're being haunted, you know, like, by a ghost?"

She grinned, and then shook her head. She found that idea amusing.

"I'll bet you never knew there are some people who can actually talk to the dead. Can you?"

She chuckled. She actually chuckled, and then shook her head.

"Okay, I take it you're not one of those either." Leaning closer to her, I grinned. "Your aunt and uncle brought you here because something happened, right?"

She nodded.

"Something *did* happen?"

Nod.

"Is that why you don't talk anymore?"

Shrug.

I leaned back. "Hmm...Well, let me ask you this. This food here is a really bad, the company is even worse, the beds are hard and there are crazies everywhere. Would you like to get out of here?"

Her face broke into a song.

"Yeah. I thought you might say that. You know, I had to bust out of here when I was a kid. Sometimes you gotta do what you gotta do to get by in this life. I'm here to help you do that."

She was still grinning as she nodded.

"Now, I doubt we will have to bust you out, but we will find a way to get you out of here. Sound good?"

Nod.

"But there's a hitch...well...it's not really a hitch, but it is the one condition you have to agree to if I'm going to get you out of here. Do you know what a condition is?"

An eye roll typical of most teenagers was my answer. The grin fell from her face and I read distrust and doubt in her.

"There's a special place and a very special woman who can teach you how to control your powers." I paused and felt her change instantly. She liked the word powers. "She taught me and many others like me how to control our abilities. Would you like to do that?"

The grin reappeared and she nodded.

"I thought so. I loved it there and learned so much. You can too."

She cocked her head in a question she didn't need to ask.

"Why did I leave? We all have to leave once we grow into our skills. But I still visit and it is still my home." Rising, I extended

229

my hand to her. "Trust me?"

She nodded and put her little hand in mind. It was incredibly warm.

"Good. Now, let me see what I can do about getting you out of here. I promise I won't leave you in here, but give me some time to make arrangements, okay?"

When I left her room, Big George was just returning with her file in his hands. "I thought you were going to stay by the door."

"No need. You got to her. I could see that. I take it that means—"

"Yep, but I can't tell what she is yet. Says she doesn't hear voices or feel emotions or talks to ghosts. Also says that she doesn't move things. It's weird."

"Mama will know."

"If we can get her there."

"That shouldn't be too hard." Big George handed me her file. "Brought in by her aunt and uncle because she would no longer talk to them. They just don't have the time to put into her because they recently had triplets. They don't really want her back."

"Then, where are her parents?"

"No clue. They failed to make mention of that in the file, but I think this is worth a try. If we get their okay, it saves us the hassle of getting her out of here under cloak of darkness."

"Fine. Let's do it right away. You get her discharge papers, I'll make the call."

He nodded.

I left, mentally wiping the heebie jeebies off of me.

When I got to my car, I called Cindy's aunt and uncle and told them I was in admissions director for a special school in Louisiana. Let's just say it didn't take much convincing with crying babies and barking dogs in the background, Cindy's aunt agreed to talk with Melika to make the necessary arrangements. I think they were thrilled at the prospect of getting rid of a problem child.

That was when I jotted down my notes for my next story. The homeless weren't the only invisible ones in our society... there were thousands of unwanted, unloved and, yes, invisible children in the United States just waiting to be written about.

After making my notes, I called Melika and told her all I had ascertained from my meeting with Cindy, which wasn't much. Some spotter I would be.

"You still don't know what she is?"

"I couldn't tell, no."

"But she *can* talk, right? She is just choosing not to at the moment."

"Apparently. I don't know why she doesn't. I suspect we will know soon enough."

"Excellent work, my dear. I will call and make the flight arrangements. I can't tell you how much I appreciate your work on this, Echo. I know you have a lot on your plate right now, but you know the importance of time in these matters. I lost a twelve-year-old telepath last week. By the time we got to him, his brains were fried. It breaks my heart every time we lose one."

"Well, I think we got to this one in time. Let me know what else you need me to do."

"I will. Again, thank you my dear. Oh...and keep at it with your story. Bishop says you are on the right track. Believe in yourself, my dear. The rest of us do."

I had two messages beep me as I was talking to Melika. The first one was Luigi, making sure I was okay. The second was from Rupert the necromancer, telling me he was back in town and offering to take me out on his boat for lunch.

I hung up and started to the police station for my meeting with the task force. I was very excited to finally have a place for my voice; to finally have someone take me seriously. This story wasn't over by a long shot.

"The boys are all aflutter," Danica said when I arrived bearing lunch.

I'd stopped by and picked up four pepperoni pizzas, and

Danica took the boxes from me. "You better feed them *after* they tell you whatever it is that has them all pumped up. Apparently, someone found something useful, but the horrid creatures won't share it with me. They are enjoying colluding with you."

We walked briskly down the hall to the Bat Cave. At the door, I stopped, took a breath, and pushed it open. "Hey boys."

"Yo, Princess!" Carl said, turning from his laptop, his hair standing on end from running his fingers through it. "It's about time. We were going nuts over here." He waved us over.

We all gathered around Carl's computer. "Okay, whatcha got?"

Pushing his glasses up the bridge of his nose, he grabbed the mouse and started closing browser windows. "We dug deep into every word of every line you gave us and you're gonna want to marry us when we tell you what we found. We struck gold with the word heliotrope."

On the screen was a flower. "What's that?"

"A heliotrope."

"I thought you said it was a stone."

"It is, but we're pretty sure he meant the flower." Carl clicked on another window. Up popped four flowers. "Gotta give Roger his props. He never gave up."

"It just stuck out there, don't you think? *Amid that swarm...* it made me think of bees. Bees and flowers. So, I punched in heliotrope and *voila*, it's a flower."

"If I said *so what*, would it hurt your feelings?"

"Be patient, Princess. There's more. A lot more. We dug unsuccessfully for a bit, until Roger typed in Circe." Both guys grinned. Franklin nodded. I was beginning to feel their excitement even through my shields.

"The Circe line ties right in to the heliotrope line. The Dragon Circe is a heliotrope."

"Okay." I looked at Danica and shrugged.

"The Dragon Circe is only found in Colombia."

Now, they had my attention. "Keep going."

"Colombia has all the puff and blow and drugs anyone

could ever want. Eighty percent of the world's blow comes from Colombia."

"So, we think your savant was trying to say that the people who are taking your guys from the streets are Colombians."

I let out a huge sigh. "That's quite a stretch even for me."

The boys exchanged glances. "Oh ye of little faith." Carl punched a few keys. "This last line," he began reading it aloud. "*...For by the bridge and on that shapeless crew I saw him point to you with a threatening gesture, and I heard him called Geri del Bello.*"

"We looked up old Geri and discovered he was a cousin of Dante's father who was murdered. When Dante wrote the story, his death had not yet been avenged."

"There are several components to this line," Carl said. "I think the bridge piece is clear. Although which bridge is anybody's guess. Could be the Golden Gate, Bay, Dumbarton or San Mateo. The second piece, which one could completely overlook, is the word *crew*."

I frowned.

"Don't you get it, Princess? He's talking about the crew of a boat. With all of the water symbolism and boat imagery, he is talking about a ship!"

"Not any ship," Franklin added. "A Colombian ship."

I swallowed loudly. "You think he is trying to point us toward the crew of a Colombian boat near one of the bridges?"

All three nodded and turned toward me. "Given what we have here, your savant was trying to tell you there's a boat near a bridge either with Colombians on it or a Colombian flag or something Colombian. That boat could be where your guys were taken. Whether or not your homeless guys are still there remains to be seen. But if you believe Smiley was trying to send a message, we think this is it."

"He hasn't repeated himself for no reason, Princess. He is circling around it. Look at the clues: puff and blow is heroin. The Dragon Circe is found only in Colombia."

I rubbed my face and sighed loudly. "Okay, okay. Let's suppose you guys are right. Why on God's green earth would anyone abduct a bunch of homeless guys and put them on a boat?"

All three guys looked at each other. It was Roger who answered. "Well, we looked up Geri, and near as we can tell, old Geri was in the ninth circle or chasm of Hell where the people were frozen up to their necks."

I waited, not getting it.

"Frozen, Princess. Geri was frozen enough to let him still live."

My lightbulb began flickering. "Smiley was trying to tell us that the guys who were taken are being frozen?"

Carl sighed like a disappointed teacher whose student just failed. "No no no. We started questioning all the reasons why you would put someone on ice."

Franklin ticked them off with his fingers. "Death, torture, and—"

"And then we decided to see what the cartel is up to these days. What's the newest trend in money-making?"

"We started digging up articles on what the Colombian cartel is into these days, and here's what we found." Carl handed me a newspaper clipping he'd printed off. The paper was translated from the Venezuela press and the headline gave me the chills. Without reading the rest of the article, I looked at the boys, my stomach feeling queasy.

"Oh my God. You don't mean—"

Danica took the paper from me and read it in silence.

"Body parts," I said quietly, shuddering.

All three nodded. "Organ harvesting is big business nowadays. You can make a killing, pardon the pun, on fulfilling people's desire to extend their lives if you can give them the organ they need."

I held up my hand for them to stop. I was a little sick to my stomach. "Wait, please."

Danica lowered the paper. "Shit. It makes total sense when you think of the clues. Smiley has been trying to tell us that someone has snatched the homeless from our streets in order to harvest their organs. Think about it! Who would miss them? No one. You said so yourself."

Shaking off my revulsion, I nodded. "That explains why none of the missing are drug addicts. Drug-riddled organs would be of no use. They would need cleaner organs to sell."

"Right. Drug use would make many of their organs unusable. Alcohol, not so much, unless they were needing a liver. Even then, I'll bet some of these guys don't overdo it."

"So our missing men are still alive." I said this barely above a whisper.

"If our theory pans out, then yeah, we think so."

Throwing my arms around Carl I hugged him tightly. "Thank you. You guys are so good."

"If your savant was trying to tell you that the men are on a ship and they are being held in a refrigerator room, the obvious question we were left with was how did he know that?"

Danica and I looked at each other. "He escaped," we said in unison.

Franklin shook is head. "Or he knows the Judas."

My heart sank at the thought that Dante or his people could have anything to do with this. "I'm going with he knew the Judas. Someone on the streets is leading the kidnappers to men who do not have drug habits. Whoever it is, knows Smiley."

"Unless Smiley *is* the Judas." This came from Danica and we all turned to stare at her. "What? Think about it. The kid could be protecting his people by turning in others and not them. If he is a savant, then he is child-like. Who better to get to point the finger at the nondruggies than a scared kid protecting his family?"

That made sense. "And Smiley travels in both cities."

Everyone was nodding now.

"Then he wasn't kidnapped?"

Roger shook his head as he pulled out a map of the Bay Area. "Where were your guys taken from? Let's see if we can deduce some sort of pattern." He pinned the map to the corkboard and I started marking red X's where the kidnapped guys hung out the most. When I was done, I stepped back and saw the picture more clearly. "Damn it."

Danica stood next to me and nodded. "BART."

I stared at the map with new eyes. "They're all near BART stations because that's how Smiley gets around."

We all stood silently as this sunk in. Smiley was not only acting as Judas, but he wanted to save the very people he was ratting out. I had to hand it to him, it was brilliant. Luckily for him, I had brilliant on my side, too.

"So, Smiley is alive. He comes and goes with these guys in the van, not on his bike, which we know is locked up." I stared at the map some more. "He points out the guys he knows who are healthier than the others. They get nabbed and taken to a boat where they are put on ice until it is time to take an organ or two. Does anyone have anything to add?"

"Only that to a savant, or a child, the dumping of a body overboard would give the appearance of a heliotrope as it hit the water."

I nodded. Perfect clues.

"Now all we have to do is figure out which boat out in the bay has your guys." Roger shed his traditional smoking jacket and ran his hands through his hair.

"If we're talking about organ harvesting, my guys may already be dead," I said softly.

"Maybe not." This came from Franklin, who was reading something on *Google*. "The reference to the ninth circle is about being frozen. They wouldn't freeze our guys because that would do damage to the organs. Organ harvesting has to come from a live, healthy human being."

Roger was by his side now, reading. "You're right."

"They won't freeze them, but they *will* keep them on ice, as it were, at least until they harvest the organs. Maybe to detox them. These guys are all drinkers, right?"

I nodded, feeling hope fill my chest.

"He didn't mean literally frozen then. They may be in a cooler or a locker where it's cold, but not frozen."

"So we're looking for a fishing boat or other ship with something Colombian on it." I rubbed my hands together.

236

"Excellent." Looking over at Danica, I wondered why she was still staring at the map. "What are you thinking, Dani?"

Slowly turning, she frowned. "I know why they have them in a boat."

"Why?"

"Body disposal. They can harvest the organs and then just dump the bodies over the side. That's the heliotrope. They turn blood red when dropped into the water; so do the bodies. I hate to say it, but that's what Smiley's seen: the dead bodies going overboard. We may be too late."

I swallowed hard.

"Not unless..." Roger ran to his computer and started pulling up more information. "The liver and kidneys are the most sought after organs. I think Franklin is right. They might wait a few days or more for those organs to clean themselves out before removing them from the bodies. After all, there's no hurry. No one is going after them, right?"

"It is more likely they are dead," Carl said. "If I'm going to kidnap a bunch of people in order to yank their organs, I'm not going to keep them around so they can plot and plan. I'm taking whatever they have that's viable and then dumping the evidence as fast as I can."

Franklin stepped away. "You're creeping me out, man."

"Just realistic." To me he said, "We've taken this as far as we can, Princess. One way or the other, your guys are or were on a boat flying a Colombian flag or bearing some Colombian markings near a bridge. It's up to you, now."

Up to me? "How confident are you about this?"

Carl looked at the others. "Pretty confident. Think of all the homeless people living up and down the West Coast, from Seattle to San Diego. They're ripe for the picking because nobody cares."

"Human cargo," Franklin said. "Human cargo would be best transported by boat because the Coast Guard is about as ineffective an organization as ever existed. How hard would it be to hide organs in a fishing boat or drop bodies over the side?"

237

Franklin pointed to a map of the United States on another monitor. "Well over twelve thousand miles of coastline, the Coast Guard can't defend much, if any, of it."

"Boats come in, boats go out and no one is the wiser. Only two percent of the incoming boats are ever boarded and investigated. What percent of outgoing vessels do you think are ever inspected?"

"Less than that?"

"Bingo. Princess, there's a humungous Black Market for viable organs." Carl undid and redid his ponytail. "The cartel is nothing if not progressive. Why sit around waiting for a hundred thousand dollars worth of cocaine to be sold when you can make that much on just one organ transplant?"

I finally had to sit down before I fell down. "I knew it was big business, but a hundred grand?"

Carl nodded. "At the bare minimum. It's not big business but dangerous company, Princess. When the word Colombia came up, the Boss wouldn't let us do anything else." He shot a look over to Danica. "She knows this warped from story to danger in the blink of the proverbial eye...which are also harvested, by the way."

I glanced over to Danica, who was staring at me with an eyebrow raised. I knew what was coming next.

"Dangerous folks come from there, Clark. Dangerous and violent criminals who destroy everyone and everything who gets in their way."

Carl nodded. "There's no beating these guys. They're like what the Mafia used to be—ruthless, efficient, unstoppable. The FBI, CIA and Interpol are helpless against them. And as the American need changes, so does the cartel's ability to fill that need. Organs are one such need."

"Right. Plenty of rich Americans are unwilling to wait for the donor list to cough up an organ. There's always been a way around that, and here it is, in our backyard."

I looked over at Franklin's computer. There was a graph showing how many Americans needed a transplant and how many organs would be available. The odds were not good. Only thirteen percent of those on the list received organs. Eighty-seven percent of our population would die before they received the transplant. Who wouldn't scrape up a hundred thousand dollars to save the life of their child? Of their spouse? I realized we were on to something really huge.

Dangerously huge.

"So they put them on ice, clean them up a bit, and then basically dissect them."

Carl pulled a couple of sheets out from a file and handed them to me. "It happened off the coast of India a dozen years ago. They didn't find them, but they did find the boat. What they discovered on that boat was something out of a horror flick."

I took the printout and scanned it. They were, as usual, impeccable in their homework.

"We think what happened in India is happening here."

Danica stepped next to me. "Listen to this, Clark: *In 2003, an illegal kidney-procurement network was uncovered in South Africa. The donors were recruited mostly from the slums of Brazil flown to South Africa where the operation was performed, compensated between $6,000 to $10,000 and returned home. The South African middlemen were then able to sell the organs for as much as $100,000.* It's big business, Clark. Big, dangerous business."

As if she'd read my mind.

I read the rest of the piece, my palms sweaty. This was happening everywhere on a voluntary basis. The Chinese government actually sanctioned the harvesting of organs from its prison population, and in one year, performed over forty-one thousand operations. "My God—"

"In South America, they actually use the street urchins because their organs are young and viable. They sell mostly to an expanding Asian market, namely the Japanese, who as you may know, have a burgeoning class of millionaires."

"Your boy Smiley is on the inside of a story that will blow your career open if you live to tell about it."

"She's not going to tell about it," Danica said matter-of-factly.

"Leave this one to the cops, Clark. Tell the story after the fact, but leave the rest alone."

I looked up at her but said nothing.

Roger kept talking. "Besides their housing boat, they may have one or more smaller boats as well because they won't want to dump the dead bodies near the ship. They'll have to dump them further offshore."

"They'll also need a smaller boat to get the guys from the dock to the mother ship," Franklin said, his fingers skimming across the keyboard.

"In other words, Clark, step away from the God—Damned—Story." Danica's voice was steel. I had only heard her use that tone twice before in our lives.

I looked from one serious face to another and, one by one, they each nodded. "Even if you are able to convince that task force of what is happening, politics would take over before justice. Even the United States government can't control the cartels. Why do you think eighty percent of the world's cocaine comes out of Colombia and yet, the United States has never imposed a Cuban-like sanction against them?"

Danica walked over to me and took my hand. "Nothing good can come of this. Tell Finn. Tell the task force, then let it go."

I stared at her in disbelief.

Danica held her hand up. "And lest you doubt the four of us really, really smart people are right, then ask Melika. Hell, ask Tip. This is not your fight, and it's not a fight you can win."

Then whose fight was it?

I heaved a huge sigh. I hated when she used Melika to back herself up. "I understand what you're all saying but—"

"But nothing, Clark. Goddamn it, you are way out of your league on this one. I'm sorry, but you really are." Releasing my hand, Danica took a folder off the desk and handed it to me. "Read this."

The boys were all nodding. "The Boss is right. Walk away. It's probably too late anyway. More than likely, your friend is a goner."

"But what if he isn't? What if there's a boat out there with our guys in it? What if everything you're saying is true and I do nothing? How do I live with myself knowing I sat cowering in the corner doing nothing?"

"The way the rest of us live with ourselves. You have to ask yourself why you are the only one willing to risk your neck on this."

I looked into Danica's eyes. I didn't have to be empathic to read her fear. Whatever they had discovered in their digging had scared the hell out of every one of them.

"Forget what they taught us at Mills and take care of yourself." Danica opened the folder and rifled through the pages. "There's a reason the cartels are still around, still powerful, still in our midst, and it's a big reason. They. Are. Killers."

I took the folder from her. "I tell you what; let me ask Melika about it. If she says—"

"Why not ask Tip?" Danica asked.

I shook my head. " No way. If she so much as thought I was going to be in danger, she would be here like that." I snapped my fingers. "Even if I didn't need her help, which I don't."

"Some day, you'll realize what Tip is all about, but for now, you need to proceed with caution. These are not the kind of people you want to piss off. You might win this battle, but these people are warlords, Clark. Warlords who seldom lose."

I nodded. "We'll see. I'll have to think about it." Gathering up the file, I looked over at the guys who were eyeing the pizza. "You guys are the best. You know that, don't you?"

"We're only the best if we can keep you alive."

"I'm going to be fine. I swear. I'll read everything in the file. I'll arm myself with knowledge, but I'm not walking away from this." I started out the door with Danica hot on my heels.

"Clark. I know how you get, and I am begging you to let this one go."

"Dani, I'm not sure what I'm going to do, but if there's a boat under a bridge, I don't know how I can turn away, cartel or no cartel."

She nodded slowly. "I have something for you in case you simply can't stop yourself."

I followed her back to her office. She opened her desk and pulled out the revolver she had threatened to buy for me. Then, she pulled out something I initially thought was a phone.

"This is your direct link to the boys' computers. It's a prototype for a machine Roger has been working on. It's also a video camera for conferencing. Has a camera, webcam capability, and uploads via satellite, not wi-fi or cable. That means it doesn't matter where you go, you are always online. We all have one. You can video conference with one at a time or all of us while also e-mailing or surfing the Internet. This way, if you need instant information, we can access it for you right away. It's just a prototype, mind you. Presently, we're having some problems with the embedded camera, but we're working on that."

I opened the tiny computer and was amazed at the clarity of the screen. Suddenly, Carl's face was on the monitor. "Yo Princess. Pretty cool, eh?"

I almost dropped it. He scared the crap out of me.

Danica nodded. "The moment you open it, all of our computers beep. The fact that it's linked to a satellite means no dead spots, no dropped calls, and has a better frequency and longer range. Opening the monitor signals the rest of us on the same vidmeet protocol. Let's just say it's our way of keeping tabs on you."

I marveled at it. "Kind of like some cyber babysitter."

"Not what it was intended for, Princess, but if it will keep you safe...safer...then so be it. Take the vidbook with you and keep in touch. Regardless of how you do this, it will keep you connected to the brains of this operation...and that would be us."

I nodded. "Fine then. Are you sure you guys don't just want to put a bug up my butt?"

Carl grinned. "Don't have to. There's a GPS system built right in."

"Of course there is."

Standing up I wrapped my arms around Danica and hugged

her tightly. "Believe in me, Dani. I can do this. It's not like I'm going out there to haul them in myself."

"Right. You're an empath, Clark, not some superhero. Remember that, will you?"

"I'll try."

Funny thing was, I wasn't sure there was a difference.

"Hi, Mel. It's me." Shifting ears with the phone, I felt my shoulders relax as they always did when I talked to her.

"I was hoping you'd call. We've made all of the arrangements to get Cindy out of there, and they are willing to release her into your custody tomorrow morning."

"Into *my* cu—"

"Just until we can get her out here. George can't come, so I bought you and the girl an open ticket. I know this is a bit of an inconvenience for you right now, but it's the best I can do at such short notice."

"I can handle it, really."

"I know you can. They'll meet you at the hospital tomorrow morning at eight."

"Eight. Got it."

"As for the piece you are struggling with, all I can tell you, all that you're *willing* to hear is that you need to do what you have always done; and that's to follow your heart. It's how you've always managed your life even when you were a young girl. I have no doubt you will do the right thing for your life...whatever that may be."

"And if I'm in danger?"

There was a slight pause. "Echo, my dear, the world we live in is fraught with danger. Just because we have extraordinary abilities does not mean we are safe from these dangers. We each must look into our own heart to determine whether or not we are willing to take these dangers on."

"Like the time you threw chicken to that alligator?"

"Precisely. Remember when you first came to the Bayou, how you couldn't believe we lived among them?"

"Yes. They were so big and scary, and I knew nothing about them except how dangerous and scary they looked."

"And Tip explained that our 'gators were no more dangerous than the squirrels in the suburbs, remember?"

I grinned. "Like it was yesterday."

"Well, now you live in a world where danger is everywhere. You can shrink from it, attack it head-on, or walk away, but regardless of what you do there will always be danger lurking behind every corner. I understand Danica's fear, why she cautions you to be careful; because you should be. But life is fuller when you follow your heart, and if your heart guides you to those dark places where danger lies in wait, then you must forge ahead with every bit of power the universe has given you. It's your way, my dear. It's simply who you are."

I became a reporter because truth was my religion, my honesty and my creed. I couldn't very well run from it just because it was hard or scary or dangerous. My truth now was that I just might have an opportunity to save the lives of people who deserved better than what the universe had given them.

I guess that settled it then. "Thanks Mel. You always did know what to say."

Sitting at the table with Tripod in my lap, I pored over the file and notes and printouts Danica and the boys had given me. I was astounded by what I read.

Villagers in a destitute part of India who sold their kidneys in a similar scheme received about $800 for their organs. At one time, Israeli organ brokers were obtaining kidneys from people in former Soviet-bloc nations and transplanting them into patients who traveled to Turkey for the operation. For the broker, there was money to be made—one Israeli middleman in the organ trade made $4 million before being caught.

Sitting back, I whistled and shook my head and kept reading.

There are 99,564 people on the waiting list for an organ transplant in the U.S. 13,813 people were lucky enough to receive an organ. More than 15,000 Americans die each year while waiting for an organ. In Europe, 25-30% die before they can receive an organ transplant. The shortage of transplant organs has caused some very unscrupulous people to take advantage of the desperate people in a race against death. Out of options, many in need of an organ are turning to an underground black market.

I started scratching out more notes.

People donating their organs to black market brokers are generally poor and from impoverished or underdeveloped countries. In December 2007, authorities in Africa and Brazil broke up one of these black markets. These are just a few of the worldwide documented cases against organ brokers that pay impoverished unassuming people to give up a kidney. Most of these cases are only brought to light when the black market harvester does not pay the donor.

I sat back, stunned. It was beginning to make sense to me now. If Americans were paying for illegally gotten body parts, the organs needed to be harvested close by. The overhead would be minimal and the harvester would not have to pay out a single cent. It would be 100 percent profit. Not only that, instead of paying forty grand for one kidney, the harvesters could get both plus a liver, heart, and anything else they felt they could sell.

My stomach twisted as I thought of Bob.

I called Finn.

"Hey, Echo. I was gonna call when I had a second, but I never seemed to get one. Jardine told me the task force is starting its homework."

"That's good. Look, I think I know what's going down in regard to my story and it's big. I was wondering what you think I should do if I came upon information the task force might need, or if I should just back off now that they're on it."

"You got more evidence after your meeting? Busy bee. Give whatever you have to Darryl. Give it to him and trust him to do the right thing with it. I can't speak for the other members of the task force, but I do know he'll do everything he can to help. You give him something to work with and I guarantee you'll get some answers. Jardine's a good guy."

"I'll do that. Thanks. Be careful out there Deputy Dog."

"You do the same, Lois Lane."

Opening the little computer, I watched as the tiny camera icon popped on and the monitor came to life. It was weird knowing that somewhere in the wide expanse of cyberspace four different people might know I had logged on to their own personal electronic universe. I had to admit that the little vidbook was pretty cool.

"Need something, Princess?" It was Carl. Then the screen split and Roger was on as well. "Hey Princess. Taking her out for a test drive?"

I couldn't help but grin. These were my bodyguards? Three geeks and a woman who feared nothing? I suppose it could have been worse. At least I had brains, beauty *and* brawn. "Hi guys. Yeah, I'm just learning how to use this thing. It's a neat little gadget."

"Want me to walk through it with you?"

For the next fifteen minutes, Carl walked me through downloading my notes to Darryl Jardine. I was really proud when I hit send. It was easier than I expected and I felt so technologically savvy. The boys congratulated me and sent me on my way, making me promise never to leave home without it. Apparently, I was worthy of my very own GPS tracking device.

Closing my eyes, I tried to go to sleep, but I had monkey mind and couldn't sleep. My life had suddenly become very full, and now I had a ten-year-old mute girl to take care of until I could get us on an airplane to New Orleans.

New Orleans.

There were times when it pulled me like a beckoning lover. Now was one of those times. I longed to be on a boat in the Bayou with the sun at my back and the alligators on the banks of the river watching with one lazy eye. I was already looking forward to going back with little silent Cindy. I wondered what she would think. I wondered how big the Bayou must look to a little girl of ten. I remembered how big it looked to me at first, but after I got used to it, it wasn't nearly as big or as scary. I hoped she would like it.

Tossing around in bed, I thought about Smiley and Bob. Was

I too late to help them even if I could? Was I even on the right track?

The file spoke for itself. This wasn't something new in our country. Our throwaways were being snatched off our streets and no one was lifting a finger to help. As of 2008 there were an estimated 700,000 children reported missing by the National Incidents Studies of Missing and Abducted Children. Over half a million missing children? Why weren't we hearing about this every day? Why wasn't someone doing something? The rest of the numbers were staggering as well, and it looked like the government simply passed many of them off as custodial abductions...too domestic for anyone to really go after.

Almost a million missing children. The number was mind-boggling. If children could disappear so easily, imagine how many other people were taken with no one around to monitor them or care. The homeless were the perfect choice to act as incubators for needed organs.

Suddenly, my eyes popped open.

Incubators.

If the organs were to be viable, they needed to be in good working condition, and almost all of the guys out on the streets had a drinking problem. If they put them on ice, then carved them up, them dumped them, they had to have a way to get the organs to their clients. What would be the best way to do this?

Chopper.

Opening the vidbook, I sent another e-mail to Jardine. If they looked for any chopper licensed in the area, they might find evidence to support my theory. Between that and looking for a ship that flew a Colombian flag, he should be able to come up with some place to turn.

I was exhausted. I had sat up thinking and thinking of ways to help Bob. So how could I just walk away? Bob was my friend. He came to me for help. After all, what would the quality of my life have *been* if people hadn't risked something to help *me*?

Rolling over, I came face-to-face with Tripod. I could see him blinking at me. "Hey there, cutie." Reaching over, I scratched him under his chin and he purred loud enough to wake the dead. Everyone had told me to put him down; that a cat with three legs couldn't get around or have a decent life. They were all wrong. He'd been a throwaway once. Against all odds, a three-legged cat had not only survived, but had become a big part of my life.

Staring into his blue eyes, I sighed. It didn't really matter what anyone else thought about this. It was no longer a story to me, but a debt I needed to repay to the universe.

I was out of the house before seven. My first stop was to the Berkeley Marina. If there was a cargo boat by the bridge, I needed to know, and there was one man I knew who had just the boat to take me there.

"*Necromancer*," I said, reading the name of the boat and grinning.

"I like to hide in plain sight," Rupert said, leaning over the railing. "I wondered who was calling this morning, but damned if I could find my phone."

"You're a hard man to track down."

"Not really. You just have to be persistent." He was dressed all in white and was wearing a white captain's hat. Salt-and-pepper hair peeked out from underneath the cap.

"Apparently, you're expecting me."

He grinned. Rupert was about fifty years old and had a year-round tan that went well with his silver hair. "I know you think of me as just a lowly necro, but I have many other powers as well."

"Then you *were* expecting me."

"I was expecting a super, yes, but you are a pleasant surprise. I got your message when I was in Catalina. I wish I had been here to help."

"Can you help now?" I walked around the side of the boat to the plank connecting the boat to the dock. "Permission to come aboard?"

Rupert tossed his head back and laughed. "Aye, aye, matey, come aboard." He reached out and helped me across the plank. "Would you like the nickel tour?"

"Absolutely."

Rupert's boat had one of the most spectacular living spaces I had ever seen. Cherrywood adorned walls polished until it practically reflected my face. Venetian tiles lay in the spacious kitchen complete with stainless steel appliances. The place was gorgeous and roomier than one might think of a yacht. Every little thing was top quality, from the doorknobs to the crown molding. If I had come in here blindfolded I would never have guessed that I was on a boat.

We went up to the deck, where he pushed a button and a table lowered from a wall while two chairs rose from the floor. "I don't care much for clutter," he said as he served me coffee. "So, I had this made to keep out of my way while I was dancing."

I accepted my mug. "Dancing?"

"Sure. I love to dance. The rumba, the salsa, the swing. Don't care much for the flamenco and tango, but the others are big fun if you have the space. Please, have a seat."

I sat down across from him and wrapped my hands around the warm mug. "You have a beautiful home."

"Thank you. It suits me." He sat down. "Now, tell me why you're really here. As much as I wish it was to engage with my scintillating and charismatic personality, I'm pretty sure this is about business." He grinned softly and looked out over his mug. "Melika business?"

"Not this time. I wanted to take you up on your offer to sail the bay."

The corners of his mouth twitched as he set his mug down. "You don't beat around the bush, do you? Not much has changed since your college days. What's this really about, Echo?"

"If I told you I needed to see if there was a certain boat in the bay, would you think I was nuts?"

"Actually, I would think you are a reporter getting a story. But if you want to use my very expensive boat, you'll have to tell me the whole story. This is my home, Echo, and if I'm going to put it at risk I need to know what I'm risking it for."

So I told him. All of it. When I finished my explanation, he leaned back in his chair. He was wearing what could only be described as a Cheshire cat grin. "So let me get this straight. You want to cruise around looking for a ship full of abducted people who may or may not have been taken by the Colombian cartel in order to carve them up for their organs for the Black Market. Does that about sum it up?"

I nodded. I couldn't tell how he felt about my request. He was a great blocker; nothing leached out. "I'll know it when I see it, Rupert. I'm sure of it."

He studied me for a minute. "When do we leave?"

I blinked several times. "That easy?"

"Sure. You're not asking me to do anything illegal; not that it matters, of course. I've done quite a few illegal maneuvers in my life. It's a beautiful day for us to sail, E. Just tell me what time and your chariot will be ready."

"You do understand this could be dangerous, right?"

"We're locating a boat, not going aboard. It's not like they'd come after us in broad daylight. I say let's see what we can see."

"I really appreciate this, Rupert."

He reached over and laid his hand on mine. "We have to stick together, Echo. I'll never forget how wonderful you were with that boy last year. He was so scared, and yet, you managed to calm him down enough so that we could get to the heart of the matter. I think your skills are being wasted on the naturals. I hope someday you realize how much *our* people need you."

"For now, there are a bunch of homeless guys who need me."

"Just name your time and I'll be ready."

"Well, I have to pick up a little girl, so how about eleven?"

"Eleven it is. I'll have the *Necromancer* up and at your disposal."

When I got back to my car, I sat there a moment shaking my head. It had been awhile since I had dealt with as many supers as I had in the past week and a half. It was weird, really. At Mills there were a couple, but we never interacted. I think they were trying to live the "normal" life. After I graduated and started at the paper, I was too busy to notice, so all this extra psionic energy was beginning to kick my ass. Rupert was incredibly powerful, yes, and I still hadn't determined the extent of his powers, but he was a great blocker and a superior necromancer. Now, I was on my way to pick up another whose powers I was unsure of. No wonder I had a headache.

An hour later, I was pulling out of the hospital with Cindy quietly occupying the passenger seat of Ladybug. Her aunt and uncle had been there and done their best to appear concerned about Cindy; sending her to a special school lessened their guilt. But I knew better. These people were relieved and practically gleeful at the prospect of getting rid of her. It was heartbreaking, really, to see how easy it was for these two to dump her in the hands of a woman they didn't even know. Whatever Cindy had done in their home had made them very afraid of her; so afraid it was palpable.

So, after filling out numerous forms and whatnot, the family said tearless goodbyes. Not even Cindy shed a single tear. She was done. Not that I could blame her, of course. It's very difficult to see any good in a human being who could dropkick you to the curb of a mental hospital. Still, there was no love lost between Cindy and her aunt, so maybe Melika's was best for her after all. At least there, she would find a family like I had.

"You're not sorry to be leaving them, are you?" I asked, looking over at her. She shook her head. "I thought as much. Didn't like living with them, eh?"

She held her palm up and then flicked it over.

"Oh, I see. It was the other way around?"

Nod and a sigh.

"Well, don't you worry because you're going to love it where you're going. I know I did. It was where I learned about my special skills and how to use them. You'll love Melika. She's a really good teacher and a wonderful friend."

At the word friend, Cindy's head swiveled toward me, her eyes two huge question marks.

"Yes, she's now my friend and she cares about me. Even

though she hasn't met you, she cares about you as well. We all will. We are like a little family who looks out after each other. I'll be like a big sister to you. Would you like that?"

Vigorous nodding.

"Okay. Now I've got some boring adult work to do, so you have to promise me one thing."

She looked at me, expressionless.

"You have to stop talking so much."

I was rewarded with a huge smile that spread across her face and made her eyes light up for the first time.

"I take it that means yes?"

She stuck her hand out to me and I released the wheel to shake hers, marveling at how warm it was. I really liked her. Maybe she just reminded me of me a long time ago, but I liked the spirit in this girl. She had *chutzpah*.

I drove a little farther until I heard this strange beeping sound. Cindy looked in my bag and pulled out the vidbook. She started to hand it to me when she realized I was driving.

"Go ahead," I said. "Open it up."

Cindy nodded and then opened it.

"Goddamn it, Clark...Oh...you're not Clark." It was Danica in all her foul-mouthed glory. "I...uh...where's Echo?"

Cindy grinned and held the vidbook so I could see it. I decided it was best to pull over so I could talk. "Hey there. What's wrong with a cell phone?"

"I'm sorry for my potty mouth. The boys wanted a test run. Where have you been?"

"Picking Cindy up. Why? Are you keeping tabs on me?"

"You know it. I know you, Clark. Until you tell me that you're letting this story go, I'm watching you like a hawk."

"Well here I am. I've got Cindy until tomorrow night. Then we're on the redeye to NOLA."

"And your story?"

"I'm taking her out on the water with Rupert and—"

"Oh hell no. You think I don't know what you're doing? You're looking for that goddamned boat!"

"No I'm not. We're just...uh...sailing around."

"I'll give you two seconds to take that lie back."

I looked over at Cindy. She was smiling. "Fine. Yes, I am looking for the boat, but that's it. If I find it, I'm calling Jardine and the task force and letting them take care of it."

"Promise that's it?"

"You said so yourself; I'm not a superhero. I just play one on TV."

"Not funny. Promise me you'll be careful."

"I will."

Her face softened a little. "How's the kid?"

"Keeps talking my ear off. I can't get in a word edgewise." I winked at Cindy, who chuckled. "I think we'll be fine."

"Let me know if you need anything."

"Will do."

"What do you think of the vidbook?"

"It's pretty cool. Does it have games? I was sort of hoping to give Cindy something to do this afternoon."

"Games? Are you insane? Who works for me? Only the biggest gamers on the West Coast. See that red arrow button? Press it."

I did and up came the boys' names as well as Danica's, only hers said DaBoss and mine said, of course, DaPrincess. "Okay."

"Scroll down to Carl's name and hit enter."

I did, and in less than two seconds, the screen split and Carl was on one-half of the monitor. "Yo Princess."

I cut my eyes over to Cindy, who had her hand clamped over her mouth because she was snickering. "Hey Carl. I've got a kid with me and she would like to play some cool games on this thing. Would you mind walking her through it?"

"No prob."

"There's just one problem. She doesn't talk."

"Sounds like my kind of girlfriend. Then all she has to do is listen. Can she do that?"

I looked at Cindy, who nodded. "She says yes."

"Cool. Hand her over."

"And Dani? Don't worry. I won't do anything stupid."

Handing the vidbook back to Cindy, I continued to the marina. A part of me considered taking her back to my apartment, but I just didn't want to leave her alone. It didn't seem right. It was bad enough that she had been handed off to someone she barely knew; the last thing she needed was to be kicked to the curb twice in one morning. Besides, this was just reconnaissance to see whether or not anything would pan out.

As I drove back to Berkeley, my mind wandered around in search of any clues or ideas that I might have missed. If Rupert and I found a boat and he could get us close enough, I would be able to sense the energy of the individuals inside. It was possible I could detect Bob's energy, but not if he was surrounded by a lot of other energy. The key, again, was Smiley.

Autistic and Down's Syndrome people have a different energy field than the rest of us. When I was in the Bayou, Melika taught me about the different kinds of emotional energies different people emanate. If Smiley was truly a savant, I would be able to pick it up...*if* we could get close enough.

Then I would contact Jardine and the task force and maybe even the Coast Guard. Danica was right that I was no superhero. I sure as hell didn't want to get in the line of fire. All I needed to do was do what I do best: feel.

Turning to Cindy, I asked if she had ever been on a yacht. She shook her head.

"Well, before we go back to my place we are going on a yacht with a friend of mine. He is...well...he's one of us. You can trust him, okay?"

She frowned a second and then pointed her finger back and forth at me and her.

"What's one of us?" I asked. She nodded. "That's a good question. One of us means that we are not like everybody else. We're special. You're special, and Melika is going to show you just how special you are. Does that sound like fun?"

She squinted and pointed at me.

"Not enough, eh? We are paranormals, which means above

the norm. We call ourselves supers because our powers are supernatural. That's what we all are."

She nodded again. I so wished she could talk. As odd as it seemed, I enjoyed the company. It was nice to have someone to talk to even if she didn't talk back.

"Rupert is a really nice guy. It's his yacht and he's taking us out so I can see if a certain boat is floating around the bay. Does that sound like fun?"

Cindy gave me to thumbs-up and a huge smile.

"It's a beautiful day for being on a boat. Of course, anything is better than being back in that hospital, huh?"

Nod. She closed the vidbook and dropped it in her backpack.

When we got to the *Necromancer*, Rupert was standing by the side of the boat, waving. "Well, who have we here?" he asked, kneeling in front of Cindy as she boarded. "Hi there. I'm Rupert, captain of the *Necromancer*. Do you know what a necromancer is?" Rupert cast a look over at me. I nodded. "A necromancer is someone who can communicate with the dead. Pretty cool, huh?"

Cindy nodded.

"Her name is Cindy."

"Welcome aboard the *Necromancer*, Cindy. Feel free to check it out."

Which is precisely what she did. She scrambled all over it, high and low, and I was worried she would get into something.

"Stop worrying, Echo, She can't hurt anything. She's just a kid."

"Thanks, again, Rupert." Looking out at the robin's egg blue sky, I inhaled the fresh sea air. It was a clear day with low swells and high-flying gulls.

Rupert rose and helped me aboard. "It's been awhile since I've had two good-looking women on my boat, so the pleasure is all mine. Now, I've got the best equipment of any boat this size, so the chances of us finding a ship the size of what you're talking about are pretty good." Rupert pulled the ropes and released the

255

Necro from the pier. "I'll get us out to the open water, Echo, if you and Cindy would bring the food up from the galley. I took the liberty of having a little spread delivered."

A little spread?

When Cindy and I went downstairs, we were treated to a buffet that included paper thin slices of lox, creamy pate, three different kinds of cheese, fruits and vegetables, muffins, bagels, lunch meats, condiments and several chocolate truffles along with chocolate-covered strawberries.

Cindy and I just stared at the food. Her eyes were as big as mine. "Oh wow. I told you he was a nice guy."

She nodded quickly.

I lightly touched Cindy's head as she set the tray down and went back downstairs. "Expecting an army?"

"This is kind of like a stakeout, and you have to have good food for a stakeout. We will not perish."

I smiled at him. He had a boyish charm I'd always found quite appealing. "What's our plan?"

"Well I think we should cruise by the Bay Bridge first. My equipment will locate all craft within twenty miles of the *Necro*. When we spot one, we can just cruise by and let you take a look. I take it we're looking for a vessel at least forty feet long that's going to hold a minimum of twelve men. I mean, if you're carrying anywhere from one to two dozen kidnap victims, they would be best in the cargo hold of a larger ship."

"Preferably the kind of ship that would go unnoticed and unbothered by the Coast Guard."

Rupert turned and studied me. "Then you're looking for a ship like this one or a container vessel. Even after nine-eleven, our ports are our weakest link. Hell, you could back a cargo ship up to any pier in San Francisco and load it full of stolen goods and no one would be the wiser. We just don't have the security, so you're looking for either really rich or really poor."

"What if it flew a Colombian flag?"

"Why not just shoot off a flare? I seriously doubt they are flying that flag."

256

He was right. But if there was no Colombian flag, what had Smiley seen? "You find the vessel, Captain and I'll let you know if there's energy in it that matches our missing guys."

Rupert looked at me. "Melika said you are powerful...but I never imagined—"

"I know, I know. Empaths don't get a fair shake from the rest of you. I mean...what's the benefit of knowing how someone feels?"

"Actually, I could see a huge benefit to it. And it must be very helpful in your field."

"It has its perks."

Rupert and I climbed the ladder to the Captain's loft, or whatever it's called. "And we'll do what when we find the boat?"

"Call the Coast Guard."

He laughed. "Um...I hate to break it to you, but they're not like cops, you know? The Coast Guard is seriously undermanned in this part of the country. It's not like they're lurking around the corner waiting for a crisis."

"Then we call the task force see if they have any power to get a boat to check it out."

"So we're just going to recon the boat and call it a day?"

"That's the plan. I don't want any trouble, Rupert. I wouldn't put either you or Cindy in danger. Speaking of which, I need to go down and check on her."

"I'll let you know when we are in visual of any boats."

Downstairs, I sat across the table from Cindy who was playing a game on the vidbook. With every passing moment away from the hospital, her features began to soften and she looked less and less like a little girl and more like a teenager. "Having a good time?"

She nodded.

"I'm really glad. Now, I want you to know that once we get you to Louisiana you can always call me, day or night if you ever feel lonely or just want to hear my voice, okay?"

Nod. Blink.

"I would never let anything bad happen to you. Do you trust me?"

257

She nodded, and to my surprise, pointed at me.

"What? Oh. Do I trust you? Absolutely. I think you're a really good thing."

This made her happy. Trust is just a hard commodity to come by when you're a ten-year-old supernatural kid whom no one understands. I wondered what she had done to make her aunt and uncle distrust her enough to ship her off so easily, but it must have been a whopper. That's how it usually happened with most of us; a display of our abilities was the straw that broke the camel's back. I wondered what her straw was.

"Coming up on a few boats, Echo," Rupert announced from above.

I jumped up as we approached.

"There are rules to water navigation, just like there are rules of the road. How close do you need to be?"

"This is good. Just keep going by it. The amount of energy I'm looking for is pretty large, so I'll know it when I feel it."

"Ten-four. I'll just keep cruising boats until you see one that fits the bill. Do you think Cindy would like to sail the boat?"

"Oh, Rupert, I think she should really like that."

I helped Cindy up the ladder. "Have a good time. Just don't crash us, okay?" She took off up the ladder as if she was born to it.

As I stood on the deck overlooking the blue-green water of the San Francisco Bay, I felt a sense of calm wash over me. I don't know if it was because I was really doing what I longed to do or because I had done the right thing by Cindy, by Bob and by Smiley. I just felt really good. I wanted this story. I wanted a happy ending for Cindy. I guess I just wanted it all.

We must have checked out a dozen or so boats before I heard Rupert cut the engines. "Cargo ship off the port side. It's not flying a Colombian flag, but you gotta take a closer look."

I looked over at the ship, lowered my shields and was nearly knocked over by a wave of energy that had not been present on the other boats.

"Umm...Rupert?"

He came down the ladder and stood beside me. "That's it, isn't it?"

I nodded slowly and pointed to the name of the ship. It was called the Juan Valdez...a Colombian coffee bean farmer in 1970's television ads. "That's what Smiley saw."

Rupert nodded. "You picking up anything?"

I nodded again. "Strong energy bundle, coupled with the kind of energy I'm looking for from a certain young man." My heart picked up its pace and I nodded once more. "That's the one."

"Would binoculars help?"

I shook my head. "Not really. My kind of energy read has a limited distance. Energy has a certain distance it can travel before it dissipates. This is...really strong. Strong and desperate There's a fear even the weakest empath would be able to pick out."

"How sure are you? You might want to...oh shit." Rupert was looking through a pair of binoculars, and before I could answer, the whining sound of a speedboat drowned out his words as it approached us. It came from behind the bow of the cargo ship. "Looks like we have company!" Rupert yelled, motioning to the approaching boat. It was one of those superfast ski boats and it was coming right at us. Super fast. "Don't see many of those on the bay!" Rupert yelled. "Better call in the troops!"

"Maybe they're just reconning us."

Rupert looked at me sideways. "Don't risk it. I'm reading death all over that boat. What about you?"

I concentrated harder than I had in a long time. I felt fear, death, hopelessness and despair. I also felt anger, wrath and boredom.

"I've got death. What you getting, Echo?"

"Unfriendly. Curious. Suspicious. Make the mayday call now, Rupert."

The speedboat cut its engines when it was about fifty yards away. Rupert had just brought the radio to his mouth, and lowered it before saying anything.

"Go below," I said to Cindy. She nodded and then slowly went down the ladder, looking over the side of the boat at the speedboat floating closer to us, eyeing us, weighing their options.

"Put the radio down," I ordered Rupert when I was hit by their dark energy.

"Nice boat!" yelled the driver of the speedboat as he pulled alongside us. The two other men on board wore postures of aggression. They were about twenty feet away now. The driver was a Caucasian male of about twenty-five, heavyset and wearing clothes that weren't right for sailing. He had on a brown leather bomber jacket, jeans, steel-toed boots and dark glasses. His right hand rested inside his jacket. Every alarm in my body was going off, so I reached for Rupert's hand and gave him a quick squeeze. Luckily, he had replaced the radio before they saw him.

We were in trouble. We both knew it too.

"Thank you. Is there something we can do for you?" Rupert asked. I was really, really wishing that my bag was up here with me so I had the little gun Danica had given to me. I thought about releasing Rupert's hand and making a run for my bag, but I'd never make it.

"Mind if we come aboard? Never been on a yacht like that baby, and I'm thinking of buying one." As the man moved to get onto the hood of his speedboat, I saw the shoulder holster and butt of his weapon.

"Actually, I don't let strangers board my boat. Terrorism and all that. Sorry old chap."

"Aw, come on, man. We're just a bunch of guys out here partying. We don't mean no harm. I'll bet your daughter would like to see the speedboat, wouldn't you, hon?"

Rupert and I turned our heads just a fraction, and there stood Cindy at the railing glaring down at him. She had just come back up from down below and was standing at the railing staring at the speedboat with an intense gaze I found hauntingly familiar.

"Shit," Rupert uttered under his breath. "No," he said to the thug, "She's seen plenty, actually."

"Don't make this hard, old man," the driver said, reaching into the bomber jacket for his weapon. This was the moment when everything slowed down to the slowest motion imaginable. As he grabbed the butt of his gun, a huge ball of fire came out of nowhere and crashed into his chest, sending him sprawling back onto the deck of the speedboat engulfed in flames. His gun hung in midair for a moment before kerplunking into the water, his screams reverberating through the air.

The thug was completely enveloped in flames, and without a single hesitation, Rupert grabbed the *Necromancer's* controls and pulled away from the speedboat as fast as the yacht could go. As I turned to get Cindy, *I knew*. And by the looks of what was happening to her now, I also knew what she was *going* to do.

And I couldn't have stopped her even if I wanted.

"We can't outrun them!" I yelled to Rupert.

"I know. But I got a mayday call in and maybe we can play some cat-and-mouse before the cavalry gets here. How is she?"

Already, there was a strange bluish glow around both of her hands. The air around her was like the heat of a motorcycle pipe and made a crackling, staticky sound. Before the speedboat's engine could turn over to give chase, Cindy raised her hands and threw what looked like two miniature balls of sun at the bow of the speedboat. The speedboat, and the two remaining men on it blew about one hundred feet in the air, sending flaming debris everywhere. Rupert closed the controls and slid down the ladder to help me put out any of the small flaming pieces landing on the deck.

When we had stamped out them all, Rupert looked to Cindy and then to me. "Well, I guess we know what her powers are now, don't we?"

Nodding, I knelt in front of her. I was surprised by how calm she was. I had never actually seen a pyrokinetic before.

"You okay?" I asked, looking for some signs of trauma. I mean, she had just killed three people; one of them directly from a burst of flame from her own hands, and she was completely calm about it.

She nodded and looked at her hands. She knew what she had done. It was no accident. She had manipulated the energy around us and created a weapon that had blown the speedboat to smithereens and she felt not one drop of remorse.

"I'm going to send out another mayday, Echo, and move us away from that boat. Where one speedboat is, others are sure to follow. We have got to get the hell out of here."

I nodded, only half hearing him. "So...that's what you've done that scares people, huh?"

Cindy shook her head and then held up her index finger. A flame jumped from it. She blew it out and shrugged.

"Someone saw you manipulating fire once."

Nod.

"And those fireballs you just threw. You've made them before. It's not the first time." Nod.

I sighed and rose. There was one last question I had to ask. It's not that the answer mattered; it would help me understand her better. "You've accidentally killed somebody before, haven't you?"

She looked at her hands and nodded.

"Oh hon, I'm so sorry. That must have been awful."

Slowly, she nodded, then she pointed to herself. "Cinder," she whispered softly.

I frowned as I felt the yacht picking up speed. "What?"

She pointed to me and said, "Echo." Then to herself. "CindER."

Oh crap. Her name wasn't Cindy, it was CindER...as in ashes... as in a fire...as in firestarter. "All right, then, Cinder. I suppose I should be angry with you for what you just did, but the fact is you just saved all of our lives. Those fireballs were...well...in a word, amazing."

She nodded and held out her hand. With very little effort, she manipulated another, smaller fireball. Then, she closed her hand and the ball vanished. I have to admit...I was impressed.

"I got a distress call out, Echo, but it looks like we're about to have more company. I'm not sure blowing up their boat was such a great idea."

Cinder and I looked over the bow and saw two more

262

speedboats racing toward us. The cargo ship had pulled up anchor and was beginning to make its way out of the bay.

"Gee, you blow up one little speedboat and look what happens," Rupert said. "Think she's got any more firepower left? Because if she doesn't, we're screwed."

"Rupert! I'm not going to ask her to kill any more people." I turned and found Cinder had already started manipulating the energy around her, so I put my hands on her shoulders and shook my head. "No more, Cinder. I appreciate what you've done, but *no more*. This is not your battle."

"Yeah," Rupert added. "They say killing is bad for your soul, and I should know. Well, Echo, any ideas about how to get out of this one without using the kid's power?"

"Can you outrun them?"

"In those boats? Not a chance. We're either going to have to turn and fight or—"

"Or what? Rupert, we can't ask her to kill people for us. She's too young and untrained. If she could just dismantle the boat, that's one thing, but she's like a baby rattler. They shoot all their venom in one bite."

"If she doesn't bite, Echo, we're gonna get creamed."

The moment I took my eyes from her, she scooted across the deck away from me but closer to the oncoming boats. Before I knew it, she had thrown two more fireballs at the closest speedboat. It managed to get out of the way without getting hit.

"Cinder, stop!"

Suddenly, bullets bounced off the railing, and I ran to get her.

"Let her do her thing, Echo! We're sitting ducks out here!"

Rupert was right. Cinder's powers were the only ones that could save us. But how do you ask a child to blow someone to bits?

"Here comes the third one, Echo."

I looked over and saw the third speedboat drop alongside the one trailing us.

"*It's now or never, kiddo. Let her kill them before they hurt you.*

You can't stop the inevitable."

I looked over at Rupert and knew he hadn't said that. It was Tip from somewhere deep in my brain. *"I can't."*

"You sure as shit can! I leave you alone for one minute, and you get yourself in this kind of trouble? Let the kid do it. She has the power... and the experience. If she's all you've got, use her, but don't get killed because of some sort of fucked-up ethical issue. Kill the bastards!"

"What are you saying?"

"You know what I'm saying. Save yourselves at any cost. She'll get over it. She already has."

She'd not only gotten over it, she was ready for round two, and before I could stop her, she sent two more balls of flame in the direction of the nearest speedboat. The first one caught the driver on fire, and he leapt off the ship and into the water. The second hit the speedboat dead-on and the whole thing blew to bits, killing everyone on board. The man in the water was subsequently run over by the trailing boat, which I am sure Cinder would have also destroyed, had she not been distracted by an odd sound from overhead.

The loud beating sounded like the blades of a helicopter. Looking up, I spotted a Coast Guard helicopter making haste for the cargo ship.

"Well, slap a diaper on me and call me Grandpa! It's the goddamn Coast Guard!" Rupert picked up his binoculars and looked at the cargo ship. "Holy crap, Echo, people are bailing left and right out of that cargo ship. Rats jumping from a sinking ship, I guess. Where in the hell did the Coast Guard come from?"

"I thought you said you sent out a Mayday?"

"I did. They never get here that quick unless..."

Cinder pointed to the table where we had been eating. Sitting open was the vidbook. "Yo, Princess!" shouted Carl. "Say something, man, or the Boss is gonna start throwing things!"

I turned to Cinder and smiled softly. "Is this what you did when we told you to go below?"

She nodded.

Picking up the vidbook, I saw the boys' worried faces

anxiously staring back at me. "Tell Dani we're all okay and her vidbook is a huge success."

"Hell, Princess, we knew that. With the GPS system, we've had you in our sights all day long. Once the kid came on with this horrified look on her face, we called the cavalry. You sure you're okay?"

I put my hand on Cinder's head. "We are now." I turned and saw three Coast Guard ships cutting through the water like torpedoes. I mean, they were hauling ass and meaning business. Then, I turned back to Carl, only it wasn't Carl, it was Danica. She was whiter than I had ever seen her.

"You know I'm gonna have to kick your ass, right? I can't believe—" She shook her head. "Are you all okay?"

"We're fine."

"And the homeless guys?"

"From what I can see, a lot of them are still alive, but I don't have any confirmations yet. My...uh...emotions are all over the place."

"Good job, then, Clark. I mean it."

I watched as the Coast Guard boats cut off the third speedboat. "How did you get the Coast Guard here so quickly?"

"Don't thank us. Thank that Detective Jardine. We made one call to him the moment we knew you were at the marina, and he was all over it. Of course, with the GPS system, we knew exactly where you were and gave him perfect directions. You are in such big fucking trouble!"

"From?"

"Everyone!"

I said a few more words of thanks to her and the boys before signing off. She could have my head later.

"More incoming!" Rupert announced, only this time, he meant that a Coast Guard ship was pulling alongside us. "Um... Echo...is there anything else I need to know? The girl wasn't... you know..."

"Kidnapped? Not hardly. Everything is in order, Rupert. Don't worry."

"Don't worry? Honey, you're a danger magnet walking around with a kid who is her own army troop."

"*Attention all hands aboard the* Necromancer. *This is the Coast Guard. Cut your engines and prepare to be boarded.*"

Rupert did as he was told and then the three of us stood on deck waiting for the Coast Guard to come aboard.

"Ready, ladies?"

I looked down into Cinder's face. She looked so young and innocent. "It's okay to feel sad that you had to do that."

She shook her head, and I knew from reading her she didn't feel the slightest bit of remorse.

"Well, these are the good guys, so keep your fireball hands to yourself, okay? Number one rule of being one of us is you don't show *them* our powers, okay?"

Nod.

When I glanced over at the Coast Guard ship, I was stunned to see a familiar face. It was Darryl Jardine and he was boarding the *Necromancer*.

"Why did I know this is how it would end?" he said as he stepped on board.

I couldn't help myself. I ran over to him and hugged him. "Boy am I glad to see you!"

Jardine backed away, a little embarrassed. "I got your e-mail. It took me awhile to decipher where you were going with it, but once I did, I realized you were onto something. Then one of your buddies called and said he thought you might be getting in a little over your head. Guy gave us perfect coordinates."

I looked over at the cargo ship. "Are they—"

"Alive? Some are, some aren't, but we got the perps dead to rights. That's a pretty damn good day in my book. Is everyone safe here?" He looked around the ship.

I nodded. "It's just the three of us."

"Good. You know, you've got a lot of friends, Echo. First, I got a call from your friend, Danielle."

"Danica."

"Yeah, her. She called me early this morning and told me

you're probably out here poking around where you didn't belong. So, I called my buddies at the Coast Guard and had them on standby. We were just headed out when your computer guys contacted us and told us what was going on. Damn, he was able to give your exact location, which by the way, is pretty impressive. You done good, girl."

I nodded. "Thank you. Then it's over?"

"Well...it's certainly over for the bad guys, but I'll bet it's just beginning for you. This is going to make quite a story."

"Honestly, Jardine, I just want to see my friend Bob again. The story takes a far-away backseat to that."

"I'm sure it does, but that was quite a tale you sent me. If you'da sent it to anyone else, they'd probably think you slipped a cog and chucked it. I figured the least I could do was look into some of your allegations about Black Market organ harvesting. Your numbers were pretty hard to ignore. You do good work, Echo. Your boss'll be proud."

Exhausted, I tried to erect my shield, but couldn't. As an experienced empath, having your shield down is a little like going out without your underwear on. I just liked having it up and feeling only my own emotions. Jardine was pumped up, and so were the other two guardsmen standing with Rupert. Their energy was exhausting and was draining me of mine.

"Look. They're taking your guys off the ship."

One by one, guys came from the hold, eyes shielded from the bright glare of the sunshine. One by one, their faces lit up as they realized they'd been saved.

"Detective," one of the Coast Guard guys said. "We need to get this yacht farther away from the crime scene. Apparently, one of their speedboats blew up as well."

Jardine nodded. "Right." To me, he winked. "You better get back to the pier. We're going to need statements from you all before I can let you write your story. This is quite an exclusive you've got in your hands. If there's anything we can do to make your story better, let me know. This is the second time you made me look good. I owe you."

267

I nodded slowly. "The girl...Cinder. She doesn't talk, so I don't want anyone hounding her for a statement. Mine and Rupert's should suffice."

"You got it. Oh, and you better give Finn a call. She'll tear me a new one if she worried one second longer than she should."

"I will. See you back on land."

In the end, the story just wasn't as important as its ending. I was just glad I could put my powers to good use.

The guardsmen came over and whispered something to Jardine, who nodded. "Time to move out. They're gonna take the victims to the ER if you want to meet them there after we get your statements."

"SF General?"

"Yeah. Guess I'll see you over there...well...you and a hundred other reporters. This is gonna be huge, Echo. I hope you're ready."

The next forty-eight hours were a complete and total whirlwind that consumed every waking hour, which was about forty of them. You couldn't turn on any channel without hearing about the breaking story. I was interviewed by every major newspaper on the West Coast, every television station and even Katie Couric. The story grabbed national attention and catapulted me into a light that was so bright it nearly blinded me. Between interviews and appearances I barely had time to write the story.

Wes was walking around like a peacock, beating his chest over having nailed such a sensational story. He was nearly beside himself with all the phone calls and back patting that came his way. Giddy would be a good way to describe how he was for the first twenty-four hours after the story broke. A story like this takes on a life of its own, and would stay on the front pages until the next life came along. Well...for three days, there were no other stories. It was an incredible rookie story, and a boon to the *Chronicle* to have a reporter thrust in front of the cameras. Everyone was excited and happy for me. Everyone, of course, except Carter.

I couldn't blame him, really. To say that I stooped to blackmail might be a little strong, but I did stoop to something. The first chance I was alone with Wes, I calmly told him he could only have the exclusive story if he nixed Carter's dirt about the mayor's maid, or whatever sleaze he was working on about Mayor Lee. I explained to Wes I'd had to pull some strings, and those strings pulled back when I needed them most. My life was in danger, and had it not been for the creation of a task force, Darryl Jardine might not have been able to respond when I needed him most. Wes agreed in a heartbeat. I guess that's what semi-celebrity gets you. He wanted the story. In the end, Carter rubbed his sore spot, bid me congratulations, and buried the hatchet somewhere else than between my shoulder blades.

For Rupert's part in all of this, he opened up the *Necromancer* to anyone who wanted a tour. He wasn't about the publicity, but his boat made the cover of one sailing magazine and the interior found its way into three home and gardens-type magazines. He just enjoyed showing off his beautiful home. Whenever any reporter tried to give him credit for our story, he never accepted it, and instead, turned all of the credit back to me. He was very sweet when pressed, but made it perfectly clear that all he did was sail the boat. He also added, that no, we were not lovers. We were friends. I appreciated that...so did Finn, who sat back quietly watching the play proudly.

Melika also kept in touch. She was very proud of me, but her concern was always for us as supers. She knew I couldn't up and fly to New Orleans; that would have been the very worst thing to do. We couldn't afford having any reporters following me, nor could we drag Cinder through a mob of reporters. We decided it was best to keep Cinder out of sight, so she stayed with Danica, who had taken her from me the moment we got to the marina. Let's just say that Cinder spent the next three days playing with three boys who had only the coolest of toys. She dug it and so did they. They ate pizza and watched movies, and they let her play with all of their coolest techno-gadgets. I loved these guys before, but after the way they were with speechless Cinder, I would have

269

eaten hot coals for them. She was having a great time.

And so was I.

Tip contacted me shortly after we returned to land from the bay. I thanked her for her concern and told her what happened. She was relieved to know that we were okay, and that we would be going to New Orleans in the next few days. She was happy for me, but I think she knew I was finally on my own, and that hurt her a little.

And so, what I thought would be a good story turned into something much larger and kept me running from one venue to the next until I finally collapsed from exhaustion, twenty-eight hours later. When I woke up, I made my way to the hospital to see Bob and Smiley, who had managed to stay alive in the belly of the boat.

Bob was dehydrated and had suffered a couple of broken ribs from a scuffle he had gotten into trying to get off the cargo ship. When he saw me, he just started crying and hugged me for a long, long time.

"You...you..."

"I just did what I told you I was going to do."

"But Jane...no one knew...and yet..."

I pulled away and looked into his face. "How did they get you?"

Bob wiped his eyes and sighed. He was a bone rack and I noticed all his hospital food was gone. I had brought him two double bacon cheeseburgers and when I put the bag on his lap, he started crying again.

"I saw these guys cruising around Lumpy while he was sleeping off a drunk. I went to wake him up so he didn't get nabbed, and they got us both. They were quick as hot snot on a greased pole. They pulled up, three big guys got out, shoved me into a panel van, picked up Lumpy, tossed him in and were gone in under fifteen seconds. It was amazing."

"You must have been so scared."

"Shitless. The worst part was not knowing what they wanted from us. None of us understood the language, so they would just jabber away and we would sit and wonder what the hell they were saying. God, Jane, it was horrible."

"But you made, it, Bobbie."

"Others before me weren't so lucky. Once a guy left, he never came back." He shook his head. "I'd say a dozen guys were chopped up before you got there, and they would have kept on cutting us up."

Running my fingers through his hair, I felt the fear he was still feeling; that he might always feel. "They were detoxing you all before the surgery."

"Yeah, for once, alcohol saved lives." He shook his head. "That kid, Smiley. Why did he do it?"

"They threatened to go after everyone in his family. They needed an ambulatory homeless person and they found him on BART with his bike. Scared the crap out of him, so he did what he thought was best to save his family."

Bob nodded in understanding. "Judas, eh?"

"That's how he saw himself, yes."

"How is he?"

"Remorseful, but finally getting the help he needs. He'll never be out on the streets again."

Bob inhaled a shaky breath and sat on the edge of the bed. "Your story has opened a lot of eyes, Jane. You done good, as I always knew you would."

As I unwrapped one of his burgers for him, I sighed loudly. "In all of this, Bob, I've discovered that opening eyes is what a journalist is supposed to do. I look forward to achieving that more and more. Now, eat."

Bob ate mostly in silence, and when he finished he took my hand. "A lot of people claim to be your friend, but you...you really proved it. Without you, who knows what would have happened to all of us?"

We both had a pretty good idea.

We visited for a little bit, and he told me he had already been offered several jobs from people in the East Bay; people who got caught up in the story. It was at that moment I realized the power of journalism and the beauty of my job. Yes, at Mills we were taught to be agents of change. I had finally seen what a gift my powers could actually be to the world.

When I started to leave, Bob nearly crushed my spine as he hugged me.

"Thank you, Jane," he whispered, choking back another sob.

"You're welcome." Pulling back, I looked at him. "We're family, Bob, and family sticks together."

Tears fell from his eyes. "You're my angel. You know that, don'tcha?"

I smiled and brushed a tear from his cheek. "Hardly. You know what I am?"

"What?"

"Your friend."

I really wanted to see Rupert before we left for Louisiana. After all, none of this would have happened had he not volunteered his now bullet-ridden yacht.

We sat on his yacht sharing a couple of margaritas and spoke quietly amid the soft lapping of the waves against the side of his boat. "I have a few more interviews," I explained. "I told Wes I had a family issue and need to take some time off after this. I've got to get Cinder to Melika."

We sat quietly for a minute before Rupert said, "Pretty wild what she did to that boat, huh? I've only seen one firestarter in my life, and he ended up setting himself on fire."

I closed my eyes and I could see the path of the fireballs as they rocketed toward the speedboat. "Wild doesn't cover it. I never suspected she was a PK. When those fireballs hit that boat, it scared the living daylights out of me."

"Didn't frighten her in the least." Rupert turned to me. "Didn't you find it odd how calm she was after blasting that guy? I mean, cool as a cucumber she was. Cool enough to belt out two more."

Opening my eyes, I nodded. "I know what you're saying. She's done it before."

"Think that's why she doesn't talk?"

"I don't know, but something happened to scare her aunt and uncle. They were all too happy to get rid of Cinder."

Rupert whistled and shook his head. "She's a rare and dangerous breed. Normally, they wind up engulfed in their own flames because they don't understand the nature of their own power. That kid seems to understand exactly what her powers can do."

"That's why I have to get her to Mel. I think there's more to her than just her fire power. We need to know if there should be any sort of containment."

"Right-o. In the wrong hands, that girl could be someone's personal army. How's she doing?"

Thinking of Cinder playing with the boys and hanging out with her new best friend, Danica, made me smile. "She's having the time of her life."

"You've done a great job of keeping her out of the press."

"Thanks, but I didn't have much choice. I needed to protect her and the rest of us. So far, no one has said anything about seeing any fireballs or bursts of flames or anything like that, so I feel pretty confident we got away with that one."

"Excellent. Hey, was that front page your friend's company? Savvy Software?"

Smiling, I nodded. "Nice write-up, huh? She was over-the-top thrilled with it."

"She ought to be. A whole page? I know guys who'd give their left arm for half a page."

As promised, Carter got Savvy Software onto the front page of the business section, and Dani's phones hadn't stopped ringing since.

"Have you spoken to Cinder about what she did?"

I hadn't. I didn't even know where to begin. "You mean about killing those guys? I don't want to have that talk until we can spend some time together. Time is something in short supply for me right now."

"Maybe in New Orleans."

"No maybe about it. At some point, she is going to feel like a killer and we can't have that. Self-destruction is *not* an option for her if I have anything to say about it." Slowly, I rose. "What better place for me to re-energize and refocus on my life than in the Bayou. I don't know who needs it more, Cinder or me."

"Well, my offer is always a standing one. You ever want to take a sail down to Mexico for a couple of days, you know where to find me."

"I'll keep that in mind."

Leaving the marina, I was heading back to the city when my phone rang. Finn.

"Hey there, hotshot! I can't believe I got a hold of the famous reporter!" Finn and I had managed to talk to each other for only a minute here and a second there, but little beyond catching up on the latest report or interview or headline.

"Hey there, Deputy Dog. How's tricks?"

"Saw you on *Good Morning San Francisco*. You looked great. Nice color choice."

"Oh, Finn, even *I* am tired of seeing my face."

She chuckled. "Celebrity bringing you down?"

"I can't stand one more second talking about me or I'll go crazy. So, if you want to talk, tell me about you."

"Me? Well...after watching the big Samoan strutting around here like he owns the place, after having to constantly hear what a fine detective he is, after answering my mother why I wasn't as good as Darryl...well...gee...there's not much left to say."

I grinned. "Should I be sorry?"

"Never be sorry for a job well-done. I just wish you were my girlfriend so I could tell everybody *Hey look, that's my girl*! You know, get a little reflected glory."

I laughed. "Don't worry, the wave is almost over."

"So, when can you squeeze in a little beat cop like me for dinner and a movie? Dinner and dancing? Dinner and dessert? Hell, I'll even take coffee and a stale doughnut"

My stomach did a little dance. "In a week. I have family in Louisiana and I thought it would do me some good to get grounded after all of this. It's been exhausting."

"But fun?"

"It was fun for the first couple of hours, but then it took on a life of its own and...well...I'm feeling a little out of balance."

"You? Echo, you're the most grounded person I know."

"I still need to get the hell out of Dodge. Even if it's just for a few days."

"I understand. Call me when you get back?"

"Try and stop me."

When we hung up, I wondered if I was being fair to her. We were worse than two ships passing in the night...we were two ships passing on different oceans.

I wondered if we'd ever connect.

Finn managed to come over in the middle of the night to see me the night before we left for Louisiana. I was so tired I fell asleep against her shoulder. I don't mean sweet, cuddly sleep in the arms of the woman you might love. No, it was more like drooling down your chin, crust in your eyes kind of sleep that made your face all scrunched up and ugly.

When I was finally tucked into my own bed, along with a note on my nightstand that said for me to have a good time, be careful and call her for that date I owed her, I was feeling like the biggest loser on the planet.

From the Bayou, twelve hours later, that date seemed a really long way away, especially when I looked up and saw Tip standing on the dock, her long black hair catching the slight warm breeze, the smallest touch of a smile on her lips. She could stand there all day looking solid and unconcerned, but I knew better. She was relieved to see me.

"What are you...I thought—"

Tip smiled as she gently helped me and Cinder out of Bones's boat. "Even in a small cavern in the Outback, your story, your face was all over the news. It took six cabs, five airplanes, two trains, a burro and a horse to get back here as fast as I could."

"Why quickly? You knew I was okay."

She grinned and lightly moved a stray hair from my forehead, her eyes soft and almost teary. "I needed to make sure no one followed you here. We can't have your successes bringing riff-raff and other obnoxious reporters out here. With all your newfound stardom, we didn't want to jeopardize Melika's place."

"We?" My stomach did that weird jump it gets at the thought of Tip with another woman.

"It's good to see you again, my dear." Melika walked down off the porch and hugged me. For a tiny woman getting on in years, she could still hug fiercely. "Oh my word, but you're barely able to stand. In all the years I've known you, I've never felt you so exhausted. Poor girl."

I made introductions. Cinder was at once taken by Tip, as most females were for the first time. Gay or straight, they were moths to her flame. If the Bayou hadn't captivated her, which it clearly had, Tip most assuredly did.

"We'll talk later," Tip whispered to me, taking Cinder's hand, who balked...Kneeling down, I took her hand in mine. She had the warmest hands of anyone I had ever met. "You're okay. This is the school and these people are my family. They'll take really good care of you, show you some really cool things, and keep you safe and happy. Okay?"

She thought about it a second before nodding.

"Good. Now Tip is going to show you to your room. It might be a good idea to take a nap."

She frowned.

"I know, you're not a baby, but everyone takes a nap when they first get here because for the first time in our lives, we feel safe and among our own. I slept for over twelve hours when I first got here."

I looked over at Tip, not prepared for the surge of emotions rushing at me. "It's really good to see you."

She grinned. "I know. It's been too long. Let me take care of Cinder here, and then it's your turn for a nap."

When they were gone, Melika took my hands in hers. "I am so very proud of you."

"Thank you. This, too, shall pass and I can go back to my job and write more earth-shattering stories."

"It's good to have you back."

"It's good to be back."

"How is the girl?"

"Powerful. She needs a lot. She blew up those men and their boat without batting an eye. I felt no remorse from her either then or afterward. I wonder if maybe she hasn't hurt someone before."

Melika nodded. "Some people can kill without much effort or regret. Cinder is one of them. Don't judge her too harshly for it, Echo. She saved your life."

"But that's awful. Shouldn't we teach her remorse or something?"

"Is it? She did it for you."

I turned quickly to her. "For me?"

She nodded. "This young girl is painfully aware how dangerous she is. She would have struck out at anyone threatening you because *you* are the first person in her life to acknowledge that she's different without being afraid of her or leaving her. In short, my dear, you are her hero and she would have blown the city up if she felt you were in danger."

Sighing, I shook my head. "I don't feel like a hero. I feel like I've just stepped off a tornado."

"Careful what you wish for, remember? You wanted to make a difference in the world. Sometimes, you can do that anonymously and sometimes you can't. You want the world to be something it can never be, but that won't stop you from trying. Your altruism is one of the things I love most about you, but it is also going to be your cross to bear."

"But you can help her, right? I mean...she's not going to burst into flames, will she?"

Melika took my bag from my shoulder as we walked toward the house. "No, my dear, she will not burst into flames. You got to her in time."

Inhaling deeply, I nodded. "How long has Tip been here?"

"Tip came the moment I knew you were in trouble. That woman actually had to commandeer someone's horse to get out of the Outback. She traveled nonstop for thirty-two hours, cussing and spitting the whole way."

"Why cussing and spitting?"

"When she knew what was happening with you, she tried to back out of going to Australia. She felt her place was here...with you."

I stopped and studied her a moment. "Mel, you know that's over, right?"

She took my hand. "I do, but you need to forgive Tip and repair whatever rift is between you. Heaven and hell couldn't have stopped her from returning here when you got back. And you know why? Because she needed to see for herself that you are all right. Whether or not you two are together as lovers has no bearing on you being family. I need my family to love each other and get along. Let bygones be bygones, Echo, and forgive her."

"She said she came back to make sure I wasn't followed by any of my pesky colleagues."

Melika shook her head slowly. "You still don't understand her, do you? What you have done in destroying the Colombian organ traffickers is shine a very big spotlight on an organization that prefers to scoot around in the darker corners of the world. What you've done, my dear, is step on the tail of a very large and vengeful snake. Whether or not that snake chooses to strike back at you remains to be seen. Tip has returned from her journey early to make sure that it doesn't. Fear the cartels. Fear the wrath of Tiponi Redhawk even more."

I blinked several times. I'd had to stop the harvesters, but I never really felt like I was in any danger after the fact.

Was I?

Were we?

Had I inadvertently put us all in danger?

"Make peace with her, Echo, because no matter where you go or what you do in this life, she will always love you. She will *always* have your back. As long as Tip breathes, she will protect you with her life."

With that, Melika started for the house, leaving me alone with my depleted energy and weary thoughts. So much had happened so fast, I'd never really had time to catch my breath or sort through the few coherent thoughts I had. I knew one thing for sure: I was exactly where I needed to be.

Climbing up the steps, I sat down at the top and looked out over my beloved Bayou. Taking a seat next to me, in a closeness only ex-lovers share, Tip stared out at the water while laying her large hand gently over mine. "You okay?"

"I know in my head I am. I just don't feel—"

"Whole?"

I nodded. "Exactly."

Tip turned to me. "That happens, I think, when a dream comes true. It's like the dream is no longer in your heart and so you feel sort of...empty. You're out of sorts."

I stared at her, thankful for her understanding of me. "That is precisely how I feel."

"Do you know what you have to do? You have to get another dream to take its place. You always said you wanted to break a story so huge it got national attention. Well, it did. Now what? What's your next dream?"

I ran my hands through my hair and leaned on my knees. "I think my next dream won't be so grandiose and sure as hell won't include getting shot at or blowing up speedboats."

This made her chuckle. "Yeah, that last one was pretty big."

"And came entirely too fast."

Turning to me, she took my hand in hers. "The problem is, while you'll acknowledge your supernatural abilities, you fail to accept your personal power."

"Personal power? Don't I have enough power as it is?"

"Accept it. You're one of the good guys."

I studied her a moment before whispering, "And you, Tiponi. What are you?"

She reached out and tucked hair behind my ear. "I'm one of the good guys' bodyguards."

279

I grinned wearily. "You can't protect me from the world, you know?"

"I know. Maybe I *can* protect you from yourself. My job is to make sure you stay in the game for a really long time." Tip gave my hand a quick squeeze before releasing it so that she could put her arm around me. I didn't move.

"You know...I'm sorta seeing someone," I said softly.

She chuckled again, but there was something soothing about the sound. "Sort of? Those are the majority of your dating experiences."

"They are not!"

"Then why hasn't anything happened? Wait. Don't tell me. Too busy. Conflicting schedules. This big story. Stop me when I'm wrong. You like the *idea* of being in a relationship, but as of yet, haven't figured out how to actually make one stick."

I took her arm and flung it back at her. "Make one stick! Ha!"

"Have you even gone out on a date?"

"Yes. No. Shut up."

She tossed her head back and laughed. "You can't, can you? Since I've known you, you've been trying to convince yourself you're afraid of being with me. Has it ever occurred to you that you're really afraid of being with *anybody*?"

I opened my mouth to fire one at her, but nothing came out. I was too tired for this conversation and she knew it. Could it be that she was right and one of the reasons I was so emotionally drained was because I was fighting off any intimate feelings I was having toward Finn? Was I just afraid of intimacy on any level?

Her arm reclaiming my shoulders, Tip pulled me to her. "I don't want anything from you. I just want to be here to give you my support and my friendship. So, please relax, okay? You can pretend to be *seeing* this Finn all you want if it makes you feel better."

I turned to her, our faces inches apart, ignoring the fact that she had read me. "How can I relax when what you say is probably true? I'm an intimacy-phobe."

Her mouth curled into a half grin and her eyes danced. "Well, the good thing about fears is that they can be conquered." Her eyes suddenly got serious. "You really like this woman?"

I looked for any sign of jealousy and saw none. "I do."

"And she's good enough for you?"

I nodded.

"Then work with Melika to find a way past that wall you've built around your heart. And if you need someone to bounce things off of or if you just need some kneecaps broken, I'm only a thought away."

Laying my head on her shoulder, I felt the last of my energy flow from my body and into the Bayou. Yes, I was an empath, and yes, Mills had taught me to be an agent of change, but no one had prepared me for how to feel or what to do once a dream comes true.

As the orange and pink of dusk crept over the blue and purples of day, and the night sounds began replacing the day sounds, my tired spirit started replenishing itself. Yes, I had made my dreams come true. Yes, I was, in fact, an agent of change; and yes, oh yes, I *did* fear intimacy.

Maybe it was time to dream that a part of my heart could actually have someone in it. Maybe it was time to have someone to share my life with.

As my body melted into hers and my eyelids turned to cement, a new dream ever so cautiously tiptoed into my heart and took residence there.

How long it would remain just a dream was anybody's guess.

Publications from Bella Books, Inc.
Women. Books. Even better together.
P.O. Box 10543 Tallahassee, FL 32302 Phone: 800-729-4992
www.bellabooks.com

TWO WEEKS IN AUGUST by Nat Burns. Her return to Chincoteague Island is a delight to Nina Christie until she gets her dose of Hazy Duncan's renown ill-humor. She's not going to let it bother her, though...
978-1-59493-173-4 $14.95

MILES TO GO by Amy Dawson Robertson. Rennie Vogel has finally earned a spot at CT3. All too soon she finds herself abandoned behind enemy lines, miles from safety and forced to do the one thing she never has before: trust another woman.
978-1-59493-174-1 $14.95

PHOTOGRAPHS OF CLAUDIA by KG MacGregor. To photographer Leo Wescott models are light and shadow realized on film. Until Claudia.
978-1-59493-168-0 $14.95

SONGS WITHOUT WORDS by Robbi McCoy. Harper Sheridan's runaway niece turns up in the one place least expected and Harper confronts the woman from the summer that has shaped her entire life since.
978-1-59493-166-6 $14.95

YOURS FOR THE ASKING by Kenna White. Lauren Roberts is tired of being the steady, reliable one. When Gaylin Hart blows into her life, she decides to act, only to find once again that her younger sister wants the same woman.
978-1-59493-163-5 $14.95

THE SCORPION by Gerri Hill. Cold cases are what make reporter Marty Edwards tick. When her latest proves to be far from cold, she still doesn't want Detective Kristen Bailey baby-sitting her, not even when she has to run for her life.
978-1-59493-162-8 $14.95

STEPPING STONE by Karin Kallmaker. Selena Ryan's heart was shredded by an actress, and she swears she will never, ever be involved with one again.
978-1-59493-160-4 $14.95

FAINT PRAISE by Ellen Hart. When a famous TV personal-ity leaps to his death, Jane Lawless agrees to help a friend with inquiries, drawing the attention of a ruthless killer. No. 6 in this award-winning series.
978-1-59493-164-2 $14.95

A SMALL SACRIFICE by Ellen Hart. A harmless reunion of friends is anything but, and Cordelia Thorn calls friend Jane Lawless with a desperate plea for help. Lammy winner for Best Mystery. No. 5 in this award-winning series.
978-1-59493-165-9 $14.95

NO RULES OF ENGAGEMENT by Tracey Richardson. A war zone attraction is of no use to Major Logan Sharp. She can't wait for Jillian Knight to go back to the other side of the world.
978-1-59493-159-8 $14.95

TOASTED by Josie Gordon. Mayhem erupts when a culinary road show stops in tiny Middelburg, and for some reason every-one thinks Lonnie Squires ought to fix it. Follow-up to Lammy mystery winner *Whacked*.
978-1-59493-157-4 $14.95

WRONG TURNS by Jackie Calhoun. Callie Callahan's latest wrong turn turns out well. She meets Vicki Brownwell. Sparks would fly if only Meg Klein would leave them alone!
978-1-59493-148-2 $14.95

WARMING TREND by Karin Kallmaker. Everybody was convinced she had committed a shocking academic theft, so Anidyr Bycall ran a long, long way. Going back to her beloved Alaskan home, and the coldness in Eve Cambra's eyes isn't going to be easy.
978-1-59493-146-8 $14.95

SEA LEGS by KG MacGregor. Kelly is happy to help Natalie make Didi jealous, sure, it's all pretend. Maybe. Even the captain doesn't know where this comic cruise will end.
978-1-59493-158-1 $14.95

KEILE'S CHANCE by Dillon Watson. A routine day in the park turns into the chance of a lifetime, if Keile Griffen can find the courage to risk it all for a pair of big brown eyes.
978-1-59493-156-7 $14.95

ROOT OF PASSION by Ann Roberts. Grace Owens knows a fake when she sees it, and the potion her best friend promises will fix her love life is a fake. But what if she wishes it weren't?
978-1-59493-155-0 $14.95

COMFORTABLE DISTANCE by Kenna White. Summer on Puget Sound ought to be relaxing for Dana Robbins, but Dr. Jamie Hughes is far too close for comfort.
978-1-59493-152-9 $14.95

DELUSIONAL by Terri Breneman. In her search for a killer, Toni Barston discovers that sometimes everything is exactly the way it seems, and then it gets worse.
978-1-59493-151-2 $14.95

FAMILY AFFAIR by Saxon Bennett. An oops at the gynecologist has Chase Banter finally trying to grow up. She has nine whole months to pull it off.
978-1-59493-150-5 $14.95

SMALL PACKAGES by KG MacGregor. With Lily away from home, Anna Kaklis is alone with her worst nightmare: a toddler. Book Three of the Shaken Series.
978-1-59493-149-9 $14.95